Typewriter Pub, an imprint of Blvnp Incorporated
A Nevada Corporation
1887 Whitney Mesa DR #2002
Henderson, NV 89014
www.typewriterpub.com/info@typewriterpub.com

ISBN: **978-1-64434-119-3**

DISCLAIMER
This book is a work of fiction. The characters, incidents, and dialogue are drawn from the author's imagination and are not to be construed as real. While references might be made to actual historical events or existing locations, the names, characters, places, and incidents are either products of the author's imagination or are used fictitiously, and any resemblance to actual persons living or dead, business establishments, events or locales is entirely coincidental.

A FIRST CHANCE AT LOVE

T. LANAY

To my readers that kept the series alive,
and motivated me with all their sweet encouragement and loyalty.
I'm forever grateful for their support. You rock, Fluffy Pups!

FREE DOWNLOAD

Get these freebies when you sign up for the author's mailing list!

https://bit.ly/TLanay-WEB

CHAPTER 1

AVERY

My teeth clenched painfully together as I stood outside for some peace and quiet, but like always, that was never going to happen. Slowly, I turned my head to shoot daggers at the boy who was consistently pestering me to no end. I growled, hoping he got the picture that I didn't want him here.

"Oh, I love it when you growl; it's so sexy," Caleb said huskily, stepping up to me to place a hand on my chest. I snatched his wrist in my grip and narrowed my eyes in warning.

"Will you just leave me be?" I hissed, but all he did was smile as he licked his lips suggestively.

"Oh come on Ave, I love it when you get aggressive." He smirked. There were a few snickers and murmurs as I darted my eyes around to see a few older and younger wolves looking at us in disgust and amusement. I really didn't care about what they thought. I was more disappointed that some would look at this blatant display that Caleb was showing in dislike when their alphas were two gay males.

I shook my head, shutting my eyes.

"Just give me a kiss," he whined, and I snapped my eyes open to glare at him again. He was pouting as he looked up at me.

"Please? One kiss, but I can't promise you that I'll leave you alone after that." He snickered. I pushed him away, causing him to stagger back as he swiftly caught his balance.

"I've told you time and time again, Caleb, that I'm not gay nor do I want to be involved," I growled at him as I stepped around and walked off the back porch. I could hear his footsteps right behind me, causing me to groan in annoyance.

"Come on, Avery. I know that you have to have some heart in that robot chest of yours," he said. I stopped in my tracks, turning around to face him and frowned.

"Excuse me?"

He skidded to a stop since he was jogging to keep up with me.

"Well, it's true. It's like you do nothing except kiss Aiden's ass. You're always there, and you only ever talk to him, or give him the time of day." He shrugged.

I rolled my eyes.

"I'm his protector, Caleb. It's my sole purpose to be there for him at all times," I told him.

"I thought that was Liam's job. You can't let your life revolve around Aiden. What about you know . . . *alone time* with a special person." He wiggled his eyebrows suggestively.

I let out a sigh. I really didn't want to go through with this right now. Or ever.

"Look, it's none of your business what I do with others; and secondly, you have a mate somewhere out there, Caleb, and I'm not going to let you ruin something that's so special between you and your mate. It's something that should never be tainted with, so keep yourself pure and you'll thank me in the long run," I said before I turned around to leave.

"Yeah right." He followed me again.

Oh my god, this kid.

"I don't want a mate," he said as he came up to walk beside me. I just frowned at him.

"You won't be saying that when you see them."

He shook his head stubbornly.

"No, I don't want to be tied down to some girl. I'll feel like I've been shackled to someone that I never want to be with in the first place," he argued.

"No. Once you meet them, all the doubt and fear you have will go away," I assured him. He didn't know how lucky he was to know that his mate was somewhere out there waiting for him.

"Plus, who said it will be a girl? Just look at Aiden and Liam," I added.

"No, I know in my heart that it will be a girl." His face scrunched up in disgust.

We made it to the side door of the kitchen only to find it empty. I trudged to the fridge and looked around. I heard the clank of the metal chain that was attached to Caleb's wallet echo as he hopped on the counter, but I just ignored him.

Spaghetti. That sounds promising. I grabbed the container and stuck it in the microwave. The only sound was the hum of the microwave as it rotated.

"You don't find me attractive at all?" Sadly, Caleb had to interrupt my sweet silence. I closed my eyes, already exhausted from this.

"I have no feelings in that department."

"Well, do you think Sandra is hot?" He was referring to one of the pack women who has a modeling contract. She was remarkably beautiful and almost every unmated wolf wanted her, but I felt nothing when I looked at her either. I turned to him and looked him straight in the eyes.

"No, Caleb. How many times to I have to tell you that I am not attracted to anyone in this house or out of it?"

Ding!

I walked over to the microwave and pulled out my hot food. I grabbed a fork and sat at the table. I then stabbed the noodles with the prongs, twisting them with my fork before bringing them to my lips. I didn't even jump when a pair of arms slowly slid over my shoulders, eventually wrapping themselves around my neck. Caleb rested his chin on my shoulder as his mouth touched my ear.

"Aren't you going to offer me any?" he whispered. His breath caressed my ear but all I felt from it was annoyance.

"Caleb . . ." I warned him. Chuckling, he licked the helix of my ear before bitting on it gently, causing me to jump in my seat.

"I'm not giving up, Avery," he said before he walked out. I just stared down at my food as I listened to his footsteps retreat. Breathing a sigh of relief, I finally bit down on my noodles.

That kid hasn't left me alone since he's got here. Every time he would find me by myself, he would try his hardest to get into my pants even though I always tell him that there was no chance of that ever going to happen. I have one reason for being in this life and that was Aiden. Caleb would only complicate my job.

Finishing off my spaghetti, I washed the dish before I walked upstairs to my room. There were kids running up and down the stairs, and I easily maneuvered around them, continuing on my walk. Sometimes, I missed the alone time I used to have when I would travel by myself. Now I was surrounded by annoying people and a kid who won't get the picture that I want nothing to do with him.

I reached to my door, stepped into my bedroom, and laid on my bed, my eyes staring up at the ceiling. The room was dark and bland like always. I closed my eyes and focused on Aiden's life force; he was happy as I watched the swirling pink mist form behind my eyes. His content energy seeped in as I opened myself up to him.

I know it's not right, but this was how I could go through my day and that was to feed off his happiness and to fill the emptiness in my body to a certain extent. Sighing, I felt the pull of a small smile form on my face.

Soon enough, the gentle pink shifted to a deep red, and I quickly pulled out from that trance, not wanting to be connected to *that* part of his life. A blush filled in my cheeks as I snapped my eyes open and sat up, breaking the link.

I ran my hands over my face then up to my hair. It's been four months since their coronation and their intimate moments have happened more often than not. I always felt like a pervert when the energy would suddenly switch up like that.

I didn't have time to dwell on it though, since my thoughts were soon interrupted by a sudden knock on the door.

I frowned; no one ever comes to my room.

"Yeah?" I called out. Slowly, the door cracked open and I saw Dom poking his head in.

"Hey man, it's time for patrols," he said. I nodded as I slid off from my bed. As time went on, I've noticed how Dom's attitude has changed tremendously. When I first met him, he was either always moping around the house or busy training his ass off. At the time, he was showing signs of a rejected wolf. The way his skin never tanned even though he was out in the sun for hours at a time during training, and the fact that he never laughed showed that he was just not happy. Then again, I'm not a talkative person myself, but the fact that Dom has never interacted with anyone and only gave one-worded answers when confronted with questions were obvious signs in itself.

One time when I was at the mall with Aiden and Sadie, I met Jeanine—the person who rejected Dom, her destined mate. Hearing that she had the gall to reject her mate even if she was human, pissed me off. I admit, I was definitely carried away at the time, especially when she grabbed Aiden so carelessly which caused me to release a nasty growl beyond my control. Nevertheless, the day when Aiden came up a way for Dom and Jeanine to get back together or at least talk was something I did not regret. As a matter of fact, I was glad to help. Hell, I was even excited when I was the one who had to tie her up and lock her in the room. Too much?

Probably, but the plan worked. Now, Dom was as happy as ever with J and his natural glow returned. What's more, a pup was soon on the way. I guess their time in the old alpha's prison resulted in that.

The sky was dark as Dom and I stepped out for patrol. A few Enforcers were gathered, waiting for us to lead the way. Liam had made it official that I was to be one of them, to which Aiden completely agreed. Since Aiden thought I should, I accepted.

"Team A, you're taking the right. Team B, you have the left. As for the rest of you, you're with Avery and I. Alright let's go." Soon enough, we all discarded our clothes, shifting quickly into our wolves before we rushed into the woods.

The night cleared as my vision sharpened and my senses heightened. We all had spread out while I was alone for the moment. I walked slowly, my eyes scanning over the trees, never missing a thing. I saw small animals running out of my way as I trotted; squirrels racing up to their cozy little holes in the trees with their families, birds sleeping in their nest, and the soft whistling of the wind as the breeze ruffled my sandy brown coat.

My muzzle lifted in the breeze trying to pick up any unknown scents, but it was clear aside from the soft relaxing smell of wild flowers and the earthy scent of the grass surrounding me. I trotted up to the border but everything was empty. As I turned around to go back halfway, I suddenly stopped. My ears began to twitch in the direction of where a twig snapped and moments later, a certain scent hit my nose and I growled in annoyance.

Damn it. I whined. A brown wolf came out from behind the trees, his tail high as he strolled up to me confidently. Growling, I lowered myself slightly in a defensive stance. He gave me a wolfish grin as he came up to me and rubbed his smaller body under my chin, arching his back like a cat.

"Avery," he purred, repeating the process as he turned back around.

"What are you doing out here, Caleb?" I snapped at him impatiently. Can't he just leave me alone?

"I saw you patrolling and I wanted to help," he said, now brushing his body down my side.

"Well, I don't need any so leave."

He snickered and pressed his muzzle against mine.

"I'd rather not," he said, licking at my face.

I was a little worried why I wasn't pushing him off. I would usually grab him before he could even touch me, but here I was, letting him rub himself against me and practically allowing him to spread his scent all over me.

I bared my canines at him, pulling myself out of the trance. I backed away, my ears pinned.

"Leave me the hell alone, Caleb!" He didn't, of course. Why does he continue to test me so? I was usually a very relaxed person and nothing could really bother me, but there was something about him that just irked me.

"Come on, Avery, play with me!" he teased and jumped at me playfully, but I was having none of it. He pawed at my face gently and I growled, staying in my spot as I glared at him.

"Caleb . . ." I warned. He continued jumping around like a puppy. I took a deep breath and did nothing as he swiped at my face again, this time his claw scraped me in the muzzle. The sting made me growl, and I immediately pounced on him, pinning him on the forest ground and snarled.

His eyes widened in shock.

"Stop!" I growled, using way more power in my command than necessary while baring my teeth. He pinned his ears back and whined in fright. His bluish brown eyes were staring up at me in disbelief. I couldn't move as the aura of something I pushed back a long time ago now began to surge through my veins for the second time in years.

"I'm sorry," he apologized softly as his gaze searched my face curiously. I watched him raise his head from the ground, and I

froze as he slowly licked the bleeding wound on my face. I felt a light stir in my wolf as Caleb's warm tongue healed the small wound affectionately.

Our eyes met as he pulled away and I realized that I couldn't avert my gaze from him. Noticing that I wasn't going to do anything, he soon took advantage of that moment and licked my cheek, causing me to close my eyes.

What is this? My wolf began stirring again, like he was curious as to where this was going but . . . no, NO. I won't have that, I can't!

I jumped away from him like he had burnt me and backed up slowly, shaking my head.

"Avery?" Caleb got to his feet.

"Go," I told him. His head tilted in confusion.

"What's wrong?" he asked, stepping closer.

"GO!" I screamed. He flinched at my tone as he froze in his tracks.

Damn it, why doesn't he ever listen?

I whined, huffing as I turned away from him and raced off, leaving Caleb and whatever that was back there.

CHAPTER 2

AVERY

I was sitting in the living room with Aiden, Robin, J, and Sadie as they discussed . . . whatever it was they were talking about. I honestly had no idea; I wasn't paying attention. My mind was more focused on what happened in the woods last week.

Ever since that incident I had with Caleb, I spent the rest of the week avoiding him. I felt pathetic that I was hiding from someone half my size, but I was confused. I have never felt anything towards another person, male or female, before. Frankly speaking, I was prejudiced against sex, especially when I knew I would never have what the other wolves have.

Caleb's constant advances never fazed me nor brought any other emotion other than annoyance. I'm not saying I felt something for him now because I don't. I just supposed being in wolf form allowed my wolf to get a little more curious than he would have when I was in human form.

That had never happened before.

"Avery?"

I snapped my head up as I was being pulled out of my thoughts.

"Hmm?"

"We're going baby clothes shopping; do you want to come?" Aiden asked. I could see the pleading look on his eyes, making me suppress the smile that was tempting to show. I nodded once and set my book down on the table before I stood. They all headed towards the door with me at their heels.

Robin threw the keys my way and I swiftly caught them before hopping in the driver's seat.

I stuck the keys in the ignition and glanced up to see Aiden and Liam share a passionate kiss. I was frowning by the time they pulled away and then Aiden headed to the back seat with Robin and J.

"Baby shopping!" I cringed at the screech Sadie made in the passenger seat.

"Banshees, I swear," Aiden muttered from the back. I smirked before pulling out on the road. Sadie was messing with the radio as J and Robin were murmuring something to each other. Aiden was quiet, so I took a quick peak in the rearview mirror to see him gaze out of his window, his head resting on his palm. Furrowing my eyebrows a bit, I focused back on the road.

"Oh my god, I love this song!" J screamed, the car swerved a bit as I jumped from the sudden screech. I growled as Sadie turned the volume up.

'The sun has gone down
And the moon has come up'

The lyrics were going in and out as I tried to ignore them.

'He's going the distance, he's going for speed'
She's all alone, alone in her time of need'
'He is haunted by something he cannot define'

Thank God, we finally we arrived at the plaza. Once we were parked, I hurriedly snatched the keys out, cutting the music off.

"Hey!" they all whined, I just rolled my eyes and got out.

"There's a Babies R Us nearby so let's start there." Sadie pointed across the street.

J shook her head.

"No, they mostly sell toys," she complained, hooking her arm with Aiden's.

"Yeah, they have the right toys alright, like cribs, strollers, bouncer seats, and blah, blah, blah," Robin said, entwining her fingers with Sadie's.

Sighing, she nodded, and we headed over.

I walked behind them, observing and keeping a close watch until they needed me. After a while, Sadie ran off with Robin at her heels as she took off to play with some of the toys on display.

I closed my eyes. *How old was she?*

Aiden, on the other hand, was always in my line of sight, never straying too far.

"Aww, look!" J exclaimed as she rushed over to the rack of clothes, evidently dragging Aiden with her.

"It's too bad I can't get any of these yet," she whined. Aiden shrugged as he shuffled through the tiny clothes.

"Well, just because you don't know the gender of your baby yet doesn't mean you can't buy those. You can always get neutral colors like yellow, white, and black."

"You're so right!" J said, her expression brightened.

"Avery, what do you think?" J asked, holding up a small black and white outfit. Truthfully, I thought the baby would look like a penguin, but I couldn't exactly say that out loud.

"It's nice," I said vaguely, looking away like I was patrolling the area. She pouted her lips, her eyes scrutizinizing the outfit for a bit before she placed it back on the rack.

"No, my baby will end up looking like a penguin." I bit my tongue from laughing out loud.

"Hey, penguins are cute!" Aiden argued. Jeanine just stuck her tongue out at him.

And this was how my day went, walking from store after store looking for baby stuff. Jeanine decided she liked the boutique that had the 'cutest' clothes and toys, so I ended up carrying a huge box with a disassembled crib in it. Robin, on the other hand, carried an infant's car seat with her, while J and Aiden had several bags of neutral colored baby clothes of all sizes.

Who knew baby shopping was so exhausting?

Once we were back to the car, I stuffed the crib in the trunk. It was a good thing we brought the SUV since the car seat fitted along with it perfectly.

"I am so hungry," J complained as we piled into the car.

"You're always hungry," Aiden muttered, earning a slap in the head. My body tensed out of reflex, but I stopped myself.

"Ow!" he cried, rubbing the back of his head with a pout. Sighing, I started the car.

"Can we refrain from hitting Aiden please?" I said as I pulled out on the road.

"What for? He deserved that!" J whined, glaring at him.

"Just don't," was all I said, and the car fell silent. Flinching from the loud music blasting through the speakers, I flicked the thing off.

"Hey, Avery. Stop at In-N-Out, would you? We need to feed that never-ending stomach of J's," Sadie said.

*   *   *

When everyone had finished, I took them back home and they all rushed inside. Dom came out and grabbed the crib, giving me a thankful nod before heading in with J. Aiden was the one who lagged behind, so I turned to him.

"What's the matter?" I asked him softly, but he didn't reply. He sat down on the porch and rested his elbows on his knees.

"Aiden?" Now I was worried. Slowly, I opened up to him and felt his anxiety before I sat next to him.

"It's nothing, don't worry about it."

I gave him a flat look.

"It's not nothing when I can feel these strong emotions building within you. What has gotten you so anxious all of a sudden?"

He kept his gaze on his hands.

"It's just that we're graduating soon, and I know that Liam has a lot on his plate right now from being the alpha. This is where he belongs." His sky blue eyes finally peered up at me, and I frowned in concern as I saw them build with unshed tears.

"And I'm not saying that I hate it here, I love it. I really do, and I know it's now my job to take care of all of you guys but . . ." He paused, running his hands through his dark hair.

"But I have worked my ass off at school to get the grades I have now so I can get into the college I wanted and become a doctor like I have always dreamed of. So what am I supposed to do now? I can't just leave Liam and the pack while I go to school; that would be selfish. I swore before everyone that I would stand by Liam's side and look out for the pack. I'm an alpha now, so does that mean everything I've worked for is unimportant?"

I gazed at him for a while as he wiped away his frustrated tears. It was killing me to know that he was so upset but what can I do?

I looked out at the scenery before me, watching people walk around while others talk with their friends. Some kids were running after each other playing tag, their joyful laughter filled the air. One of them kept trying to catch up with his friend, but I noticed that one of his laces were untied and soon enough, he tripped and fell down, his loud cries echoing around the vicinity.

Not even a second later, Aiden was up, racing towards the kid.

"Oh no, are you ok?" he asked the kid who couldn't form a single word as he wept.

"Alright, let me see," Aiden said holding out his hand. The pup was clutching his arm close to his chest.

"It hurts," he whined, tears streaming down his face. Aiden nodded and scooted closer, gingerly taking his arm in his hand, and examining it. It was bleeding badly from the torn skin.

"Ow!" he cried.

"I know," Aiden cooed, helping the kid to his feet. "We're going to take care of it and all will be well again." He smiled down at him and the kid nodded, sniffling. I followed them to the kitchen as Aiden turned the faucet on, allowing the cold water to run all over the kid's arm.

"What's your name?" Aiden asked him softly. The pup's eyes widened with pain, but he looked up at Aiden with trust.

"Jeremy, Alpha." He sniffled.

"Well, it's nice to meet you Jeremy," he told him reassuringly, lifting him up so he could sit on the counter. Aiden looked over at me first before pointing to the cabinet right next to me.

"I think there's a first aid kit in there; can you hand it to me?" I turned towards it, rummaging through the messy cabinet till I spotted the white box.

"Alright, Jeremy. This is going to sting but you're a big boy, right?" The boy nodded, biting down his bottom lip. Aiden ripped the disinfectant wipe package with his teeth before dabbing the red and swollen wound with the gauze.

"Ahh!" he cried, flinching back.

"How old are you?" Aiden asked, distracting Jeremy as he continued to work.

"Eight," he answered, his voice wobbly as he tried to hold back his tears.

"Wow, you're practically a man now!" he exclaimed with a wide grin, although his eyes were trained on Jeremy's arm as he cleaned the deep scratch. After he was done, he smeared an ointment on it before finishing it off with a large band-aid.

"See? We're all done now," he said, stepping back to admire his work with a proud smile. Jeremy hopped from the counter and wrapped his arms around Aiden's waist.

"Thank you, Alpha."

"Just call me Aiden." He chuckled, rubbing the boy's hair playfully. "Now go out there and play with your friends."

I moved aside as the kid raced out. Children are so bipolar, I swear. I smiled at Aiden.

"What?" he asked. I walked over to the counter and began to put away the supplies he left.

"Who said what you learned was useless?" I responded, placing the kit back in the cabinet. He frowned at me.

"What do you mean?"

"What I mean is, you can still get the education you've been striving for, but make use of what you studied with a different species." I leaned back against the fridge, crossing my arms over my chest. Slowly, his expression turned from confusion to understanding.

"You mean . . ."

I nodded.

"You already have a fantastic physician right under your nose. You can ask Dr. Kindlier if you can work under him. It may not be what you expected but it's still medical training, only in the supernatural sense," I told him. He looked thoughtful as he stared down at his fidgeting hands. Soon after, he looked up at me with a huge smile.

"I like the sound of that; I should go tell Liam," he said, his face bright with excitement. I watched him rush out. Shaking my head in amusement, I headed upstairs only to find Caleb leaning up against the wall next to my room. His arms were crossed and his head was down but he soon looked up when he noticed me.

I closed my eyes with a sigh before looking back at him expectantly.

"What are you doing here?" I asked, feeling slightly agitated. Well, there goes my 'avoiding Caleb' streak.

"Well, I live here, duh." He smirked. I wasn't in the mood for his cocky attitude.

"Go away, Caleb," was all I said before I walked in my room, but he caught my arm, staring straight into my eyes with a serious expression.

"Avery—" He opened his mouth, but nothing came out.

I frowned at him, his dark hair hung over his eyes as he seemed to be in an internal debate with himself.

"Why have you been avoiding me? Ever since that night in the woods, you've become even more distant." I didn't answer and instead just kept my face clear of any emotions. His bluish brown eyes were searching mine as he stepped closer to me.

"What happened that night?" he asked. Gritting my teeth, I snatched my arm from his grip.

"Nothing, absolutely nothing," I growled and closed the door in his shocked face. I walked over to my bed, glaring at the door. He was still there, I could smell his unique earthy scent linger for a moment before I heard him sigh as he walked off.

Finally. I relaxed. *When will he just leave me be?*

CHAPTER 3

CALEB

He won't look at me. I don't understand what the hell I did wrong, but I'm not one to give up. I have made Avery my current target, and I'm going to get what I want—I always do.

I was walking down the halls of Portland High. I hate this damn school so much. It felt like I was in a sea of ignorance as I watched the glares and hateful looks they spared at Liam and Aiden, despite the fact that they were too scared of Avery and Liam to really do anything about it. That image alone, caused me to snicker as they showed their true colors when their backs were turned.

I haven't really made it known that I was gay, but it's not like I was hiding it either. Nevertheless, if they were to ever find out then they can kiss my happy gay wolf fluff! I huffed at the sudden anger I felt as I walked into history class I shared with Robin.

I took my seat next to her, and she nodded her head in greeting to which I did the same. I was happy for her that she found her mate and a bit envious that she found herself a woman to love since she was a lesbian and all.

Lucky. I dreaded meeting my mate because I knew that I wouldn't be so fortunate; I never was.

The school knew that Robin was also gay, and I did my best to fend them off. She was my sister and no one talks sh*t about her unless you have a death wish. Casually, I looked around the class at the numerous bigoted students here. I can't wait for graduation; school was never my strong suit.

"Did you see them? They were making out in the hallway, it was so disgusting!" I heard some girl whisper with another. Slyly, I peered into their direction only to see some blonde bimbo talking with another brunette airhead.

"I know, I saw them kissing in the football field," the brunette said.

"It's so not fair that Liam doesn't swing our way." The blonde pouted, and I rolled my eyes.

Dude get over it! I felt like yelling. It's been four months already, don't they have something else to talk about?

"So Sadie and I are going on a date tonight and I'm so excited!" Robin said, making me focus on her. Her face was bright with excitement and her eyes glistened with love. I felt the little green monster threaten to come out but I sighed it away.

"You and Sadie go on a date every week, Robin. It's nothing new," I muttered, looking down at my desk as I started to carve random things on the wood with my fingernail.

"And it's perfect every time!" she exclaimed.

Oh god, here were go.

"Uh huh." I tried to make my tone apathetic as she stared rambling on and on about how wonderful her mate was.

"Stop!" She swatted my hand way from the desk. I glared at her.

"You are going to get caught. How are you going to explain that you can carve a deep ass picture in the wood with a fingernail?" she reprimanded while I shrugged it off.

"I drink a lot of milk?"

Robin rolled her eyes, obviously not amused before she faced forward and rested her chin on the palm of her hand. Right then the teacher came in.

"Morning class," Mrs. Peterman greeted us with a huge smile. There were a few mumbles but that was about it. If you were to ask me, this teacher was way too cheery.

"Well let's get the class started!" she told us, grinning like a fool which was my cue to zone out.

The class went on, my focus clearly elsewhere as the boring lecture went on and on. The only thing I heard was the bell ringing at the end, causing me to jump up from my seat, and I ran towards the door for sweet freedom.

"Cal, wait!" Robin called out. Sighing, I skidded to a stop as she walked up to me and hooked our arms together.

"So, are you going out tonight?" she asked. I scoffed before I smirked at her.

"Well duh!"

She shook her head.

"Come on, Caleb, there's more to life than just clubbing and partying."

I raised an eyebrow.

"Like what, dear sister?" She pushed me before she continued.

"Like finding your mate and helping around our new pack house." I scrunched up my nose at her suggestions.

"I don't see the 'more to life' in that, only too much work, so I think I'll just stick to my awesome life of clubs and parties."

"You know what? Whatever," she said, pulling her arm out of mine before walking off dramatically.

Oh Robin, Robin, Robin . . .

I walked out towards the football field, knowing full well that Liam and Aiden would be out there which means that Avery would be out there too. It was spring which means football season was over, but Liam and Aiden loved to sit on the bleachers.

Pushing the double doors to the back of the school open, I walked out to the field, and immediately spotted the two lovebirds, who appeared to be all cuddled up together while sitting on the top bleachers.

My eyes scanned across the field. I was really looking for Avery and soon enough I found him leaning against the metal bench at the bottom, clearly giving the alphas their alone time.

Avery must have heard me coming because he looked up with his usual grim expression when I was around.

"Hey," I greeted, stopping in front of him. He didn't say anything and just sighed heavily.

My eyes wandered over to his frame. This man is a god! He was built like a freaking tank, and through his tight, gray shirt I could see his muscles which were straining against the seams of the fabric. He also towered over me with his 6'2 frame while I only stood at 5'9. His skin was tan, and his hair was cut short which had this beautiful blondish brown shade. His eyes were a gorgeous deep brown as well, which reminded me of puppy dog eyes.

I noticed the tick in his jaw as he glared at me. I cocked a brow at him. Clearly, he's not very happy to see me.

"No 'hello'?" I taunted.

"Bye, Caleb," he said, looking over my head as he ignored me. I huffed. Well, that won't do, will it? Stepping closer, I ran my fingers up his defined chest that could make any straight guy drool. He snatched at my hand tightly.

"Go away," he growled through gritted teeth. I smiled, molding my body against his harder one. I looked under my lashes, turning on the charm.

"I really get under that skin of yours, don't I?" I said huskily, wrapping my free hand around his neck as my fingers tangled in his soft hair.

"I swear, Caleb, if you don't leave me the hell alone . . ." he threatened.

Chuckling, I buried my face in his neck, his pine and sandalwood scent assaulted my senses. He did smell good.

"What are you going to do, handsome?" I purred in his ear. I felt his body shiver against mine and I smiled triumphantly. There was no way he could be able to resist me for so long.

"If you don't get off me right now, I'm going to break your damn hand." He forced out through clenched teeth. His hand tightened on my wrist, squeezing it painfully. Wincing, I pulled away from him, yanking my hand away from his grip before I glared up at him.

"Well, that wasn't very nice." I pouted, cradling my throbbing hand to my chest. Rolling his eyes, he turned to Liam and Aiden, but they were too busy lip-locking. I saw some kind of pain flash in Avery's brown eyes before it was gone.

I bit my lip in understanding; he could never have that. He would never have a mate to fawn over. I still didn't understand the whole situation with him and Aiden, but I knew it was a completely platonic one.

"So how long do you plan on waiting for Mr. and Mrs.?" I asked.

"As long as they want." His tone was clipped and annoyed. His eyes were void of all emotions as he averted his gaze from me.

Well, I certainly know when I'm not wanted. Shrugging, I turned without a word and headed to the front of the school. Levi stood by his car as he waited for me. I met him at the pack house and we hit it off as friends. He was totally cool with me being gay considering he was bi. I think he was the only one in that house who actually had some variety in his intimate encounters. I was ecstatic when I found him out of the hundreds of pack members.

"Cal," he greeted with a nod. Smiling, I walked up to him.

"What's up man?" I said, leaning against his car. He shook his head with a gorgeous smile on his face. His long light brown hair was gelled up loosely to the side. He was beyond beautiful. He wasn't buff but he had a decent amount of muscle on him. If I wasn't trying to pursue Avery, I would have snatched this piece of eye candy up a long time ago.

"Checking me out again?" he asked, wiggling his eyebrows suggestively. I smirked and moved closer to him to get up close and personal.

"You know it," I whispered huskily. He smiled pushing me away.

"Well do it from afar." He laughed before hopping in his '78 Mustang. It was gorgeous. It had black parallel racing stripes running along the top, while the rest of the car was white. He once told me that he and his dad bought it from a junkyard and restored it to its beautiful self now.

I climbed in the passenger's seat, pulling the seat belt over my chest as I examined the hood from the view of the window.

"Dude, your hood is so huge you can have sex on the thing," I commented. I turned my head to see him grinning like a fool.

"You already did, didn't you?" He kept his eyes on the road as he pulled out of the school parking lot, licking his smirking lips. I chuckled as I stared out the window. The town was quickly passing us by, the shops and restaurants were practically a blur. The green of the trees were in full view now, and I couldn't stop thinking about the time when I used to dread them. I hated it because I could never go out and run or else I would have put Robin and myself in danger.

We've been on the run for far too long that it was weird being in the same location for this long. I studied the woods as we zoomed by. There hasn't been a single rogue since then and I was glad. I know that they were only after us because of Zack, but I still get shivers whenever I think of their red eyes as they stared at you, ready to rip you apart. I closed my eyes as I suppressed the quivers in my body at the thought.

"So, are we going to Crank?" Levi asked, interrupting my thoughts. I looked at him as he waited for my answer.

"Yeah, why?"

He shook his head.

"I was just asking."

He parked at the pack house before we got out and walked inside to my room. Levi jumped to my bed and landed on his back.

"What are you going to wear tonight?" I shrugged as I rummaged through my closet.

"So, how's operation 'capture Avery' going?" he asked another question, rolling over to his stomach. I sighed, picking out a black button-up shirt with dark blue jeans and tossed them on the bed next to Levi.

"The same. I try to make an advance and he shoots me down. I mean seriously, am I ugly or something?" I turned to him, holding my arms out so he could observe me. He looked deep in thought as he placed a pointer finger to his chin, tilting his head to the side.

"Well . . . ?" I was glaring at him now. He just chuckled and shook his head.

"No man, you're hot. That's why when we go to the club, you're going to get laid and I'm going to be the one going home alone." He pouted.

I rolled my eyes as I strolled over to him and ruffled his perfect hair.

"Hey!" he exclaimed, swatting my hand away.

"Levi, you are sexy as hell. You would have no problems getting a lay for the night. You just never do it," I told him.

He sighed dramatically.

"I'm just too precious for just a lay," he said before he smirked. I bit the inside of my cheek from laughing, and instead, just nodded my head and looked at him up and down in a rude manner.

"Oh I see, and I'm just some man whore or something?" He opened his mouth to answer but he thought better and closed it, slowly giving me his usual cute innocent face that I always crack from.

"Back to Avery." He changed the subject. "Maybe he just doesn't swing that way."

I shook my head.

"I don't accept that," I said stubbornly.

"I know." He sighed.

* * *

It was eight o' clock by the time Levi and I arrived at CRANK. It was one of the few gay clubs in town where the hottest men on earth roamed the entire vicinity. After our arrival, we walked up to the bouncer with a nod.

"Morris," I greeted.

"Hey guys." He smiled, nodding for us to go in. I've been coming over here ever since Robin and I came to town. I got Levi to come with me a few months ago and he loved it so much that it became our weekly thing. Morris never gave me trouble, which I suspect is because he fancied me. If I wasn't eighteen, I think he would still let me in.

I patted his chest. "Thanks, big guy." He just grinned.

Walking in, we were soon greeted by a heavy bass techno song playing along with red strobe lights that illuminated the entire room, making the mass of bodies out on the dance floor look like crazy fun.

I needed to get in there. Levi was standing next to me and was also looking out on the dance floor. He turned to me and wiggled his eyes suggestively. Tilting my head towards the dance floor, we managed to make our way through the crowd.

The room was hot, and I was bombarded with an abundance of scents from every body in this place. The song switched to Battle Flag by Lo Fidelity Allstars, a song I loved.

Making our way to the middle of the dance floor, I grabbed Levi close to me before I wrapped my arms around his tall frame. He was as tall as Avery, standing precisely at 6'2. I sometimes hated that everyone was a towering giant . . . well besides Aiden. He gripped his hands around my hips and pulled me closer.

This is what we did till someone decided they wanted some of this. I know it's cocky but it's the truth. I began swaying with the music eventually grinding myself against him provocatively, which only caused him to throw his head back and laugh. This is why I considered Levi my best friend; we always had fun. Bending to his knees, he slowly stood back up, running his hands up my body seductively.

From the corner of my eye, I noticed a lot of people watching as they danced. A few of them were biting their lips as they watched us with lustful gazes. I don't blame them, we werewolves are very attractive creatures. I shook my head as he came back up to eye level.

"You've drawn in a crowd." I smirked. Chuckling, he brought his mouth close to my ear.

"That's the idea," he purred. I could hear the smile in his voice, and not long after, there was a tap on my shoulder,

"Do you mind if I get in this?" a deep voice said. Turning so my back was to Levi, I got a good look at the person. He had golden blond hair, gray eyes, and a face that had to be sculpted by Michelangelo himself. He also had the body a Greek god would be jealous of.

I smiled seductively. "Not at all."

He came forward so now I was between him and Levi in the sexiest man sandwich ever. Levi's hands were on my hips, while I had my arms resting on the guy's shoulders. He was grinding his lower half on mine and I was getting a bit excited.

"I can see that I'm not needed," Levi whispered in my ear as I turned my head a little to meet his knowing eyes. Smiling, I winked. Shaking his head in amusement, he backed away till I didn't feel his presence anymore.

I took a deep breath as the guy pressed his body fully against mine. Closing my eyes, I let the beat of the music sink into my system, filling me like a hypnotic drug, coupled with the guy's hardness against mine. I was practically in heaven.

"You're so damn sexy," he yelled in my ear which only made me cringe as his voice blared through my eardrums. Smiling, I pressed my face against his and whispered in his ear.

"So are you," I purred. He smiled, showing his cute dimples. Oh god, I have to have him! The song soon switched, and I pulled him closer against me, holding him as his arousal wafts up to my sensitive nose, and I suppressed my hungry growl.

"Let me buy you a drink," he offered.

Even though I wasn't old enough to drink, I wasn't going to to tell him that, so I gave him a nod. He took my hand and guided me through the tight crowd. At the bar I saw a couple eyes on me but when I set my sights, it was only for one person and this guy was my prey for tonight. The bartender set down two shots each in front of us and we chugged them quickly.

Slamming my glass on the counter, I looked to find him gazing at me hungrily. He leaned in closer to me and pressed his soft lips to my neck. I closed my eyes at the feel of his tongue running up my skin. I was unable to suppress my moan.

What can I say? A werewolf's spot was always the neck.

I tilted my head back, giving him more access before finally putting a kiss under my ear.

"You want to get out of here?" he asked. Grinning, I hopped off the stool and grabbed his wrist.

"Thought you'd never ask."

He chuckled and followed me out of the club. I caught Levi's eye before exiting, and he nodded in understanding. We walked to his car parked someway down the street and hopped in. Grabbing him by the collar of his shirt, I smashed my lips to his and raked my hands through his silky blond hair, pulling hard enough to get a sexy little groan out of him. I smiled triumphantly against his lips.

"Your place or mine?" he asked huskily against my mouth. I looked at him.

"Definitely yours," I purred, pulling back from him. I leaned back in the seat as I slowly started unbuttoning my shirt, doing one button at a time, all the while gazing at him lustfully through heavy lidded eyes as I nibbled on my bottom lip.

He bit down on his own lower lip, watching me closely.

"Shit," he cursed heavily and started his car which peeled out with a screech.

Oh, this is going to be fun.

CHAPTER 4

CALEB

I came home early in the morning. My hair was ruffled from the rough play last night and my clothes were wrinkled as I rushed out of the guy's—I still don't know his name—house before he woke up and did my walk of shame, which I certainly wasn't ashamed of. It was a fantastic night, and he really knew what he was doing.

I trudged through the door as I headed up to my room. Halfway there, I bumped into someone who shot their hand out to catch me before I toppled back down the stairs. I gripped their arms as they pulled me against them. I felt their muscular arms flex before their scent hit my nostrils.

"Caleb?" His deep voice caused me to look up at him.

"Hey Avery," I greeted him as he stepped back, letting me go. I saw him frown and his nostrils flare. A blush crept up in my cheeks. He could smell the guy from last night.

"How's your morning?" I asked him cheerfully, trying to ease the embarrassment of this awkward moment. His lips drew thin as he stared at me without blinking. I squinted my eyes as I looked around anywhere but him.

Well, this isn't awkward at all.

"Okay then." I walked around him and up to my room to quickly rinse myself off. Stripping off my shirt, I hopped in the shower, letting the hot water soothe my muscles as I washed my hair and body. I took my time before I stepped out an hour later. Wrapping a towel around my waist, I opened the door to see Levi lying on my bed. He was staring at the ceiling before he propped up on his elbows and gave me a knowing smile.

"Hey!" he greeted cheerfully. I nodded in greeting before walking over to my dresser. I grabbed a pair of boxers and slid them on.

"What's up?" I asked, tossing my towel over his head. He scowled as he snatched it off.

"Well, I came in here to see how your night was," he explained, wiggling his eyebrows. I tilted my head to the side for a second and shrugged as I bit my bottom lip.

His eyes brightened.

"Oh, that good eh?" He grinned as I put on a black shirt.

"Really good." I sighed dreamily, laying back on my bed with him.

He laughed.

"I'm guessing you were the bottom this time?" I didn't answer, but he could read it in my eyes. Hell yeah, I was the bottom and that guy was a great top!

"How old was that guy anyway?" he asked.

"Hell if I know, maybe twenty something. What happened with you last night?" I asked, leaning up on my elbow. He furrowed his brows.

"Nothing? Why?"

I groaned.

"Oh, come on! You didn't even make out with someone?"

He shrugged. "Well, there was this one guy"

"Uh huh and . . . ?" I pushed him, his cheeks flushed, and he averted his gaze, refusing to make eye contact.

"What did you do?" I asked, excited. He mumbled something that even my sensitive hearing couldn't pick up.

"What? Boy, speak up!" I demanded, causing him to huff.

"I let him go down on me!" he said louder, causing me to have the biggest grin in history.

"Oh really? That seems like more than nothing. How was it?" My eyes widened, hungry for juicy details.

He sighed and answered, "Really good,"

I punched him in the arm playfully.

"That a boy! You're finally living!"

Levi just rolled his eyes.

* * *

Levi and I both walked down the stairs together before I left him behind the lounge so I could take a walk. I made it outside in the back for some fresh air where I spotted Robin sitting just before the tree line. Frowning, I walked up to her and plopped down Indian style next to her. She didn't look up and, instead, just stared out straight in the woods with a placid expression.

"What's up sis?" I asked softly as I wrapped an arm around her. Her bright red hair was up in a ponytail; she was wearing my old black Ozzy T-shirt and a worn-out pair of jeans.

There was still no answer.

"These sort of questions require answers," I said, trying to get a smile on her face, but it wasn't working.

"It's their anniversary today," she whispered to me. I froze, closing my eyes.

"Yeah, I know," I muttered looking back at her. She turned to me, her beautiful blue brown eyes mirroring mine.

"I miss them so much, Cal." Her eyes filled with tears. I pulled her in a hug, burying my face in her hair.

"So do I, Rob," I told her softly. I let her cry in my shoulder as I whispered some comforting words while I rubbed her back in support. Eventually, she stopped crying and pulled away before throwing a punch on my arm.

"Ow!" I jerked back, rubbing my arm. "What the hell?"

"I told you not to call me that!" she chided me, her face stern, but I could see the ghost of a smile play on her lips.

"Man hands." I pouted. She rolled her eyes.

"Don't be jealous because I'm the man in my relationship."

I scowled at her.

"Hey, just because I like to be a bottom on occasions doesn't make me the girl!" I said pointing my finger at her face. "Just half the time. Plus, who said you wore the pants in the relationship anyway? Has Sadie consented to that?"

She bit her lip and avoided my gaze.

"Exactly," I whispered tauntingly in her ear. She pushed me hard, causing me to fall on my back as she hopped to her feet.

"Well, you've ruined my moment of silence, jackass." And with that she stomped off.

Climbing to my feet, I watched her storm off. I sighed and leaned against the tree as I rubbed my eyes.

How could I almost forget that it was the death anniversary of my parents? I growled in frustration. I have to be the worst son ever to forget something so important.

Robin and I always made sure we pay our respects the best we could, ever since we were on the run. I walked through the trees; it was quiet and peaceful. The forest has always been considered a no entry zone because of Zack and his rogues. However, since I knew there were good guards on the lookout, I was okay . . . I guess.

The sky was slowly darkening with rain clouds, though I didn't mind it. Leaves crunched underneath my shoes as the memories of when my father would take me out hunting with the pack came back to me. I would be stuck to my father's side like I was glued there while he would give me tips on how to catch my prey even though I couldn't turn yet. I loved it. I loved watching the pack prowl the lands in their huge wolf forms. Dad would stay in his human form when I was around, pointing at fellow pack members on the hunt.

My sister, on the other hand, would stay with mom whenever we were out even though she really wanted to go. It was on one of those hunts when I had dropped the 'gay' bomb.

Six years ago

"Dad," I said when we were pretty far behind the others. He turned to me.

"Yeah?"

I remember how my palms were sweating as I looked up into the same identical eyes that my twin and I inherited from. Brown and blue, it was a unique blend of colors, for eyes anyway.

"I need to tell you something." He waited as we stopped to look at each other.

"Okay, what's up?" he asked.

Would he hate me? Would he look at me in disgust if I told him this? I didn't want to lose the love of my father over something that I couldn't control. Those were the things going through my twelve year-old mind at the time as I bit my lip and fidgeted.

"Can you promise me you won't hate me? Please . . ." I pleaded desperately. I know I was too young for realizing the sexual orientation of my life, but I just knew that I wasn't like all the other boys or my friends for that matter. Dad's face turned to worry as he stepped forward, placing a gentle hand on my shoulder.

"I could never hate you, Caleb; that's impossible. You're my son," he reassured but it wasn't really working. When I didn't continue, he urged. "Come on, out with it."

Sighing, I bowed my head, unable to meet his gaze.

"I think there's something seriously wrong with me, Dad," I confessed softly. He didn't say anything, so I continued.

"I look around and I feel funny when I'm around . . . certain people," I muttered.

My dad shuffled his feet before he bent to one knee, staring at me in concern as he kept at my level.

"What are you talking about, Caleb?" he asked, cupping the side of my neck with his hand. I began fidgeting with my fingers as I stared down at them. The panic was setting in at how this conversation could go. I heard stories about people being kicked out of their homes for this. I was panting now and my vision was becoming blurry with unshed tears.

"Caleb." His tone was beyond worried now.

"I-I . . ." He's going to shun me out of my pack. I know it.

"Damn it, Son, spit it out!" he ordered, his tone a tad frantic. A sob ripped from my chest and I let it out.

"I . . . think . . . I like . . . boys," I stuttered through my tears. I felt him stiffen and my world began to crash. I knew it. I threw myself in his still arms as I wrapped my arms around his neck, getting one last hug in before I was getting kicked out of the pack.

"I'm sorry!" I sobbed against his neck. To my surprise, I felt him hug me tightly.

"Oh Caleb," he whispered into my hair.

"I'm so sorry, Daddy." I wept. His hands cupped the back of my head pressing me further into his shoulder. "I can't help it."

"No, no, no. Caleb, stop it," he cooed. I was gasping for breath. "Why are you crying?" he asked me softly.

"Because you hate me now." I sobbed onto his shoulder. That's when he began to chuckle.

Pulling back, I stared at him stunned.

"I don't hate you," he told me like it was the hundredth time he'd said it to me. "I told you that I could never hate you, Caleb. I love you with all I have."

"Really?" I asked as he wiped my tears away with his thumbs and nodded.

"I have no idea how on earth you would know this at your age, but I couldn't care less if you were gay or straight. It doesn't matter, you're my blood, Caleb. My family. My son. And there is nothing in this world or the next that could make me stop loving you." He gave me his usual happy-go-lucky smile, and I melted in his arms with relief as I hugged him again.

"Thank you," I whispered shakily. Now, how is he going to feel when Robin tells him her little secret?

I stopped walking as the memory ended and found that I was in the middle of the forest. Blinking, I looked around my surroundings.

How the hell did I get here?

Sighing, I turned around, ready to go back when the sky decided to open up and let the rain pour. This caused me to growl in annoyance.

"Really?" I said to no one in particular. I trudged back to the house, getting soaked in the process. This had to be punishment for almost forgetting about my parents. The water was dripping from the fringe of my hair and into my eyes.

"Ugh!" I exclaimed, slicking my hair back with my fingers. I was almost at the house when I felt a strong figure knock onto me.

"Ah!" I screamed as I fell on my back, my head hitting the mud as I heard a grunt from the other person. Groaning, I rolled onto my side and tried to catch the breath that had been knocked out of me.

"Sh*t that hurt!" I whined before I propped myself up on my hands and knees, shaking my head from the impact.

"I-I'm s-sorry." Came an unfamiliar voice, causing me to raise my hackles in defense. I snapped my head up to see a boy no older than fourteen picking himself off the ground. He had shaggy blond hair and bright green eyes that were currently clouded with fear. I frowned at how ragged his clothes were; they had rips, and old dirt caked on them. His big frantic eyes met mine and he scrambled on his knees and crawled towards me.

"Please! Help me!"

CHAPTER 5

CALEB

"Why is it that every lone wolf decides to come to this pack for help?" Liam grumbled while Aiden took a seat next to the boy. After bumping into him, I kind of had to sneak him into the house because I couldn't just leave him out there in the rain, now could I? But of course, Avery caught me.

I watched as the boy's eyes darted from face to face while our alphas; Avery; Dom, the beta; and Robert, Liam's dad, surrounded him. He was scared out of his mind and I wanted to know why. It didn't really help that he wouldn't talk to anyone. The only thing he has said since he's been here were the three words he told me earlier.

"Caleb, can I talk with you?" I looked up, surprised that Avery had finally acknowledged my presence. Frowning, I stood up but a hand snatched me back. As I turned around, I saw the boy kept a firm grip on my wrist, his eyes wide with terror.

"I'll be right back. I'm just going to be right outside that door, okay?" I reassured him. His large green eyes stared up at me for a long time before he finally loosened his grip.

I smiled.

"Be right back."

Turning my gaze back to Avery, I walked with him out the door before he shut it quietly behind him. Turning on my heel, I leaned my back against the wall. Avery's face was calm, but I knew he was anything but calm.

"Yes?" I asked. His brown eyes were hard as he glared at me.

"Why would you bring some random kid here?" he whispered. My face was blank as I looked at him.

"Well technically, he brought himself here. He ran into me," I explained. Sighing, he crossed his arms, his legs spread as he stood in his usual intimidating stance which incidentally didn't work on me.

"You could have put Aiden in danger. Heck, he could still be in danger," he scolded. Rolling my eyes, I pushed myself off the wall and stood up straight in a challenging gesture.

"How is he dangerous, Avery? He's just a kid, and he hasn't even hit puberty yet," I scoffed.

"He could be a danger by bringing people in here, Caleb. Do you ever think? Don't you remember when you came here with the same problem?" he growled.

I stepped closer so I was up in his face, or at least I tried to. He was so much taller than me.

"Well, do you remember when I was being chased by a mad man and needed help?" He nodded, not even fazed that I was inches away from his face.

"Yes, and I remember that Aiden was kidnapped in the process." I shook my head at his stubbornness.

"He's only a kid, Avery, and I know what being on the run feels like. If there is a way to help him, then I want to do just that," I said firmly. I glared up at him, barely noticing the faraway look crossing his face. My glare then slowly turned into a frown.

"Well, it's not up to you to make that decision, Caleb. That belongs to your alphas and it needs to be respected." I rolled my eyes. Here we go again with his 'oh so righteous' speech.

"If they think that this boy is going to bring trouble then you have to obey their judgments." He continued. I tilted my head back in exasperation, letting out a loud sigh.

"Oh, can you just cram it about the alphas for one second?!" I groaned, exasperated. His hand snaked out and gripped my chin tightly, forcing me to look at him. His brown eyes were hard with annoyance and his face set.

"Caleb, quit being a brat and be responsible for once." He forced out through gritted teeth.

"I am being responsible by helping this kid out, Avery. He needs it badly, I just know it," I retorted jerking my chin away from his fingers. He sighed, closing his eyes.

"We don't bring suspicious wolves in the pack; that should be a reasonable rule to follow by now. But if Aiden and Liam are okay with this, then you're going to have to keep an eye on him," he ordered. "You're on babysitting duty." I never got to answer as the door opened, causing me to back away from Avery, who also moved away from the door.

Everyone came out at once, leaving the boy alone in the room.

They closed the door as I stepped closer. "Well, did he say anything?" I asked.

Aiden shook his head.

"He wouldn't say a damn word," Liam spoke, frustrated.

"We tried to get him to tell us what was wrong with him but he's not budging. He's a stubborn little thing," Aiden explained, making me frown.

Why the hell would he come all this way asking for help and not try and get it?

"I can try," I offered but Robert shook his head.

"No, I think we should let him rest for a while. Let him take a shower, get some food, then tomorrow we can try and get some answers."

Everyone agreed but me, but I had no say in the matter so I'll just leave it for tomorrow.

* * *

AVERY

The days passed, and the mysterious kid still wouldn't say a thing to anyone. The only person he seemed to give any fleeting attention to was Caleb, but he wouldn't talk to him either. Whenever he was around, the kid would give him a pleading look, as if silently begging him not to leave before he constantly reached out to grab his hand to keep the older boy from leaving.

There was something about the kid that I couldn't put my finger on; nothing bad though, just different. When Monday came around, Liam said that it was best to enroll the kid at the school to keep a close eye on him, but the problem was, we still didn't know his damn name. Good thing the principle was a pack member and knew the situation, so we got him in under a false name and such.

"Avery." Liam came up to me, bringing the kid by his arm. "I want you to take care of him. I know your soul purpose is to look after Aiden, but I need you to do this. I've already informed Caleb, and he will be looking after him as well." I stared at the long-haired blond kid and didn't protest but gave a stiff nod imstead.

"Good, don't lose him," he joked. I kept my face blank as Liam walked off with Aiden while I stared down at the small boy. He kept his eyes on the ground while his hands fiddled with his backpack straps.

How the hell did I get stuck with babysitting?

Sighing, I placed a hand on the kid's back and guided him to the school building.

I helped him get his schedule, books, and locker number. As I waited for him to open his locker, I spotted Caleb standing with Levi and they started laughing about something. I don't know why but it reminded me of the other day when he was out all night and came home covered in some other male's stench. The thought alone irked me. How can he just go and mess around with someone knowing that he had a mate out there waiting for him?

"That's not really the reason is it?" my inner voice asked.

I sighed. No, that's not the entire reason, but there's nothing I can do about it except let him find his better half.

"But do you really want that?" Again, my conscience was contradicting me. Damn, why am I so confused? I need to keep my beliefs strong and turn my back on this distraction that was everything 'Caleb'. But somehow the annoying male was starting to seep deeper into my consciousness and it was scaring the sh*t out of me.

Fortunately, the sound of the locker slamming shut brought me back to the present, and I looked down at the boy who stood there, still staring at the floor. Straightening from the row of lockers, I again placed my hand on his back before leading him through the busy halls to his class. We knew he was around thirteen or fourteen since he was an unchanged wolf, so we put him in the freshmen classes.

"I will be here when the bell rings to take you to your next class. And from now on, either Caleb or I will be escorting you to your classes, understand?" I told him gruffly. He gave me a nod before disappearing into his classroom. With that, I turned to head to Aiden's first class. On the way there, I saw Caleb again with some random guy he pinned against the wall, eyeing him like he was his latest prey.

"We should go to the club sometime," he told the guy who looked like he was going to faint at any minute. I noticed Caleb did have that effect on people. I'm not going to lie, he was very attractive, and he definitely knew it and often used his looks to his advantage.

"Um . . ." the guy stuttered. Chuckling, Caleb dragged a finger down the guy's chest and I could hear his breath hitch.

"Sure . . ." he sighed, looking at Caleb with lustful dark eyes. Smiling, Caleb leaned closer to his ear, and I watched the guy shut his eyes tightly, suppressing a moan.

I gritted my teeth. I had no idea why I did it, but I marched over towards them and grabbed the back of Caleb's shirt, yanking him off.

"Hey!" he exclaimed as I glared at the guy, causing him to jump in fright before running away. Caleb jerked his shirt away from my grasp before turning around to scowl at me.

"What the hell, Avery?"

I didn't reply because I couldn't. *Why did I do that?*

After straightening his clothes, Caleb looked up at me expectantly.

"Well?"

I collected myself as I hardened my features.

"Have some common decency, Caleb. You know how this school is with same sex displays of affection," I scolded.

He narrowed his unique brown and blue eyes at me.

"Like I care, Avery," he said, rolling his eyes. "What are they going to do? Burn me at the stake?" Shaking his head with a scoff, he was about to storm off when I grabbed at his arm roughly, pulling him back a bit too hard which caused him to fall against me.

He gasped, gripping my shoulders to keep himself from tumbling as I wrapped an arm around his waist. Our faces were too close, and I could feel his suprisingly sweet breath fan across my face. We both seemed frozen in that moment; I watched as his gaze flickered back and forth from my eyes and down at my lips. His clean but earthy scent hit me. He smelled like freshwater orchids and the sweet scent of spearmint; and as weird as it was, it was a very captivating scent.

My heart was pounding. Why am I acting like this? It didn't make any sense. I have never been affected by anyone before, but now Caleb was slowly capturing my attention.

His eyes darkened and his teeth seized his bottom lip. I guess he thought this was something else now because he pressed further into my body, molding himself into me. I felt the caress of his hand move up the side of my neck to the nape, his fingers playing in my hair, where amazingly my usually uninterested and subdued wolf came alive, inwardly purring. I never expected him to be so curious and open.

The warmth of Caleb's breath on my neck shook me from my thoughts and I held my breath.

Get away from him, Avery!

Push him away!

GET A GRIP!

The shrill ring of the school bell blasted, just when his mouth was pressed under my ear. Tearing myself away from him, I stared at him for a second in astonishment. He frowned at me as I kept stepping back, shaking my head.

"Avery?" he questioned, and I spun on my heels and walked away. I hate the pathetic feeling of running away from my problems, but this was all I could do. I don't know what was happening to me. I've let things get too far whenever he's near me, and I almost forgot all of my principles.

What the hell is he doing to me?

CHAPTER 6

CALEB

"Apparently, the humans are beginning to complain to their parents about Aiden and Liam," Levi said as he set his tray down and took a seat at my lunch table.

I looked up to him with a frown, my fork inches away from my mouth.

"What are you talking about?" I asked before I shoved my food into my mouth. Levi nodded a greeting over to the blond boy next to me. He still hasn't said a thing to anyone, much less his name; although, his false name was Andrew but no one seems to call him that. It didn't really fit him so I've decided to just call him Blondie.

"I'm talking about the complaints that the principal is receiving from parents. Something about their children being subjected to immoral sinners in our school," he scoffed before eating a generous amount of mashed potatoes.

"So what are they going to do? They can't kick them out; it's their last year," I retorted.

Levi shrugged and placed his spoon down.

"I don't know, but I do know that a few people saw you and Avery the other day and it caused a major uproar along with the alphas," he explained, and I rolled my eyes.

"This school is beyond ridiculous! Don't they have their own lives to worry about?" I growled. Looking around the cafeteria, I only just noticed the weird stares I was getting from people. I couldn't help but chuckle at how this was turning into another Aiden incident, despite the fact that there were a ton of differences between me and him.

One: I was no puny human that you could push around; and

Two: I was proud to be who I am. They could whine to their parents all they want, but it's not going to change my ways.

"You're laughing?" Levi asked, his expression clearly amused. I shrugged before shaking my head.

"Why not? I think it's hilarious that they think glaring at me is going to scare me off, or that running off to their parents like a bunch of spoiled little brats is supposed to intimidate me." Levi didn't say anything, so I continued finishing my lunch.

My thoughts went back to that day in the hall when Avery and I had a moment. I was beginning to realize that every time Avery and I would get really close like that, he would run away. The looks that crossed his face in those moments were clear as day. He was scared of something, but what? Was he scared of admitting his feelings towards me? Or was he scared of being close like that to someone in general?

I do know that since he's a wanderer, he's never held those kinds of feelings for anyone. But was he really that terrified to even try? I couldn't accept that. I wouldn't. I had set my sights on Avery and I planned on getting what I want, but was what I was aiming for had more than what I planned it to be? Was I just looking for a quick lay with Avery? No, I wanted more than that. To think, of all the people I've slept with, I have never once made a relationship out of them, but it was different with Avery for some reason.

Ever since I saw him, I was attracted to him and I knew that I wanted to have more than just a one-night stand. It was difficult, but I was going to tear down those walls he has built and tread across new waters. I think he's worth it.

"Hey, are you going to take the kid to class?" Levi asked as I stood up.

"Yep."

*   *   *

Since I was stuck on babysitting duty, I couldn't exactly go to the club today which sucked. We all piled in Levi's car after school and drove home. Once we entered the house, Blondie rushed to his room, keeping his head down the whole time.

Sighing, I slapped Levi on the shoulder and went to my room. Throwing my bag in the corner, I collapsed on my bed with a hardy sigh.

Why do I feel like my life is getting more and more complicated by the minute?

First, Avery won't accept me; then this mysterious boy comes along; and now, the whole school might one day become an angry mob with pitchforks and torches that planned on chasing us off for who we are.

My lids slowly dropped along with the day's exhaustions. The last thing on my mind was the all-time question: Who was this kid and why the hell did he come here begging for help?

*   *   *

AVERY

"Can you please tell us your name at least?" Aiden begged the kid. I posed by the door as Aiden continued his questions, hoping to get at least something out of him, but it was a lost cause. He just sat there, looking at his feet without giving any sort of indication that he understood.

Sighing, Aiden hung his head.

"Why won't you talk to me?" he muttered, a bit exasperated. Just by looking at the kid, I knew that he never would—not to Aiden anyway or Liam. But I do know that he would eventually talk to Caleb.

"Alpha," I interjected. Aiden turned to me with curious blue eyes. I shook my head at him. "He won't ever speak a word to anyone unless he's the right person," I told him.

Frowning, Aiden got out of his kneeling position from the kid.

"Why do you say that?" he asked. I peered at the kid again, his big light green eyes peaked up at me from his peripheral.

"I just have a feeling."

Aiden's brows scrunched up as he turned his head back to the kid.

"Well, that's all good but Liam is going to want answers soon, so how are we going to find this 'one' person out of the seven billion people in the world?"

A ghost of a smile played on my lips. "You're going to have to narrow that down to a few hundred. That person is here but it will still take time for him to talk."

"Who?"

I looked back at the kid and kept my mouth shut. Sighing, Aiden threw his hands up in frustration and left the room. I stood there watching the boy as the door shut. He wasn't looking at me anymore. His focus turned to the blackened fireplace in the room, a blank stare still evident on his features. I wasn't going to lie and say I wasn't curious on what was on his mind at the moment. I was getting a weird feeling from him but not in a bad way.

I was ordered to stay and watch the kid till someone came along and took over. Eventually, my mind began to wander a bit—to a place filled with bright green grass and huge mountains. The cold breeze hit against my skin as the joyful giggles of my little sister echoed in the wind. The sky was a grayish blue color as I lay in the grass staring up at it. We lived in the country side of England where we were able to run free in our wolf forms, but I was too young for that and so were my siblings.

James came rushing towards me. I was fourteen at the time, just one year off from hitting my full maturity, while James was twelve. He had bright blonde hair and blue eyes that he inherited from our mom. My six year old sister Delilah, Dee for short, had the same dirty blonde hair and brown eyes as me. Today, her hair was pulled back into a ponytail, although the soft tendrils still flowed down her back. She wore a cute peach colored dress which fit well with the scenery.

"Avery!" she exclaimed as she dived into me, causing me to grunt in pain. "Why are you over here by yourself?" I couldn't help but smile as her words were mashed together by her baby voice, it was adorable.

"I don't know, Dee," I said, feeling James sit next to me.

"You're always like that, bro," he told me, and I turned to look at him.

"What do you mean?" I frowned. I watched him start to pick at the grass while he kept his gaze down.

"You're always so distant from us."

"No, I'm not," I argued defensively. Delilah settled down on my lap, reaching out to play with a strand of my overgrown dirty blonde hair that hung in my face.

"Yes, you do," she agreed. "I always find you alone somewhere whether it's in the house or outside. You like to be by yourself big brother." Her attention was still focused on my hair as she spoke.

Was I really like that? I won't lie, I did like my space, and I felt like I needed to learn to be on my own. It felt like a huge forewarning in my subconscious. I suppose I was distant, but it wasn't like I was the best person to hang out with, so I figured I was better off solo.

"Well I'm sorry Dee, James." James just shrugged while Dee jumped in my lap.

"It's alright Avery, we understand that's just how you are." This caused me to smile and I pinched her flushed cheeks.

"Well thank you for your understanding, Dee." I laughed. She threw her arms around my neck.

"You're so very welcome, big brother!" she exclaimed rather loudly in my ear. Looking over to James, I saw him stare out into the mountains.

"I heard it's going to rain tomorrow," he randomly said.

I chuckled. "It always rains James, that's far from something new."

He smirked.

"What do you want to do for your birthday this week?" he asked, glancing over at me. I grimaced, I didn't know why but I was dreading for my birthday.

"I really don't want to do anything."

"What? We have to celebrate dummy!" Dee exclaimed, grabbing my face between her small hands. "Mummy has this big surprise party for you—"

"Dee!" James scolded cutting her off, Delilah's eyes widened into saucers as she slapped her little hands over her mouth.

"Oops," she whispered. James huffed a loud sigh.

"Oops is right you little brat." I was trying my hardest not to laugh.

"A party huh?" I teased.

"At least be surprised, I was told to keep it a secret, but I let it slip to Dee and then she went up and spilled the beans, the little twerp," he pleaded, ruffling up her hair. Again, she had my face in her hands.

"Please big brother, keep it a secret. Mummy is working really hard on this and so is Papa." She gave me her signature puppy dog face. I chuckled but nodded.

"Okay, I'll act completely shocked just for you," I said, tapping her nose playfully. She giggled while James looked relieved. I did all but begged the Spirits to help me with this birthday. Not only was it the day that I finally turn but it was also the day that would set me on my life's path.

What was mine going to be like?

* * *

"Hey Avery!" I was brought back to the present by Dom, who poked his head in through the door.

"Yeah?" I asked.

"I'm here to take over," he said.

"Oh," I looked back at the kid who was fast asleep on his bed. Nodding, I walked passed Dom and went down the hall with a frown. Why did that specific memory have to come back? It was one of the happier times of my life with my family.

"Ave." I turned and saw Aiden come out of his room.

"Yes?"

"I'll be going out to visit my parents tomorrow."

I nodded once. "I'll be ready to leave Alpha, what time?"

He sighed. I knew he hated it when I was so formal, but it was a force of habit that was beyond breaking now.

"Three, we're having dinner."

"Is Alpha Moore coming?" He shook his head.

"No, he's going to be busy tomorrow." He frowned. I nodded again.

"Okay." And with that, he walked back to his room.

Great, now I have to put up with Aiden's crazy mother. Lucky for me, I loved her craziness.

CHAPTER 7

CALEB

"Why are you poking my face?" I asked Levi. We were sitting on the couch. The TV in front of us was mute, and Blondie was on the other side of us, curled into a chair. His eyes stared at the floor as Levi pushed his finger into my cheek again as he faced me.

"Why?" He started. "Because I'm bored and you're my entertainment for the moment."

"Ugh!" I exclaimed, leaning my head against the back of the couch, clearly annoyed.

"Poke, poke, poke," he continued saying. It should be illegal to poke somebody this many times.

"Oh my God, I am going to bite your damn finger off!" I snapped at him, lifting my head up to glare at him. He gave me an innocent look, his finger still pressed against my cheek.

"But your face is so soft," he whined, leaning his head closer to mine before rubbing our cheeks together.

"Ahh," he sighed.

"You are so weird," I muttered to which he giggled.

I tried to watch the TV show; not really knowing what the hell it was about, probably because Levi's hair kept getting in the way. Soon after, the sound of footsteps approaching caught my attention before their scent did.

"I'm so bored!" Kyle's voice boomed next to me.

Oh, Kyle. He and his father had gone off somewhere a couple weeks ago. I kind of missed him, he was my video gaming buddy after all. It was no fun playing without someone to boast to unless it was Kyle. Levi couldn't play to save his life and neither could Aiden.

"Yeah, well you and Levi should go and be bored together. Go up into your room. Who knows what the possibilities have in store for the two of you?" I teased, pushing Levi off me and onto Kyle who was sitting on the couch.

"Ew." Levi made a face before scrambling off and fell on the floor away from Kyle, who had a disgusted look on his face.

"Yeah, okay I'm trying real hard to look past at all the gay sh*t in this pack and be cool with it since my sister is one of you. So let's not add any awkwardness to it shall we?" he proposed as he leaned back and rested his arm on the back of the couch. I rolled my eyes.

What he said was true, it had taken him a while to get used to the Alphas, along with his sister and mine, and even me to some extent. Eventually, he did become more comfortable with me more than anyone else for the past few months and we've grown especially close, practically making us brothers now . . . well technically speaking, we *are* brothers since our sisters were mated.

"So, bro," I joked. "Where did you and dearest father go?" I saw the slight frown on his face as he looked over to Blondie.

"Um, to some neighboring packs. Who's the kid?" I noticed his frown had deepened.

"We don't know, he doesn't talk much," I told him, my curiosity spiking. "Why?"

He tore his gaze away from Blondie and raised an eyebrow at me.

"Well it's kind of hard not to ask when you've got somebody you've never seen around here before, but I think I have," he said.

"Hey kid have we met before?" he asked him. I watched the kid's green eyes widened as he looked up at Kyle. Kyle pointed at him. "We have!" but he frowned again. "But where?"

I watched Blondie jump up from his chair and run out of the room.

"Blondie?" I called after him. Levi, who was still on the floor, sat up and watched him leave.

"You know him?" I asked.

Kyle shook his head.

"No, I don't know, but I never forget a face and his is very familiar, I don't know why though, he's just a kid."

I sighed.

"Well if you do remember tell me okay? We've been trying to get him to talk for weeks now and he won't say a thing to anyone."

Kyle just shrugged.

"Where's Sadie?" he asked.

"Probably with Robin," I huffed, laying down across the couch before I put my feet on Kyle's lap, causing him to narrow his eyes at me.

"I think they said they were going out on a date or something." Levi added.

"So why did you and Daddy go to those packs?" I asked. Kyle shrugged, staring down at my feet.

"Robert asked my dad to come visit at the Lunar pack. Apparently, they were curious as to why we had two males for Alphas instead of a Luna. It was the most boring thing my dad has ever dragged me on. We tried to explain the best we could about Liam and Aiden's position to them and just when we were about to leave, Robert called us to go visit another pack. That's why we were gone for so long."

"So, it's just us with same sex mated members in a pack?" Levi asked.

"Yeah I guess, because every pack we went to were either grossed out, curious, or awed at what we had to say. I just hope that they don't come barging in on us to wipe us off the face of the earth for this."

I rolled my eyes.

"Oh, come on. They know that we're one of the best allies to have on their side so why the hell would they even try and get rid of us? We'd wipe the floor with all of them. Gays rule!" I insisted.

"Yeah, whatever. Now why the crap is the TV on mute? What's the point of having it on if you can't hear it?" he growled, snatching the remote off the side table. Levi sighed, getting to his feet before he plopped down on my lap.

"Oof!" I grunted as Levi settled himself comfortably.

I could tell Kyle was frustrated about something, but as usual he would never tell anybody what was on his mind.

* * *

AVERY

We pulled up to Aiden's house. The drive was quiet and pretty much uneventful.

"Your brother is here," I said, turning the car off. Aiden nodded.

"Yep," he said excitedly before hurrying out. We weren't even on the first step to the door yet when it came flying open and a blonde blur ran out to attack Aiden with a hug.

"My baby!" she yelled.

"Ow Mom!" Aiden complained. "I can't breathe!" He wheezed. This woman needs to learn some restraint. She stepped back away from Aiden and turned to me with her usual big smile.

"Avery!" she exclaimed, jumping towards me before she pulled me into another huge hug.

"How have you been, honey?" she squeaked in my ear, making me wince.

"Ahh . . ." I whined, putting a hand over my ear.

"Jeez Grace, the boy has sensitive hearing! You can't go screaming into his ear like that," Mr. Carlisle said, before he walked out to hug his son.

Grace pulled back with a small pout.

"I'm so sorry I forgot," she whispered. I nodded

"It's alright ma'am," I told her. She slapped my shoulder,

"What did I tell you about calling me that? It's Grace or Beautiful but I don't think my husband would approve with that last one." She giggled behind her hand. I couldn't help but chuckle. This woman was something else, no wonder Aiden was the way he is: lovable and caring.

"Will you quit flirting with the man Grace? I'm getting jealous over here," Mr. Carlisle hissed playfully before grabbing her towards him. He wrapped his arms around her as he buried his face against her neck. Grace slapped at his arms.

"Quit it!" She giggled again. Aiden gagged dramatically and sidestepped past them to walk into the house.

I could tell they were soul mates just from the look of them, I suppose even humans can find their other halves.

"Well come on in, son," Mr. Carlisle told me, waving me inside. Once I was in the house, I saw Aiden pressed on the floor with his sister on top of him.

"Aiden, I missed you!" she screamed. Nash was sitting at the kitchen table with a dark-haired girl on his lap. He stood up, holding his hand out to me.

"Hey man," he said as we shook hands. "This is my girlfriend, Cassie."

I smiled, nodding to her.

"Cassie, this is Avery," he introduced us.

"Nice to meet you," I said.

"Same here." She smiled. She had a nice small-town girl persona about her. Her hair was cut short to her shoulders and she wore a nice yellow Sunday dress.

"Okay everyone!" Grace called out loudly. "We have dinner on the stove waiting for us, so Connie get off you brother," she said, stepping over them before she skipped to the kitchen.

"Con, quit smothering Aiden," Mr. Carlisle told her, walking around them as he followed his wife's example.

"I'm smothering him with love!" she complained.

Cassie scoffed. "That's a first". I raised an eyebrow at the biting sarcasm in her voice. Connie looked up from Aiden to glare at her.

"Just because I don't show any of it to you doesn't mean I don't have any to give." She stuck her tongue out at her while Cassie rolled her eyes.

"Whatever, you little brat."

Nash laughed, pulling her into him before he wrapped his arms around her waist, slowly rocking her back and forth.

"You guys are like rabid wolves whenever you're around each other." Cassie sighed relaxing back against him.

I held in the snicker at how ironic that was since both Cassie and Connie didn't know anything about us.

"Avery." I heard Aiden whine. I walked over him, lifting Connie off away from his form before taking Aiden's hand and slowly pulled him to his feet.

"We're waiting!" Grace called out from the kitchen, the sound of plates clanging against each other echoed as she set the table.

Once we were at the dinner table, all I could hear were the clicking and clanging sounds of forks and knives. Grace was asking Aiden as many questions as she could without revealing too much, while I sat there, quietly observing the two. Their playfulness and loving relationship towards each other made me feel happy for Aiden yet somehow even lonelier than usual.

I know I had Aiden now to preoccupy my time with, but it didn't stop the longing I had for the one thing I missed deeply. My family.

Grace reminded me of my loving and caring mother. I also missed my funny and protective father who taught me everything he could before I left, along with my crazy eccentric little brother and cute baby sister. I missed them so much that sometimes I feel like running straight back to England, but I knew that I couldn't, not after what I did. After all, I left them all without leaving a single word. Still, it was the right thing to do and I have to keep telling myself that.

"So, Avery . . ." I heard someone call my name, causing me to pull out of my melancholy thoughts as I looked up at Grace.

"Yes?"

She smiled.

"Anyone special?"

"Mom!" Aiden whined.

"What?" she asked her son before turning back at me. "Any cute girls? Handsome guys maybe?" She wiggled her eyebrows suggestively.

"Mom!" Aiden snapped.

"You never know these days, honey," she said with a shrug.

I smiled. "No ma'am."

"Ah, what did I say?" she warned, pointing her finger at me.

"No, Grace," I corrected myself as I grinned at her.

She gasped. "Why, you're so handsome I bet both men and women are falling all over themselves just to be with you," she said. I felt Aiden's frustration, so I looked up at him. His eyes were sad as he watched me. He knew there was no one I could ever connect with with the same way that he and Liam had.

"Sorry." He mouthed as I nodded my understanding.

"I'm just not interested," I told her. She leaned over to pat my hand.

"All in due time and it'll be real soon I bet," she reassured as she gazed with her honest blue eyes. All I did was force a smile on my face and continued eating.

I really don't think it will be.

CHAPTER 8

CALEB

I made my way down the stairs in the kitchen to get a snack when I noticed Avery leaning in front of the sink. His head was bent down and his back was facing me. I felt the drool seep from my mouth as I watched him in those tight jeans. The muscular cords on his back were tense and prominent against his smooth bronze skin.

I bit my bottom lip, keeping the whine from escaping them. A smirk eased on my mouth as I slowly crept up to him. He still hadn't noticed me yet. As I moved closer behind, I pushed up on my tiptoes and licked his neck up to his ear. He jumped away from me with the cutest squeak I've ever heard.

"Damn it Caleb!" he growled. I just smiled.

"Hey there, lover boy," I purred, stalking up to him. He rolled his eyes at me.

"Stop," he said but I shook my head.

"No chance." I pushed him against the counter so he was trapped.

"Caleb," he warned harshly.

"Ooh, how many times do I have to tell you that I love it when you say my name?" I was pressed up against him, a little surprised that he allowed me to be this close, but I didn't dwell on that.

"Say it again," I whispered.

"Get your ass off me," he growled.

"Where were we the other day?" I asked, breathing into his skin, my nose ran along the column of his neck as he shivered, making me grin.

"My, my, is someone enjoying this?" I teased, kissing his collarbone. His skin was so soft and warm, and his woodsy scent engulfed me. I looked up to see his jaw clenched and his gaze focused anywhere else but me. It was in that moment that I thought of something. It was the way he was always awkward when I was too close or was teasing him relentlessly.

"Avery? Have you ever been kissed before?" I asked softly, dragging my finger along the hard muscular ridges of his stomach and watched them quiver under my touch.

"That's none of your business," he told me stiffly. My fingers reached the waistband before it hooked into his jeans, pulling his bottom half towards me until there was no space left. I leaned my face closer to his, lips inches apart; his breath smelled of mint toothpaste and just him. Delicious.

"I can be your first, if you'd like," I whispered huskily. His brown eyes stared down into mine, and his expression was blank as always.

"I think that you should get out of my face, Caleb," he said softly, his warm breath fanning against my cheeks. My hand pushed further down into his jeans till he quickly caught my wrist before I could reach my wanted destination.

"Now!" he growled lowly in my face. With a shrug, I licked at his lips playfully, getting nothing from him, not even an expression.

"You're missing out, Avery," I told him. I leaned close to his ear. "I could rock your world; you have no idea," I whispered, wiggling my fingers that were still trapped in his jeans till he yanked them out.

"Don't you have babysitting duty?" He changed the subject and sidestepped away from me.

I rolled my eyes.

"Don't you?" I countered, then my face lit up. "Hey, how about we take junior to the batting cages? You can teach him how to swing, honey," I said while I mimicked swinging a bat. He rolled his eyes before making his way out the door.

"No? Maybe we can take him on for a bike lesson!" I yelled after him. "A two-wheeler this time!"

He didn't reply.

"What? Was it something I said?"

Chuckling, I walked over to the fridge, grabbing whatever looked appetizing which was fried rice from the other night and carried it out to the lounge where Kyle was sitting.

"Why are you always in here?" I asked, plopping down next to him before I threw my feet up on the table.

"Because I can," he huffed. I raised my brows up for a second.

"Wow very clear and straight to the point," I commented sarcastically.

"You know me." His voice flat and void.

"Wow something must have crawled really far up your anal canal." I chuckled before stuffing my mouth with cold fried rice.

"I bet you'd like to try and find it," he huffed. I bumped my shoulder against his.

"Just because I'm gay doesn't mean I like to be up in just anyone's ass," I joked.

"Hey what happened with you and that Avery guy? Did you snag him or what?" he asked.

Kyle, besides Levi, was the only one I told on how I was going to capture Avery's attention and make him mine.

"Yeah, well he's tougher than I originally thought he would be," I said nonchalantly, even though my feelings on how I first wanted to approach him changed. Back then I just wanted to get him in bed, but now, I wanted to keep him all to myself and never let go.

"Hmm . . ." was all he said.

"So, have you found anything about Blondie?" I changed the subject.

Kyle sighed, slouching further in the couch as he kept his eyes on the TV.

"No." There was a long silence after that, so I just shrugged and stuffed my mouth with more rice. Right when Kyle's football game was about to start and my brain was starting to fry with boredom, Levi came in.

"Hey Caleb, are we going to CRANK tonight?" he asked before sitting in my lap. I raised my container over his head so he could get comfortable, and circled him in my arms.

"I was planning on it, I need to get laid! We haven't gone since Blondie came here," I said to him. "Maybe you can get sucked off again tonight like last time." I wiggled my eyebrows suggestively. I watched as his face brightened with a red flush and his body stiffened.

"Caleb!" he exclaimed as I heard Kyle growl.

"Seriously can you take that f*cking nasty ass fag talk somewhere else?!" he snarled at us before he shot up to his feet and stormed off. I rolled my eyes at his retreating back.

"He has a troll up his ass," I told Levi who said nothing.

"Have you talked to your sister today?" Levi asked after what seemed like a long pause of silence. I frowned at him.

"No," I said slowly. "Why?"

He shrugged innocently but wouldn't answer me.

"Levi," I warned him like a strict parent, causing him to widen his eyes.

"Because she told Alpha Aiden and Liam that you were coming to dinner with her, Dom, J, and Sadie tonight," he explained in a rush. I froze and stared at him like he was freaking crazy.

"Why the hell would she do that?!" I yelled.

Dinner with the Alpha family? Great.

"Don't yell at me, ass!" he snapped, getting off my lap.

I sighed. "Sorry."

He crossed his arms before pouting. "Whatever, anyway they're probably going to some new gay friendly restaurant."

I groaned dropping my head back on the back of the couch.

"Let me guess, my sister recommended it."

He nodded.

"Figures." I sighed again.

* * *

So after my sister cornered me right when they were ready to leave, she dragged me to Sadie's car and threw me in the back seat. We were meeting Aiden and Liam there, so we didn't have to take the same car and get crammed together.

Once were pulled up to the restaurant, I let out a loud groan. The sign said, "Rain and Bows" with a rainbow flag hanging out. It was a homey looking place, but I seriously didn't want to go in mainly because it was too corny.

"I'm too cool for this!" I cried silently.

"They better have some damn good food," I muttered, slamming the car door.

"Hey! Don't abuse the car asshat!" Sadie growled at me, narrowing her eyes. I stuck my tongue at her but continued to follow my happily skipping sister. The door chimed as we walked inside and a waiter greeted us.

"Hi! Welcome to Rain and Bows, how many will be joining you?" he asked.

"Actually, our friends are already here," Robin told him to which he nodded.

"Go right on ahead then." He waved his arm for us to walk ahead.

We found Liam, Aiden, Blondie, Dom, J, and Avery sitting at a large table. A small smile crossed my lips upon seeing Avery, maybe it won't be so bad with him here. Walking a little faster, I took a seat in front of him before I flashed a huge grin. He looked up at when the sound of the table grunted at my abrupt arrival.

"Hey, lover boy," I whispered only for his ears. He sighed and looked away from me. I pouted as I leaned forward on my elbows to talk with him.

"So, were you dragged here too?" I joked. He slowly looked back at me.

"No," was all he said.

Geez, why is everyone giving me one-worded answers today? I focused on him a bit harder, noticing something was off with him. He was being more detached and depressing lately. His brown eyes were dull as he looked around the restaurant with his usual watchful eye. I desperately wanted to ask him what was wrong, but that would have been a waste of time. He would never tell me anyway. He was just a bundle of secrets.

Everyone settled in their seats before they ordered their food. Eventually the table errupted into lively chatter as we waited for the appetizers to come out.

"Oh my God!" J exclaimed causing everyone to tense up. Dom touched her ever growing round stomach and gave her a worried look.

"What's wrong?"

She giggled, lifting a forkful of Caesar salad to her mouth.

"It's so good," she moaned around her food.

There was a collective sigh of relief that went around the table as we all relaxed.

Dom sighed, hanging his head. "You scared the shit out of me," he breathed.

Jeanine patted his back. "Aww sorry baby but I couldn't help it," she told him before she went back to eating. Aiden chuckled, throwing a piece of bread at her.

"You b*tch! You scared us all!" he exclaimed. Jeanine gasped picking up the offensive piece of bread and threw it back.

"No need for delicious food throwing, fairy!" she hissed playfully. I watched as they kept throwing the torn piece of bread back and forth at each other until Liam snatched it out of the air as it came flying Aiden's way.

"Okay stop before we get kicked out," he ordered, using his Alpha authority, putting the game to a complete halt which caused Aiden and J to pout.

"So how do you like the place?" Sadie asked everyone. They all agreed it was nice and they'd come back again. The only thing I really like about this place was the men. I had about four guys hit on me with their eyes since I came in, and since I wasn't going to CRANK tonight, I might as well snag one of these yummy humans up.

Our main course came out, causing the table to immediately quiet down with all the small talk. I guess that was a sure sign that they had tasty food, but then again, anything food-related would have any werewolf chowing down.

Halfway through dinner, I moved my foot across the space under the table to the other side, touching Avery's boot. He snapped his head up to glare at me, but I kept my eyes down on my plate. Growling, he kicked my foot back to my side.

I suppressed the grin as I did it again but this time I slipped my shoe off and ran my foot up his pants leg, touching his bare skin with my sock covered toes. I was innocently cutting into my steak as he reached down and pushed my foot away again with his hand.

Oh, this is too fun. I thought as I did it again but this time I roamed further up, touching his thigh and kept going up till my foot was pressing against a very large and semihard extension of himself.

I felt him jump when I touched him there, catching the attention of Aiden.

"Are you alright Ave?" he asked, concerned. Avery snapped his gaze to him and nodded his head.

"I'm fine, Alpha." He used his formal tone, but I heard the hitch in his voice that no one seemed to notice. Aiden smiled and went back to talking quietly with Liam. I saw his chest heave slightly as he turned his brown eyes back to me.

I smiled, noticing the drastic change in them. Gone was the dull void that was ever present in them which was now replaced by a fiery gaze. I didn't know if it was for sexual arousal or annoyance, but it was there, and I was glad.

"Move your foot." He mouthed. I raise a brow and rubbed my feet against him. Again, he jumped but not as noticeably this time. His jaw was clenched, showing off the strong muscles that were just begging for me to kiss them. I smirked as I felt him harden against my foot. His hand rushed down to my massaging foot, gripping it in his hand. Our eyes met, his gaze turned into that mysterious royal blue like it did the other night when I had followed him out in the woods. It still gave me chills, just the intensity of them burning through me like that had me harden.

I bit down on my lip and pushed harder, his grip on my foot tightened and to my surprise his eyes fluttered shut as he allowed me to continue pleasuring him. His arousal hit me, and I was relishing in it. It was a musky yet delicious scent that had my mouth watering. Growling low, he pushed my foot away from him and quickly excused himself.

I remained seated there but all my wolf wanted to do was jump up and chase him, I'm pretty sure that only a few seconds ticked by until I realized I couldn't take it anymore. I slipped my shoe back on quickly and stood up before heading towards the restroom.

The sound of a loud bang caught my attention before I quickly slipped in where I spotted Avery facing the wall and large crumbling hole of plaster where he had just hit it. His back was tense, possibly from knowing I was there.

I scanned the stalls, finding no one else before I locked the door.

"Go back Caleb," he told me, his voice hard and low. Rolling my eyes, I strolled closer to him.

"What are you afraid of?" I asked, ignoring his command. This caused him to turn around sharply, glaring daggers at me.

"I'm not afraid of anything," he stated. I took a step forward as he took one back till his back was pressed up against the wall.

"Right, of course not," I said sarcastically.

"Stop fighting me Avery," I whispered, looking up at him. When he didn't say anything, I continued. "I know that you're scared, I can sense it and I see it in your eyes. What do you have to be scared of Avery?" His chest rose quickly.

"You don't get it do you?" he said, making me frown. "You continually try to pursue me, and you never learn. I can't be with you Caleb, I can't be with anyone. That is my fate. We're not humans, we can't just have a regular relationship and live happily ever after. You will soon find your mate and I will have to give you up. There is no point in even trying, so let. it. go." His words were stern and harsh but lonely and miserable.

"What did I tell you before? I said I don't want my mate," I explained, closing the distance between us, but he pushed me back.

"And what did I say about once you find them that all that will go flying out the window? Take Alpha Liam and Aiden for instance, Liam tried to stay away but they ended up falling in love, succumbing to his mating instincts, so don't tell me that you'll be able to fight it because if your Alpha couldn't, how can you?" he asked as he towered over me with a hard expression on his face, looking like his regular intimidating self but I wasn't affected.

"I love you, that's how," I said boldly.

He scoffed at me before laughing humorlessly.

Anger rose in my veins at how he could brush off something I've never said to anyone before. Growling, I punched him in the face, his head snapped sharply to the right. I didn't have time to step away before he let out a vicious growl of his own and I was roughly slammed on the floor with Avery on top of me. His eyes shifted to royal blue again and his canines extended. But I was far from scared, I was beyond pissed.

"I tell you that I love you and you laugh!" I screamed in his face.

"You don't know what love is," he snarled.

"Neither do you!" I countered. His hold on my shoulder loosened and his face contorted in pain.

"I don't just throw that word out to just anyone jerk! Why can't you just live in the now with me Avery? Let me show you how to love, what it feels to let someone care for you!" He said nothing, his frame stayed bent over me as he froze on the spot. His eyes were slowly going back to normal.

"I can make you feel something Avery; I can give you a taste of what living is like. Quit worrying about things that don't concern us right now. When the things you're so concerned about do happen, then we'll face them when the time comes, but for now, just let go with me, is that so hard?" I asked him.

Slowly I reached up and ran my fingers over his soft dirty blonde hair. Cupping the back of his head, I gripped the hair at his nape and brought his forehead against mine, our breaths irregular and uneven together.

"Live with me Avery?" I asked him softly. He wore a tortured expression as he gazed into my pleading eyes.

"Let me love you."

CHAPTER 9

CALEB

He never got to answer me, there was a knock at the door causing Avery to shoot up to his feet.

"You're not allowed to lock the bathroom door. Sorry, but I'm going have to ask you to come out now," a voice called out on the other side.

I let out a sigh as I stood up, looking over to Avery who unlocked the door and brushed past the man who was going to say something. The guy turned towards me to say something, but I didn't stay to listen.

My heart was beating loud and hard in my chest. I had opened up to him, leaving myself vulnerable for the first time to anyone. He now had the upper hand; and could either crush me to pieces, or let down some of those walls he built and give into me.

It was all a waiting game now and I couldn't take it; I was too impatient for it, but I would let him because that's how much I have fallen for him. Avery was back in his seat, refusing to look me in the eye and it hurt.

"Caleb?!" I heard Robin call out to me, but I ignored her and stomped out into the streets and power walked down the sidewalk, heading for the woods that was a few blocks away. Once I hit the tree lines, I immediately shifted, my clothes shreding off as a result. It had been way too long since I last let my wolf run free.

The woods still scared me but right now I didn't care, I needed fresh air.

My paws pounded the forest ground as I ran my heart out. I still couldn't believe that I left myself open to him like that. I didn't know that I was in love with him till the words flew from my lips. Trees blurred by me and my breaths left fog in the air. When did it get so cold?

What if he didn't agree to be with me?

I whined as I could already feel the humiliation and pain of his rejection. I know he wasn't my mate but that didn't stop me from wanting him like he was one. So what if it didn't have the connection like everyone else describes: the sparks and the undying love for each other? Who said that two unmated wolves couldn't learn to feel that way? If Avery would let himself, then I had a feeling he would love hard and be just as protective and loving as the next mated were. He was after all, still a wolf with the same traits as one.

By nature, werewolves are possessive and protective of what was theirs, and would be damned if someone were to take something of ours without a fight, and that was how I felt. I had this possessive streak when it came to Avery, I just hoped it was the same for him about me.

"Ugh!" I sound like a lovesick puppy. Growling, I pushed my legs harder, running out all my frustrations.

I was in love with Avery Chandler.

My ears perked up at the sound of another set of paws behind me, my hackles rose as the familiar sensation of fear at being chased after locked in my muscles and I ran faster. Flashbacks of rogues came back to me when Robin and I were on the run and my wolf took over, switching to survival mode.

Taking a sharp left, I ran along a stream, panting as my lungs felt like they were going to burst, but the wolf behind me was picking up speed and continued till I felt the sharp snap of their teeth on my tail. I yelped in surprise before I was tackled to the ground with the large wolf perching on the top of my back.

I struggled and continued to growl and whine, trying my best to get them off me but to no avail.

"Stop!" Avery's voice commanded, causing me to freeze instantly. Again, this heavy aura surrounded him like that time in the woods, making me wither beneath him.

Slowly, I rolled on my back to look up at him, showing my belly in submission. There was no use trying to fight him off, he was too big for me to do anything. I watched closely as he huffed from the chase.

"Why the hell did you run?" he growled.

"Because I was being chased," I said like it was the most obvious answer in the world. He shook his head, staring down at me. It was then that I realized that he had followed me.

With that little revelation, my heart skipped a beat.

Does that mean he cares? Is he finally going to answer me?

With a sigh, Avery backed away and sat on his hunches allowing me to get back on my feet.

"Why are you out here?" I asked him. He didn't answer for a while and instead just watched the trees.

"I don't really know," he finally said.

I cocked my head at him.

"Well there is a reason," I told him.

"Yeah well, I don't know what that is either."

I felt angry again. If he didn't come out here for me then can't he just leave me alone?

"Well why don't you go and find out then!" I snarled, whipping around and trotting off. He growled before he pounced on me again, causing us to roll over the ground as I fought back this time, but in the end, he just pinned me down.

"What do you want from me, Caleb?!" he yelled at me, his eyes glowing blue. *"You know why I'm here,"* he growled.

"No, I really don't unless you say it." I challenged knowing it was dangerous to do so with him.

"I don't know what to say. I don't even know what to do with what you've asked of me." His gaze on me was tortured and helpless. I didn't say anything and just stared up at him.

"I've left Aiden's side to find you, don't make this hard Caleb," he told me with a whine. My face softened at this. He was like a newborn trying to walk for the first time. He had never done anything like this before, much less know how to approach me correctly.

"I can't tell you that I'm in love with you, because just like you said I don't know what that is. I don't know why but you stir my wolf's curiosity like no one else can, but I can't ignore the fact that you have someone out there waiting for you and neither can you. Soon you'll be stolen from me and I'd have to let it happen."

With a whine, I lifted my head up to nip at his ear.

"I told you to not think about it," I whispered. He cocked his head, giving me more possession of his ear.

"How can I not?"

I growled, pawing at his chest.

"Stop," I demanded. *"The more you dwell on it, the harder it becomes, just let all of it go."* His look of uncertainty was ever present. In an attempt to make him feel better, I began to purr and lick at his muzzle softly while he stood above me awkwardly, watching me closely with unease.

He was walking in uncharted territory, agreeing to be with me and I wanted to make him as comfortable as I could. I nuzzled my head into his large warm neck, still purring and his body began to relax. Wiggling myself out from under him, I stood before him, my tail wagging playfully. He gave me a frown as I crouched down low. With a growl, I pounced on him causing him to fall backwards but he retaliated faster than I thought he would and he pinned me again.

"What are you doing?" he asked, his blue gaze shining like a hunter after his prey. That gaze alone cause shivers to trail down my spine in delight.

"I'm playing with you." I chuckled. He watched me amused.

"Like a pup?"

I grinned wolfishly.

"Well yeah."

He shook his head in amusement.

"Haven't you ever played when you were a pup?" I asked him curiously. I watched his face drop as he backed off.

"We should head back," he said, turning towards the pack house's direction.

I frowned getting to my feet. He's shutting me out, I knew it.

"What's wrong?" He shook his head and started to run. I sighed and followed him a few feet behind.

Just as I figured, more secrets.

* * *

AVERY

I couldn't watch him leave the restaurant by himself. My wolf was oddly against letting Caleb be alone especially when he's angry. I kept seeing his face invade my head from the time when we were in the restroom earlier. The blazing color of his brownish blue eyes as he glared at me in anger, or how his face softened when he told me he loved me. Both expressions were plastered in my mind and I couldn't let it go.

Was I wrong for wanting him to do the things he just said? Having someone care for me and love me made my chest tighten at the mere thought.

Can he break through the walls I've had all my life? The same ones that have made my life so empty by preventing anyone from getting in or me getting out? I was a wanderer with a purpose and that was to protect the reason for my existence, the same one who held my life in his hands: Aiden.

So how did Caleb fit in? Why was it that my wolf stirred whenever he was around? Why does it make me angry to smell another male on him?

I knew he wasn't my mate, that simply wasn't possible so what the hell was happening to me?

I followed him after telling Aiden that I would go after him, knowing that Caleb's storm out had caused some worry among the table. Once I had his scent and I could sense it growing stronger, I knew that he had shifted and I did the same. Here I was now, agreeing to this absurd fling or whatever it was with him, knowing in the end that I'm the one who was going to get hurt.

Caleb followed me behind as we ran back to the house. It was quiet and I was avoiding the question he asked me moments ago, not wanting to get into my past with him, or anyone else for that matter.

Thirty minutes had past when we finally arrived home. Robin was the first at the door, and ran past me to hug her brother before giving him a slap.

"What the hell is wrong with you? How could you run off like that?!" He just huffed at her and trotted up the stairs, purposely brushing against me. My wolf growled within, wanting to follow him but I held back his yearn for Caleb's submission. Squaring my shoulders, I went up behind him to go to my room.

* * *

"Avery." I looked up from my book that I wasn't really reading to find Robert standing in the doorway to my room.

"Sir?" I asked, setting my book down before I stood up.

He smiled. "Call me Robert, son," he told me to which I just smiled gently. "Anyway, the Greenfield pack is coming down in the next two weeks or so. I've told Liam about this, but I thought that you would also like to know since you're Aiden's defender and all," he said.

I frowned.

"What is the nature for their visit, sir?" I asked him. He shook his head at me with a small smirk.

"They've caught wind of our Alphas being two males and were merely curious as to how we run things. They're just going to be observing."

I frowned deeply.

"And what gives them the right to watch us like some circus show, sir?" The tone of my question was harsher than I intended. Still, I didn't like the idea of some random pack roaming around ours like we were freaks to laugh and point at.

Robert walked up to me before placing a calming hand on my shoulder.

"Cool it, son." He gestured for me to sit back on the bed and did the same. "There are bound to be inquisitive packs wanting to know how we function around here without a Luna. Packs need a Luna and the thought of a pack without one, and instead having two males made them interested in our lifestyle. It's out of the norm so I can be sure we will lose allies from this just from the ignorance in the world, but we werewolves know that mates have no choice. They were destined by the spirits and that's how things will be, and the fact that we have more than one homosexual couple in our pack is going to gather more attention."

"Plus, the Greenfield pack may be a bunch of narcissistic superficial power hungry bastards but they are still one of the powerful packs in the US and when they ask to visit, you simply don't turn them down." He shrugged.

He was right about one thing, this pack was a gay magnet. From Liam to his mate Aiden, then Robin and Sadie, plus Caleb being gay and Levi being bi. It was bound to gather some unwanted attention. Plus there was me, who was never attracted to anyone until Caleb wormed his way into my wolf's interest.

"Alright, do you know how many will be here?"

He nodded standing up.

"Alpha Collin, his daughter Lynn, and a few others, so not that many."

Sighing, I nodded to him.

"You're telling me this because you think they might harm Aiden in some way?" I asked.

His face hardened.

"You can never be too cautious so yes I'm telling you to keep an eye on him while they are here. I can't trust anyone that isn't from this pack Avery, it's our wolf instinct to be wary of others. Although I doubt that they'd try anything, especially when they're being surrounded by wolves who have sworn to protect him."

"I understand. You know it is my soul purpose to protect Aiden when his mate is unable to."

He smiled at me.

"Thank you, son," And with that he walked off, closing the door behind him. It was ten at night, so the house was asleep. I streched my arms over my head, letting out a yawn before I grabbed my checkered pajama bottoms and walked into my bathroom to turn the water on. Discarding my clothes, I threw them in the hamper and checked the water, the room was filling up with steam causing the mirror to fog up.

I moaned in delight once the water hit my skin. I loved hot showers. They always made me calm and relaxed me like they're meant to. I stood there, letting the warm water cascade down my back and in my hair. Grabbing my shampoo, I started to scrub my hair while my mind wandered back to Caleb, I hadn't seen him for the rest of the day since he went up to his room. I wondered if I made him mad, but I didn't have the desire to find out. If I had, he surely would have let me know at least.

Did me not answering his question really bother him that much?

"*Haven't you ever played when you were a pup?*"

My answer would have been no anyway. My wolf at the beginning of my maturity was always distant and detached; unlike the rest of the wolves around me at the time. I never stuck around long enough to know how to act like a carefree pup with the newly turned wolves. It all seemed inconsequential to my wolf since he knew that he had more important things to do like trying to find ways to survive.

The water cooled down so I shut it off and stepped out, wiping off my dripping body with a towel. I slipped into my pajama pants and climbed into bed.

Out of habit I began to focus on Aiden, this time the mist was a relaxing and calming blue which appeared as he slept. I let his energy seep into mine and I instantly felt tranquil and calm.

Closing my eyes, I let Aiden's calming aura pull me into a deep and peaceful sleep.

CHAPTER 10

CALEB

Blood.

Blood was everywhere and it was soaking the ground. Their screams filled my ears making them ring terribly. As I watched on, I saw my best friend Kaid getting attacked by a huge wolf. The latter was on his back before his teeth sunk into Kaid's neck, causing dark red blood to pour out from his wound as he sunk to the ground.

I could hear his cries die in his throat as he followed. I clamped my hands over my mouth as I watched in horror. Just earlier today we were playing video games, where we even had a soda drinking contest to see who could burp the most. Now his fifteen year old lifeless body just laid there, his empty dark eyes staring straight at me.

I listened to the heart-wrenching roar as his father came rushing to his son's side. I could feel the pain and agony emit from his grieving father right from my window. I watched his father slowly turn rabid, eventually taking on as many wolves as he could till he was killed off in the midst.

Why were they doing this? Why were the friendly wolves of the Redwood Pack attacking us? Why was my uncle killing my friends and family? Robin was weeping next to me as I covered her face in my chest. I refused to let her see the damage that our supposed uncle was doing.

A body was thrown at our window, producing a loud bang that caused both of us to jump while Robin screamed. Right then and there, I looked up to see a pair red crazed eyes staring back at me with such hatred.

Zackary.

* * *

"Ah!" I shot up from my bed. Sweat was pouring down my face while tears stained my cheeks. Why do I keep having this damn nightmare? He was dead so why was he still haunting my dreams? My chest was heaving rapidly as I tried to calm down but that didn't work.

I threw the covers off my legs and got out the door and into the hallway. I didn't know where I was going but I just went, and before I knew it I was at Avery's door. Taking a deep breath, I turned the knob slowly and slipped in as quietly as possible, closing the door softly behind me.

Avery was lying in bed, his covers bunched at his waist. He was on his back with one arm over his stomach while the other rested across the other side of the bed. He looked so peaceful and inviting so I tiptoed to the empty side of his bed and climbed in. I really hope he doesn't get angry at me for this, but I just needed something to take the torment of that night far, far away.

Settling down, I placed my head on his arm, using it as a pillow and pressed my body up against his side, soaking up his warm and earthy scent.

Take them away. I thought quietly to him and fell back into a grateful dreamless sleep.

I awoke to the feeling of slight movement below me. I opened my eyes, wincing at the light that streamed through the curtains. I groaned, burying my face further into my warm pillow when I realized it was really hard.

"Caleb, what are you doing in here?" Avery's soft voice caused me to jump up and look at him. His brown eyes were watching me inquisitively. His hair was disheveled from sleeping and was sticking up on all ends. It was adorable. He didn't look mad that I was in his bed and that made me relax a bit.

"I-I . . ." I stammered. *Should I tell him about the nightmares I suffered from every other night?* The one from last night was too much for me to take alone so I snuck in here so I wouldn't be alone. Sighing, I averted my eyes before it settled on his sculpted chest.

"I didn't want to be alone is all," I confessed. He didn't say anything for a long while.

"Why did you come here then?" he asked. I bit down on my bottom lip as I reached out and drew circles against his abs with my fingertips.

"Why not? I mean you said yesterday that you would give us a try, so what better way to break you in by sleeping in the same bed?" I didn't want to tell him about my dreams, they make me feel weak, and compared to him I was. I didn't want to come off as a pathetic, fragile, damaged wolf like I really was.

His body tensed up against mine.

"Right," he said. I sat up, wrapping my arms around my legs before I changed the subject.

"So, what do you want to do today?" I asked him. He frowned sitting up against his headboard.

"What do you mean?"

I laughed at him.

"I mean, what do you want to do for our date today?"

He raised an eyebrow.

"Date?" I rolled my eyes before I pushed him by the shoulder.

"Quit questioning everything I say."

He stood from the bed, giving me a clear view of his checkered pajama pants that was riding low on his hips. I could see the deep 'V' indentation dip into them.

"Caleb, I can't just leave Aiden like I did yesterday. I wasn't thinking clearly and leaving Aiden goes against my very instinct. So, honestly I don't know how this thing between us is going to work."

I shook my head. *Oh no he didn't! He was trying to back out of this!* I just got him and I wasn't going to let him go that easily.

"Quit making excuses Ave. Aiden is surrounded by pack members who would rather die than let him be harmed, so I think you can take the day off."

He had an uncertain expression on his face.

"I think that we should forget about this. It isn't going to work, Caleb," he told me.

I huffed, irritated. He was breaking up with me and we hadn't even started yet.

"No!" I exclaimed, jumping off the bed and stormed towards the door before I turn to face his shocked form. "Let's see what Aiden has to say about your day off!" I snapped and ran towards Aiden and Liam's room.

"Caleb!" Avery yelled after me and I could hear his feet stomping as he followed me quickly. I pushed my legs harder till I reached their door. I banged loudly, listening to their murmurs from the other side.

"Aide—" A hand came over my mouth, cutting off my call and my body was lifted into the air before it was firmly pressed against a hard one.

"Leave them alone, Caleb!" Avery growled in my ear, causing shivers to travel down my spine and not the fearful kind either. I struggled in his arms when the door came flying open. Liam stood there, shirtless and irritated.

"Is there a reason you're bothering us?" he snarled.

"I sincerely apologize for the disturbance, Alpha," Avery told him. I rolled my eyes, mouthing off in his hand which only came out as muffles.

"We're leaving."

Liam stood there, watching us with an unamused frown, right when Aiden appeared behind him. The latter poked his head under his mate's arm to see what was going on with big curious blue eyes. From the looks of them both, who wore nothing but crooked boxers and sported messy hair, I could tell that I had definitely interrupted them in the middle of 'something'.

I kicked my foot back into Avery shin hard, causing him to grunt and loosen his hold on my mouth.

"Can I steal Avery away today?" I rushed out before he recovered. Aiden stared at the both of us in interest. His eyes moved to Avery who clamped his hand over my mouth again.

"Mmm!" I complained in his hand.

"I don't see why not," Aiden told me slowly. "I think Ave deserves a break. Go ahead Caleb take him," he said with a knowing smile.

"Alpha, I don't think that it's a good idea, sir," Avery told him but Aiden merely shook his head.

"Go Avery, you work too hard you need to loosen up," he said. Avery sighed behind me and nodded.

"Yes, Alpha." He set me back on my feet while Liam watched us with a weird frown.

"Is that all?" he asked us. I nodded my head vigorously.

"Alright then, go away." And with that he closed the door in our faces.

"Liam!" I heard Aiden snapped at him from behind the door for being so rude.

Smiling smugly, I turned towards Avery sticking my tongue up at him childishly.

"You have no more excuses to try and weasel your way out of this now," I said and poked my finger in his chest. He glared at me as I walked away from their room and back to mine. I turned around to check on him, noticing that he was still standing by the doorway, looking very uneasy about all of this. My face softened to sincerity as I stepped closer to him.

"I want to get to know you Avery, I want you to become comfortable with me. The better we know each other, the easier it'll get to be together. Isn't that what you want? What you came after me for?"

His eyes dropped to the ground.

"I don't know what I want Caleb."

I smiled reaching up to lift his chin. Those puppy dog brown eyes met mine and I melted.

"That's what I'm here for," I told him softly. "Now get ready, I have some brainstorming to do."

He nodded before leaving.

* * *

"You seriously got him to finally be with you?!" Levi exclaimed, as he sat cross-legged on my bed. I had just gotten out of the shower and was towel drying my hair. He had come in a few minutes after Avery had left and I told him everything.

"Well, he's still really iffy about the whole thing and I want to open him up a bit you know. So, I need to find a place that's perfect for a first date."

"I'm amazed that you even got him to leave Aiden's side at all."

I chuckled.

"Yeah I had to ask Aiden myself because he was having second thoughts."

"So, what are you going to do today then?" This earned a shrug from me.

"I have no freaking idea! I'm new at dating too, I usually get it in then bounce," I cried as I slipped my black shirt over my head and pulled a pair of semi dark blue skinny jeans.

"Why don't you go to that fair they just set up about a week ago on fourth and Langston? They start at six," Levi suggested. I scrunched up my face,

"Do they have clowns at these things?" I asked timidly, causing him to frown.

"You're practically the big bad wolf and you're scared of clowns? How f*cked up is that?"

"It's just not normal!" I exclaimed.

"Yeah, a majority of the world would say the same about your date with Avery."

I glared at him.

"Whatever," I huffed yanking a brush through my wet hair. "Stupid white-faced, red-nosed, big-footed, ugly clothes wearing freaks," I muttered to myself silently, but Levi heard and started laughing hysterically as he rolled around in my bed. Growling, I threw my brush at his stomach making him grunt and curl into himself.

"Jerk!" he wheezed, throwing my brush back which I caught easily. Snickering, I turned back to the bathroom, wiping the steam away from the mirror and continued to comb my hair including the fringe that hung in my face. I walked back out.

"Do you think I should cut my hair?" I asked him seriously. It was well past my ears and stray strands were hanging over my eyes nearly reaching my upper cheek.

Levi gave me an incredulous look.

"Hell no! Your hair is hot Caleb. You've got this whole bad boy messy hair thing going on and its perfect! Have you seen mine? If I don't fix it up like I do everyday I'd look like the Ring chick."

I chuckled, and dropped down on the bed to lie on my back right beside him.

"Your hair could never be that long," I told him. Laying on his side, he rested the side of his head on his hand.

"I know that you've wanted to be with Avery for a long time now and are excited that he finally cracked, but what are you going to do when your mate comes along? You'll have no choice but to leave to be with them, and what happens to Avery, Caleb? I don't think it would be fair to him."

Oh no, here comes the practical Levi.

I groaned loudly.

"Seriously? I've told you just like I've told him; I don't want my mate! They'll just end up being a disappointment. Why do I have to give up my rights to choose who I want to be with because of some stupid fate sh*t that the Spirits came up with? It's not fair, and it's certainly not right for Avery to never be able to experience love for being what he is," I ranted, my blood began to pump faster at how angry I was about all of this.

"What part of that is sensible? Screw what the Spirits have planned, I'm making my own!" And with that I got out of the bed and grabbed my jacket, leaving Levi to sit there, staring at me sadly.

It was around six thirty when I had cooled off and Avery came out of hiding. He was sitting on the bottom step of the front porch when I came, so I sat beside him.

"So, are you ready?" He didn't answer or look at me and just continued to stare into the trees. Sighing, I slid off the steps and knelt in front of him till he was looking straight at me. I took his hand and stood up, taking him with me.

"Come on," I told him softly, pulling him towards his car. I knew that he was uncomfortable with this, so I didn't mind being the dominant one for tonight if it help him loosen up towards me. I reached into his pocket and pulled out his keys.

"I'll drive," I said. He gave no protest.

The car ride was quiet and awkward. Every time I tried to come up with something to talk about, all I had gotten were one-word answers. I didn't know how to make him open up to me. All of this was just as new to me as it was to him but he was making it a bit more difficult.

We soon arrived at the fair and Avery gave me a weird look.

"What?" I asked, stepping closer to him so we could walk together to buy our tickets.

"A fair?"

I bit my lip.

"You don't like fairs? We can go somewhere else if you'd like," I offered quickly, grabbing his hand and pulling him back to the car. He sighed before drawing me to a stop.

"It was just a question Caleb, I don't care," he reassured me. I scratched the back of my neck, letting out a nervous chuckle.

"Oh." Shaking his head, he walked me back to the ticket booth and bought both of our tickets. While standing there I noticed that he hadn't let go of my hand. I looked down at them, his was warm and so much bigger than mine. It gave me a sense of security with him so close to me.

"So do you want something to eat?" he asked as we walked around.

"Um, a soft pretzel?"

He nodded.

After telling me to go sit down, I watched him stand and talk to the guy at the booth. I took the opportunity to perv him out. He was wearing a tight gray t-shirt that stretched over his muscles, and a pair of well-fitted blue jeans making his ass noticeable, plus a pair of his black Harley Davidson steel boots. His hair was in its usual messy style. I remember this morning waking up on top of him, the way his body fitted perfectly with mine, and how smooth his skin felt under my fingers. Oh, and don't even get me started about that deep 'V' indention in-between his hips.

By the time he came back, I was hard as a rock. He set down our food taking the seat across from mine. Not soon after he had settled his head that he shot up and looked at me in surprise.

Crap, he could smell my arousal! I felt the blood rush towards my cheeks as I picked at my pretzel, playing it off like I didn't notice.

"So . . ." I started, trying to distract him from my embarrassing horny scent. "Do you like to swim?" I asked randomly. He was still looking at me knowingly, but answered evenly.

"It's okay I guess."

"Do you prefer one sport from the other?" I asked, popping another torn piece of pretzel in my mouth.

"Football—or should I say soccer."

This caused me to frown.

"Why would you say football if. . . wait, where are you from originally?"

He tensed at my question.

"The UK," he said moments later.

My eyes widened.

"But you don't have an accent."

He chuckled softly.

"Aiden said the same thing." I lifted my foot on to the bench that I was sitting in, letting my knee rest against the table.

"You've told Aiden all this?"

"Of course, there is nothing I can hide from him," he confessed before biting his food. My brows furrowed.

"Why Aiden?" I asked him. He peered back at me with those damn brown eyes.

"Why ask Caleb? I have no control over who I was meant to protect. I just searched till I found him."

"Like you had no control over your mate," I muttered. He placed his pretzel down and looked away from me.

"Yes," he whispered.

I sighed, feeling like an ass.

"I'm sorry," I apologized, reaching out to take his hand in mine. "I didn't mean to upset you." He looked back at me, his face serious.

"Now do you understand how lucky you are?" he asked me. His hand tightened in mine.

"Avery, don't start," I warned him, trying to take back my hand.

"No, you are privileged to have a person who could make you whole Caleb. A person to make you happy for the rest of your life. The perfect person for your wolf, his mate for life." I gritted my teeth.

Damn it! We're going two steps back instead of forward. I stood from the table and yanked Avery up with me. Storming back to the car, I pushed him up against the gate of where we parked and grabbed his face.

"Stop! Stop telling me what to do! I want to be with you Avery. No one else. What is it about that that is so hard for you to comprehend? I've been chasing you all over this damn town and you have rejected me every step of the way until now. You're letting me in and I will be damned if you pull back now! I'm going against the Spirits and love you even if you're not my mate. I announce to the high heavens here and now that I will love you unconditionally and screw what 'they' have to say about it! I'm declaring you my life mate!" But once those words had left my mouth, my wolf suddenly took over my body, complying with my declaration.

Growling, I felt my canines extend and I bit down in-between his neck and shoulder, injecting my essence deep within his body, making him mine and no one else's. I felt his knees give in for a second, so I grabbed the gate, pressing him into it further.

A soft moan left his mouth as I growled with the taste of his blood on my tongue. It was so sweet but strong and powerful, giving me a high like I had never experienced. His arms circled around my waist and lifted me off the ground, holding me close as he withered under my teeth while I refused to let go.

"Mmm," I moaned against his skin. Finally, I unlatched my canines from his neck before licking it to heal my mark. I slid down his body as he slowly let me go. Our chests were heaving as we tried to catch our breath. I licked his blood off from around my teeth and mouth and gazed up to meet those mysterious wide royal blue eyes.

"What did you do?" he asked huskily, pressing his hand over his neck.

"I-I don't . . . I don't know."

CHAPTER 11

AVERY

Where was he?

After that night, Caleb had run off after biting me. I wanted to follow him, but I kept myself rooted to my spot as he shifted before he ran off.

I was sitting in one of Aiden's classes, watching closely as he talked with his friends J and Eric. I knew he was worried about Caleb as well. He had been gone for two days now and my wolf was pacing back and forth, wanting out to find him. Robin had told us that it would be impossible to find him now until he was ready to come back. After all, being on the run for four years, teaches you on how to become invisible when needed.

"What happened?" Robin had exclaimed. Aiden told her that he was with me and when I came home alone, she went crazy.

"Why didn't you go after him? Now it'll take a miracle to find him." She slapped me in the shoulder, but I kept my face blank and solemn.

"Why do you say that?" Liam asked.

She glared at him.

"Have you forgotten? We knew how to mask our scent, why do you think it took you so long to figure it out that we were wolves?" she snapped before returning her focus back to me.

"He better come home soon or I'm going to beat the living sh*t out of you!" She pushed me, making me stagger a few steps back. A growl tore through my throat as I rushed towards her.

"Avery!" Aiden's frantic voice stopped me as my hand came around her throat. I felt him grip my arm and pulled on it.

"Let go," he told me softly.

Snarling, I jerked my hand off of her, my breathing rough from her challenge and turned my body towards Aiden's. His sky blue eyes were filled with worry as he looked up at me.

"Calm down Avery." He turned his gaze to Robin, "and if what you say is true then I guess we'll have to wait. I'm sorry for this Robin, I feel responsible somehow."

I shook my head.

"If anyone's responsible it's me, Alpha," I told him.

"You damn right it is!" Robin snarled.

"Robin!" Liam warned as I growled dangerously at her, ready to grab her again, but Aiden's grip tightened. Still, I kept my glare on her just as she did the same.

Since that night, we haven't exactly been on the best terms, not that we have ever really talked before.

The bell rang at the end of class; I walked up behind Aiden as we headed for the door.

"Avery, can I speak to you?" Mr. Simons called. I looked at him as he stood up from behind his desk, then back to Aiden who walked into Liam's waiting arms as the latter stood in the doorway, ready to take him to his next class.

"Yes, Elder?" I asked, walking up to him once everyone else was gone.

"You don't have to act so formal," he told me. I inclined my head down in compliance. With him being an Elder I couldn't help but be respectful. I watched him step up to me and gave him a frown as he reached for the collar of my shirt and pulled it down, showing Caleb's bite that was slowly healing. He had an inquisitive expression on his face.

"Have you heard anything from Caleb yet?" he asked, letting go of my shirt before leaning back on his desk with his arms crossed. I gazed at him curiously.

"No, sir."

He nodded.

"How are you Avery?" His question sounded like it had a double meaning behind it.

"I'm fine, sir." I was seriously confused, I wasn't used to being the reason for someone's concern.

"Are you sure?"

How did he know about Caleb biting me? Was that what he was asking about?

I heard his sigh.

"I can smell him, Avery. You don't have to hide it from me. Tell me what happened," he said calmly.

I shook my head.

"I really don't know, sir. He constantly tries to be with me and I finally agreed to go on a date with him. I keep trying to make him see that he needs to wait for his mate. Am I wrong for doing that?" I asked him before I continued. "Am I wrong for wanting him to experience something so special that only his true mate can give?"

His face softened as he looked at me before placing a comforting hand on my shoulder.

"No, Avery, you're not. It's just your deep belief that everyone who can have a mate should never go against them in any way. You're a wanderer and like every wanderer out there, they all have the same feelings about it. But not every mated couple has a happily ever after, Avery."

"There are wolves out there that have gone crazy with agony and pain because they have been rejected by their other half, or experienced their death. Most of the rogues that roam this earth are how they are because of that."

I scoffed.

"Yeah I know, but Caleb hasn't been rejected or witnessed his mate's death to become one of those unfortunates. He hasn't even met them yet and already wants nothing to do with them. I just don't understand that, I don't get how you can push someone away who could love you so deeply and unconditionally."

"Maybe it's his desperation and need to have a choice," he said softly.

"Sir?" I asked.

"Some werewolves don't like the thought of never being able to have a choice; that they're not in control of their own fate. And maybe Caleb's past has some major role as to why. He had no choice but to run to save his and his sister's life from Zackary, so he never got the chance to settle down and live a normal life. Now that the threat is gone, he has a say in what he does and what he wants from now on, and I guess he wants you."

He pointed to my neck.

"And judging from that bite on your neck, I'm pretty sure he's serious in claiming what he wants."

Without thinking, I reached up, fingering the indentation of his teeth marks.

"It's not possible for him to bite me and make me his mate. You can only have one and I'm not it," I said stubbornly.

Mr. Simons nodded.

"That's true, you're not his genuine mate but from the look of things he wants to love you and I know it's hard for you to forget everything you believe in and let him. Plus, on top of protecting Aiden like you were born to do, I think it would be the best thing to ever happen to you if you let Caleb in."

I was silent for a while and looked at the ground in thought.

"Is this coming from the wise Elder side of you or the genuine good guy?" I asked him a while later.

He smiled. "How about both?"

I sighed again but gave a short nod.

"I'll try, but what happens if by some miracle I fall for him, knowing that I shouldn't?"

He watched me with a sincere expression.

"Then fall Avery and relish in the opportunity that none of your kind has ever experienced, the feeling of knowing what it's like to love."

Once I left his class, I stood out in the front of the school looking out into the never-ending vast expansion of trees that held Caleb within them. I was finally willing to be with him like he wanted, but now I had to wait for him to come back to me.

CHAPTER 12

LEVI

Why me? Why did I have to end up with . . . ?

With a groan, I fell back on my bed, glaring at the ceiling in frustration.

It wasn't fair!

My dad and I came to this pack after escaping our last one. The Alpha was vicious and evil, along with the people who didn't care for anyone else but themselves. The Alpha there had killed my mother when she spoke out of turn and defied against him. It took five wolves to hold my dad back as they made us watch. I could still hear my mom's screams and my dad's anguished cries as the Alpha ripped her heart right from her chest. I watched as he just walked away, while the others left my dad to crumble to the ground where he crawled to his mate and cried against her.

I was frozen, unable to move. That night after burying her, my dad told me we were leaving. We snuck out past the patrol and shifted into the night. Being rogues on the run was not at all fun. We ran all the way from Iowa to Portland, trying our best to start our life over. We knew we were safe from our old pack because they wouldn't try and follow us. We weren't worth it.

We were found roaming around the Blue Moon pack's land a few weeks before Liam and Aiden were made the Alphas of the pack. My dad and I thought they were going to kill us but they were in fact, very gracious after hearing our story and let us stay in the pack. It was really weird and amazing to find a pack that had two males as future Alphas, plus they were also mates. It gave me hope that I could find a nice, handsome male mate to love me for life since I knew that I was attracted to both genders. Still, I had always leaned more towards the male population than female.

I wasn't ashamed to say I was more sub than dom, but I had my moments when called for. That's when I met Kyle. The moment our eyes met, I knew he was the one. The only problem was that he was hell bent on avoiding me. I still remember the moment I saw him, my heart was pounding and I was lovestruck. My wolf was screaming, "Mate!" And I was head over heels for him instantly.

Well since his future Alphas were gay, I thought that maybe it was okay with him too, but it turns out I was wrong. I had walked up to him, my stomach fluttering with butterflies and my wolf jumping in excitement when I got closer. He smelled so good and so masculine. We were standing in a vacant hallway so I was hit with a bit of shy confidence. When I was a few feet from him, I could feel an electric current flow between us, which was a sure sign that he was definitely my mate.

I hadn't even opened my mouth when I saw him step back and looked at me venomously.

"No!" he growled. I froze to a stop, watching him with a shocked expression.

"No?" I questioned, confused on why he chose that as our first words to each other. I frowned, stepping towards him a little bit more timidly, which only caused him to back away again.

"Stay the f*ck away from me!" he growled again. His beautiful grey eyes were stormy and glowing with repulsion. I stumbled back from him, stunned. I felt my wolf whining at his instant hatred towards me. If I was in wolf form, I would be low on the ground with a paw over my muzzle in torment.

"I-I don't understand . . ." I whimpered. His lips were drawn in a tight line as he glared, he was visibly shaking.

"Just keep your damn distance from me f-fag!" And he stormed off, leaving me standing there to stare after him. His rejection was fresh and it pierced deep into my soul. All my excitement and joy were now gone and replaced with an ache that was gnawing at my heart.

He rejected me.

* * *

Since then I stayed clear of him, never even touching him to keep ourselves from moving on to the second phase of the mating process and to keep things at a standstill. That was until he came back from his errands with his dad and idiotic Caleb pushed me on him. With that one touch, it felt like fireworks were exploding against my skin, but I played it off with an 'ew'.

On the inside, I was dying to do it again. I wanted to jump Kyle right then and there, so I could touch him everywhere, kiss those delicious looking full lips of his, and run my hands through his silky blonde hair, and hold on for dear life.

Now, I can't stop thinking about him even more than before. No one knew that Kyle and I were mates and he liked it that way. I didn't think he knew how much it hurt to deny how I felt about him. How every time I saw him in school with some new tramp on his arm, it killed me a little inside, or how he would leave the room when I was in it.

Why the hell would the Spirits put me and him together? We weren't even compatible.

A bisexual and a homophobe simply don't mix.

I rolled over on my stomach and buried my face in my pillow screaming out my anger and agony. Where was Caleb when I needed him?

I remember when Avery came back home without him. I was going to the kitchen to get a late night snack, when I overheard their conversation.

It's been three days since he disappeared, but I knew once he came back, I would be beating his f*cking ass in for scaring all of us. I just prayed that he would come soon. What caused him to run off like that? I'd ask Avery but I was terrified of that guy. He was huge and intimidating and I knew he could kick my ass all the way up and down this house.

Ugh!

Getting up, I went to do something productive than spend my time in my bed. I walked out, only to bump into something hard, I didn't need to see who it was because the tingles were a dead giveaway. I held my breath as I caught my balance. I heard his growl before I was shoved back in my room, the door slammed behind him.

"Quit f*cking touching me fa—dammit!" he growled through clenched teeth as I stared at him. We were at the same height, but he was way more muscular compared to my skinny frame. My breath hitched as he stood no more than a few inches away from me, his grey eyes were bright and annoyed.

"I-I it was an accident Kyle," I explained to him. The current that connected us was making me shake with want.

"You're doing it on purpose Levi and you better stop, now!" I dropped my gaze to my feet, refusing to look at him so he couldn't see the hurt in my eyes.

Why was it like this with us? Why the hell did he hate me? He was supposed to love me and care for me with his life and I him. I can say I kept my side of the bargain, I knew for sure that I would risk my life to save him even though he was a homophobic jerk.

"Why because you won't be able to ignore me anymore?" I challenged, peering back up to meet his stormy gaze with my own.

"Because you'll start wanting me just as much as I want you?" I stepped closer to him as he sneered at me. "We're mates Kyle, that's what we're supposed to do!" I exclaimed.

"F*ck you Levi, there's no way in hell that I would want you. Not ever!" His words hit me hard and I could feel the knot in my throat tightened.

I hissed in anger as I pushed him as hard as I could. I felt it before I knew it came as his fist connected with my jaw. I flew back landing hard on the floor from the force of the blow. Cupping my throbbing cheek, I looked up at him, shocked.

His eyes were huge as he stared at me like he hadn't known what just happened.

"Levi?" His voice was strained as he stood there. When he knelt down quickly to reach for me, I scooted away from him.

"Leave," I said, glaring him.

"Levi," he said again with desperation in his voice.

"Leave!" I screamed. His worried expression disappeared as he stood up with that familiar look of disgust I was used to.

"Gladly!" And with that he stormed out and slammed the door behind him.

I stared at it with hateful unshed tears in my eyes.

He hit me. I never thought that he would actually hit me in anger.

He really despised me but I loved him . . .

Still.

CHAPTER 13

CALEB

The rain pelted against my fur as I marched up the back porch. Shifting back to two legs felt so weird as I opened the door and walked up the stairs. The house was quiet with sleeping wolves, but all I could focus on was his scent. It was wrapping itself around my senses as I trudged up the stairs and stopped at his door.

I had run off a week ago, like a coward.

After biting him, I watched the worried and wide-eyed expression on Avery's face grew as I pulled back from his neck.

"What did you do?"

I didn't know, but I could smell myself seeping into him along with the smell of his fear and arousal from what I did. I couldn't take him looking at me like I was some kind of freak, so I ran. I know it was cowardly of me but I was so overwhelmed with such strong feelings that I couldn't take it. All the emotions that rushed into me were never there before or they weren't as prominent so when I couldn't take it, I ran. I ran to every place my legs could take me but not before rolling myself into a rare plant that disguised my scent. It was an old pack secret that Robin and I had learned from our grandparents.

I had stopped running when I reached the California border. It was there that I knew I had to go back, my body was telling me to go back to him, so I did, and here I was.

Quietly, I opened his door and walked in stark naked. He was there, sleeping on his back with the covers low on his hips. Softly closing the door behind me, I walked over to him. His dirty blonde hair was tousled from sleep while his body shone in the moonlight from the open window that blew in a cold draft, making his muscles look as if they were sculpted in absolute perfection.

My eyes followed down his chiseled abs to the dip in his low riding pajama bottoms and sheets. The light golden hair that trailed from his navel to his groin which nestled into his pants hit me hard.

I couldn't take it anymore, I came back to have him for myself and I would be damned if I didn't get what I wanted. Slowly, I climbed in the bed trying my hardest not to wake him up just yet. When he stayed where he was, I gently crawled up to him and straddled his hips, leaning closer to his face in the process. Quick as lightning, his hands shot out gripping my arms in a painful grasp as a growl tore from his throat. His brown eyes snapped open and glared dangerously at me, his face mere inches from mine.

I just sat there in his lap, staring down at him.

"Caleb?" he asked, shocked. His grip loosened on my arms as he relaxed. "Where the hell—"

"Shh," I replied and closed the distance between us before I pressed my mouth to his. I felt his body grow rigid beneath me but I ignored it. His scent consumed my senses and I nipped at his bottom lip. He pulled away in surprise, staring at me wide-eyed. I kept my face blank as I averted my gaze to his mouth then back up.

His brows were drawn together as he peered up at me. It was silent and every second we stared at each other made it harder for me to resist him. This time he leaned up, pressing his forehead against mine and pecked softly at my lips. I let out a content sigh from the contact, he then did it again but lingered for a moment.

Pulling away with our foreheads still touching, he just gazed into my eyes for the longest time. Not a word was spoken because there wasn't any need for it. We both knew what was going to happen and we weren't going to stop it.

I felt his large hand cup the back of my head before he kissed me so softly that I thought I might weep. My hands roamed down his chest, fingering over every ridge of his hard stomach. His lips were slowly becoming rougher as he deepened the kiss, getting more into it. I laid myself completely over his body, leaving no space as he wrapped his big warm arms around my much smaller form.

I moaned gently against his lips. I could tell he was having a problem on how to go further. With him being inexperienced at this, I decided to help and licked his lips seductively.

His breath hitched as he gasped and I swept my tongue inside.

Geez, he tasted like heaven!

Suddenly, he captured my tongue with his teeth and I jumped before I rubbed myself against him in pleasure. A growl slipped from his mouth as he gripped my rain-soaked hair in his hands and tilted my head for better access. Our surroundings soon slipped away and all that was left was us. Our bodies were beginning to gather sweat from the hot session we were in while our breaths turned rough and irregular. Even the cold air couldn't stop our heat.

Avery rolled us over till he was on top, where he was slowly losing himself in the passion. His eyes were closed, his lips were hungry for more, and his body was slowly moving against mine in an intimate motion. The friction from his pajamas rubbed against my bare, hardening shaft. I arched my back in want, causing Avery's mouth to detach from me.

He didn't let that bother him as he trailed soft kisses down my neck and chest.

Moaning loudly, he nipped at my nipple. I had to bite my lip to keep myself from waking up anyone. I threw my leg over his back, pushing his lower body into mine again as I relished in the delectable feeling. I pulled Avery closer to me before I smashed my mouth to his. \

"Stop teasing me," I growled at him, biting into his lip hard enough to taste blood, and man was it sweet. He growled roughly, biting me back.

"Mmm," I arched against him in pleasure.

Using my feet, I pushed his pajama pants down his legs till they bunched at his feet. Flipping us over, I moved myself down his body, kissing every space of flesh I could see. He let his head fall back as he breathed harshly and moaned. I licked his navel and watched his gorgeous stomach flex, so I moved further till my lips were pressed against the dip in his groin. His scent was so strong here that I could feel myself grow weak from it.

My mouth watered as I lapped and bit at his inner thigh which were mere inches from the heaven I was moving towrads. Delicately, I took his pants off with ease and threw them somewhere on the floor.

His hand came down on my head, tightening his fingers in my damp hair.

"Caleb!" he said through clenched teeth, his voice low and raspy with lust. He was losing all control, I could feel it.

Smiling against his thigh, I gave him what he wanted. Shifting myself closer, I finally took him in my mouth and shivered at the deep and powerful growl that left his lips which vibrated throughout his entire body. His hands were gripping my hair painfully now and I hardened further from it. I took him as far as I could, but he wasn't at all small and I was having difficulty. My tongue caressed the underside of his shaft, causing a jewel of liquid to fall from the tip and I lapped it up slowly.

"Ahh," he moaned sexily, bunching his legs up further so I could have more access. I gripped the bottom of his large member in my hand and moved it in sync with my mouth.

"F*ck," he groaned, arching his back and I knew he was ready for release. I ran my teeth down him gently, teasing him before bringing him to his first orgasm. He released in my mouth and I stayed between his legs, taking as much of him as I could. I watched him fell back against the bed, panting and totally spent from pleasure. Licking my lips, I began to kiss up his stomach and chest until I reached all the way up to his mouth.

"How was that?" I asked him huskily. He opened his eyes to look at me, not saying a word but I knew he enjoyed it very much. I smiled smugly and leaned down to kiss his lips deeply as I maneuvered my body in a sitting position so my ass was in his lap and rested against his still hard member.

I looked down at his deep brown eyes as he stared up at me intently. Reaching out, I stroke his face gently, peering at him with a kind expression.

"I want you Avery," I whispered.

With those for words, I watched in excitement as his brown eyes blaze into that sexy royal blue shade. He took my hips tightly in his large hands and moved me against him. He sat up, pressing his head into my neck as he kissed and nipped at my sensitive skin. I threw my head back moaning loudly.

I couldn't take it anymore, I reached down to grab him in my hands and placed him against my entrance. Our heavy breathing was the only thing filling the room as we never looked away from each other's eyes. I slowly lowered myself on him, gasping at the size of him as he filled me.

I groaned looking down at his face, I loved the pleasure that consumed his expression. His eyes closed and mouth open in a silent moan. I crashed our lips together, dipping my tongue into his sweet warm mouth.

When he pushed up to bring himself completely inside me, I lost it. My arms wrapped around his neck in response, holding him close as I began to move with him. We both gasped at how wonderful it felt being together like this. It helped that I could also smell his overpowering lust and arousal that filled the room which easily mixed in with mine.

Sweat was dripping from the both of us as things got faster and more aggressive. Avery's grip on my hips dug into my flesh painfully as he took over my movements, lifting me up and down on him at the speed he wanted. I didn't say anything nor did I complain because I loved that he was taking control along with hearing his growls and moans as he lost himself with me.

This was what I had longed for so long, seeing him pull down his walls and show me the emotions that were hiding behind them. I also wanted to feel the emotions that were bound to show themselves. I wanted to see them for myself, to be the one to bring them out and share the ones that Avery had.

His thrusts became so forceful that I had to brace myself, I held on to his shoulders, my nails biting into his skin.

"Yes!" I whined into his ear right when his tip hit that one pleasurable spot that had me come undone. Avery had to wrap an arm around my back to keep me firm against him as I shifted wildly.

"Yes, right there!" I screamed till his mouth blocked out my loud moans.

Soon he picked me off his lap, getting an unhappy whine from me before he laid me down in front of him, my head at the bottom of the bed while he pressed his body on top of mine. Spreading my legs he nestled in-between them and pushed his member back into me, causing us both to sigh in delight. At this angle I could easily look up at him and all his glory. Licking my lips, I stared up at his blazing blue eyes and wrapped my legs around his waist, pulling him fully into me as he closed his eyes.

"Move baby," I whispered to him when he just laid there. He looked back at me and did as I asked. I sighed softly, turning my head to the side as he moved gently and slowly. The sheets were cool against my flushed cheek. I felt his wet lips on my neck, leaving sweet loving kisses all the way up to my ear.

"You feel so good," he said breathlessly. My heart soared at his words. Those were his words, his first comment to me. I smiled to myself, relishing in happiness. Wrapping my arms around his broad back, I had one arm across his waist and the other gripping his hair, holding him so close, never wanting to let go.

The aggressiveness from earlier soon turned to slow passionate love making. His hips brushed against mine lightly with every slow thrust. Our chests slick and hot from the constant friction as I arched against him, I felt like I was on the edge but not fully ready to fall, I want to do it with him, I want to release together.

I felt him move his head towards mine so I turned to meet him as he sought out my mouth for a sweet passionate toe-curling kiss. I cupped the back of his head, keeping him there as I moved on him, causing him to moan helplessly in my mouth. I tore my mouth away from his as he thrust deep and hard and I bit down my lip to keep myself from screaming when he hit my spot again.

With that, we couldn't go slowly anymore, we were hungry for release. He was plunging in deep and fast, practically bringing me off the bed with the each and every strength he had. I bit down into the mark I had left, reopening the once healing wound. He growled deeply and lowly from the feel of my teeth and moved faster. Every thrust brought me closer to the edge, my stomach was tightening, and my heart was pounding so fast and loud that I could barely hear Avery's moans or my own.

My nails dug deep into his back when I couldn't take it anymore and dragged them down, drawing blood.

"Ahh," he moaned, arching from my nails. I stared at him intently, watching his royal blue lust-filled eyes glow at me. His canines had extended from the throngs of passion.

"Take me Avery," I growled at him. He had never stopped his delicious pounding into me as his eyes focused on what I knew he wanted, and without a second thought he swooped down and bit into my shoulder. My body arched up as I held him close, my mouth open in a silent moan as I fell into the delights of release, Avery followed me to the depths of pleasure, growling and moaning into my neck without ever unlatching his teeth.

Once our bodies relaxed a few minutes later, he finally released my neck from his hold and lapped up the wound to heal it. I never got to do that before running off that night. I looked down at the mark I opened moments ago, the blood dripped down to his chest in such an inviting way that I couldn't stop myself from shifting up to clean up his sweet blood to close it up this time.

Laying back against the bed, I peered up at Avery, his eyes reverted back to its delicious deep chocolate brown. Beads of sweat were running down his face as his hair stuck to his forehead. I brushed back his wet hair making it stick up a bit in the front.

Why was he so beautiful?

The moon was again lighting up his bronze skin along with the perspiration that coated his body. He moved to lay behind, wrapping me in his arms, I felt him nestle his face into the back of my neck and inhale deeply before we both fell asleep.

The last thing on my mind was that I was completely in love with this man.

CHAPTER 14

CALEB

I nuzzled my face further into the warm earthy scent surrounding me. Sighing in content, I was about to fall back asleep when I felt something tighten around my waist. My eyes shot open as Avery's sleeping face came into view and I immediately relaxed as I stared. He was so handsome and beautiful, then I remembered what happened last night and my cheeks flooded.

He was unlike anyone I had ever had; I even dared to say that he was the best I ever had. The way he was rough and soft at the same time, and how he made me lose myself. I wonder if he had other lovers before because he knew just what he was doing. No one had ever made me do that before, and it made me want him again.

Smiling, I snuggled further into his arms, pressing my face into his neck as I breathed in deeply. The fact that my scent was mingled in with his had my heart soaring. This was how it was supposed to be. He hadn't woken up yet so I took advantage of the situation and nipped at the flesh of his collarbone before licking at it. He moaned softly but didn't wake. I continued, trailing my lips down his hard chest to his nipple, circling my tongue around it before I took it in my mouth.

I felt his body stiffen beneath me before I was yanked up to his chest, my body was laying against his suddenly, his face only a few inches from mine. I gave a yelp of surprise as I braced my arms on either side of his head, our legs tangled with each other's.

"Morning," I spoke after a long silence. His brown eyes were staring at me lustfully as I watched his nostrils flare like he was taking a deep breath. He still never said anything as he buried his face into my neck and inhaled deeply. I frowned as I was just about to ask him what he was doing when he pulled his head back, his eyes were a blazing blue.

"Mine!" he growled and threw me off of him so I landed on my stomach.

"Oof," I grunted in surprise and excitement as I lifted my upper half up with my arms. I felt him climb on top of me.

"Avery?" I asked him curiously. This wasn't normal behavior for him, this was predatory, even wolf-like but then again why the hell am I complaining? I thought as his tongue raked from the middle of my back up to the nape of my neck.

"Ahh," I moaned, quivering from his soft wet tongue against my skin. His teeth raked the bite he gave me last night and I immediately hardened, dropping my head forward on the bed in pleasure. His large calloused hands ran up from my hips, towards my ribs, then back to gripping my hips again.

His body was hot and hard against my back, I moaned from the feeling of his member resting between my ass, causing me to arch as I tried to get him to hurry it up. His deep chuckle above me had my body shivering from delight. I had never heard his laugh before in such a carefree nature.

"Do you want it, Caleb?" he whispered, his voice low and deep at the back of my neck while his breath felt like a warm caress.

"Yes," I whimpered desperately.

"How badly?" he teased as he nipped at my ear, pulling it a bit. I don't know what had happen that made him such a playful tease but I actually loved it.

"Really bad," I said helplessly as he lay his whole body on me, preventing me from moving though that didn't stop me from grinding my ass into his excited shaft. My arms collapsed from his weight as I realized we were still at the foot of the bed. His shaky breath told me I was doing something right.

"Come here," he growled, gripping my head to turn it to the side so he could capture my lips in a hot searing kiss. I barely noticed him lifting off me for a second until I felt him push into me completely.

I moaned into his mouth. He never stop devouring my lips as he began to move. He filled me like no one had ever done before and I loved it.

I sucked his tongue into my mouth as he pleasured my body before he thrusted into that one spot that had me burying my face into the sheets and screaming my little heart out. His growls were vibrating off the walls in the room which grew louder with every thrust.

"Don't stop! Please!" I begged him wantonly.

"I wasn't planning on it," he growled.

Grabbing my hips, he plunged deeper and harder, milking whimpers and moans from my withering body. The air was heavy with the delicious smell of his desire and lust that had me leaking like crazy. My heart was beating at a dangerous rate and my body hummed with pleasure. I tried to muffle my cries by biting my lip but this just caused Avery to growl.

He leaned in closer until his face was right next to mine and I could feel his heavy breathing labored in my ear before he nipped at it.

"I want to hear it," he spoke huskily. I shook my head as I pressed myself into the mattress, balling the sheets roughly in my hands to stop the screams from leaking out. He didn't like that, so he gripped the back of my hair and lifted my head up, pushing himself deeper and deeper until I let go and climaxed beneath him.

"Oh f*ck!" I cried.

"Yes!" he growled, delighted before he sank his teeth into the mark he left on my shoulder, thrusting a few more times before he met me in release. In that moment, I was thrown into another amazing euphoric and stimulating sensation as his canines sank deeper into my skin.

Avery collapsed beside me as we both tried to get our breathing back to normal. We were both looking at each other in sedation. His royal blue eyes were slowly fading back to his deep brown.

"Why did you leave me, Caleb?" he asked after a while. He was laying there on his side and covered in sweat. His hair was sticking to his forehead and his nape while I internally asked myself the same thing.

Why would I leave this beautiful man? The one I worked so hard to make mine?

Sighing, I reached out and ran a finger over one of his perfectly shaped eyebrows. He didn't pull away or move and just stared at me expectantly.

"I can't answer that because I really don't know myself," I told him which caused him to frown.

"You can't just run off without some valid reasoning, Caleb." I closed my eyes as I rolled on my back, my arm up against his hard chest as I stared up at the ceiling.

"I-I guess I was scared of what I did," I confessed. He never said anything and just laid there silently like his old self so I continued.

"I didn't know what the hell came over me for biting you like that," I stated, "but that doesn't mean that I regret marking you Avery, because if it came down to it I would do it over and over again." I sat up to look down at his frowning face.

"I love you, Avery, and I know that you don't feel the same but I claimed you as mine that night and last night as well and I'll be damned if you reject me! Not after this." I motion towards the ruffled bed sheets. "You can't tell me that you don't feel something after that."

He watched me with his normal stoic expression.

"I don't know what this is Caleb, but I showed you last night and right now that I'm willing to agree to this. There is something about you that my wolf is attracted to and that is saying something; especially when my wolf never really concerned himself with anything unless it's about Aiden," he confessed.

"Really?" I asked, surprised. He simply nodded. I bit my lip thoughtfully. "So we're really doing this? No backing out this time?" I asked him accusingly. This caused him to smile softly as he lifted himself and brushed his lips across mine.

"Yes, Caleb." I couldn't help the huge grin that spread across my face. I grabbed his head and gave him a real kiss, leaving us both breathing hard when we pulled away.

"Good."

"So I think it would be for the best if you get dressed and show your sister that you're alive and well so she'll stop giving me the death glare," Avery said, standing up from the bed in all his sexy glory before he pulled on his checkered pajama bottoms.

I groaned, rolling over on my stomach as I glared at him.

"Do I have to?" I whined. He gave me his usual stern expression.

"Yes." And with that he walked into his bathroom, closing the door behind him.

"Fine," I grumbled to myself but I knew he heard me.

* * *

Once I was all showered and squeaky clean, I prepared myself for Robin. I had never run off without her before. We had made a promise that we would never leave each other and that we would be each other's rocks; but she had someone else be her rock now, she didn't need me to be with her at all times.

I made my way quietly down the stairs into the kitchen since I was starving my ass off. I walked through the door and was met with everyone looking in my direction.

I froze in the doorway, staring at all of them.

Oh crap.

Seconds later I was tackled into a bone-crushing hug.

"Oof!" I grunted as the small body slammed into me. I peered down to find Blondie hugging me like his life depended on it. His face was buried in my chest where all I could see was a messy nest of blond hair. I frowned but smiled at him, wrapping an arm around him as I patted his back. The kid was really short.

"Hey kid, what's the deal?" I teased.

"He's been on edge since you left," Aiden said.

"Speaking of leaving, what the hell is wrong with you?!" Robin yelled at me before she jumped from the kitchen counter. She then marched towards me with a look of anger that would have had anyone running for the door. I grimaced, reaching down to pick up Blondie. He didn't protest and just readjusted his arms from my waist to my neck.

"Are you going to attack someone with a kid in their arms? Oh Rob, I'm so ashamed of you." I shook my head in mocking disappointment. This just caused her to become angrier.

"Oh shut up you idiot! I should rip you a new one! You had us all worried sick with your runaway episode!" she growled at me. I tightened my hold on Blondie. God, she's super scary right now. I heard someone sigh and looked behind Robin to see Liam standing beside Aiden.

"Well the real question is, are you okay?" he asked me. I tilted my head and sighed dreamily.

"Aww, you care, you really care!" I said dramatically. Robin growled again and reached over to slap the back of my head. I gasped at her with a shocked expression.

"I have a precious bundle in my arms, Robin. You want me to drop him or something?" I scolded. She narrowed her bluish gray eyes.

"No the real question is, why the hell did you run off for like that?!" she exclaimed, smacking me in the head again. I let out a loud and long sigh.

"I really don't think I have to explain myself to you," I stated, setting the kid on his feet but he didn't want to let go so his arms went right back around my waist. He was like a magnet. I looked down at him with a curious look but shrugged it off.

"Like hell you don't," she growled again, her hands were balled in fists but I could see the worry and hurt on her face. I cursed silently.

"I just need some me time. Is that a crime?" I watched Sadie take Robin's hand in hers as she whispered soothingly in her ear. Robin visibly relaxed and I sighed in grateful relief. Robin was a force to be reckoned with so when she was in one of her moods, I definitely tried to stay out of her way at times like these.

"I didn't mean to worry you guys so much. I didn't think it would bother any of you so badly," I confessed.

"Yeah, well it did!" Robin snapped and pushed past me out of the kitchen, Sadie at her heels. I watched her retreat with a long sigh. I'll talk to her when she calms down a bit. Everyone else was still staring at me till Liam stepped forward with a frown.

"You are part of this pack now Caleb, and for you to up and leave like that after everything we have been through. You were out there unprotected and we couldn't even find a scent trail of where you went because you masked your scent like last time. I will not lose a pack member out of stupidity." His voice was deep and assertive, placing his Alpha influence into every word. I shrank back a bit and again tightened my hold on Blondie. I nodded and kept my eyes down away from his powerful gaze.

"Good, don't do that again Caleb." His word was final and I couldn't disobey. "Come on Aiden," he said, his voice a lot softer now and I heard Aiden walk beside his mate. I sneaked a peek from underneath my curtain of dark hair and saw Aiden gave me an apologetic smile before he left with Liam.

Dom and J were sitting at the table before they stood up. Dom placed a firm hand on my shoulder.

"We're happy that you're back." Jeanine smiled at me then looked down at Blondie. She touched his back lightly.

"Let's go, hun," she said softly to him but he just tightened his arms around my waist and shook his head against my chest.

They both frowned at him then looked at me.

"I guess he wants to be with you. At least he's showing some interest in something," J said.

I nodded. "Yeah sure, I can look over the kid." They thanked me and left.

Sighing, I looked down at Blondie and laid my hand on the top of his soft shaggy hair.

"Are you hungry?" I asked him. He looked up at me with those bright green eyes. "I'll take that as a yes." I motioned him to sit at the table while I rummaged around in the fridge and cupboards. I couldn't find anything that looked good and where I didn't have to cook. I mean I didn't want to kill the kid with my horrible cooking so I shrugged and grabbed a bag of top ramen.

"Are noodles fine with you?" I asked him looking at him over my shoulder. He nodded.

"Cool, do you what chicken, beef, shrimp . . . ?" This was a test to see if he would answer me as I held the bags up but all I got was a finger point at the chicken bag. I sighed. Well, it was worth a try. I prepared our breakfast or lunch, whatever you want to call it at eleven something.

A few minutes later, I placed his bowl down and leaned in front of him, holding a fork in one hand and a pair of chopsticks in the other.

"Do you want the chopsticks or the old reliable boring fork?" I asked him with a raised brow. I watched as he tried to stop himself from smiling and reached for the fork.

"Ahh so boring man," I whined playfully. I settled down beside him as we ate silently. I would occasionally watch him out of the corner of my eye, trying to figure him out.

"How was school without me? Did you get on Avery's nerves for me?" I chuckled. He kept his eyes on his food as he slurped it up, giving only a head shake as an answer.

"Boo, you should have."

Was there someone after him that he was running away from? Well, anyone would think that especially after hearing the desperation in his voice when he asked for help and his dirty appearance. Then again he could just be a rogue abandoned by his pack, but why would they leave a pup that hasn't even matured yet? A frown deepened on my face. Could he be like Robin and I? His family killed off like ours? There was a sorrow so deep in me as I watched him eat, his long shaggy hair in his face. He was so young to be on his own like this. I felt a strong protectiveness towards him and I knew that no one was going to hurt him or make him unhappy if I could prevent it.

"Would you like to go swimming at the lake today? It's a perfect day for it." I offered, taking our bowls to the sink and washing them out. He looked a bit shocked at first before recovering and nodded. I smiled at him and guided him towards my room, grabbing two pairs of swimming trunks.

"Here you go, you can use my bathroom to change." He took the trunks and closed the door behind him. I could feel the excitement coming off him in waves and it pleased me that I could make him happy.

*   *   *

The lake was shimmering clear and beautiful as the sun shone on it, making the water look refreshing and inviting. I motioned for Blondie to go in as I took his towel from him and laid it out on the grass next to mine. Sighing, I settled down on my towel and leaned back on my elbows to keep an eye on him as he dove in for a bit.

Isn't it girly to bask in the sun like this?

Shrugging, I laid all the way back and closed my eyes while I focused on the splashing. The sun was warm and welcoming and I felt my body begin to relax further till my mind began to wander.

And where else would it go but Avery?

I could still remember the feel of his warm sweet mouth on mine as we kissed. I could also remember the way his body felt on mine and the way his muscles dominated me in such a way that it made me weak. The feel of his large hands on my sensitive skin gave me goose bumps and let's not forget his teeth!

The way they sunk into my flesh, it was painful yet pleasurable, and my body was tingling all over from the memory. Unconsciously, I reached for the mark and fingered every groove his teeth left. I couldn't believe that he actually agreed to be with me. After all this time, he wanted to do this thing for real. A smile pulled at the edge of my lips at the thought, he was mine and there was no way that I was going to let him go. Not now. Not ever.

The sun was suddenly blocked, causing me to open my eyes in surprise, where I found a large dirty blonde wolf standing over me upside down. I squeaked out a very unmanly sound and placed my hand over my racing heart.

"Damn Avery, warn a person. Geez!" I huffed. I watched him tilt his head at me like I was overreacting.

Well, he did sneak up on me like a freaking ninja without making a single sound so what did he expect?

I glared at him as he laid down, he was still upside down so he laid his head on mine covering my entire face. I crossed my eyes in annoyance.

"Seriously," I muttered into his chin and it came out muffled. He laughed wolfishly, still not moving. Growling, I pushed his giant head off me and sucked in a large breath.

"Are you trying to suffocate me?" I accused him, glaring at him playfully. He just stood and walked around me before he laid his head down on my lap and stared up at me with his big deep brown puppy dog eyes.

I shook my head at him and rolled my eyes, but inside I was ecstatic at his playfulness. He had never been so laidback before. Reaching out, I began to smooth his soft fur with my fingers as we looked at each other. Finally taking my eyes off him, I peered up to the lake to see Blondie floating on his back.

Oh yeah, I could get use to this, everything was just perfect.

CHAPTER 15

CALEB

The next day I let a deep breath and made my way to my sister's room. Gulping, I raised my hand up to knock but was met with a growl.

"Go away Caleb!" she yelled from the other side. I dropped my hand in defeat. Damn, I could never sneak up on her. I heard some muttering as Sadie and Robin argued before a loud sigh sounded. The door opened and Sadie came out giving me a 'go ahead' smile with a thumbs up. I shook my head, she was so weird.

Summoning up the courage, I pushed open the door hesitantly and saw my sister sitting on the bed cross-legged with a pillow hugged to her chest. She refused to look at me but it didn't stop my advance towards her until I was sitting on the edge of her bed.

"What?" she asked with a biting tone in her voice.

"I'm sorry," I apologized. She huffed, turning her head the other way before laying it on the top of the pillow.

"Whatever."

"I know I hurt you Rob, and I am truly sorry for that. I just need to have some time to myself," I explained as best I could. She didn't answer and just stubbornly ignored me. Growling irritably, I snatched her pillow from her causing her to fall forward.

"Hey!" she shouted. I grinned mischievously. Her eyes narrowed at me.

"Forgive me, butthole!" I demanded jumping to my feet away from her reach. Stray strands of her red hair were framing her face as she glared daggers. She kind of looked like a pissed off lion.

"Why the hell should I forgive you for this?"

"Because I said so."

She rolled her eyes.

"Who are you to deserve my forgiveness so easily?"

I gave her an obvious stare.

"Caleb, your twin brother duh."

"Yeah, the twin brother who just up and left me to worry about. Do you know how much I was scared for you? What if rogues got you and we would never know because you just left without saying a damn thing to either of us?! How could you be so reckless? Even Avery didn't know where you were going and he was the one with you! And why he didn't follow you pissed me off to no end!" she exclaimed.

"I said I was sorry, what else do you want from me, Robin?!" I demanded.

"A real explanation Caleb, you never just left without telling me first and you always brought me along."

"What, would you have left Sadie to run away with me?" I asked her seriously. Her expression faltered for a moment. "Exactly."

"If you must know, because you're so damn nosey, I was running away was from myself. I was confused and scared at something I did and I ran like the coward that I am okay? Are you happy now?" I sighed in defeat as I plopped back down on the bed.

Robin frowned at me.

"What were you running away from? Did that big oaf hurt you or something because you know I'm not afraid of him, not one bit and I'll take him down for you," she said, determined and serious. I shook my head and looked down to avoid her eyes. I began to pluck at her hello kitty pajama bottoms absentmindedly. She was silent for my sake as I built up the courage to say it. I took a deep breath, still messing with her PJs

"I . . . kind of . . . marked Avery," I muttered the last part. She didn't stir, I thought she hadn't heard so I looked up at her and saw her shocked face.

"No way . . ." she finally said in disbelief. "How do you know if it was like 'for reals'?" I tilted my head at her.

"What do you mean how do I know if it's *'for reals'*? I was the one who sank my teeth into him Robin, I think I would know something like that," I said irritated.

She shook her head.

"No not like that, I mean how do you know if it worked? I thought you had to be mates."

I nodded.

"Me too but I can smell our combined scents in his blood and his skin." Her face began to flush red. "What?"

She averted my eyes.

"I thought that was because you two were . . . you know, last night," she responded. My eyes widened in realization.

"H-how do you know about that?" I demanded, practically mortified. She caught her bottom lip in-between her teeth.

"The whole house knows about that Caleb, you guys weren't exactly subtle in his room. The smell you guys were producing had the whole house recognizing what kind of 'mood' you guys were in, if you know what I mean." She winked.

I turned, slamming my body into the bed before I buried my face in the comforter.

"Oh God" I groaned, humiliated.

"Oh especially this morning—"

"Robin stop!" I begged.

She chuckled.

"Okay, so you ran away because you were confused that you marked Avery even though he's not your mate, and you were scared?" I nodded into the blanket.

"I needed to think," I said, my voice muffled. I felt her small hand on my back.

"Fine, I forgive you now, but if you do that again you better tell someone you butt wiping cow turd." This caused me to lift my head up at her in shock.

"Butt wiping what?" She giggled, her bluish brown eyes shining.

"Butt wiping cow turd, Sadie used it on me and I couldn't stop laughing. That girl just kills me sometimes." She laughed.

"Yeah, she'd kill me too but literally." I teased with a grin. She huffed and smacked me in the head.

"Don't talk about my snuggle bottom like that!" she chided with a mocking stern expression.

"Snuggle . . . bottom . . . ?" I stared at her in disbelief as she nodded stubbornly. "Okay, I'm leaving you and your weirdness since 'Crazy Sadie' is rubbing off on my poor sister." I scrambled off the bed as she dove for me and made it by the hairs on my chinny, chin, chin as she pounced and landed on her stomach at the edge of the bed. I laughed boisterously and hightailed it out of that crazy loony ben.

I made my way down the stairs and into the lounge, hesitating for a moment.

What if everyone's eyes were on me knowingly? That would be so embarrassing!

I stood there before squaring my shoulders and straightened my back. Screw it, it's not like I've ever cared about what people have to say.

I nodded in confidence as I strode in and spotted Kyle at the pool table.

He looked up when I approached and gave me a grimace.

"Well if it isn't Mr. Sex Hormones, we can smell what you two gross wolves were up to last night and this morning. Why don't you try and keep that outside so the rest of us can get some damn sleep?" he growled. I stopped at the sudden harshness in his voice.

"Whoa, jealous much?" I tried to tease, holding my hands up in surrender. All I got was a growl as he returned back to his game.

What happened to him in the last few days?

"What's up man? Are you okay?" I asked. I know Kyle could be a jerk at times. Okay, most of the time but I know when he's joking and when he's serious and right now something was definitely eating at him.

"Nothing." He bit out. I stood there with a frown before making my way around the side of the table to stand beside him.

"Is it that time of the month again dude? Cuz my sister can help you out with some pads or tampons. Your choice." I grinned at him. He scrunched up his face and pushed me out of his way, leaning down on the edge to position the stick thing—whatever you call it, at the white ball.

"You have problems," he said, not looking at me as he hit the ball into a striped one, sending it into one of the holes. He straightened up, "I just have a lot on my mind right now and don't feel like talking about it to you or anyone else for that matter." He walked away from me to the other side of the table to repeat the process all over again.

"Well, since you already know what I was doing last night, I finally did it. I got Avery!" I cheered excitedly.

"Congratulations," he said dully, striking the ball a bit too hard and sent it flying through the air before it stuck straight into the wall.

"Damn it!" he snarled, throwing his stick on the table before he walked towards the wall.

"How about we go for a run, I think you need some time to cool off from whatever's bugging you," I suggested, walking over to him cautiously. I wasn't oblivious to his status, even though he wasn't Liam's right-hand man, he was still a Beta, a very mad and irritated Beta who could strike at any moment.

He yanked the ball out and tossed it to the pool table.

"Whatever," he huffed before walking out with me to the back yard.

We shed our clothes in a pile by a tree and shifted quickly. I shook out my body as I accepted the change and stretched. After being so long in this form for the last week or so, I missed the feeling. I watched Kyle do the same thing with his blonde fur before we both took off.

The wind rushed through our fur which was soothing and calm as we raced past through the trees. The grass was fresh and its earthy set made the run much more enjoyable. The sense of freedom was prominent in the air, causing our wolves to howl as the sound rang through the air. Calling out to all our pack members, the trees were just a blur as we raced by them where they resembled mere streaks of green and brown. The birds were singing their joyful songs, adding to the beauty of nature.

Animals were scurrying out of the way as our paws pounded their way through the forest, dirt flying out with every step. We both cleared a fallen tree that lay in the way and continued on. The setting sun was warming down on my dark brown fur, while the sky was blue as it could be with a little pink hue from the retreating sun. It was beautiful and pure. This was one of the perks of being a wolf, the freedom that comes with running till you tire out and then collapse into the soft green grass.

Finally we slowed down till we came to a stream. I was huffing and panting out of breath as I trotted over to the crystal clear water, dipping my head down to lap at it for a moment before I laid my body down on my side, staring at Kyle as he paced the edge of the stream. His blonde coat shone from the light that was streaking through the openings in the trees that shaded the area. His sleek muscles bunched under his fur as he paced. His gray eyes clouded with an abundance of emotion that I couldn't quite figure out. I knew I saw anger and confusion, guilt if I'm right, and defiance.

"Come on Kyle what the hell?" I sighed through the mind link. *"This was supposed to clear your mind not bring more into it, just tell me what is bugging you man."*

He huffed, shaking his head as his eyes trained on the ground.

"I agreed to go on this run but I'm not letting you into my head," he growled. *"I don't need you to help me with this, I've already made up my mind."* His voice was determined and stubborn. Too bad for him, I can be very, very persistent.

"Uh huh, I think you're being an asswipe. I'm your friend . . . at least that's what I thought and you're not going to let me help you out? Maybe I know how to fix your problem." He faced me, his lips pulled back in a snarl showing all his pointy sharp teeth.

"Let it go Caleb!" His chest rumbled with a low feral growl. I narrowed my eyes at him and climbed to my paws with fluency that only a graceful wolf had. Baring my teeth at him, I refused to think he could intimidate me with his brutal methods to demand submission from others.

*"You're not my Alpha or my Beta Kyle so I suggest that you calm the f*ck down right now!"* I demanded. His ears lay back against his head as he crouched.

"I am a Beta!" he growled out.

"Dude, don't do this!"

I knew my pleas and demands were useless towards him. This was how he coped with things, the abrasive and aggressive way instead of the reasonable and human way of talking it out. I groaned inwardly, knowing I was going to have to fight him and try to prevail. There was no way I was going to back down, my wolf wouldn't let me. I still had my pride to consider.

"Fine tough guy, go ahead an attack the only person that gives a damn about you!" I growled, trying to make him feel a little guilty and to think this over but he's too hardheaded.

He charged at me faster than I thought he would and tackled me down. I yelped as his claws stuck into my shoulder. Pushing my paws up against his chest, I raked them down his skin. He jumped off me and changed his tactic, going for my legs. His teeth sank into my hind leg, bringing a whimper from my mouth.

Growling, I turned sharply and slashed my claws at his face the hardest I could, and was rewarded with a pain-filled howl as he backed away and shook his head. I took the opportunity to jump on his back and run my sharp nails down his sides.

He began to spin and buck trying to get me off, but I wasn't loosening my grip till he saw reason.

"This is stupid Kyle! You're fighting with your friend because you're too stubborn to ask for help," I chided, out of breath.

*"Shut the f*ck up! You know you're weaker than me Caleb, just submit and let it alone!"* He fell to the ground and rolled roughly, making me gasp as the air rushed from my lungs under his heavy weight. My grip loosened and he jumped to his paws. I didn't have time to recover my breath as he dove for my neck.

I shut my eyes tightly waiting for the pain when the air was interrupted with a vicious and spine-chilling growl. There was a yelp that followed along with a loud thump.

I opened my eyes, forcing my sore body to its feet to see two blonde blurs. I heard the loud snapping of the teeth as they fought. My wolf began to whine, wanting to run to the aid of the other wolf and I knew that it was Avery who came to help me. I watched in shock at how dangerous he was, he was fast and agile in his attacks as he bit into Kyle's shoulder and legs, drawing blood and howls of pain from his victim. Avery was lethal when he wanted to be and I knew that if I didn't do something he was going to kill Kyle.

Kyle was no match for Avery's strength but he tried anyway, and it was quickly turning into a losing battle. I caught Avery's movements towards Kyle's neck and I barked sharply while I screamed at him through the link.

"Stop!" Immediately, Avery was frozen, his canines inches from Kyle's neck.

"Stop," I said again, my tone exhausted. *"As dumb and idiotic as he is, he's still my friend Avery,"* I begged.

Growling, he snapped his teeth at Kyle in warning as he backed off him and ran to my side as my body wobbled from blood loss and weakness. The bite in my leg had me collapsing to get my weight off of it. Avery whined, pushing his muzzle against my cheek tenderly.

Glaring, he snapped his head over to a panting Kyle.

"Go!" It was a clear command, one that wasn't easily ignored. Kyle growled, forcing himself towards his feet and limped slowly away back towards the house. I shook my head mentally at him, whatever it was to make him this way was only going to eat at him further if not treated. I knew if that happened, something dangerous was going to happen. Kyle was normally an intolerant, short-tempered guy where the littlest thing could set him off and for him to be so angry and on edge more than usual was going to cause some serious ripples.

I felt the warmth of something on my shoulder and averted my eyes from Kyle's retreating form towards Avery's gentle attention to my wounds. His tongue was lapping at the bloody gashes. I lay back on my side.

"Are you ok?" he asked, his voice laced with worry. Shifting back into my human form, I let his tongue have better access to my skin without the fur.

"I'm alright now." I smiled at him reassuringly.

I lay back, staring up at the trees surrounding us which blocked the sun as much as it could. I jumped at the feel of his tongue on my upper thigh. But once he was done healing my wounds, he too shifted till he was kneeling beside me, and reached down to cup the back of my neck, pulling my tired body up and to his hard and demanding lips. I let out a whimper of pleasure, gripping his biceps to keep myself from falling back.

Slowly, he laid us both down with half of his body over mine. Our mouths never separating until he had his fill. When it was hard to breathe, he pulled back and met my eyes with a fierce expression.

"Stay the hell away from him or I might just have to kill him next time." His words were final and hard but I just stared at him.

"He's my friend, Avery," I told him again. He growled, his eyes teetering from brown to blue.

"I wouldn't care if he was the President, he doesn't go near you or I'll rip his worthless throat out! Friends don't attack each other like that."

"That's just how he is." I winced at the pathetic whine in my voice. I should be agreeing with him instead of defending that jerk but I was loyal and once I made a friend, which wasn't very often, it was hard for me to see past trying to help them out at any cost.

Avery could see the defiance in my eyes.

"I'm telling you now that if you continue to be around this guy I'm not sure if you'll be able to stop me from finishing the job." It was a clear warning and I took it into serious consideration.

"No, you won't." I smiled teasingly.

"Caleb," he warned again.

"How did you know I was out here?" I changed the subject. He sighed, brushing my hair from my face.

"My wolf was worried about you, he knew you needed us," he said. I watched him through the curtain of hair that fell back into place.

"Really?" I asked with a frown. "I thought only mates felt their mates in trouble."

He shrugged.

"I guess not, because I knew," he answered.

I didn't say anything after that, I just looked out into the undisturbed clear rushing water.

"Thank you," I whispered. He nuzzled his face in my hair.

"Anytime," he said softly.

CHAPTER 16

AVERY

Was this how it felt to have a relationship? To have a mate? Was the fast beating in my heart, one of the symptoms of having affection for somebody that isn't someone I'm sworn to protect?

No, I would protect him, I would risk my life for Caleb just as I would for Aiden but this was a different feeling than what I felt for Aiden. I was loyal to Aiden and protective of him like a brother would be or a loyal knight to his king.

With Caleb, I felt an immense possessiveness that consumed me, the thought of him in trouble or being around someone who I thought was no good caused me to react in a way I never had before. I was so used to being in control of my feelings that I never acted rash or lost control.

I was void of emotions for the longest time, that when Caleb came around I was confused with the unusual actions of my wolf. His curiosity, protectiveness, possessiveness, anger, joy, and most of all his sudden lust for Caleb all consumed him and me.

I lay there in bed with Caleb who was snuggled close to my side. His head rested on my chest which was his makeshift pillow. One of his arms wrapped around my waist, and I shifted slightly from the feeling he was causing me. There was a tightness underneath the sheets which I knew now all too well what it means.

His body was so warm and his scent was wavering up to my nose and my senses were going crazy.

I was not used to this need to be with someone like this. I was a solitary creature, a lone wolf compared to the normal weres that need a pack and I was comfortable that way. I never talked to anyone in this pack nor associated myself with them ever. Aiden and the Alpha were the only exempted ones because I had to. If I didn't need Aiden to live then I would still be out wandering like I was created to.

I remembered all the places I had roamed to in my search for a reason on why I was still on this earth. How it felt to know that I was forever alone, and never got to experience the love my parents had for each other with someone made just for me was something I had grown used to. If I were still in England, I would watch my brother and sister find their chosen ones while I carried the constant emptiness in my heart for all time. My wolf would be the silent and lifeless attachment to my already desolate soul.

Then I finally found what my wolf needed to survive, something that gave him purpose. I was extremely grateful that Aiden had accepted me even though he had no idea what he was doing. From then on, he was the only one I gave any thought to but now Caleb had wormed his way in.

I shook my head at that. His persistent, annoying little ass couldn't take a hint, and in a way I'm glad he didn't. If he had, I would never had felt such an overwhelming feeling of affection for someone, nor felt this burning in my blood when he looked at me with those unique eyes of his as they darkened with passion. The same eyes that showed me how he was bold in the ways of our lovemaking, telling me how, when, and what he wanted me to do to him, and how to please him.

I had never made love to anyone or had sex before because I didn't have the drive for it, nothing interested me in that area. Now I was insatiable, I couldn't get enough and neither could he from the way he yelled and screamed in pleasure. I had heard others in the middle of sex and always thought it was annoying to hear all their loud moaning and hollering, but now I knew it made you feel empowered. Knowing that you were pleasing your significant other to the point where they could no longer hold it in and needed to voice their passion was something that made me feel truly alive. Now, I hunger for his moans and whimpers and often demanded that he scream for me.

My hand was caressing his soft dark hair as he slept. I didn't love him, I knew that but I cared a lot about him. It was a shock to me but it was true. Of all the times I had avoided and pushed him away, he ended up growing on me. Now the thought of him with someone else tore through me. This was what I was afraid of because he was going to leave me soon and there was nothing I could do about it. So now, I was just going to listen to our Elder. I was going enjoy the time I had, knowing it would never be enough with him and cherish our numbered days together.

I swallowed down the rising emotions I felt in my chest and grabbed Caleb's long hair, pulling him up my body. He moaned in protest in his sleep as I pressed my lips against his in desperation, savoring every moment with him, relishing in the feelings he gave me. I pushed my tongue against his parted swollen lips and massaged our tongues together in an erotic dance. Caleb was slowly and unconsciously complying to me.

From the moment of our very first kiss, I became infatuated with his taste. Was it normal to taste like strawberries? He straddled me, still half asleep. His eyes were closed but his mouth was frantic and hungry on mine.

Smiling against his soft sweet mouth, my hands roamed down his smooth back, the cords of his muscles flexing under my palms. Caleb wasn't in any way buff, but he was fit and had the body of a swimmer: lean, tight and fit. Most werewolves had the same built if they were in lower ranks, unlike an Alpha who was much larger than the rest of his pack or a Beta plus Enforcers.

He was moving against me restlessly, his naked body hot and ready. We had just finished our last hot session not too long ago and I would have let him rest but I couldn't stand the separation. I needed to be attached to him in this way to know he was mine . . . at least for now. I growled possessively, a sign my that wolf didn't like the way my thoughts were going. I recently learned that he was a very selfish wolf. He didn't like to share and I knew it was going to be torture to keep him from acting out when Caleb had to leave.

The room became sharper, the dark was as clear as day as my eyes changed, letting my wolf out but only a bit. I gripped at Caleb's bottom, moving him against my demanding body till my tip was at his entrance. Caleb let out a whimper of impatience that boosted both mine and my greedy wolf's egos tenfold.

Slowly, I teased him and pushed him down on me as I watched his face intently. His brows knitted together in desperation, his eyes hooded and I could barely see his beautiful bluish brown eyes. His mouth parted wider in a silent moan the further I went till he caught his bottom lip with his teeth. I dropped my head down as I sank to the hilt. He was always so warm and tight, and I was quickly losing control. Gritting my teeth, I let him sit on me and adjust.

"Avery," he moaned. His hands were against my chest to keep himself up as I moved my hands to his hips.

"Move Caleb," I ordered softly. "Let me feel you." He watched me with lust-filled eyes as he began to do as I told him. It was slow and sensual and I never took my eyes off him. I loved the way his stomach muscles flexed from the movements, how he closed his eyes when everything got too much for him, and how he couldn't keep his delicious rhythm going. My fingers dug deeper into the soft skin on his hips and pulled him off me to the tip before bringing him down.

"Ah!" he yelled, throwing his head back in pleasure. The sweat was building on both of us, and the room filled with our combined scents, making it that much harder to not let my wolf take full control and end up hurting Caleb. I could feel him scratching at me to let him out, to take what was his the way he wanted to. The animalistic way of mating with a true mate. He was strong and made everything so difficult, I was never used to this kind of demanding and wild behavior from him that I did slip and he burst forth.

Caleb gasped as I pulled him off me and flipped him on his stomach. I jumped off the bed and pulled Caleb by his hips towards the edge of the bed where I stood.

"Get on your hands and knees," I growled deeper than normal, a sure sign that my wolf was with us at this moment. Caleb was stunned as he stared at me in shock, but did as I said like a good little mate. I bent down and ran my tongue up the middle of his back to his neck as he let his head hang for me to get access.

"Good boy," I rumbled. A shiver of delight wracked his body and his arousal slammed into me, making me practically howl in pleasure. Taking hold of his hips again, I slammed myself into him without warning and he screamed out loud and long. I threw my head back at the beautiful sound.

"Oh God," he panted.

I began to thrust into him hard and fast, unable to leash my wolf back. Growls erupted in the room which belonged both Caleb and mine as I took him wildly and relentlessly. Judging from the sounds coming from him, he didn't seem to mind. I could feel my wolf smiling with pleasure at how our little mate could handle us in the throes of passion and the hard way we took him.

Caleb's arms gave out on him and his chest and face were pressed to the mattress giving him a look of total submission, indicating we had complete control. Leaning forwards, I gripped his shoulders and pulled him up against me so he had no chose but to step back on the floor and stand against me.

"Avery," he whimpered breathlessly. I buried my face in his neck where my mark lay close and it gave us immense joy. He was ours. I continued to move in him, never slowing and only increasing my pace and friction.

"Do you submit to me Caleb?" I growled in his ear, licking at the lobe.

"Yes," he moaned through clenched teeth and dug his nails in my outer thigh pulling me into him harder.

"You're mine," I stated firmly, pushing him back down again so he held himself up over the bed. I pistoled in, going deeper till felt I was getting closer.

"Tell me Caleb, say you're mine and that you belong to me," I growled deeply, bringing my mouth to his shoulder while hovering over my mark.

"Yes, I'm yours!" he exclaimed desperately. Grinning with satisfaction, I bit down, bringing him to a world-changing climax for the both of us. His scream rang off the walls and my canine howl roared deep and true, letting everyone in the house and beyond know that Caleb was mine and mine alone. My wolf had staked our claim and I would kill anyone who tried to take him from me.

We collapsed on the bed, exhausted, panting, and deliciously sated.

Slowly, I lifted my heavy weight off him, ready to ask if he was okay but he was already asleep and worn out. Smiling lightly, I removed myself out of him reluctantly and lifted him in my arms and under the covers. Curling in behind him, I wrapped my arms around his waist and buried my face in his hair and nape. My scent was mixed into his skin and I couldn't help myself from lapping at the newly opened bite on his shoulder, closing it lovingly.

I felt him shiver slightly and I licked it once more just to let him know that he was mine before I settled down and let sleep come and take me.

* * *

I felt movement from the waking house pull me from my sleep. My eyes refused to open as I snuggled deeper into Caleb's hair. He giggled softly, swatting at my hair.

"Stop, your hair tickles," he muttered softly. I sighed contently, tightening my hold on him.

"Sorry," I whispered huskily.

"Your hair tends to stick up in all places when you sleep." He yawned before pressing his flushed body against mine and nuzzling his head into my shoulder. We lay their silently for a while till he stretched lazily, flinching a bit as he did so. The gesture brought me back to last night and reminded me on how rough I had been with him. I opened my eyes and watched him closely.

"Are you okay? Did I hurt you?" I asked him, concerned. He looked up at me with bright blue eyes, the brown specks in them making them all the more beautiful.

"I'm great Avery, and no it's more of a delicious sore feeling." He smiled sleepily. I wasn't convinced all the way.

"I think I was too hard on you, I'm sorry Caleb," I said, combing his tangled dark brown hair from his eyes with my fingers. He shook his head and took my hand in his.

"I loved every minute of it so don't worry." He pushed my shoulder lightly and wiggled his eyebrows suggestively. "To tell you the truth I like it rough and wild. It's normal for us wolves, Avery."

I closed my eyes.

"Yeah, my wolf surely made that clear last night."

"I know, I felt him. You should let him out like that more often." He grinned shamelessly. I shook my head.

"He's too rough Caleb, he could have hurt you—*I* could have hurt you." I continued. Rolling his eyes, he rolled on to his stomach before lifting himself on his elbows then laid half his body on me.

"Well, we could always go full wolf but I think we'd end up tearing this whole room up," he said, his eyes laughing at me. I just gave him a flat look.

"Don't give yourself gray hair, Avery, I was fine with it and I expect it to happen again and again and ag—" I growled and silenced him with a kiss.

He chuckled.

"If thats your way of shutting me up, I like it," he whispered against my lips, kissing me a little longer. Reluctantly, we pulled away.

"Are you hungry?" I asked him softly. He nodded but placed his head back on my chest and started making designs on my stomach with a finger.

"I have a question," he said. I raised a brow at him and waited. He looked up at my expectant face. "Have you ever . . . you know, with anyone else?"

I knew what he was asking but I just frowned in confusion.

"What?" I asked innocently. His face set in a cute pout.

"You're going to make me say it aren't you?" he accused. I didn't react to it.

He sighed. "Have you had sex with anyone before?" There was a deep blush building in his cheeks and I was surprised. Caleb was the bluntest and crudest person I have ever met and for him to blush at such a question was laughable.

I chuckled softly and shook my head.

"No," I answered truthfully because there was no way I could ever lie to him.

His brows shot up.

"Really?"

I nodded.

"And you're like what, twenty two?"

"Twenty three and really," I corrected. There was silence for a minute before he interrupted it once more.

"Okay, how about making love?" I furrowed my brows. "There's a difference," he assured me. I was quiet as I stared at him before I suddenly rolled us over so I was hovering over him, my face serious as I looked deep into his eyes.

"No."

I watched his gaze flicker down to my mouth before he licked at his lips. Smiling lightly, I leaned down to give him what he wanted. He sighed into my mouth, wrapping his arms around my neck as I let my body slowly settle down on his.

"Good." He grinned selfishly. I chuckled and kissed down towards his neck.

"Avery?" he asked a bit breathlessly. I lifted my head to look at him, he met my gaze with a thoughtful expression.

"I was serious when I said I was yours, and you're mine."

Blinking, I stared into his handsome face.

"I know," I said in a voice barely above a whisper before I shut the world away from us and let the burning flames lick our skin again.

CHAPTER 17

KYLE

*This is bullsh*t! It wasn't right and it sure as hell wasn't going to happen!* I thought, internally cursing the spirits as I stormed away from the house. I didn't know where I was going but wherever it was, it was definitely going to be far away from Levi. I couldn't take being around him or his damn scent lingering in every space in that house any longer. It was a reminder that was constantly kicking me in the face.

The spirits have a seriously messed up sense of humor. There was no way that I was going to let some guy be my mate.

*I'm not a f*cking fag!*

This was all Liam's fault. He just had to mate with that damn human boy. Now the whole pack was turning into a freaking fairyland.

First Liam, then my sister, well that wasn't true. It was Liam and his damn human!

A growl ripped from my throat as I remembered that day . . .

During Liam and Aiden's Announcement

It was completely disgusting to think that the guy that was supposed to be our future Alpha was a d*ck sucking fairy. I remember standing in the back of the room as Aiden and Liam stood there announcing their mating. I had to hold back the bile that rose in my throat. I rolled my eyes as Aiden decided to grow a pair of balls out of nowhere and tell us off.

Where did that little gay boy get off telling us to leave our home?!

I watched as a few pack members stepped up to leave. I would have done the same but I couldn't leave my sister. Even though she was older than me by a year and in college, I still felt protective of her because let's face it, my sister is weird and careless.

After the announcement, everything went back to normal but only to a point. Not everyone was okay with our new Alphas being fags, especially me. It was just disturbing since I was next in line for the Beta position which means I would have to take care of them with my life.

A few days after that, I heard from my dad, the pack's Beta, that there were a few rogue wolves walking around our territory and that the Alpha was letting them stay. I didn't think much of it till that day. I was coming in from hunting with my dad when I smelled something weird. It was unfamiliar but I was drawn to it. My wolf was practically jumping off the walls, figuratively of course and I knew I had to find it.

What was it? I raced down through the house, following the scent that reminded me of apples. I rushed around a corner and came to a stop when I noticed it was getting stronger, closer. My ears picked up on the light footsteps headed my way.

Who was it? My wolf whined loudly in my head, scratching for release. I was confused. He had never acted so anxious before, it was making me beyond curious.

Then *'he'* came around the corner.

He was tall and lean. His hair was ridiculously long that he had it gelled up in a messy combed back style. His skin was lightly tanned and flawless. He also had deep brown eyes that captured you with one look.

MATE!

My wolf exclaimed in my head.

I was frozen in place.

"No." I choked. I watched the other guys face lit up like I was Christmas morning.

No this wasn't right, it couldn't be.

He took a step closer to me and my wolf rammed at me to get out and go to this stranger.

MATE!

He screamed at me, not understanding why I wasn't moving towards the guy.

"No," I growled more at my wolf then the guy who was getting closer. His smell was consuming my senses, wrapping around me like a pair of welcoming arms. I wanted to inhale more and more of it, it reminded me of my mom's delicious apple pie.

"No?" His melodious voice sounded, crashing through the terrible ringing in my ears. This caused my wolf to whine louder and my body tightened in delight.

"Stay the f*ck away from me!" I glared at him, reproachful. I blamed him for making me like this. It was his fault that my wolf was demanding me to take him in my arms. I refuse to be like our fag Alphas.

I'm straight dammit!

"I-I don't understand," he whimpered, his handsome face contorted into confusion and anguish and it shattered something inside me. I hurt him, the guy's wolf was sending radar waves of pain into me like knives.

"Stop hurting him and go comfort our mate!" my wolf demanded.

No!

"Just keep your damn distance from me f-fag." I stumbled on the word as it caused me physical agony to even call him something so cruel. I couldn't do this, it wasn't right for us to be mates. It was wrong.

I turned abruptly away from him and stormed off. Away from his damn intoxicating scent that called my body and wolf, and triggered a boiling sensation in my blood that felt like an insatiable fire.

UGH!

*   *   *

When I was out of sight of the house, I ran, shifting midair. I can't be in that house with him, I can't concentrate. He's everywhere and it's driving me crazy. Growling, I pushed my legs and broke out in a run taking in all of the fresh air.

The sun had gone down some time ago and the night had blanketed the earth, covering everything. This was where a wolf should be, this was his real habitat, out in the night, in the wild doing whatever he wanted.

A noise caught my attention, my ears perked up, and I crouched low. Inhaling deeply, I could pick up the fading scents of the Enforcers who had scouted this area a while ago, the smell of water from the stream was not too far from here, along with the undeniable scent of prey.

Lifting my lip, I snarled lowly, my wolf ready for the hunt and what better way to blow off some steam than by hunting? I kept my body close to the ground and moved forward, my feet expertly avoiding any twigs or leaves that would give me away too early. I came upon a bush and looked through to see a deer grazing the bright green grass in the moonlight. A wolfish grin spread on my lips, I just love the chase.

Purposely, I swiped at the bush causing the dear to snap its head up in my direction before bolting away. Howling, I jumped through the bush and took off after it. He was quick as he hopped over fallen logs and rocks but I was faster. I pumped my legs, welcoming the burn as I mimicked his every move, staying on his tail the entire time. He cleared the stream in one graceful jump, I could have ended it at any time but I enjoyed the exercise. I basked in the excitement and the rush it gave me and my wolf.

When I thought it was enough I pushed my back legs hard and propelled myself on top of the deer's back, digging my claws into its sides before I went for his neck.

I trotted over to the stream once I was finished to clean the blood off my muzzle as well as lap up some of the cool refreshing water. The last time I had been here was with Caleb. I closed my eyes at the memory, I was such an ass, but I told him more than once to let it go. It was just like Caleb to try and get his way until that jackass boyfriend of his had to come along.

In a way I was glad for the intevention, I didn't want to hurt Caleb and I feel bad for doing what I did, but I would never tell him. It's bad enough that I feel that way.

Sighing, I lay my body down at the stream's edge and stare at the rushing water. I didn't want to go back to the house; I didn't want to be constantly reminded that I was a werewolf with a guy for a mate. I was meant to have a girl like all the other normal wolves, where we'd breed and have pups. I was meant to grow old together with my 'female' mate, then watch my pups do the same.

How was I supposed to do that when my mate was a guy? It wasn't right; it wasn't fair.

Why were the Spirits punishing me?

CHAPTER 18

CALEB

Something wasn't right today. I don't know what it was but I just didn't feel right. Something was wrong and I was going crazy because I was on edge all day. I was currently searching high and low for Levi.

I hadn't seen him since I came home a few days ago. I wanted to tell him that I was finally with Avery and I was the happiest I'd ever been in my life. I don't know how Avery felt about all this, but I hope he felt the same. Plus, let's not forget our sex life was to die for. I would have never guessed that Avery was such an animal in bed.

I bit my lip as I suppressed a goofy grin from spilling on my face.

Okay Caleb, stop thinking about him now or you're going to steal him away from Aiden and have your naughty way with him.

Climbing up the stairs that were on opposite side of the staircase I walked down earlier, I made my way through where the adults's rooms were. Who knew looking for my best friend would be this difficult?

Lifting my nose in the air, I caught his scent located at the far end and I sighed in relief. I then jogged to the room that was on the end of the hall and knocked on the door. I heard a pair of feet shuffle before the door opened, revealing a man with familiar dark brown hair and brown eyes. His face was sporting a stubble, his hair was messy from sleep, and his clothes were rumpled and unkempt.

Marten Blackman.

Mr. Blackman had always looked this way even from the moment I came to this pack and became friends with Levi. His sorrowful bloodshot eyes, deep lines in his face, and disheveled clothes stood out to everyone around him. Levi once told me about his old pack and what happened to his mother and I always felt sorry for Mr. Blackman. He had to watch his mate get murdered right in front of him, but I also admired him for taking Levi away from that horrible place.

"Morning Mr. Blackman, I'm looking for Levi. Is he with you?" I asked softly. He tried to form a smile but it just came out as a grimace.

"Caleb, for the last time call me Marten." He sighed.

I grin sheepishly.

"Right."

"And about Levi, I don't think right now is a good—" The door swung open and Levi stood there looking every bit like his dad from the messy hair, bloodshot eyes, and wrinkled clothes. They matched each other down to a T.

"C-Caleb." It came out as a whimper and I instantly knew something was wrong.

"Levi? What is it?" My voice immediately taking a sharp tone. He shook his head, his usual perfectly gelled hair was flat and hung right in front of his eyes.

"Caleb!" he cried and rushed into my arms. I wrapped my arms around him as he threw his around my neck, burying his face in my shoulder. He was bent over since he was a few inches taller than me. I looked past his shoulder and looked towards Marten in concern but he only had a sad expression on his face as he looked at his son. I tightened my arms around him in response.

"Levi what's wrong?" I asked softly. He didn't answer and just cried quietly.

Mr. Blackman cleared his throat.

"I'm just going to leave you two alone for a while," he told us as he edged around us in the doorway and walked down the stairs. Slowly, I walked a sobbing Levi back into this dad's room and closed the door behind us, all while he was still clutching to me. I turned us around and laid back on the bed where he followed my every move and lay with me.

I stared up at the ceiling and let him cry out into my neck before I asked what the hell happened. After who knows how long, he finally quieted down.

"I m-missed you so much Caleb." He sniffled. I closed my eyes in guilt. I felt horrible that I just left him to whatever it was that was bugging him so badly.

"I missed you too Lee. Now tell me, what has gotten you like this?" I demanded softly. I pulled away, sitting us up. His face contorted in pain, his eyes filled with more tears, and it hurt my heart. Levi had never acted like this. He was always a loving person who cared for others and loved to have fun. I had never once seen him so sad and full of anguish that was enough to cry over.

"I heard you and Avery are together," he said, averting the question.

I narrowed my eyes at him.

"Levi," I warned. He sighed and sat up, hugging his long legs to his chest.

"It hurts too much Caleb," he whispered.

I frowned in concern.

"What does?"

His eyes were on the bed while his chin rested on his drawn up knees.

"What you want me to talk about, it rips me apart and I just want it to end."

My mouth was drawn in a tight line.

"Damn it Levi! Just tell me!" I demanded. Levi shut his eyes tightly and buried his head in his knees.

"I don't understand how he could do this to me. How he can just ignore me like this. He was so uncaring of my feelings despite knowing that I love him," he whispered.

"He? What are you talking about? Is this over some guy? Levi you have never acted like his before because of a guy."

"This is different, completely different, and it's too much to take."

"Okay tell me what he did. Did he take advantage of you?" I asked, my voice holding a threatening note. If someone hurt him, I was going out for blood. He shook his head as I waited, I was losing my patience but I kept myself leashed.

"No, he hasn't touched me. Well, not in the way that I want him to. Caleb am I ugly? Repulsive enough to run away from? Do I have a horrible personality?" he asked, snapping his head up at me expectantly.

I frowned in confusion.

"What?! Hell no! You are gorgeous Levi and you're one of the sweetest and most caring people I know," I answered. His eyes watered again.

"Then what's wrong with me?!" he cried out and raked his fingers through his long greasy flat hair. When was the last time he took a shower?

"You're going to have to start from the beginning because you are losing me Levi," I told him softly.

He sighed, turning his head away from me to look out at the open window that blew a gentle breeze into the room.

"I found him Caleb," he muttered quietly. I had to strain myself to hear him.

"Found who?"

"And he doesn't even want me." A lone tear slid down his cheek. My heart squeezed at the sight. Reaching out, I wiped the tear away and cupped his face in my hand turning him to face me. I knew then, the hurt and sorrow was clear on his face. Looking at him at this moment was like looking straight into Mr. Blackman's face.

"Your mate?" I whispered. His eyes misted up, his chin trembled as he bit down on his lip.

"How did this happen, Caleb? Finding your mate is supposed to be the best experience we can ever ask for. Finding your other half is meant to complete you but all I feel is emptiness. It isn't right Caleb. It's not fair. I can't take this, I'm not strong enough," he whimpered weakly, letting the tears fall.

I bit my lip, swallowing down the lump in my throat. He was right, it wasn't fair. He had dreamt of finding his 'one'. He believed in it completely and for it to be ripped away from him like this was cruel.

"Tell me who it is so I could talk to them." He shook his head, wiping his face with his hands.

"There is no talking to him. He's the most stubborn person you'll ever know," he argued.

I rolled my eyes.

"Just tell me his name Levi." He averted his gaze from me. It took him a few minutes but he finally said it.

"Kyle."

I froze.

No.

"Oh God Levi, no," I whispered.

He nodded.

"He hates me Caleb, there's nothing I can do about this. It was over before it even started." My heart dropped to my stomach. How could this happen? Kyle may put up with all the gay relationships in this house because he had to but that didn't mean he liked it. He was definitely against anyone who came on to him who wasn't a girl. He was a homophobe and I could physically feel myself hurt for Levi. He didn't deserve this, he didn't deserve Kyle. He deserved someone who would love him with all their heart unconditionally, someone who didn't care about gender and cherished everything about Levi.

Squeezing my eyes shut, I took Levi in my arms.

"I'm so sorry. I'll talk to him okay?"

He shook his head that rested against my shoulder.

"It's no use Caleb, don't even waste your breath."

I buried my face into his hair, Kyle was going to let Levi waste away into nothing and I couldn't have that. I was going to talk to him and he was going to listen. I pulled back, taking Levi's hand. I walked him into his dad's bathroom then turned the water on warm. I hugged him to me.

"Take a shower and I'll get you spare clothes okay?" He nodded, his face exhausted and void of emotion. I tensed my jaw in anger,

Damn it Kyle!

* * *

I left him a clean pair of pajama bottoms along with one of his band T-shirts and went down to find Kyle. I caught his scent down in the living room. Gritting my teeth, I marched towards him having every intention of punching him right in his ungrateful face. I turned sharply into the room where he stood alone, his head down and focused on his phone. Once I was close enough I pulled back my fist and slammed it hard into his oblivious face. The phone flew to the floor and he staggered back, tripping over his feet as he tried to catch himself from landing on the ground.

"How could you?!" I screamed at him. He looked up at me in shock, his gray eyes wide in surprise.

"What the f*ck?!" he hissed, hopping to his feet swiftly. I knew he could overpower me in a fight. He could easily kill me but I didn't back down. I stood there as he stepped towards my face intimidatingly. His eyes dark with anger,

"You unappreciative bastard!" My glare sliced through him harshly.

"What the f*ck is the matter with you Caleb?!" he growled.

"You, you're what's the matter! How could you be so heartless and let Levi suffer like this?!" I growled back. He backed away, not expecting that. I felt a moment of satisfaction at this.

"You don't know what you're talking about," he said stubbornly. I glared.

"I know exactly what I'm talking about and so do you!"

"This has nothing to do with you Caleb so why don't you stay out of it and mind your own business!" he yelled.

"How can I when you broke my best friend's heart?! No, I'm going to tell you where my business lies and it's right here!"

"Oh really?" he snarled, his canines extending. I was shaking, I was so mad that I did the same and showed mine as well. I was not about to back down.

"Yes, Kyle you're a scared little pup," I spat. He narrowed his eyes but I continued even though he was inches from my face. "Grow a damn pair and go to your mate! How could you let him suffer like this? You have been doing this ever since he came here all those months ago haven't you?" I said in disgust.

"You know nothing Caleb." His chest rumbling in anger.

"I know enough that there is no Levi without Kyle. You're a murderer and suicidal on top of that." He furrowed his brows in rage.

"Shut up!" he hissed as he pushed me. I staggered but retaliated with my own shove.

"What, you don't like to hear the truth?" I taunted. "That's what you're doing, you're slowly killing him and yourself, you assh*le."

"I never asked for this!" he yelled at me.

Suddenly I heard a vicious familiar growl. I spun around to find Avery standing in the doorway, his eyes a blazing blue of violent justice. He marched towards us in deliberate strides.

"I thought I told you to stay away from him!" Avery growled at Kyle. Kyle snarled showing his canines.

"He's the one barging in here, bugging me about things that's none of his business." Avery wrapped an arm around my waist possessively as he glared daggers at him.

"Levi is my business! You need to fix this, he's your mate!" I repeated, trying my hardest to make him realize what a great person he has for his other half.

"You're rejecting your mate?" Avery asked in quiet revulsion. Kyle groaned.

"I don't need your input bodyguard, just take your damn boy toy and leave me the hell alone."

I gasped.

"Excuse me, I'm trying to help your worthless ass!"

"No you're trying to be a pain in my ass and I don't like it very much so why don't you back the f*ck off?!"

"I'll be the thorn in your side, the pain in your ass, and the pounding in your head. Hell, I'll be your damn conscience until you realize that Levi is what you really need and want. I'll be here to constantly remind you of how stupid you are for rejecting him!" I yelled.

"You're getting on my nerves damn it!"

"Good!" I screamed.

"Caleb," Avery's voice whispered in my ear as a soft warning. I never got to respond as a deep rumbling shook the walls and windows.

"What the hell is going on in here?!" I cowered back into Avery's side as he tightened his hold on me. I turned my head to see Liam glaring at all of us with Aiden by his side and a burly looking man standing on the other.

They all walked in the room.

"We apologize, Alpha. It was a minor argument that could have been taken elsewhere," Avery said formally.

"No, it's over so excuse me!" Kyle snapped, snatching up his phone as he strode past Liam like he wasn't there. Liam glared at Kyle before turning towards me with sharp hazel eyes.

"I try to show my guest around and this is the first impression they get." His voice was disapproving and strong. I bowed my head.

"I apologize, Alpha, I was just so angry. If I had known you were having people over, I would have waited to talk with Kyle." He shook his head with a sigh.

"Kyle is hardheaded and can make you lose all sense at times." I nodded, knowing he completely agreed with me. I was relieved. I was about to turn towards Avery to tell him I wanted to go upstairs when I heard a gasp and my body froze. I snapped my head up in horror as my eyes landed on a pair of wide baby blue ones.

Then it happened, my wolf stirred.

"*Mate.*"

CHAPTER 19

CALEB

Her blonde hair fell down in waves around her face. She was beautiful. That was easy to see. My wolf stirred again.

No!

I stepped back further into Avery's arms and the raging in my head and the pacing of my wolf calmed.

"Caleb?" Avery asked, looking down at me in confusion. I looked up at him in terror then back at her. This couldn't be. Kyle's words suddenly came to mind.

"I didn't ask for this."

This girl couldn't be my mate, it wasn't possible. I was gay, I have never been attracted to women.

She moved forward, walking towards me with confidence in her step which had a bit of arrogance if you ask me. She looked from me to Avery whose arms I was still wrapped up in. Something flashed in her eyes but I couldn't catch what it was because it happened so quickly.

"Caleb, is that your name?" she asked, her voice was so soft that it caused my wolf to whine. Avery tightened his hold on my stiff form.

"Caleb, what's wrong?" he asked, his face suspicious. His voice made my wolf whine too.

What was going on? I felt like I was being tugged in two different directions. My wolf was becoming so confused.

"I'm Lynn, your mate." The room suddenly went still. I felt Avery stiffen, I wanted to turn and scream at him not to listen. I wanted to run away as fast as I could, to get far away and take Avery with me. Instead, I stared at her and shook my head.

She frowned.

"Yes." She pushed, nodding her head. "We're mates Caleb. Can't you feel it?" I whined aloud. She held her hands out and I just stared at them as I grabbed at Avery's hand.

"Come to me Caleb," she said softly, like she expected me to listen. I shook my head as Avery gripped my hand harder, I felt the turmoil raging inside of him as if it were all my own, but it just added to my chaotic thoughts and feelings.

"I can't," I whispered.

"What are you talking about? I'm your mate Caleb you have to come." She frowned. I glared at her. Who does she think she is? I don't have to do anything especially for her.

"No, I don't!" I snapped and pulled a shocked Avery out of the room.

"Caleb!" I heard Liam call, but I ignored him and walked faster. Avery didn't protest, he just followed me outside. I rushed through trees as we ran. I had to get away from there, from her.

What was happening? Why did she had to show up now? Right when everything was perfect?

Ugh! I felt like such a hypocrite for yelling at Kyle back then. Was this how he felt?

My throat tightened from all the emotions swirling around within me. I stumbled more than once, but Avery caught me. Finally we burst from the woods and towards the lake that glistened peacefully. I stared at it for a while, wishing my life was like this: tranquil and calm. Sighing, I turned around, facing Avery and reached out to take his face in my hands and push his lips against mine. I needed him to make me forget all about this. I didn't care about her, it was all about Avery and I. She had no room in our relationship and never will.

Avery's lips were unresponsive, I pulled back a little to look into his dazed eyes. I knew what he was thinking and it hurt. He was pulling back from me again.

"Avery, please don't," I whimpered against his mouth, pressing them together again. He just stood there, unmoved. I closed my eyes, tears building in them.

"Please don't do this to me now. I need you Avery," I cried, not bothering to wipe the fallen tears. His eyes were filled with so many emotions that I couldn't decipher all of them. Without warning, he shot his hand out to grip the back of my head before he smashed his mouth to mine. Passion filled my senses and I was lost. My wolf howled inside, utterly confused with all the feelings bombarding us, he wanted his mate but he wanted Avery just the same.

The kiss became needy and desperate like Avery could feel the chaos of my wolf and wanted nothing more than to make him realize it was him that he needed. I was frantic as I pulled his shirt over his head.

"I want you Avery, only you." I looked him straight in the eyes, every word to him was serious and true. I wanted him to see that. He held my gaze for a long moment till I bent over to kiss his chest, his stomach, and every piece of skin I had access to. I hurriedly unbuttoned his jeans and pulled them down to pool at his feet along with his boxers.

God he was beautiful. I thought.

The sun was shining on all of him like a beacon just for me. He was mine and I was not going to give him up for anyone. Quickly, I took him in my mouth while I watched him, needing his taste. His eyes closed and his head was thrown back in pleasure. I continued to move on him as I reached down and took my jeans off. I pulled off him for a second to tear my shirt off then took him back.

"Caleb," he moaned, sliding his hands in my hair and gripping it tight. He began to move me against him faster, using me to his will. I loved it, I loved him. I caressed his thighs up further, feeling his muscular bottom.

My tongue quickly flicked out, causing him to buckle his knees and tear himself away from my wanton mouth. He sank to his knees with me and took my mouth in a searing kiss before laying me down. I wrapped my arms around his neck and wrapped my legs around his waist.

"Now," I said, practically begging. "Please, now!" I cried. He buried his face in my neck and thrust into me.

I screamed in pleasure, digging my nails in his back. His hands took hold of my hips, lifting them off the ground to better suit his deep penetrating strokes. I was lost in all the feelings I had of him while he was inside. My heart was hammering against my chest from the deep emotions he always brought out in me. I gasped for air, hearing his labored breathing in my ear which was hot against my neck.

"I love you, Avery," I whispered to him as I reached my first peak of climax. His grip on my hips turned painful, and I felt his mouth on my shoulder as it roamed up my neck and back down. I slowly came down as he still kept his thrusts even and persistent. Sweat was building up between us, the grass was soft while our arousal was high and strong. His teeth grazed over his mark and I bucked against him, bringing him further inside He let out a sexy groan and sunk his canines into me.

I screamed, throwing back my head at the euphoric feeling of his teeth and my body shook with another climax, joining Avery this time. His growl rumbled between us, and he slowly pulled back, hovering over me with his beautiful blue eyes.

"I don't need anyone but you, Avery," I told him softly, reaching up to move his sweaty hair away from his forehead. He didn't say anything, just leaned down and licked the scar he left on my shoulder. I peered up into the clear blue sky and sighed as he tended to his mark lovingly.

My wolf was sated, quiet, and content. He like being here with Avery, I felt the love he had for this male wolf. It was like he connected with Avery on a level that was impossible to comprehend, more complicated than any other mated couple. He loved him, just as I do, and this girl who seem to come out of the blue had confused him to a point where he couldn't take it. Avery had fixed it like he was meant to, we were meant to be together.

My eyes wandered back to him and to the scar I had left on him not too long ago. This was proof that he was mine. I had marked him. I wouldn't have been able to do so if I wasn't supposed to be his. Unable to control myself and my wolf stirring with me, I leaned forward and bit into him, needing the permanent truth in the mark we shared together. Avery yelled out and I felt the warmth of his seed erupt inside me again.

He collapsed on top of me, panting for breath. Lapping to heal the scar, I pressed my lips to his ear.

"You bear my mark Avery and I bear yours, don't forget that. There's a reason for it and I'm not letting you go."

He sighed, kissing my neck.

"I don't want to let you go Caleb," he told me quietly. I reached up and combed my fingers through his dirty blonde hair soothingly.

"Then don't. That's all I ask for. Just be with me because I'm never letting you leave me," I whispered possessively. I wanted him to soak in my words and hold on to me forever.

"Caleb," was all he said as we lay there holding each other as if our lives depended on it.

* * *

They were here! Why? Where was Caleb? I needed Caleb! I rushed down the stairs and flew past the room they were in and threw open the door. I ran down the steps. I looked around frantically, I couldn't breathe right, and my vision was blurred with tears as I trudged through the woods.

I ran to the lake, hoping he was there. I burst through the bushes and spotted Caleb lying naked with Avery. I would have blushed and turned way if it wasn't for the erratic chaos in my body. Ignoring their current position, I rushed over to Caleb, who had shot up with Avery covering himself with discarged clothing. I dove into him without hesitation, hugging him close as I hid my face in his chest.

"What the hell?!" Caleb exclaimed sharply. He wrapped his arms around me. "What's wrong Blondie?" he asked, worried. I looked up at him with tear-filled eyes.

"Keep them away from me, please Caleb," I whimpered.

"Help me."

CHAPTER 20

CALEB

I sat there, shocked out of my mind. He just talked to me. Blondie talked to me and the words coming out of his usually mute mouth were unnerving. I frowned, pulling him away before I stood up and pulled my clothes on fast.

"Who Blondie?" He looked scared to death.

"Them," he whispered looking around him cautiously. I spared a quick worried glance at Avery who was fully dressed now and looking every bit of a serious warrior. His brown eyes were trained on Blondie as he watched the boy shake with fear. He took a step forward and bent low on his knee.

"Who is '*them*'? Are they the ones you were running from?" he asked softly. Blondie looked up at him and nodded.

"They found me Avery, and I need to get away before they realize I'm here." He stressed. I frowned, following Avery on his knee.

"You're talking about the people who just arrived aren't you?" I stated. He nodded, his shaggy hair flying all over the place. I looked at Avery again and we both had the same protective expression. Whoever these people were, they weren't getting anywhere near this boy.

"Okay, come on," I said, rising to my feet and taking his hand. Avery stood as well and walked close to us in a protective manner, he was on alert now like he always was with Aiden.

Aiden. I peered up at Avery.

"Avery you have to go to Aiden, if these people are bad then you need to protect him," I told him. His face was stoic.

"He has Liam with him and the whole pack surrounding him. Right now he's safer that anyone else in this whole town." His eyes were ahead of him as he did an occasional sweep around us. I sighed as Blondie's hand tightened in mine.

"I'm taking you away from your duty to him aren't I?"

He frowned at me.

"Caleb, you're in need of me more than he is right now. I will know if Aiden is in trouble. Trust me, these people are not going to do anything." I nodded and focused on the walk towards the house. Blondie pulled me to a stop.

"I don't want to go back in there," he whispered, looking at the house as if it was going to eat him. I grabbed him by the shoulders and turned him to face me.

"They aren't going to touch you. Nobody is," I told him sternly. He gazed at me for a long moment then nodded slowly.

"Promise me?"

I smiled down at him and ruffled his hair.

"I promise and so does Avery." He looked over to Avery who inclined his head in agreement.

So my supposed *'mate'* was the one who caused little Blondie to run. Well I don't know about you but she was looking worse in my eyes, and I was going to get to the bottom of this.

* * *

They day was coming to an end and the sky was getting dark. We snuck Blondie in through the back and into our room which used to be Avery's, but since I never sleep in my room anymore, I call it ours. Come to think of it, I should just move my clothes in here too.

Blondie was sleeping in the middle of the bed. He had worn himself out with all his stressing and worrying. I sat down on the edge of the bed and began to smooth his hair back. He was so young and innocent that when I looked at him, I got a glimpse of myself and Robin. He was running from someone and apparently they found him just like Zackary and the rogues had found Robin and I.

His face was calm in his sleep. What had these people done to him to make him like this? To scare him so bad that he ran and refuse to talk for so long?

Sighing, I took off his shoes and socks and tucked the blanket up to his chin.

"You care about him a lot don't you?" Avery asked in a low tone to not wake the boy. I didn't look up at him and just kept my gaze on Blondie.

"I do. I don't know how to describe it. I feel like I'm responsible for him in a way you know?" I whispered.

"Like a parent?" he asked. I peered up at him. He was standing against the wall watching us.

"Do you think?" I questioned.

He smiled.

"The way you're with him and how he's so attached to you, I would think you were his mother," he teased.

I glared at him.

"Shut up, and what are you, his father?" I laughed. He didn't answer and just stood with a blank expression. He was doing it again, pulling back.

Sighing, I stood from the bed and walked towards him. He didn't move and just watched my every move with a careful eye. I came to a stop in front of him.

"You're running again, Avery."

He frowned at me.

"I'm right here," he stated.

I nodded.

"But you're not here," I said touching his temple. "You're pulling away from me and I refuse to let you." He stared at me silently. I bit down on my lip and cupped the side of his face. He closed his eyes, leaning into my touch. My heart fluttered from the action.

"I just want you and no one else," I told him again and I would keep telling him the same thing till he got it through that thick skull of his.

"But I can't have you Caleb," he said softly. I didn't say anything and just stared at him.

"We weren't meant to be and you know that."

I shook my head.

"No, you were meant to be mine Avery. Don't do this to me," I retorted, my voice strained. He took my hand from his face and pulled it down but kept it in his.

"How was I meant to be with you when your mate is in this very house?"

I sighed, stepping closer so our bodies were pressed together.

"You're right, my mate is in this house." He nodded looking away from me and let go of my hand.

"I'm glad you finally see."

I never stepped back.

"So am I because I'm standing right in front of him."

His brown eyes snapped back to mine.

"Cal—"

"Stop Avery!" I exclaimed softly so I didn't wake Blondie. He gazed at me stubbornly but said nothing.

"I'm not doing this again, I have worked my ass off to try and get you, and this *'girl'*," I said it like it was a curse, "means nothing to me because I have deep feelings for someone else and she's not going to change that. It's too late, I'm already in love."

His eyes flickered a moment.

"You'll learn to love her. She was meant for you Caleb, not me. Our time is up and it's time for me to back off now."

I growled.

"Don't you dare! Whoever she is, she hurt this boy and I'm not a bad judge of character so I know that something's not right with these people. My wolf may recognize her as his mate but he's confused Avery, and I don't think wolves are supposed to be confused with their true mates. So I'm following my instincts and keeping away from these people and that girl."

"Your wolf is confused?" he asked with a frown.

I nodded laying my head on his chest.

"He knows she's his mate. He told me but he's giving off these crazy disorderly vibes and the only time he's calm is when we're with you," I confessed. I moved my face so I was looking up at him with my chin on his chest. He was looking down at me in confusion.

"This is all too much, Caleb. I think we need to talk to someone about this," he said.

"Alright, but just hold me Avery," I muttered in his chest. Slowly, his arms wrapped around me and I smiled.

He's not going to get away from me that easy.

* * *

AVERY

It felt so right to have him in my arms. He was warm, real, and solid against me. I wanted to forget about today but I couldn't. My conscience wouldn't allow it. She was here, she had found her mate and intended to take him away. It all happened so fast, I barely had time with him before his mate showed up. I should have listened to myself when I refused to be with anyone. If I had done that then I wouldn't be feeling like my heart had just been ripped out. He was going to leave. Something I had feared all along, the only thing I have ever feared.

I took a deep shaky breath and tightened my hold on him. I buried my face into his neck, taking in his unique scent of water orchids and spearmint. I bit my lip as a lump rose in my throat and out of their own accord, tears spilled silently from my eyes.

What was wrong with me? I knew this day would come, not this fast but I knew it would, so why was I acting like this?

My wolf began to whine at the emotions swirling inside of me. He was as reluctant to let Caleb go as well. Caleb was his mate in his mind and he howled at me to fight for for what was ours.

I wanted to do just that but it wasn't right to take someone's other half, to steal what was never rightfully yours to begin with. I still had my principles. My cheeks were wet now and tears spilled on his shoulder, but he didn't notice. My fingers combed the back of his hair absentmindedly.

I love you Caleb.

Damn it what the hell am I going to do?

Should I let him go?

CHAPTER 21

CALEB

"You can't be serious!" I exclaimed in a whispered tone. Alpha Liam and Aiden had brought me in the sitting room to talk privately. Avery was guarding the door with his oh-so-usual stoic expression. I fell back in the couch as I stared at them in disbelief.

"Yes," Liam said, watching me closely. "They are staying for a while. Since you are mates, Alpha Collin thinks it's the best thing for the both of you since you two live so far apart."

I narrowed my eyes at him.

"I don't give a damn what he thinks, I don't want her here and that's final!" I practically yelled.

Liam glared.

"No that's not final because I'm Alpha here Caleb and I give the 'final' say," he said.

Everything was quiet for a while before he sighed.

"She's your mate Caleb, why are you being like this?" His voice was tired. I turned my face from him stubbornly and eyed the wall remaining silent.

"Caleb if you're not willing to tell us what's wrong, we can't help you," Aiden said in a soft caring tone.

I shook my head.

"It's just these people. There's something not right with them," I confessed.

Aiden frowned looking up at Liam.

"Why do you say that? You haven't even been in the same room for more than a minute," Liam sighed.

I opened my mouth but nothing came out. Should I tell them about Blondie? He hadn't told me what they have done to him and I didn't want to betray his trust in me.

"Caleb?" Aiden questioned. I closed my eyes tightly. If I told them, would it cause problems for Blondie? Would they take him away from us? Who the hell were they to him?

"Well if you're not going to say anything, then I guess they are staying," Liam said in a tone of finality. I bit my lip. "Make sure you get to know Lynn, Alpha Collin is expecting you two to be together in the next week or so."

My eyes snapped open as I stared at him with wide eyes.

"What!?"

He raised a brow at me.

"Watch your tone, Caleb," he said sternly. I ignored him and shot to my feet.

"Why the hell are you doing this to me? You know damn well that I'm gay!" Liam got to his feet in a fluent motion.

"Tone," he growled. My head was raging.

"I'm not doing it," I exclaimed. "You can't make me"

"She's your mate, so I guess you're not as gay as you thought," he said. "You can't fight the mating Caleb. It's inevitable, trust me."

"Bull!" I screamed. I didn't have time to see what happened before I was knocked on the table with a strong grip on my throat. I stared up at Liam's bright yellow eyes.

"You do NOT talk to your Alpha that way!" he growled, his canines extended. My hands reach out to grip his arm but it was like steel. My breath was coming out in gasps.

"Liam!" Aiden yelled.

Then his hand was gone. I gulped in air as my vision cleared, my senses were coming back and I heard a growl. I looked up to see the hem of a black shirt above me.

"Don't. Touch. Him." Avery growled dangerously. He was crouched over me in a protective manner, glaring at the Alpha.

"Tell him to have respect or he'll keep getting the same treatment," Liam snarled at him.

The room was tense and suffocating.

"Guys," Aiden said. I scooted out under Avery. He straightened his stance but kept himself in front of me. When I was standing, I watched the two glare at each other.

"I thought you were supposed to be protecting Aiden," Liam growled.

"Well he doesn't need it at the moment," he answered. Aiden walked in front of Liam and placed his hands on his chest.

"Liam," he said softly, causing him to look down at his small mate. "I think we all just need to calm down. Let's go outside for a bit okay?" Aiden said, grabbing at his hand to pull him out of the room but not before Liam turned to face me once more.

"They are staying." Was all he got out as he was tugged out of the door. I sighed, collapsing down on the couch in defeat. Avery turned from the door and looked down at me.

"Are you alright?" he asked, kneeling down in front of me as he lifted my chin to examine my neck. I jerked my chin away from his grasp, placing a hand over my sore throat.

"I'm fine." My voice was a bit raspy. He didn't look convinced but he said nothing else.

"You know what? I'm not fine. I don't want them to stay here!" I exclaimed, staring straight into his brown eyes. "I don't want them near Blondie at all."

"There's nothing we can do about that, Caleb. Alpha Liam says they can stay and that's what they're going to do unless you tell him that they are the ones responsible for the boys's behavior," he stated.

"Yes I know that," I said, a bit irritated. He tilted his head to the side with a questionable expression.

"Then why didn't you?"

I looked up at him.

"Because I don't know if Blondie is okay with us telling anyone about this, plus we don't even know what they did, but whatever it was sent him running."

Avery looked thoughtful for a moment before he grabbed my hands and lifted me to my feet.

"Well then just go up to him and ask him what happened."

I nodded.

"Just that easy?" I teased.

He smiled. "Yes, I'm just as curious to know."

I sighed, walking towards the door.

"Fine." I turned to him once more and stood on my toes and gave him a gentle kiss. "I'll see you later," I whispered against his mouth. He nodded, reaching up to brush some of my hair away from my face.

With that I walked out, making my way towards our room where Blondie was hiding. He refused to come out since yesterday so I had to grab all of his clothes from his room to ours. Lately, all he has been doing was huddling in the middle of the bed with covers thrown over his head, sleeeping, or staring at the door. He hasn't spoken since last time, and I was afraid he was retreating back to his old self.

I was on the top step when Lynn popped up from nowhere. I jumped with a yelp. Placing my hand over my fast beating heart I held myself up by the stairs banister.

"Sh*t!" I exclaimed, glaring at her. She had a sickly sweet smile on her face and I glared at her cautiously.

"Hey babe," she purred. I scrunched up my face at her nickname.

"I'm not your *babe*." I sneered, moving around her. She started to pout.

"Of course you're my babe, we are mates after all." She reached out to grab my arm and I jumped back from her touch. She watched me with wide innocent eyes.

"Why won't you let me touch you?" Her voice was shaking with sadness. My wolf stirred again, telling me to comfort her. I shook my head and reprimanded him.

"Because I don't want you to, so if you don't mind, you're in my way," I said rather rudely as I walked around her and rushed towards the room but I heard her right behind me.

Ugh!

"Do you understand that I'm your mate? We are meant to be together," she pressed. I rolled my eyes.

"No, why don't you tell me about it a hundred more times?" I growled sarcastically, slowing my pace. I didn't want her near Blondie and I paused.

"What are you doing up here anyway? The guest rooms are downstairs." I turned towards her accusingly. She shrugged.

"I wanted to explore." She circled her arms around my neck and pressed her body up against mine. I had no time to dodge her. I looked down at her shorter form nervously. Reluctantly, my body was reacting to hers.

"You can show me around can't you?" My wolf was purring at the feel of her small curvy body. I was breathing hard as she got closer towards my face.

What the hell was wrong with me? I can't believe she was affecting me like this.

"I-I really don't have the time right now," I stuttered. Her hand reached out and she ran a finger slowly down the side of my face.

"You have time," she whispered. Her warm breath inches away from my mouth. I needed to pull her off but my body wouldn't move away. A shiver wracked through me as her hand played with the hair at the nape of my neck.

"The first on our tour should be your bedroom." My wolf scratched at the surface, desperate to get out.

Damn what was wrong with him? He can't want both Avery and Lynn!

Closing my eyes, her lips were barely brushing against mine when I pulled away from her roughly and pressed my back up against the wall. I tried to get the havoc of my senses back under control.

"I need to go," I stressed before I ran from her. I was relieved that she didn't follow me this time. I got to Avery and my door and ran in, slamming it shut behind me. I let out a shuddering breath and slid down against the wall, resting my head back.

This was not normal behavior for a wolf. Why was I so torn?

"Caleb?" A small voice sounded from the bed. I looked up to find Blondie looking at me as he peeked through his spot in the middle of the mattress.

"Hey kid," I greeted forcing a smile on my face.

"What happened? Did they find out?" His voice was cracked from fright as he stared at the door behind me with wide green eyes.

I stood up, shaking my head in reassurance.

"No, you're safe." I made my way to him, planting myself on the edge of the bed before I reached out to move his shaggy hair away from his face. His thin shoulders sagged.

"Blondie, I have to ask you something." He looked at me innocently and waited. "Can you tell me what they have done to you?" A look of uncertainty suddenly crossed his face.

"I-I don't know," he said shakily. I nodded.

"I wouldn't be asking you this but for us to help you, we need to know what happen so we can take it to the Alphas." He looked down at his clenched hands.

"Will they really help?" he asked.

"Yes, if they heard your story then they'll boot those guys out of here and tell them to never come back," I told him with a smile. He was silent and thoughtful for a long moment. I waited patiently, rubbing his back affectionately.

"Um, t-their m-my family." He forced out. I stared at him in shock.

"I'm different from the rest of the pack." He continued.

"What relation are they to you?" I asked softly. He ducked his head.

"They are my cousin and uncle. My parents died when I was eight, the Alpha took me in after that."

I nodded.

"Okay, so why do you think you're different?" His bright green eyes looked straight at me.

"Because I don't . . . like . . . girls," he muttered in a low tone. I was taken aback.

Did he just say he was gay?

I frowned.

"You're telling me you're gay?" I asked. His cheeks brightened.

"I guess," he whispered. I got some serious flashback from the time I told my dad the same thing, the feelings and uncertainties from that moment came slamming back. I was a little younger than him but I understand now.

"So what did they do when you told them?"

"They told me that I was no longer their family," he whispered. Anger was building up inside of me.

"So they disowned you and you ran away?"

He shook his head.

"Not right away, I hoped they would love me again but it just got worse."

"What got worse?" I asked cautiously. He hesitated before answering.

"First, it was the names they called me. I was lowered to the omega position so I was treated badly. I had to clean every one's messes. They would h-hit me. Hit me so hard that I wouldn't be able to get out of bed for days but they forced me to anyway."

Growling, I grabbed him in my arms.

"Oh Blondie!" I said. "How long did this go on?"

"Two years, I was too scared to run away but I couldn't take it anymore. I didn't know where I was going but I ended up here," he confessed to me, tears flowing down his face. I pulled his head into my shoulder as he cried silently. I sat there, gritting my teeth as I glared at the wall opposite of me. How dare they do this to him? He's just a pup and was no older than twelve when this started!

"Tomorrow, we'll go to Liam and Aiden okay and you can tell them what these people did to you." He shook his head suddenly.

"I-I can't tell them all that, c-can you do it, please?" His wide green eyes stared up at me with such trust that I easily gave in. I nodded, holding him close to me.

"I'll do anything for you kid, all you gotta do is ask." He settled into me further and soon he was asleep.

Well these people have certainly overstayed their welcome. It was time for them to go!

CHAPTER 22

CALEB

It was midnight and Avery hasn't come to the room all day. I think he's trying to avoid me. I turned my head to make sure Blondie was still sleeping. I needed Avery near me, he was like my anchor. He kept me grounded in a good way.

Quietly, I slithered from the bed trying my best not to wake him. Slipping away from the room, I walked down the hall trying to follow his scent from all the others filling in the house. I picked up Levi's faint scent from the other side of the hall; he was still with his dad since I last checked on him the other day.

I sighed, this wasn't going to happen with Lynn and I right? Because this girl had to go, especially after what she had done to that poor boy.

I wanted to go talk to him, console him, but there was nothing I could say after what I had already said, and talking with Kyle just made me feel like a huge hypocrite. Then again, Kyle hadn't been in my shoes where his wolf was drawn to two people. I knew deep down that Avery was my one and only. Even if Lynn was my "true" mate, I couldn't be with someone like her. Avery's scent drew me to one of the few empty guest rooms on this section of the house.

Taking a deep breath, I pulled open the door to find him sitting on one of the window sills staring out at the night sky.

He turned to look at me in the doorway.

"Hey." I smiled at him. His blank expression softened as he watched me move further into the room and closed the door behind me.

"Hi," was all he said. I whimpered softly and rushed the rest of the way towards him, taking his sandy blonde hair in my fingers as I pressed a hard passionate kiss to his lips. He answered back, gripping my hips with his hands before he pulled me in-between his legs.

"I missed you," I whispered against his mouth.

He let out a soft chuckle and rubbed his hands up and down my sides. He laid his head on my chest and sighed deeply.

"I missed you too, Caleb." I held his head close to me, combing the back of his hair with my fingers soothingly. I looked up towards the window, the moon was half full and its cleansing, mysterious light reflected in the room.

I smiled.

"Gosh Avery you just saw me a couple hours ago, getting clingy much?" I teased in his hair. His body shook slightly as he laughed. My smile grew wider, I was beyond happy that I could be the one to make him laugh so freely. I started to trail my other hand's fingers down his neck slowly.

"I guess I'm obsessed with you," he teased. I gasped dramatically,

"Was . . . was that a joke coming from your mouth?" I questioned, amazed. He pulled his head away from my chest to look up at my standing figure with those beautiful chocolate brown eyes of his.

"You're rubbing off on me. I think you're becoming a bad influence," he told me. I wiggled my eyebrows and took his face in my hands.

"I'll be glad to rub on you, where would you like it?" I whispered the last part to him. A twinkle sparked in his eyes and he stood up, easily towering over me. I had to tilt my head back a bit to look up at him.

"I think you have a sex addiction." He smiled. I rolled my eyes, shaking my head.

"There's no such thing," I purred, pushing my body against his as I rubbed on him like a cat. "It's just that you're really good at it," I whispered and bit his ear.

"You think so?" he asked huskily. I nodded, trailing my tongue around his ear then down to his neck.

"Oh yeah, you make my body scream with passion, and have my wolf howling for more." His hands ran down my back over my shirt, leaving traces of heat that followed his touch.

"Is that so?" he growled softly in my ear. I bit down on my lower lip, closing my eyes as he buried his face in my neck and did the same things that made my knees buckle.

"Uh huh, and when we're done you leave me feeling so satisfied." I giggled.

"You know what I want right now?" I asked him, quietly stepping back away from him in a teasing manner. He watched my every move like a predator stalking his prey.

"What?" he asked, his voice strained. My legs hit the back of the bed and I sat down slowly.

"You."

That was all he needed as his eyes changed to that dangerous and sexy royal blue, he was on me in an instant.

* * *

I shifted in my sleep as the sun shone in my face. Groaning, I turned around burying my face in Avery's chest. I inhaled his strong masculine scent, replaying last night or more like this morning. He was so aggressive the first time but then he was beyond sweet the last two times throughout the night as he woke me up. I opened my eyes to look up at him, and saw him gazing at me with a soft expression on his handsome face.

"Morning," he said, his voice rough from sleep. Smiling, I stretched out and gave him a little kiss on the mouth.

"Morning, my love," I said in the best English accent I could muster. This caused him to grin down at me. We lay there for a while in each other's arms till I leaned up to face him, my body half on his.

"Do you miss it?"

He frowned at me.

"What?"

"Home." I stared at him in silence before he reached out to brush the hair away from my face.

"Doesn't everyone miss their homes once in a while?" he said.

"How long have you been away?" He continued playing with my hair as he sighed.

"A long time."

"Why did you leave?" I wanted to know more about him. He was a total mystery to me, and never opened up to anyone. I wanted to be that person he was comfortable with, the one who he could trust with his life and his heart.

"I left because they didn't need me." He shrugged.

I frowned.

"What are you talking about? Family always needs each other."

"I was just a nuisance, always in the way of every one so I left." His eyes were focused on his playing fingers.

"Avery Chandler, a nuisance? I never thought I would hear those two words in the same sentence." I teased.

"Well it was true."

"Tell me why you feel this way?" He finally met my gaze with a raised brow.

"What are you Dr. Phil?" he asked humorlessly. I shrugged.

"I just want to get to know you better, is that a crime? And if I can help you along the way then that's a bonus." I winked at him. He was thoughtful for a few moments.

"I guess if you want to know, I was . . ." He paused, taking a deep breath. "I was never really a part of my family in the same way everyone else is. I loved them dearly but I was always detached in a way."

I stayed quiet and listened as he continued.

"I always had a feeling that I was different than the rest of my pack. I was never one to play with others as a pup or enjoy the little things. I guess I always knew deep down that I would have to grow up faster than the rest," he told me.

My eyes roamed over his face, taking in every groove and line.

"So why do you call yourself a nuisance?"

"Because I had responsibilities that I would never be able to do. My parents needed me and I would fail them eventually because I'm not . . . I'm not whole." I furrowed my brows in sadness as I watched him. He was vulnerable right now. I was seeing him in a whole new different light and my heart broke at his grief. "And because of that, I was just in the way. A disappointment and I couldn't take that, so I left on the day after my fifteenth birthday."

I widened my eyes.

"So you told them you were leaving once you hit maturity and they let you go?" That was new, usually parents protected their pups till they were able to protect themselves in both forms. He shook his head.

"No, I left during the night," he confessed. I closed my eyes.

"You don't know if they miss you? What if they are worried sick about you?"

He frowned, glaring at the door.

"I can't think about those kinds of things Caleb. What I did was for the best for both of us."

I bit the inside of my cheek.

"You were to be Alpha, weren't you?" His eyes widened as he stared at me in shock.

"How did you—"

"You're no ordinary wolf, Avery. It all adds up. You say you have responsibilities at home. You're stronger that everyone in the house, well besides Liam and the former Alpha, which I'm sure you're evenly matched with, and let's not forget the fact that your eyes change colors. Only Alphas have that ability," I told him.

He gazed at me with a smile.

"Very observant. You're really smart Caleb."

I shrugged.

"But yes, I was in line to become Alpha," he answered.

I nodded.

"And you can't be an Alpha without your mate by your side," I stated. He inclined his head in agreement.

"Did your parents know your situation before you left?" I asked. He shook his head.

"I don't think so, I could tell they knew something wasn't normal with me but they didn't know what."

"Go back Avery," I said softly.

He sighed.

"I can't do that Caleb. It's too late, they probably hate me now."

I rolled my eyes.

"It's never too late. You're their son and they will love you regardless on whether you're a wanderer or not, Avery." He looked uncertain and doubtful.

"I have a job to do here, this is my responsibility. Aiden's my responsibility now," he said firmly as he pulled away from me and stood up.

I stayed on the bed, laying there as I stared at his broad back while he stretched.

"I think we should get back to Blondie before he notices he's alone and see if he hasn't already," I said, changing the subject to ease Avery's tension on the recent conversation. I would try later but I'll let it go for now.

He nodded while he pulled on his jeans.

"I called the Elder to come talk to us about the thing that has been happening to your wolf lately," he said, turning his gaze back at me.

I rose in a sitting position, the blanket falling down to my hips.

"Do you think he would know?"

Avery shrugged.

"He is an Elder, they are supposed to be wise, he has to know something. He told me that he might be here tomorrow, but he had to go to the council so he doesn't know when he'll be free." I nodded and held out my hand towards him. He went to me without any hesitation and sat down next to me taking my hand in his larger one.

"I love you," I whispered, leaning in and kissing him softly. He responded by cupping the back of my neck to pull me closer to him. I opened my mouth when I felt his warm wet tongue and gladly obeyed. The fire in us was quickly building up and I tore my mouth away from his demanding lips.

"We should stop now," I said breathlessly against his mouth.

"I thought I make your body scream with passion," he teased, nipping at my bottom lip. I felt my wolf growl with impatience at wanting to jump his bones.

"You do and if you ever want to leave this room, now would be the best time," I stressed through clenched teeth.

He grinned.

"If you say so." He then gave me a hot breathtaking kiss before he stood up and pulled on his shirt. I glared at him and slid from the bed.

I followed him in getting dressed; he told me he had to go back to Aiden before he gave me another kiss goodbye. I walked to our room, Blondie was sitting in the bed and watched me walk in with an apprehensive look which soon disappeared when he realized it was me.

"Hey, morning Blondie," I greeted walking to the bed. He smiled lightly.

"Morning," he whispered.

"So I have a few things to do today but we will be talking to Liam as soon as we can," I told him. He nodded, plucking at the blankets. I stood up and rummaged through Avery's drawers and grabbed a shirt and pants to take a shower in.

"Connor." I heard before I could even open the bathroom door. I frowned, turning around to face Blondie.

"What?" I asked.

He licked his lips and peeked up at me from under his shaggy hair.

"Connor, that's my name." I blinked at him for a while. I wasn't expecting that, I mean it shouldn't be a big deal but I felt lighthearted at the answer that all of us have been searching for. I finally knew the name of this kid whom I had grown so close to.

"Well it's nice to meet you, Connor," I said giving him a gentle smile.

He blushed, ducking his head down.

"I'll be back." He nodded, still looking down. Chuckling, I continued to take a shower.

* * *

I went searching for Liam and Aiden but I had heard from Dom that they had left to see Aiden's parents. Avery was with them so I was stuck at the house with the mate from hell. Trying my best to avoid her, I quickly made sure Connor had food before I went on my mission to find Levi. I hadn't seen him in so long, so I knew it was the right time to see him. I also knew that he hadn't been in his room for some time so I went to Marten's room where both of their scents were strong.

Taking a deep breath, I knocked on the door, hoping that Levi was better than last time. I hated that he was having such a hard time with this and there was absolutely nothing I could do to make Kyle accept him or take his pain away.

The door cracked open and Mr. Blackman looked down at me before opening it all the way.

"Is Levi here?" His eyes were tired with dark circles, even more so than usual.

He nodded.

"He's here." He sounded exhausted as he stepped back for me to come in. Levi was sitting on the bed, his eyes staring at the window. I looked over at Marten then back to Levi before I made my way over to the latter.

"Hey," I said softly, wrapping an arm around his shoulders. He didn't look at me and just stared out the window with a blank expression.

"He's gone." His voice was raw and scratchy. I frowned down at him.

"What do you mean?" I knew he was talking about Kyle.

"He left." I frowned, concerned.

"How do you know, did someone tell you he did?" He shook his head.

"I just know, I can't feel him here anymore," he said, the words coming out strained. I closed my eyes and shook my head.

Damn it, what do I do? What can I do? I hated seeing him suffer like this. I looked over to Levi's father only to see the look of pain on his face as he watched his son.

"I can't stand to see him this way," he said. Marten was very close to his son since the death of his mate. Levi was the only thing keeping him alive on this earth and for him to see his son so broken like this must hurt so much.

"Can I take him off your hands for a bit?" I asked him. His brown eyes met mine for a moment before placing them back on Levi. He nodded.

"Yes."

I smiled at him reassuringly.

"I promise I'll take good care of him." And with that, I grabbed Levi's hand and pulled his stiff body up from the bed before I dragged him out of the room and out of the house. I had no idea what we were going to do but I thought he needed some fresh air, so I took him down to the lake. I stopped by Robin's room to tell her to meet us there. I also asked Connor if he wanted to come but he shook his head, scared they would see him.

The lake was about a ten-minute walk from the house and when we got there, I was already ready for a swim. The water was glistening under the hot sun, making it look like a million diamonds floating on the water. Levi sat on the edge, holding his legs close to his body as he stared out over to the lake. Sighing, I came to sit next to him and wrapped an arm around his shoulder.

"You'll be okay, I'll always be here," I said softly. He didn't respond to anything so I just waited for Robin.

Not long after, I heard footsteps coming in our direction. Standing up, I watched my sister, J, and Sadie come to us dressed in swimsuits.

"Woah, I haven't swam in so long!" Sadie exclaimed, jumping up and down while she clapped. Robin shook her head with a smile before looking over at me.

"So what's with the sudden get-together?" she asked before throwing her towel and stuff on the grass. I shrugged.

"Can't a brother ask his sister to hang out with a few friends?" She narrowed her eyes at me suspiciously.

"Uh huh."

I smiled innocently.

For an hour or so, I watched the girls play in the lake. What is up with women and squealing when they're in water? I can't see how men could find that attractive, I just thought it was hella annoying.

Shaking my head at the sight, I sat by Levi who still sat motionless and stared out at the water. There was nothing but forlorn on his face.

"Come on Levi have some fun or I'll throw you in the lake," I teased, bumping into his shoulder.

He shook his head.

"I don't feel like it Caleb," he muttered.

"Hey what's wrong Levi?" Sadie asked as she walked out and grabbed her towel.

"Nothing," he said. She didn't look convinced.

"I haven't seen you in forever Levi, where did you disappear to?" Robin came up beside Sadie.

"Around." He wouldn't meet anyone's gaze. J waddled next to him, struggling to sit before Levi finally moved to stand and took her elbow in his hand to help her sit down. J settled down with a light blush on her beautiful mocha-colored skin.

"How embarrassing I can't even sit down now without help," she whined.

"Well I'm sure Dom enjoys helping you whenever you need it," Sadie said wiggling her eyebrows. J glared at her playfully.

"Yeah, he helped make it so he better help me," J grumbled.

"Oh the hormones are coming through," Robin teased. J ripped out a handful of grass and threw it at her. Robin squeaked and hid behind Sadie who was on the receiving end of the grass and dirt onslaught. We all watched Sadie sit there with grass on her face as she started to spit out some pieces that managed to find its way in her mouth.

"Sorry Sadie," J apologized with a sheepish grin on her face. I heard Levi chuckle quietly and a small smile formed on my face. Finally, that was what I brought him out here for. He needed to get his mind off things.

"So has anyone seen the visitors lately?" Sadie asked, wiping her face off with a towel. J nodded.

"Yeah, that Alpha guy gives me the creeps," she said, shuddering. Robin nodded along with her.

"I heard that the girl who came with him is Caleb's mate," J said. I snapped my head towards her.

How the hell did she know?

"What?!" Robin exclaimed, looking at me with wide eyes. I closed my eyes tightly.

Sh*t! Of course she would know, she was mated with Dom, Liam's best friend. I opened my eyes to see them all looking at me in shock. Except J who looked guilty.

"Sorry I thought you told everyone."

I shook my head.

"It's okay J," I told her with a reassuring smile. Levi was staring at me in shock.

"So what are you going to do about Avery now?" he whispered. I could only wonder what he would feel if I told him, probably disappointed. If I told him that I was sticking by Avery through whatever was thrown in our way and a mate wouldn't change that then he would surely be disappointed in me.

Before I could answer, Robin interrupted.

"So is it true?" Her face was serious as she asked. I knew what she was talking about so with a long sigh, I nodded.

"Yep." Her mouth formed in a hard line and her eyes narrowed.

"That b*tch!" she yelled. I frowned.

"Why, what happened?" I asked. Sadie began to rub her back but stopped when Robin started to pace.

"I can't believe her!" she exclaimed.

"What?"

Robin's blue brown eyes met mine with a furious fire behind them.

"I was walking back to my room last night and I caught her scent in some guy's room from the sound I heard. I didn't think much about it, but now that you told me she's your damn mate, she was getting it on with some other guy while you were in the same house! That's just not right!" she yelled.

Everyone was silent as they looked at me.

I stared at her in shock. *What? She was sleeping with someone else?* Somewhere deep down I was broken, hurt. My wolf howled in pain at the betrayal and growled in anger. I know I was doing the same with Avery but she knew from the start that I didn't want to be with her. If she was sleeping with someone else, then why the hell is she trying to get with me too? She hasn't even been here for more than three days!

Growling, I glared in the direction of the house, at least I told her that I didn't want her but she was being a slut behind my back and the Alphas, who were oblivious to these horrible people. Did she think I was just going to drop everything just because we were mates while she did whatever she wanted? Hell no!

Well she certainly made my decision to stay with Avery easier now.

CHAPTER 23

CALEB

"So tell me Caleb, why are you trying to avoid me?" she purred behind me. Rolling my eyes as I turned to face Lynn, and waited for my wolf to scratch at me wanting her like usual but it didn't happen. Instead he was growling at her in disgust. She repulsed us. Her beauty didn't affect us at all anymore.

"Well it was either that or rip your slutty throat out," I growled and bared my teeth at her. To my pleasure I watched her eyes widen in surprise and she stepped back away from me.

"W-What?"

I smiled maliciously.

"Oh yeah, I heard about you. Did you think that you could just spread your legs in this house and not be found out? As a matter a fact I can smell him all over you." I sneered at her.

Her shocked face soon changed. Those innocent blue eyes flickered, flattening out into a glare while her mouth turned down in a frown that looked as if it belonged permanently to her face. Her whole expression contorted into a menacing one. Her true colors were finally showing.

"Oh like that mutt's repulsive stench isn't clinging to you like a disgusting second skin!" she spat at me.

I narrowed my eyes at her.

"Now we see the real you, don't we?" I taunted. Rolling her eyes she pushed at my shoulders.

"You think you can just reject me huh? No, I don't think so. I get what I want Caleb and I am getting you."

I glared at her, pushing her back.

"I'm nobody's pet Lynn so you can turn your skinny little ass around and march it out this pack house today."

"Well we'll see what daddy has to say about that," she growled. I laughed.

"Oh okay you go run to daddy like a spoiled little pup but I'm telling you now that I will never accept you. I will never let you be my mate so go back to your boy toys because you won't be getting it from me," I hissed, turning around to walk away before I was tackled onto the floor. Lynn's body was lying on my back as I shifted my weight and threw her off.

"What the hell is wrong with you?!" I exclaimed, climbing to my feet.

"I'm so tired of you faggy wolves. You can't be gay Caleb!" she said, stomping her foot childishly as I watched her in disbelief. "You're supposed to be mine, to do everything I tell you, and do whatever I want!" she screeched, stomping her foot again.

I looked at her with wide eyes.

"What the f*ck kind of world do you live in because it's not reality, I'm not your damn slave b*tch!" her face was turning bright red.

"This was not how meeting my mate was supposed to go!"

I chuckled, humorlessly.

"Yeah well you weren't what I wanted either and never will be so just go pack your crap and leave!" I ordered. "Oh and take daddy dearest with you." I sneered and walked away. I made sure that I was ready if she tried to attack me again. She didn't.

Sighing, I walked down to the kitchen to get something to eat. I had waited for Avery all throughout the night last night but he never came home. They had stayed the night at Aiden's parents's house so I was excited to see him today. I couldn't wait to tell the Alphas who these 'visitors' really were. I pushed open the kitchen door and came to a stop as a smile formed on my face. Crossing my arms, I propped my hip up against the doorway to see Mr. Simons raiding the fridge.

"Well if it isn't the Elder food monster, here to raid the fridge of all its yummy goodness," I joked. Mr. Simons peeked his head up from over the fridge door to roll his eyes at me. Straightening his form, he closed the door and held a container full of leftovers.

"Well if it isn't the oh so 'respectable' Caleb. For your information, I never got to eat anything because I was too busy with council meetings all day yesterday to do anything about it."

I pushed off the door frame and stepped in the kitchen.

"Don't they have snacks or something over there? I mean come on, you guys are 'all powerful' and stuff so they had to have a sushi bar or raw steaks set out," I teased with a grin. Mr. Simons shook his head and pulled the lid off the container before sticking the food in the microwave.

"Yes well, I'm not one for sushi." He shuddered. "I had my mind preoccupied with more important things," he said, the microwave dinged and he took it out.

"Like what?" I asked curiously, grabbing a bucket of leftover KFC chicken as I took over the microwave.

"You know that's confidential council information."

I shrugged. "It was worth a try." He shook his head before taking a seat at the table.

Once my food was warm, I took a seat next to him.

"So what brings you here? Don't you have a home?"

He smiled. "You know why I'm here, I'm the one who's curious as to why I'm here," he said.

"I guess it has something to do with me."

He nodded.

"So do you want to tell me your problem? Avery talked to me over the phone saying he needed me over here but didn't want to get into it without meeting face-to-face."

I bit into my chicken.

"I think we should wait for Avery, he deserves to know just as much as me."

Mr. Simons looked at me for a long while then shrugged.

"It's up to you. I'm here to help to the best to my abilities. Meet me in the Alpha's office around five, I'll be with my brother," he said, finishing up his food as he got up and washed his dish. I nodded.

"Thank you for this," I said. He smiled at me.

"You're welcome."

And with that he left.

* * *

When it was close to five, Avery finally came home and I rushed to him and jumped into his arms right in front of the Alphas.

"Warn a person when you think about staying out for so long!" I exclaimed, burying my face into his neck. He held me up, rubbing my back in comfort.

"I'm sorry, I didn't think about it."

I scoffed, pulling away a bit to look into his eyes.

"Yeah, well you better think about it!" I glared at him. He smiled and gave me a small kiss.

"Okay."

I nodded in satisfaction with a smug grin. I slowly slid down his body till I was standing.

"So that's it?" Aiden asked stepping up to us. His blue eyes peering at us in awe. "This is why you've been acting different lately and why Caleb's reluctant to give into his mate?" A large grin spread across his face.

"You're in love!" he exclaimed, rushing into Avery's arms and hugging him tight. I looked up to Avery, who hugged Aiden back awkwardly. His eyes shifted to me begging for help. I smiled, shaking my head as I held in in my laughter.

"Oh yeah, he's deeply in love with me, huh babe?" I teased. Aiden squeaked and hugged him tighter.

"Aww you guys even have little pet names!"

Avery glared at me. Finally Liam came and pulled his mate from Avery.

"Wait, I thought that wasn't possible?" Liam asked, gazing at Avery.

"It's not." We all turned to see Mr. Simons walking towards us, his focus solely on Avery and I.

"Uncle Jim, what are you doing here?" Liam asked happily. They embraced in greeting.

"I'm here for these two." This caused Liam to frown and looked at all of us.

"Okay, what the hell is going on?" His voice was full of frustration.

"That's a good question." Mr. Simons answered. "Can we use your office for a while?" he asked Liam.

He was still confused but threw his hands up in the air.

"Yeah sure whatever, but I want an explanation for all of this," he warned.

Avery nodded. "Of course," he told him.

"You'll be getting more than an explanation, trust me," I added. Aiden was still smiling at us.

"Go, go! I want to know everything later okay?" he asked excitedly.

I shook my head and chuckled.

"Alright."

We filed into the office and took a seat while Mr. Simons seated himself in the Alpha's chair. He folded his hands in his lap and leaned back against the seat.

"Alright, let me have it, what's the problem?" My gaze shifted over to Avery who was sitting straight and tall in his chair, waiting for me to speak. His face was blank, and he was being his usual observant self. I cleared my throat and leaned forward, meeting Mr. Simon's curious gaze.

"Umm, well we asked you here because we think there is something wrong . . . with my wolf," I muttered the last part, a bit embarrassed that I had such a humiliating problem. But then again I guess since Lynn was a slut, it was best that he was confused between her and Avery.

Mr. Simons straightened from his relaxed position before placing his folded hands on the desk right in front of him.

"Oh, in what way?" he asked.

"In the mating way." He raised a brow before he looked over at Avery for a moment then back to me.

"I'm not quite following. Is this about you not being able to mate with Avery? Because you're not destined mates you know this." I shook my head then glance at Avery for support and he nodded reassuringly.

"That's just it, Mr. Simons—"

"Jim, please," he said cutting me off with a smile.

I nodded awkwardly.

"Jim, my mate showed up the other day," I said bluntly. Jim's face brightened.

"Congratulations."

I shook my head, giving him an unhappy expression.

"Actually it's not."

He frowned again.

"For one it's a she, not a he and I'm pretty sure that I'm an all-around gay guy. Then there's the part where my wolf is confused. Oh and my so-called mate is a complete and total—" I was cut off from my rant again.

"Confused?" he asked, suspiciously. I let out a frustrated breath, remembering what my sister told me about Lynn.

"Yes," I answered. Jim shook his head, raising his thumb to his mouth to bite at his nail thoughtfully. He was looking down at the table before looking back at me.

"Wolves never become confused with their mates, a wolf knows automatically. There is no denying a mating bond. Why do you think he's confused?"

I shrugged.

"I was hoping you could answer that," I said.

He nodded.

"Yes, but you are the one with the confused wolf. Tell me what he feels, what's conflicting him." I bit into my bottom lip and looked over at Avery who was sitting there in silence.

"Avery," was all I said.

Mr. Simon's eyes instantly shifted towards him. I could just see the gears turning in his head from the expression he had on his face.

"Avery." He wasn't talking to us but more so to himself. I watched him raise a curious brow at the Elder. Then Jim sighed, chuckling a bit as he shook his head.

"How didn't I see this before? How do you feel about all this?" he asked him. Avery straightened further.

"This isn't about me, I asked this meeting for you to help Caleb not me, Elder."

Jim nodded with a knowing smirk.

"Of course." He glanced back at me for a second. "But then again everything that concerns Caleb is important to you, right?"

"Yes," Avery said without hesitation and I saw him look taken aback for a moment himself. I blinked at him in surprise. Jim smiled knowingly again.

"But I thought Aiden was the one who was the most important person to you Avery. I mean he is the one you're tied to. You are after all his protector." I could hear the ulterior motive in his voice. I watched him suspiciously.

"He is." Avery's voice was firm.

"Uh huh and Caleb is too? Isn't that a bit confusing for you Avery? To be loyal to these two boys?" Avery growled glaring at Jim.

"What are you getting at, Elder?" His patience was wearing thin and his mouth was set in a hard looking expression. Mr. Simons didn't seem to notice and shrugged.

"I'm getting at the fact that I didn't notice this before about you, like the aura you emit when the time calls for it, especially now when your principles are being questioned, your power elevates to a level that is impressive. It makes me wonder just how powerful your wolf really is, Avery."

We sat frozen as we stared at Jim. Avery didn't say anything and just waited.

"So?" I interrupted. He smiled but never looked away from Avery.

"You're an Alpha," he said. Avery licked his lips before speaking.

"No, I'm not. I left that life behind me a long time ago." Jim raised his finger to point at him with a grin.

"Ah but that doesn't free you of the Alpha gene, Avery. Your wolf is an Alpha and he is finally speaking up isn't he? After all this time?" I was impressed at how Mr. Simons mind worked so fast. I guess it was an Elder thing.

"Okay yes, but that has nothing to do with Caleb's wolf," Avery said, a frustrated tone building in his voice. Mr. Simons held his hand up.

"It has a big part of it."

We frowned at him like he had lost his mind.

"How?" I asked. He leaned back with his usual gentle smile.

"It's simple, Alphas are meant to have mates. You can't be a very good Alpha without one. Think of it this way, a mate is like a rock and you're a shaking piece of paper. They hold you down keeping you from making rash decisions that could end up disastrous. An Alpha 'must' have someone to keep them in line or the power gets to them. Otherwise, they begin to think they can do anything.

"I'm sorry to bring this up Caleb, but Zackary was a prime example. He lost his rock and the grieving threw him over the edge to the point of insanity and power lust. He thought he could come here and take over this very pack which is ludicrous. The Blue Moon pack is one of the most powerful in the US and he thought he could recruit a group of rogues and win." I cringed at the name but held back my angst.

"I understand but I have no mate Elder, he or she was lost to me before I ever knew them, that is the reason I am a wanderer." Mr. Simons nodded.

"That is true you did lose your true mate but you have gained a new one," he told us calmly.

"What are you talking about?" Avery asked, confused.

"By marking Caleb you have claimed him as your mate. It's an old custom and found in all the old history books in the council library but not totally lost," he explained. I scooted further in my seat along with Avery.

"Wait, Avery can still have a chance?" I asked. He nodded.

"An Alpha has the power to claim over anyone who isn't their mate, but they can't go around just biting anyone and everybody. It has to be someone they can connect to, be close to. It only happens if their true mate is no longer among the living, but most Alphas don't know this."

"So you say that I'm Avery's 'substitute' mate?" I didn't know how to feel about that. Should I feel happy or hurt that I'm just a last resort. But then again, he never did have the chance to be with his real mate before me.

"You can say that, yes but I'm curious as to why Avery is a wanderer in the first place though. It's unheard of for an Alpha wolf to become a wanderer. They are the sole purpose of the survival of their packs. It's an interesting case, I've never heard of anything like yours, Avery."

I looked over to Avery who had a confused but hard expression. He didn't look happy which hurt me much harder that I thought it would. Was he not happy to have me as a mate?

"By me biting Caleb I have somehow confused his wolf from the one he was truly meant to be with?" His voice was strained and angry. His brown eyes were staring into Mr. Simons with such emotions and I was shocked. He was always a blank sheet with everyone around him, never showing his true feelings. It has only happened with me a few times but this was more than I had ever seen.

"It's possible. Caleb, tell me your side of all this. How do you see your mate, your true mate?" he asked, turning his attention back on me. I met his gaze squarely.

"I feel like I could puke from just the sight of her face," I spoke bluntly. Mr. Simons was clearly taken aback from the stunned face he made. I kept my expression unmoved, completely serious.

"Wow," was all he said. Avery peered at me with a frown.

"Why would you say that? Don't you think that's a bit overkill?" he reprimanded. I rolled my eyes.

"No, I think it was called for."

"You don't even know her yet!" he snapped.

"Neither do you!" I argued back.

"Caleb, you're being unreasonable to her without even getting to know her. She is your mate, she can't be anything bad to you. It's not possible to wrong one's mate," he shot back at me. I glared at him, shooting to my feet.

"Oh yeah then why was she sleeping with some male behind my back? I would mark that as a big f*ck you to my face wouldn't you?" Avery sat there, his head cocked to the side, a grimace formed on his beautiful face.

"I'm sorry to interrupt this argument but what was that?" Jim asked curiously. I sighed before collapsing on the couch that was beside the door. I threw my arm over my eyes.

"She's been sleeping around behind my back. I mean at least I had the decency to reject her from the start, she's just a conniving b*tch." I sighed, feeling drained all of a sudden. "She's not the angel everyone thinks she is." I continued.

"How did you find this out?" Avery's voice was soft and deep as he watched over me with so much comfort.

"My sister told me, plus I bumped into her this morning and there she was, covered in some guy's scent." I growled, my wolf furious at the wh*re who was our supposed 'mate'. I quickly pulled myself to a sitting position to look at the both of them. They both sported concerned expressions but Avery's was confused and sad whereas Mr. Simons was curious and thoughtful.

"Do you believe she had the gall to practically call me a slave? Like I was meant to serve her hand and foot? What do I look like to her? She has lost her freaking mind! She can take that somewhere else for all I care. I just want her gone!" I yelled, falling back on the couch.

It was silent for a while before I felt a hand brush the hair back from my face. I opened them to find Avery sitting by my head, giving me a sympathetic look.

"I'm so sorry Caleb. I didn't know a wolf's mate could be so wrong to their other halves," he spoke softly. I peered into his beautiful brown eyes.

"And it's not just me, she's been horrible to Blondie for so long, her and her father," I confessed shakily. I could feel a lump build in my throat, his eyes softened as he leaned down and kissed my lips gently.

"If you want them gone, then they are gone Caleb. Whatever you want I would do it for you. Just as the Elder said, you are important to me, your needs are mine. But getting rid of this girl would kill you Caleb. You'd suffer something no wolf should go through and I just can't see that happening to you," he told me softly.

I closed my eyes with a sigh. *What do we do?*

"Maybe not, you two. You have marked him Avery, meaning he's your mate also, and being an Alpha could make the mating strong enough to withstand the separation, but I'm not entirely sure. As I've said before, this kind of mating is an old custom not familiar to us in centuries."

We sat there, thoughtful for a second.

"Anything is good enough. I just don't want her anywhere near me or Connor," I said. They frowned.

"Connor?" they asked together.

"Blondie, he finally told me his damn name." I laughed.

"Caleb I understand your human feelings about this girl but what about your wolf? What does he have to say about this?" Mr. Simons asked.

"He agrees with me one hundred percent; he can't even stand the thought of her being anywhere near us. To be honest all I'm feeling from him is hatred towards her," I answered truthfully. Jim's brows shot up, his eyes wide.

"Really, he truly hates his own mate?" he asked astonished. I nodded.

"Yes." I watched him get out of his chair and pace, the gears in his head turning more and more. Both Avery and I stared at him.

"Your father was an Alpha wasn't he?" He started talking to himself. "But this is so rare I doubt . . ."

"Mr. Simons?" I asked.

"Jim," he corrected me, still distracted.

"Jim, what are you going on about over there?" I pushed.

"Tell me Caleb, what was it like when you bit Avery the first time? What was going through your mind?" He came to a stop in front of me.

"Um . . ." I hesitated for a bit. I didn't even know he knew about that.

"Just describe to me the feelings," he insisted.

"A feeling of need, I guess. I needed to mark him, needed to make him mine," I said, peering over at Avery who was still beside me as he gazed at me. "I wanted no one else, just him forever. I loved him from the beginning," I told Jim but mainly to Avery as he smiled at me.

"So your wolf just took over, intensifying the need to mate with Avery?" I nodded, taking Avery's big hand in my smaller one.

"Yes."

Everything was silent for a moment before he spoke again.

"Caleb, I'm going to tell you something that is very important and it must not leave this room if this is what I believe it is." This caused me to snap my eyes at him. He slowly knelt down on one knee in front of me so we were at eye level, his face serious.

"What is it?" I could tell this was beyond important. Avery had tensed beside me preparing himself for whatever was to come.

"There are a group of wolves, a very small group. There's only a few that live in selected packs today who have been betrayed by a mate as you have. Some have had worse than others. It's a horrible fate for these few but they are the ones who have been on the wrong side of the Spirits's mistakes."

I raised a brow at him.

"The Spirits don't make mistakes Jim," I told him. He shook his head.

"That's not entirely true. The Spirits don't make many mistakes but there are a rare few. They aren't perfect but they do fix them. If you are who I think you are, then you are a rarity, Caleb."

I was worried as I stared at him. Avery's hand tightened in mine.

"Then what am I?" I whispered. He smiled before placing a comforting hand on my knee.

"A rare class of an Elder."

My eyes bulged as I stared at him.

"I'm a what?!"

He chuckled softly.

"An Elder, Caleb." I was speechless, my mouth was hanging open but nothing was coming out. Avery helped me.

"How is that possible? I thought you knew at maturity. Caleb's past that stage as you can see."

Jim nodded.

"Yes, I can see that. This is why I say rare. This Elder power doesn't show its true self until he or she has been wrong by their mates."

"That is so messed up," I muttered. He agreed.

"That is why your class of Elder is called a curse and a gift," he said.

"How the hell is this a gift? I mean I might not have wanted a mate from the beginning but others deserve happiness don't you think?"

"Because now you know grief, what all these wolves who have lost their other halves or who have been rejected feel. You have been there, you can help," he told me.

I shook my head.

"What are you talking about? Help? How is that even possible? There's nothing I can do for them," I said.

"There is a thing about these certain Elders. They have no specific names to them like most of us. Take me for example, I'm a telekinetic which means I can move things with my mind. Others can become invisible, teleport, and the list goes on and on, but all of us have a label. You may not have quite figured out your label yet but since we needed something to put beside your names, we call you healers in a way."

"Healer."

He grinned.

"Yes, you have the ability to take grief away from people, not all of it but good amounts where they can finally breathe again and move on to a certain extent. Maybe start a new life with someone, if they want. Your gift is to give rejected and mourning wolves a new start. You help heal their souls."

I gazed at him in awe.

"Wow," was all I could say. Avery was speechless as well, looking over at me with something close to amazement and love.

"Wow is right, but your gift doesn't stop there. Unlike us normal Elders who have just one ability, you also can heal yourself but beyond the help you give others. You can mate with someone of your choosing."

My jaw dropped.

"Like an Alpha?" I asked. He shook his head.

"Alphas are limited, you are not. You can have anyone. You don't have to be connected to this person but most healers choose those that are. I mean, who wouldn't?" He laughed. I let out a long breath I didn't know I was holding.

"So me, I'm an Elder." I had to say it out loud to get used to that.

He nodded.

"Yes you are, and a special one at that." He sounded proud of me.

"How do I heal people?" I asked curiously. He smiled.

"The old fashion way Caleb, you take a big ol' chunk of them," he teased before rising to his full height and stretched.

"That's it? Just bite them?"

"Yes, well they also have to be willing for the help Caleb or else you're taking away their free will. It's their choice or it won't work."

I nodded in understanding.

"So I hoped I answered your questions to satisfaction," he said.

"Yes, thank you Elder," Avery said and stood up to shake Mr. Simon's hand.

"You're welcome Avery, and Caleb, you and I have lots to discuss. Now that we know that you're an Elder and a rare one at that, you are officially under council protection. Meaning you can tell no one till we have everything situated with you."

"What do you mean by 'situated'?"

"This is one of the bad things about being an Elder, we are in danger. Hunters are always trying to find and destroy us."

"Why would they hunt you? Elders are like pacifists aren't they?' I didn't know much about Elders since Robin and I had to leave our home at such a young age.

"We can be but when the time calls for it we can be a force to be reckoned with and that scares the hunters. We have powers that can be more lethal than an Alpha and his pack. They think all of us as monsters and needed to be eliminated. This is why our identities are kept secret and we have different names in case they start sticking their noses in where they don't belong," he explained, leaning against the desk with his arms crossed.

"Well what about the pack? They know who you are, can't they rat you out?" I asked.

Jim nodded. "They can, but why? They would have to go and search for a hunter and they are dangerous people who don't give mercy to anyone. They don't care. They wouldn't believe you and if they did, they would still kill you. It's a suicide mission."

I took a breath. Okay, my head hurts.

Talk about information overload.

Shaking my head, I looked at Avery.

"So he and I are real mates now," I whispered, changing the subject to gaze over every plane on his face. He smiled at me gently.

"Yep, the Spirits have given you two a second chance at love," he told us. I couldn't look away from my mate's face. This was so surreal. Avery reached up and cupped my cheek softly.

"In my case, it's more of a first chance at love," he whispered then claimed my mouth with one of the most heated kisses I have ever experienced. My knees would have given out if it wasn't for his arm snaking around my waist that pressed me against his body.

"Mmm . . ." I moaned while he growled lustfully. I could feel the bond between us now that my wolf wasn't torn between two people.

"Alright alright, enough lovey dovey, I don't mind you guys expressing your love for one another but could you wait till I'm out of the room before you suck face?" Jim whined.

I pulled away from Avery with a laugh. He had a grin on his face as well.

"Don't you have a mate somewhere?" I asked turning my head towards him. Jim raised a brow.

"Why yes I do but someone was oh-so-desperate for my help now wasn't he?" he teased. I rolled my eyes and hugged Avery, burying my face in his shaking chest as he laughed at us.

Avery was my mate, my *true* mate.

CHAPTER 24

CALEB

The air was cool and soothing as Avery and I raced beside each other in our wolf forms. After all that we learned today, we needed a break for a while. The moon was full and bright tonight, causing Avery's sandy coat to shine beautifully. The sound of water from the small stream ahead of us roared in my ears.

I glanced at Avery and grin mischievously, well the best I could while being a wolf. Slyly, I scooted closer to him before ducking under his running form causing him to tumble to the side.

He caught himself faster than I thought he would and gave me a menacing glare. I yelped in surprise, pushing my legs harder to get away from him. I felt him right at my heels, his hot breath fanning against my hind legs. Hopping, I nearly fell on my face. Avery laughed wolfishly shooting past me.

"Show off!" I growled at him.

He continued till he came to a complete stop in front of the water of the stream which glistened like flowing crystals. Panting, I trotted up to his smug form and pawed at his face gently.

"You're a sore loser Caleb," he simply implied. I glared at him.

"I am not!"

"Yes you are. For an Elder you're a pretty pathetic one," he teased but kept all expression from his eyes.

"Pathetic one huh? So me giving you a chance at a mate is pathetic, I see how it's going to be jerk. I should just go back and leave you here . . . ALONE," I growled and turned, whipping my tail in his face in the process. I had to stop the snicker from coming out as I made my dramatic exit but was stopped expectedly. Avery climbed up on my back, holding me by my shoulders as he pushed me forward into the ground.

"No, I'm sorry. I am beyond grateful, you know that Caleb," he whispered into my ear. My tense body relaxed under him until I was lying flat on the ground with him comfortably on top of me. He rested his chin over mine as he lay there.

"You're really okay with this? I know that I'm not 'the one' but you're fine with me as a substitute?" I chuckled slightly, trying to lighten the mood a bit.

"You're not a substitute Caleb. You're my true mate . . . to me at least." My heart seemed to lighten up all of a sudden. He thought me his true mate. If I could smile right now, there would be a huge grin on my face.

"Thank you," I whispered. He nuzzled the back of my neck and licked behind my ear, making me shudder. The air shifted from a calm and innocent atmosphere to a tense-filled one. But it wasn't awkward tension, no this was sexual tension. My body was tingling all over before it burst into flames.

I whimpered, rubbing my face against the grass as I wiggled my body underneath Avery's. He seemed to notice and stood up to stand over me.

Quickly, I rolled on my back, showing my stomach in a submissive manner.

He was frowning as he watched me. The moon rose higher in the sky and in my eyes as I stared up at him.

"Caleb?" he questioned me just as the trees spilled moonlight on me and he stiffened.

Why the hell was my body burning like this? I just wanted to rub on everything to loosen the tension that was building up in me.

"Do you feel that?" I asked him, whining in my throat. He nodded, burying his muzzle in my neck. I heard him inhale deeply and a deep rumbling growl spilled from his chest.

"God, you smell delicious Caleb," he said in a raspy tone, licking the fur at my neck. I couldn't stop myself from shifting back into my human form so I could feel that large soft tongue of his.

"Ahh . . ." I moaned at the amazing sparks that emitted from his touch on my sensitive bare skin. "What's happening Avery?" I groaned, gripping his long soft fur in my hands. I looked back into his face to meet his bright royal blue eyes. Slowly, he changed back before laying his naked body over mine.

"I have no idea but I don't care at the moment," he growled, capturing my mouth with a rough kiss.

It was like our bodies were no longer ours, like they were being taken over by some other force. It was our wolves; they were too close to the surface to be ignored. Our wolves wanted each other badly, worse than normal and the only way we would feel better was to let them have it.

Avery pulled away and flipped me over in one move. I grunted at the weight of him on my back as he mounted me. I jumped when I felt his hot mouth trailing down my skin, causing shivers of pleasure to spill out of me.

I moaned, encouraging him. I felt him smile against my back as I raised my hips, making him groan.

"You're just asking for it aren't you?" he asked huskily into my shoulder.

I chuckled.

"No, more like begging," I whimpered. I turned my head to look at him behind me. His blue eyes were roaming up and down my back in appreciation, making me hotter and harder.

"You are the most beautiful creature I have ever laid witness to, Caleb," he said seriously. I sighed resting my forehead back on the grass.

"Well, you sure were hard to get in the beginning, nothing seemed to faze you," I whined. He laughed, licking the mark on my shoulder. I tightened under him in response, biting my lip.

"I have a good poker face," he teased. "Even then, I wanted to tear your clothes off sometimes."

"You want to know something else about that?" I asked, breathless.

"What?" he groaned, pushing his hips further into me which pressed a certain hard *something* into a place where I wanted it to be. I reached back with one hand and grabbed his hard hip.

"I have no clothes on at the moment," I growled, which in turn made him growl along with me.

He lifted my hips up better to accommodate him.

"I noticed," he whispered as he bit into my ear before he thrust hard and fast into me.

We both let out our pleasure and pain-filled screams. Right as he entered, I knew what this was and why we had to. It was the reason I was burning like gasoline to a fire, why I had an amazing pull towards Avery. We were commencing in a ritual as old as time under the bright full moon. We were claiming our right as mates to the Spirits. A forever bound mating.

Avery's thrusts were fast and powerful as his wolf consumed him, while my wolf did the same. We were just in the background, letting them get this out of their system. The heat was rising between us more and more and before we knew it, I was clinging to him for support as I screamed out my climax. He leaned down quickly and sunk his extended canines into the mark on my shoulder, joining me seconds later before he collapsed against me.

I was panting hard, my body was slightly hurt but I was happy. So happy that I could feel a single tear fall down my cheek.

He couldn't get rid of me now.

*   *   *

AVERY

His scent was imprinted in my nose. Every breath I took was spearmint and fresh water orchids mixed with mine. He was mine, forever. I knew there was no way in hell that I could let him go, not after this. I was tearing myself up at the thought of him being taken by this girl but I refused, my wolf refused. She no longer had the power over me, nor did she have the power to take away the only thing I knew I lived for now. I had mated with Caleb; a real mating under the moon, given to me by the gracious Spirits.

Lynn had to go, Caleb didn't want her here and I definitely wanted her gone soon as possible. Whatever Caleb had gotten out of Connor must have been serious for Caleb to act that way towards her.

Caleb was warm and solid in my arms, the moon gave him an otherworldly gleam. His perfectly shaped dark eyebrows were drawn in a bit as I watched him curl further into me. He had fallen asleep a while ago but I didn't have the heart to wake him so we could start heading back. I knew that Connor would be feeling anxious being all alone in the room without Caleb, but I had to have him once more.

Slowly, I leaned close to his slightly parted full lips and nipped at the bottom one. He shifted but didn't wake. Smiling, I rolled him slowly on his back to keep from jarring him, never leaving a gap of space between us as I now lay on top of him without adding too much pressure. I reached down and guided myself back into my haven that was Caleb. Being one with him was a mind-blowing experience.

I could stay like this for years, I thought as I pushed myself into him gently.

This caused him to stir, and he woke up with a beautiful moan.

"Avery?" he moaned softly, like he wasn't sure if he was awake or still asleep. I chuckled, burying my face into his neck and nipping lightly. I felt him pull his hips up to meet mine unconsciously.

I lapped at his ear.

"Wake up, love," I whispered. His back arched suddenly and his hands reached up to hold me closer. His blue brown eyes opened sluggishly, enjoying the pleasure I was giving him.

"Just let me take care of you Caleb," I whispered against his parted lips before taking them with mine. His kisses were always a pleasure to experience. He was so sweet and warm and I couldn't get enough of them.

His tongue snuck out and slid across my bottom lip innocently as I slowly opened them up for him, sucking in his tongue which caused him to groan deliciously. I kept our kiss steady, our sweet rhythm taking us to new heights. His face was full of pleasure and my heart soared.

He was mine, and that was all I could say now.

"Mmm," he whimpered, holding me closer. I felt the grooves of his teeth skim across my skin and my body shivered in desire. I started to thrust faster in anticipation. He was driving me crazy with that sexy mouth of his.

"Do it Caleb," I whispered in his ear, resting my head next to his. He sighed lightly before he bit down, causing me to slam into him and we both fell over the edge. His moans were loud in my ear but I bet so were mine. We lay there for a minute before I pushed myself up on my elbows to look down at his sweat covered body. His hair was sticking to his forehead. I smiled and brushed it back.

"We have to head back," I told him reluctantly. He nodded looking none too pleased about it either.

"I guess," he muttered, nuzzling my shoulders. Slowly, I sat up and kissed his forehead.

"Come on," I said as I got to my feet and held my hand out for his.

We shifted back to our wolves and headed towards the house; we had left our clothes by some trees earlier and quickly changed into them. I grinned as Caleb wouldn't let me put my shirt on while he kept sneaking kisses on me. First it was my lips, then my chest, then sneakily down to my stomach where it was a bit too close to my groin.

"Caleb," I warned him in a husky tone. He smiled as he reached up on his tiptoes to kiss me again. The feel of his lips caught my focus once more as I raised my hands up and took his hair in my hands, gently pulling him closer for a more passionate kiss.

Eventually I pulled away, breathing hard. He pouted at me with such an adorable face that I was tempted again to take him again right then and there. I shook my head and quickly pulled my shirt on.

We were walking up the steps when a horrible scream rang through the air and caused both us to freeze.

"Caleb!"

CHAPTER 25

CALEB

I rushed back inside the house the minute I heard Connor's screams. Chills ran throughout my body. My heart was racing in fright at what could have happened.

"Connor!" I yelled back once I was inside. There was a crowd gathering by the stairs that led up towards the teens section of the house. Liam and Aiden were at the foot of the stairs looking up, while I spotted Mr. Simons leaning against the banister with a hard look.

"What do you think you're doing Collin?" Liam demanded. Frowning, I came to a stop right beside them and looked up at the top of the stairs to see Alpha Collin and Lynn each holding one of Connor's arms. My heart dropped.

No.

"This boy is part of *my* pack, Moore," Collin growled. "This is considered kidnapping."

Liam narrowed his eyes at him.

"Yes well, the boy doesn't talk to anyone."

"Were taking him back with us!" Alpha Collin snarled.

"No you're not!" I exclaimed, moving past Aiden and up the steps. Lynn scoffed, looking down at me like I was beneath her.

"Oh and what are you going to do Caleb? You were the one hiding him in your room."

I gritted my teeth at her.

"Well, I wonder why," I said in a mocking tone.

"What's that supposed to mean?!" she sneered.

"You boy, need to learn your place. You are her mate and you better start acting the part," Alpha Collin reprimanded me. I shifted my eyes to him.

"Excuse me?"

"That's not true." Mr. Simons interrupted and we all looked over at him. "Just because they are mates doesn't mean he has to stay with her," he explained calmly.

"And who the hell are you, mutt?" Collins sneered. Everyone froze wide-eyed. No one had ever talked to an Elder like that but then again he didn't know who he was. Jim's face stayed blank as he stared up at him.

"Hey! You don't talk to members of my pack that way Collin! You need to show some respect while you're in my territory!" Liam ordered. We all shrank back from the powerful tone in his voice. I didn't need to turn to know that his eyes were glowing their usually fierce yellow. This caused Collin to glare down at him.

"Are you challenging me, pup?" he growled, his eyes shifting from brown to a silvery gray of his wolf's form.

"No, I'm warning you so you better start changing that attitude towards my pack," Liam growled. The room was shaking at the heavy aura of two powerful Alphas. It was unnerving to say the least.

"Okay guys can we work this out without pounding our damn chests?" Aiden interrupted, taking ahold of Liam's arm who had stepped forward.

"There's nothing to work out, we're leaving." Lynn snapped and started dragging Connor with her down the stairs. Her grip was tight and I knew that would leave a bruise. I saw Connor wince in pain as his big green eyes found mine, begging for help. A growl spilled from my throat as an unknown protective instinct overcame my wolf.

"You're not taking him anywhere!" I snarled. "Let. Him. Go." I stuck my arm out, preventing her from moving any further as she stopped inches away from my arm and looked at me straight in the eyes with a nasty expression.

"Oh and what are you going to do Caleb?" she sneered.

"Well, I'll be happy to tell my Alphas on what you've been doing to this poor kid," I threatened her through gritted teeth. Her eyes widened at a fraction of a second before she regained her composure back.

"Thery're lies." She pressed, I rolled my eyes.

"I doubt that." She froze before looking back at her father then at me. I didn't give her a chance to say anything as I turned around to meet Liam's gaze.

"I was planning on telling you in a much less public setting, Alpha but these two have been abusing this boy till he finally had the courage to run away from these monsters." There were gasps but I kept my attention on Liam though I did noticed Aiden's eyes widen.

"What?" Aiden whispered, moving his gaze to Connor while Liam frowned at me.

"How do you know this?"

"Connor told me, this is why he has been hiding out in my room. He was scared that this would happen." I motioned towards the two on the stairs.

"The boy is a pathological liar," Collin quickly responded.

"Oh really? Then tell me how he found his way here scared out of his mind!" I growled.

The Alpha's silver eyes narrowed at me dangerously.

"You better watch yourself kid, I don't take kindly to disrespectful little brats," he warned me. "The boy ran because he was caught in one of his many lies and didn't want to face his punishment," Collin explained.

"No, Caleb," Connor whined, staring at me with pleading green eyes.

"I think you're the liar." I reached out, snatching Lynn's hand away from Connor's arm and threw it down, causing her to stumble back in shock. I took Blondie's hand and pulled him behind me.

"Who the hell do you think you are?!" Collins snarled, marching down the steps in front of me. He reached his hand out towards me, grabbing the front of my shirt in his grip. "You need to realize your place," he growled in my face.

"It's right here assh*le, between you and him." I grinned at him mockingly. He then lifted me off my feet, his glowing gray eyes piercing mine. There was no way he was going to take Connor away from me. Soon enough, an arm flashed out of nowhere and gripped Collins's arm tightly, causing him to wince and let me go.

"Don't touch him," Avery said. I looked up to see him standing right in front of me. Collins's eyes narrowed.

"Well if it isn't the bodyguard to the rescue." He smirked at Avery, snatching his arm away from his grip.

"I suggest you leave." His voice was low and deep as he glared at Connor and Lynn.

"I think that's a perfect idea." Liam added. "And the boy stays, apparently you have done something to him to make him act this way. If you hadn't then he wouldn't have been scared to speak to us or run away in the first place."

"This is bullsh*t! He's ours and we're taking him!" Lynn shrieked.

"No he's not yours and he's staying here if he wants," I argued.

"You are the worst mate anyone can ever have!" she screamed at me.

I chuckled.

"I was never your mate to begin with Lynn so don't worry too much over it. Now I think you guys have overstayed your welcome." I turned then and took Connor's hand, guiding him down the rest of the stairs to stand by Jim who was far away from the two angry wolves who were glaring at all of us.

"You think you can just steal a member of my pack?" His voice was furious and irritated. His gray eyes met mine again. I didn't move, just stood still and blank-faced.

"I'm not stealing him from you, he's the one who decided he no longer wants to be with you," I explained.

He suddenly smiled.

"Well then that means he has to die. Wolves can't just leave my pack, they know too much to live," he said it so simply that it caused a shiver to run down my spine.

"What? You would kill your own nephew?" I shrieked. There was a loud gasp and a whimper. I looked behind me to see Connor, shaking like a leaf.

"Nephew? You abused your own family? " The voice was small but the devastation in it caused me to glance over at Aiden. His head was lowered, his long black hair covered his face, but the anguish was felt through us all.

Alpha Connor was at a loss for words as was Lynn, and they just stood still, watching us in shock.

"Why?" Aiden's voice broke as he looked up at them.

"That's really none of your business is it?" Collin mumbled.

"No I guess it's not but you can forget about taking him from us because I would rather die than let you lay a hand on him," Aiden growled at him, a fire building in his eyes.

"That can be arranged, *'human'*," he spat the last word out with disgust. With those few words, the whole house suddenly sparked with angry tension. Liam and Avery both crouched in front of Aiden, glaring with different colored Alpha eyes.

"You dare threaten my mate?!" Liam growled, his voice deep, low, and more deadly than anyone had ever heard him before. His canines slowly extended into view while Avery did the same. Collin just made the biggest mistake of his life, who only had his daughter with him and was surrounded by the whole Blue Moon pack that would defend their Alpha to the death.

"Like I said before . . . leave," I ordered, pointing towards the door that suddenly swung open at the demand. I had to suppress the smile I would have given to Mr. Simons for the extra dramatization. "And take your tramp of a daughter with you." I gave them a sweet smile.

"Don't ever come back on my territory again, Collin. You are not welcome here . . . ever!" Liam snarled at him, his body shaking as he stood in front of Aiden defensively. Someone took the time to pack their stuff and throw their bags at the door.

"You have no idea what you're doing," Collins growled at us. His sharp gaze kept still on the Alphas and Avery before it landed on me at the last minute. He stood up tall and walked towards the door, trying his best to keep his pride intact. Lynn was cowering close to him, her glaring eyes shifting all over the angry and disgusted faces of our pack.

"You can keep that fag cousin of ours for all we care. He'll fit right in to this disgusting freak show pack of yours anyway," she sneered at us. Liam growled loudly, causing the room to shake with its force and Lynn yelped and ran out of the house. Alpha Collins snatched the bags off the floor and turned towards Liam.

"You've just made yourself a powerful enemy, Moore," he said.

"So have you," Liam said through clenched teeth as he pulled Aiden to his side. Once Collins walked out, the door slammed behind them. Liam sighed, relaxing his posture before he turned his head towards me.

"I'm sorry I didn't listen to you before Caleb. If I had known, they would have left the moment they got here." I didn't answer and kept my head down, silently accepting his apology.

"But wait, what are you going to do about your mate Caleb?" Aiden asked.

"She was never my mate to begin with," was all I said as I turned to look down at Connor, who peered up at me.

"See, I told you I wouldn't let them get you," I said smiling down at him, his big green eyes were brimming with tears under his blonde hair. He then reached out and hugged me close and tight.

"Thank you," he whispered to me. I closed my eyes and wrapped my arms around him.

"Anytime kid."

This felt right. It was like he was mine. I was the one who was supposed to protect this boy, both me and Avery. With that thought, I opened my eyes and saw Avery watching me with the tiniest smile on his face and softest expression in his eyes as he peered down at us. I knew he was thinking the same thing.

"I guess you're stuck with me then," I told him with a smirk. He chuckled lightly and shrugged.

"I can handle that," he said.

I shook my head.

"I wouldn't be so sure about that," I teased, giving him a mischievous look. He tilted his head slightly and walked towards me, towering both Conner and I. He leaned in close, his face a few inches away from mine.

"Give me all you got," he whispered before planting a tender kiss on my waiting lips.

CHAPTER 26

AVERY

"Come on," Caleb whined as he pulled my arm and tried to get me out of the car. We had arrived at the airport about ten minutes ago. I had no idea he was taking me here, he just told me that we were going on a road trip. I was reluctant but Aiden demanded that I go so I begrudgingly did as he said. Now I was here.

"What the hell are we doing here Caleb?" I asked, keeping my butt firmly in the front seat. He rolled his eyes.

"Quit asking questions and get your butt out of the damn car Avery!" And with a strength I didn't know he had, he managed the force my body up in the air and out of the seat to land teetering behind him.

"There. See? That wasn't so hard, now was it?" he said with an innocent smile.

"Yeah, you know I'm not getting on a plane to anywhere with Aiden here unprotected," I told him firmly, staring straight in his beautiful unique blue brown eyes. He stuck his tongue out at me.

"Yes you are, I already paid for our tickets so all you had to do is walk that sweet little tush of yours over to the plane, now move it! Plus Aiden has a whole pack to take care of him and one loving powerful Alpha as a mate. I think he's the safest human in all of Portland," he said, stealing my own words as he gave me a push towards the entrance of the airport causing me to stagger into a man. I hopped on one foot a couple times around him to get my balance back before snapping my head at him and glared. Again, he had an innocent smile on his face.

Oh God, what am I going to do with this guy?

I groaned then turned towards the man.

"I'm so sor—" I stopped mid-sentence as I got a clear look at him.

"E-Elder?"

Mr. Simon's shining green eyes looked up at me.

"It's Jim, and what's up?" he greeted and corrected me with a smirk.

I blinked.

"What-why are you here?"

"Jim?" Caleb exclaimed, rolling our bags over to the side as he walked around the Elder to get a good look.

"Wow, what are you doing here?" he asked, surprised. So Caleb didn't plan this either.

"Well, I called Liam earlier to ask about you and he told me that you and Avery were heading to the airport this morning. You should have told me you were taking a plane ride somewhere, you're not allowed to be by yourself Caleb. You're an Elder now and are priority number one on the hunters list if they found out about you. You need protection." Mr. Simons shook his head at him as he spoke with a hard glare. Caleb of course, rolled his eyes and turned towards the entrance.

"I don't need a damn babysitter, plus this is Avery and Caleb time. Don't you have a mate out there somewhere?" And with that he rolled our bags into the opening doors.

"Hurry it up!" he yelled before the doors closed behind him. Mr. Simons sighed and lifted his suitcase.

"I could be with my mate if it wasn't for your impulsiveness," he muttered.

"Do you know where he's taking me?" I asked, hoping he knew but Mr. Simons only looked over at me and said nothing.

"Sorry, but I'm sworn to secrecy by Aiden." He smiled gently. I let out a huge sigh. Great, that was helpful.

The building was bustling with several people rushing to get to their cars outside. The entire area hummed with voices, which frankly hurt my ears as the sounds were magnified by my sensitive hearing. I dragged my feet as I trailed behind Mr. Simons.

"Get a move on you two!" Caleb yelled from a boarding line. Once I stood next to him, I took one of the suitcases he had, still unsure how he was able to pack them without my knowledge. Little sneak.

As I stood there moving with the line I was anxious at the thought of leaving Aiden by himself. It was against my nature and that of my wolf to leave someone as close to me as Aiden. I was connected to him. What would happen if I wasn't near him for too long? I was pulled out of my thoughts by a forceful tug as Caleb grabbed my hand and hauled me to the plane.

Jim took the seat on the side of us while Caleb and I had seats besides each other.

Okay this was getting ridiculous, where the hell were we going? It was important for me to know if we were going to someplace foreign so I could prepare the right things, which I never got to check my bags for. I just slumped back in my seat, there was no use trying to figure it out when Caleb was trying to be a sneak, but something told me I wasn't going to like it.

Soon after everyone was boarded and settled, the stewardess strutted over to the intercom and held it to her smiling mouth which looked strained.

"Welcome aboard to Blue Skies Airlines," she said as she went through all the safety rules while I drifted off.

If I was Caleb where would I secretly take me? Florida? No too hot, he hates the heat. New York? No too busy, he's not a people person and neither am I. California? Maybe, there's a lot to do over there.

"Hope you have a comfortable flight and we will be arriving at The Royal Crown Airlines in thirteen hours so relax and enjoy your flight. If you need anything we will be with you momentarily so just raise your hands. Thank you." And with that she went back behind the curtain.

I sat there, frozen. She said "The Royal Crown Airlines". There was only one airline with that name in the world and it was located in the one place where all my nightmares and shame reside. It was where my past continues to haunt me to this day, the one place that caused most of my regrets and where my independence began when I built up the courage to leave. Now Caleb was taking me back to the place where the most painful times of my life happened.

Slowly, I turned my head to glare at him as he hid his face behind a magazine that had the picture of the United Kingdom flag on the cover.

"You're taking me to England?!" I whispered harshly through clenched teeth. My body was shaking and I had the urge to strangle the mess out of him for being such an insensitive idiot. He moved the magazine down till his eyes were looking over at me apologetically.

"You need to go home and make things right Avery," he whispered lowly. I growled dangerously at him which caused some of the passengers to gasp in fright as they looked around for the source. He didn't move an inch and just kept staring at me.

"You went behind my back Caleb, you damn well know that I don't want to be here!" I bit back another growl as I stood up to move past him but the stewardess stopped me with a questionable look.

"Sir, you'll have to sit back down. Is there something you need?" she asked. I gave her a steady frightening glare.

"Yes, I need you to open the door so I can get off," I snarled. She was visibly shaking but I couldn't care less at the moment. Eventually, she managed to shake her head.

"I-I'm s-sorry sir, but the plane is about to take off, you'll have to take your seat." She tried to be firm but her voice was squeaking the entire time. I bared my teeth at her, contemplating on pushing her frail form away so I can tear the door clean off its hinges, but I decided against making such a public display.

Growling lowly, I turned around and sat back besides Caleb. I felt like a caged animal being carried away to his demise.

How could he do this to me? He knew my family brought back such painful and lonely memories. I've worked years to stopped thinking about them, but he was ruining all those hard years of work by bringing them right in front of me, effectively showing me all the pathetic shame I suffered from for being a coward by not telling them I was leaving or why. I left my Alpha position behind because I wasn't worthy of it and they were going to hate me for it. They all would probably just turn their backs on me just as I did them and spit at me in disgrace.

"Avery, you're tearing the armrest apart," Caleb said in a soothing voice. I looked down at my hands and saw that my claws were extended and were digging deep into the leather. Slowly, I retracted them back one by one.

"Caleb, don't speak to me right now," I said in a flat, expressionless tone. I couldn't handle his betrayal at the moment. I kept my eyes on the headrest in front of me and dared not move in fear of lashing out at him and regretting it later. Taking deep breaths, I tried to leash in my raging wolf from the anger that rose as the plane lifted off the ground.

The moment the lady told us it was safe to move about, I felt Caleb stand and kneel beside Mr. Simon's chair. The Elder bent his head down towards him before nodding, I knew they were planning something but my anger was still flared and I couldn't care less. Not soon after, Mr. Simons was sitting beside me while Caleb took over his seat.

"What happened, Avery?" The Elder asked, settling down in the chair and getting comfortable as he looked over at me. I never moved my eyes from the headrest. My body was still tense and shaking.

"Now is not a good time," I snarled through clenched teeth. Jim raised an eyebrow at me.

"Okay, but it's kind of my duty to protect the people of this plane and you're showing some sure signs of wolfy frustration," he teased.

"I'm not at all frustrated Eld—Mr. Simons, I'm furious. There's a considerable difference between the two," I growled.

"I see and what is it that is making you so angry?"

"What do you think?" I snapped, glaring at him for the first time. He was sitting calmly, watching me with intelligent eyes.

"It's not about what I think. It's all about you right now, Avery." His voice was smooth and even, unaffected by my attitude.

"I don't want anything to do with me!"

"You can't put off yourself for the rest of your life, Avery. Why are you mad?" he asked again, ever the helping Elder even when he wasn't wanted. It wasn't helping me at all, and it only made me feel worse.

"I don't want to go. Caleb knows I don't, but he betrayed me by forcing something on me that could very well destroy my entire being," I confessed in a low tone. My stomach was turning at the thought of what horrible things lay ahead.

"Caleb knows this."

My head snapped up to look at him wide-eyed.

"He wants to destroy me?" I frowned in confusion and hurt but the Elder shook his head.

"No Avery, he would never want to hurt you and *"destroy"* is a very strong word. I think you're overreacting. Caleb knows that if you don't face them, you will never be at peace and that you will always feel broken. If you face them head on that at least you'll know and that you can finally move on from this foreboding chapter in your life and live."

"That's ridiculous, I've already moved past all of this. I finally pushed it away and could breathe. Going back is only going to cause it to resurface and I've worked very hard at moving on."

"No. It's true that you pushed it away but that's just it. Pushing away isn't going to solve the problem, it's only going to prolong the pain, the worry, and the constant 'what if's' you'll be asking for the rest of your life. Caleb wants you to have some resolve and I think so do you," he said, placing his hand on my arm.

I shook my head.

"It hurts too much, Mr. Simons" It barely came across as a whisper. My body slumped over as my anger left and was soon replaced with a sense of dread and sorrow that I knew would come after this stupid trip. I bowed my head in defeat.

"What's life without pain Avery?" he asked, leaning his head towards my view. "We all learn to heal from the things that hurt us the most in this world and hey, you have no idea how they'll react. This could go well if you have some faith in your family."

I said nothing and just kept my eyes on my lap.

What he said was right, but how do you live with the fact that your family might tell you that they hate you to your face? I deserve it for leaving them. After all, I dropped all my responsibilities to their shoulders and left without a single word.

"Avery." The voice this time was soft and musical, and it rushed over my skin like a summer breeze that always felt amazing and beautiful. Slowly, I looked up to find Caleb who had moved to kneel down, his face peering up through the fringe of his dark brown hair while those captivating blue brown eyes meet my brown ones.

"I would never intentionally hurt you if I knew that it would end up that way. I have a feeling that all will go well, I just want you to patch things up with them. They're your family and family is the most important part in anyone's life. So don't let fear get in the way of getting to know them again. Like you said, you have a brother and sister who love you very much and they're all probably waiting for you at this very moment."

I said nothing but continued to look at him.

"If I had a chance to see my family again, I would snatch the opportunity up in a heartbeat so don't let this go to waste. Even if it doesn't go well, I'll always be your family, Avery. I'll be here for you forever, to love you when you think no one else will, to hold you when you're feeling lonely and be beside you through it all. Let me be your shoulder to carry some of the burden, alright?"

I ducked my head again, not wanting him to see the tears that began to blur my vision. There was an unfamiliar tightening in my throat. What did I ever do to deserve someone so perfect? I felt him wrap his arms around my neck and I buried my face into his shoulder as he stroked the back of my hair.

"Okay," I muffled softly into his shirt, feeling the most vulnerable I had ever been but it was okay. Things will be okay.

CHAPTER 27

CALEB

Avery has been quiet throughout the whole plane ride and I was worried. I knew this was going to be hard on him but I had a feeling that everything would work out fine in the end. Still, he was putting me at a distance, and I learned along the way that this was his usual way of keeping himself safe from everything around him. He also kept a blank expression and played off like nothing affected him which meant that he was seriously scared.

I gave him a soft smile and took his hand in mine, looking up at him with as much reassurance as I could possibly give him. I noticed the tiniest lift at the corner of his mouth as he peered down at me.

The taxi ride was silent, Jim sat in the front while Avery and I were in the back. I had refused to let go of his hand. His eyes were focused out to the window, his expression as calm as ever but I could feel the turmoil in him building up like a storm. My wolf cried at me to comfort him so I tightened my hold on his hand, causing him to turn his head at me questionably. I leaned forward and brushed a kiss on his shoulder before meeting his beautiful deep brown eyes.

"I'm right here," I whispered. He said nothing and just stared at me before he let out a deep sigh and nodded.

We were driving on a long dirt road surrounded by bright green grass, tall trees, and hills as far as the eye could see. It was beautiful and I had an instant feeling of home. With all these rolling hills and vegetation, it was practically like a welcome mat for a wolf like me.

The sky was bright and blue, where a light breeze blew into the crack of the windows, filling the cab with its sweet and musky aroma of earth and grass. I stared out the window with a smile, this was a sure sign that everything was going to work out just fine for Avery. It just had to.

Soon enough the pack house came into view, the deeper we got into the woods although it resembled more like a rustic mansion while the trees that surrounded it made it look like its shield.

The house was a good distance away from all civilization for the pack to have its privacy. Before we left, I asked Liam for the directions leading to the pack house. Since he was Alpha, he had to have everyone's territory written down somewhere.

"Well this is it," the cab driver said, his mouth open in awe as he looked around.

"Thank you," Jim said, handing him his fare before we all got out and grabbed our bags from the trunk. The cab drove back down the road as we stood there and gazed at the amazingly breathtaking house. I again reached down and took Avery's hand in mine.

"Are you ready?"

He peered down at me, emotions swirling in his brown eyes. I knew he was dying to turn and run away from this place but I tightened my grip on him.

"You can do this," I said, moving the few inches between us to close the gap and cupped the back of his neck. "I don't have to keep telling you the obvious do I?" I teased, rising up to my toes as I pressed my lips lightly on his. He quickly answered back by wrapping his strong arms around my waist and pulled me against his solid body.

A whimper escaped my lips at the sudden hunger in the kiss as it escaladed with his tongue invading my willing mouth. My hand bunched up a handful of his short silky dirty blonde hair. I felt him harden before I smelled his delicious arousal which assailed my senses. I knew I had to pull back but it was hard when he was desperate like this. It had been a while since we had alone time. Damn, I should have pulled him into the plane's restroom and join the mile high club, that would have been awesome.

Avery pulled back a little, our lips still touching but we were both heaving for air as our breaths fanned each other's faces.

"Don't leave me," he whispered. I frowned before smiling.

"I told you already, I'm not going anywhere. I'll be right here, always," I said breathily, leaning in as I gave him one more long kiss.

"Guys, do I need to leave and come back later?" Jim asked, the amusement clear in his voice.

"I don't mind that at all. Why don't you meet up with us at the house in an hour or so?" Avery suggested as he tightened his arms around my waist.

I chuckled before I stepped out of his grip.

"Or we can go now and get this over with." I readjusted my bags and grabbed Avery's hand to march up to the door.

It suddenly hit me that no one was guarding the house or maybe they were hiding in the trees. I scanned the woods as I raised my hand to knock when it suddenly ripped open and a tall older blond woman stood there. She was beautiful, if you were into that kind of thing. Her eyes were blue and bright as she looked at us before her face molded into a look of complete shock.

"Uh . . . hi, um, I know we didn't call ahead but we came here to talk to Alpha Chandler and his wife," I said to her but it seemed like it wasn't getting through.

Okay let me try again.

"We came from Blue Moon—not the beer but the pack. We have something important to discuss with the Chandlers," I told her.

"Caleb," Jim said with a light snicker. I turned to him and he pointed at the woman then Avery. "This meeting has already started," he said. Frowning, I look at Avery then to the woman then back to Avery again as I noticed the tears in her eyes.

"Oh." I mouthed and took a step back and stood beside Jim to get out of their way and let them at it.

* * *

AVERY

Was this really happening? Was my mother really standing in front of me?

"A-Avery," she stuttered, her voice still sweet and soft like all those years ago. I watched her step towards me hesitantly as I stood frozen to the ground.

"It's you isn't it?" she whispered as tears began to stream down her face. I couldn't get my mouth to work, it was practically filled with cotton at the moment so I nodded to her stiffly and she flew at me. The shock of it all rocked me to the core.

This was real. She really was here where I could see her, touch her, and smell her. Her arms came around me fiercely, holding me tightly as her face buried into my neck.

"My Avery, you came back to me," she whimpered against my skin and I felt a foreign object lodge itself in my throat, making it harder for me to breathe. I couldn't form a single word so I wrapped my arms around her, breathing in her scent.

Home, she smelt like home.

She was home.

"Mom," I choked out before I crushed her to me. "I-I'm sorry." I cried, bringing her down on the porch with me as my legs gave way.

"It's okay baby, it's okay," she whispered to me, stroking the back of my hair soothingly as I buried my face into her chest like I used to do when I was a child. I didn't know how much I missed her till she was standing here right in front of me. It felt like a dam had broken and every emotion I had bottled up came pouring out, flooding everywhere around me.

My house, my family, my country, I missed it all like hell and it hurt like hell too. How could they forgive what I had done to them all? I abandoned them and they had to deal with everything on their own along with the heartache and responsibilities I left on their shoulders.

I didn't know how long we sat there on the floor but mom slightly pulled away when a pair of heavy footsteps came behind her.

"Ivy, what are you doing?" The deep smooth voice sounded in curiosity and concern and I almost had the urge to hide behind my mother. Me, a twenty-three year old man, hiding behind my mother's skirts, but he was the one I was dreading the most to see.

"Lucian, he came back to us," she cried, turning back to me as she got up to her feet. I followed her, taking a deep breath before walking past mother to come face-to-face with Lucian Chandler, the Alpha of the Sky Raven pack. He was a dominant man and his presence always demanded respect from those around him. He was not one to be easily fooled and if you made an enemy out of him, then those who had would be running home with their tails between their legs. He wasn't just the menacing authority figure though, he was a fierce lover and protector and a trustworthy friend. His family was his core and he loved them more than anything else in the world. If it came down to it, he would gladly give his life for this mate and his children and would go down with his pack if he had to.

But what would he do to his very son who ran and turned his back on everyone he loved?

We stood there in silence for a long time as it continued to stretch on, causing my heart to beat erratically fast. This was the moment of truth. If Lucian shunned me away then I would shatter into pieces and I know I deserved it. His dark eyes looked over at every inch of the man that stood in front of him, possibly measuring my worth. Slowly, the blank mask started to crack on his face as he stared at me, meeting my gaze.

"Avery," he whispered softly, his deep voice catching at the end. I knew I had tear stains on my face, and my eyes were red but I kept my gaze on him, trying my best to look strong in front of him.

"Dad." I nodded stiffly.

"Oh my God, Avery," he cried, taking a few strides towards me before he enveloped me in the strongest, warmest hug I had ever received in my life. I was a little taken aback by this reaction. I was so sure that he would kick me out while he screamed at me and told me how worthless I was, but then again, that was never my father at all. Where did that huge exaggeration come from?

The scent of pine and the fresh English air after his runs surrounded him. How I missed this smell too.

"You're so big," he choked out, tightening his arms as he held me closer. I pressed the side of my face against his, relishing in everything I longed for so long.

My family.

"I've grown a bit," I muttered into his shoulder, trying to stop the flow of tears that just wouldn't quit.

"I'm so happy, we've missed you Avery." He pulled back holding me at arm's length. "I'm happy you decided to come back to us." I nodded, I couldn't take my gaze away from his dark eyes as they filled with unshed tears. He was crying, this was the first time I have ever seen tears in his eyes and they were for me.

"I missed you too dad, I missed all of you," I told him weakly. He smiled patting my arms.

"Come on, let's go inside and talk, I know that your brother and sister will be happy to see you." I nodded, turning towards Caleb before I held out my hand. I gave him a soft smile as he wiped tears from his eyes and quickly picked up our bags before reaching for it. His grip was warm and soft as his hand slid in mine and I was overcome with joy. He was right, he had told me that they would welcome me and they had and he stood by my side the entire time. He was amazing.

Lucian noticed this but said nothing and just stood aside and let us in.

"Jim, is that you?" my dad asked from behind us. I watched Jim smile and clap him on the back.

"Yes it sure is. How have you been Lucian?" he asked as he walked towards my mom to give her a hug, "and you Ivy? You're as lovely as ever."

"Well you know, a few rogues trying to sneak in but besides that minor annoyance, nothing has happened until now and what a surprise it was. Why did you come along?" Dad asked as he led us to his office.

I had an overwhelming sense of nostalgia as I walked down the halls of my old home, my childhood memories came flooding back as I tightened my hold on Caleb's hand.

"I'm looking after that one," Jim said pointing at Caleb. Caleb turned to glare at him.

"I told you 'Jim' I don't need a babysitter," he growled. Jim just smiled.

"Sure you don't." Rolling his eyes Caleb turned back marching further away from him.

"Whatever Grandpa," he muttered.

"Hey I'm not that old!" Jim complained.

My dad laughed softly. We all arrived at his office door and he opened it, letting my mother in first before the rest of us.

I remember when I was a kid that I would run around here with my father. The latter would chase me around the big wooden desk, all because I refused to take a bath while my mother would stand by the door and laugh at us. Other times, I would come in and sit on the desk while my father talked to his Beta about pack issues.

The wall behind my father's chair was covered with books from past generations. Those were the journals from all the previous Alphas that had run this house before. All the bindings were worn as my eyes ran over them. It was tradition to put your thoughts down during your reign as Alpha till the next generation took over. As I looked around, nothing seemed to have changed.

"I'll go get your brother and sister," Mom said excitedly and ran out. I took a deep breath, my stomach constantly doing nervous flips. Now that I knew my parents were happy to see me, the crazy nausea I had earlier had calmed down but it was slowly starting to return at the thought of my brother and sister. What did they look like now? Would they hate me for leaving?

"You look good, Avery." I looked over at my dad as he leaned against his desk, his toned arms crossed over his chest. He looked the same as he did before I left. His hair was still dark and full, and was cut at the nape where a few strands hung in his face. I spotted a few wrinkles around his eyes, but if you weren't actively looking for them then you wouldn't notice. Werewolves generally start to age slower than humans once they hit their eighteenth year, so our looks lasted a little longer than theirs. However, if you were mated to a werewolf, the mark would change your DNA, slowing down your aging to match your partner's. So if you were in your fifties you would look like you were in your late thirties, maybe early forties, and both my parents were in their late forties.

"You too dad. You haven't aged a bit," I told him.

"Well you sure have." He smiled but it didn't reach his eyes all the way. "So what made you want to come back?" he asked me. I bit my lip, glancing at Caleb who still stood by my side.

"That was me sir," he spoke up. Dad raised his brows as he looked over at him.

"Oh."

Caleb nodded.

"He was too nervous to come by himself so I took matters into my own hands," he answered, squeezing my hand gently. Lucian looked down at our hands again.

"Who are you?" he asked Caleb politely.

"Oh, I'm Caleb Carmichael, Avery's mate." My dad's eyes widened as his eyes shifted from him to me.

"M-mate?" The shock was evident in his voice.

"Yes, sir." I felt Caleb stiffen beside me, ready for an outburst.

"How is that possible, I thought . . ." He frowned over at Jim, who was seated on the couch and nodded.

"This is one of those special cases, Lucian," he answered. Dad looked back at us.

"You're no longer a wanderer?" he asked, stepping towards us.

"I guess not, I marked Caleb without knowing I could and he did the same to me," I explained. He shook his head, hugging us close.

"I don't care how it happened as long as you're not suffering anymore," he whispered in my ear. He pulled back and clapped Caleb on the back. "Thank you Caleb."

"Well I try," he joked with a shrug. Dad laughed as the door opened and I was soon knocked to the floor as someone jumped on me.

"AVERY!" The scream had to be one of the most beautiful things I had ever heard. Soon after, a pair of arms wrapped themselves around my neck tightly, making it hard for me to breathe.

"Delilah," I whispered to her as I sat up holding her close. She was so big now, I pushed her back from me a little as my breath got caught in my lungs. She was beautiful. Her hair was long and wavy which lay past her shoulders. Her brown eyes were shimmering with tears as she stared at me with such joy and excitement. She smiled at me and I saw the prominent gap between her front teeth and laughed, pulling her back to my chest.

"I missed you so much, big brother," she said, her angelic voice shaking with emotion.

"I missed you too," I whispered, unable to strengthen the tone of my voice. "You have grown so much, Dee." I stood up, bringing her up with me. "And you're completely stunning".

"Where have you been brother? We've missed you terribly. Why did you go?" she asked, wiping her tears away with her sleeve. I felt the lump form in my throat again.

"That's a hard question to answer at the moment Dee, but I can say that I've missed you all so badly that it hurt sometimes," I told her. She nodded before scrunching up her nose.

"What happen to your voice Avery?" she asked, stepping back but still keeping ahold of my hand. I smiled.

"Time has washed it away."

"You sound so American." She giggled.

"I feel American," I said, beyond happy that I could finally talk to and see my little sister again.

"Well we'll have to change that won't we?" My dad added. I looked over at him with the same smile that refused to leave my face. I can't remember ever smiling this much in my entire life.

"Honey, why don't you have a seat and tell us how you've been," Mom said, gesturing at one of the large leather bound chairs. I nodded and took Caleb's hand in my free one and sat him in the chair while I leaned against the armrest. Dee leaned up against me, refusing to have even the littlest ounce of space between us.

"How old are you now Dee?" I asked looking down at her upturned face. She smiled again.

"Fourteen," she said proudly.

"Seriously? You look much older than that," I teased.

"I age well," she joked, causing me to laugh aloud.

"She's been signed up for a modeling contract this year, she's extremely excited about that aren't you dear?" Mom said.

"Mum," Dee whined, "I wanted to tell him that."

I laughed giving her a side hug.

"That's fantastic Dee, I'm proud of you."

She ducked her head as a blush rose in her cheeks.

"Thank you," she whispered.

"Avery, aren't you going to introduce us to your friend here?" Mom asked. I turned my head and saw Caleb smile expectantly.

"Of course, mom, Delilah this is my mate, Caleb Carmichael."

When I didn't hear them say anything, I looked up to see them both with wide eyes and gaping mouths.

"Y-your m . . . mate?" Mom stuttered slowly. I nodded. Dee looked from Caleb to me than back to Caleb again.

"Oh . . . my . . . God. That is so cool! You guys are so cute together!" She jumped up and down before pushing past me to sit with Caleb on the large chair.

"So like how long have you two been together?" she asked, her brown eyes shining with mischief. Caleb chuckled.

"Oh I don't know, a few weeks now I think though it took months to get him to notice my existence."

Dee gasped.

"Brother, how could you be so cruel? He's your mate!" she exclaimed.

"It was complicated, Dee," I answered her. I could see my mother turn her awestruck gaze towards my father.

"How? But I thought—" she said as Lucian walked over to her and placed a hand on her shoulder.

"We'll get an explanation soon," he told her before he leaned down to place a kiss on her temple.

The room was loud with Delilah and Caleb's adamant conversation. I sighed as I suddenly realized they were going to be trouble together. Just what I need, Caleb having a partner in crime. I then noticed something between all the excitements of my home coming.

Someone was missing.

"Mom, dad, where is James?" Once the words were out of my mouth, the room ceased of all noise and my heart dropped in my stomach.

"Well, look who decided to show his face again." The deep voice was void of all emotion except one: anger.

Swallowing, I turned towards the door to see my brother standing in the doorframe with balled fists and sharp blue eyes.

"James."

"How long has it been, *'brother'*?"

CHAPTER 28

AVERY

The room was silent and heavy with tension. James was still glaring at me while he stood in the doorway. I watched him with a blank expression but inside I was torn apart. I knew there was someone who held animosity towards my departure and what better person than my little brother who I was so close to? We were only two years apart so we did everything together when we were little and me leaving that night caused a deep rift in our relationship. From the look in his eyes, I knew it was no easy fix. He hated me for what I did and I don't blame him.

The silence dragged on till he finally moved, taking slow purposeful strides towards me. He finally stopped in front of me, his eyes hot with malice. It was like a sharp blade cutting through my stomach. I never meant to cause him pain, but I knew I caused them all pain. His full lips were drawn into a tight line. I didn't stop it even though I already knew it was coming. The force of his fist driving into my cheek sent my head snapping to the right, causing my neck to crack in the process.

"James!" my mother gasped, Delilah did the same.

"Avery." Caleb's worried voice filled me with strength.

"It's alright," I told him quietly and turned back to look at my baby brother again. His blue eyes flamed with justice as he socked me again, this time blood rushed into my mouth as my cheek snagged against my teeth. When he went for a third time, I caught his wrist in my hand with a vise grip. There was only so much my pride could take.

"I deserved that but don't think I'll let you get away with it a third time, James," I growled at him in warning.

"You deserve so much more than that. You caused this whole family to suffer with your selfishness, Avery and don't think I'll ever forgive you for that," he snarled back, ripping his wrist from my hold. "You should just go back to wherever it is the hell you came from and quit giving my family grief." And with that he turned and strode out with hard angry strides.

I watched him go as the sorrow took over. Was I doing more harm than good by coming here? Before I could contemplate further, a sleeve came up to my lips and gently wiped away the blood that was dripping from my mouth. Looking down, I caught Caleb's worried yet angry expression.

"What an assh*le," he muttered.

"Avery, are you okay?" Mom exclaimed, standing next to Caleb. I nodded with a smile.

"I knew that had to come sooner or later," I told her, taking Caleb's hand in mine to stop him from ruining his shirt further.

"No, Avery let me clean it," he insisted, his eyes shining with anger.

"I'm fine," I pressed, intertwining our fingers together. He huffed but didn't let go of my hand.

"So . . . that went well," Dad said, shaking his head.

"I'll go talk to him." Mom's skirt whipped around as she turned to leave.

"No Ivy, let him cool off first." Dad sighed, then looked at me. "He's had the hardest time coping with your disappearance. We tried to explain your unique situation to him but nothing helped. He was very close to you Avery." I looked at my family and saw the same pain that they lived with all this time. I closed my eyes.

*   *   *

"Was he right, should I leave?" I asked Caleb later after we were settled into my old room. I was sitting on the edge of the bed while Caleb packed our things into my dressers. My questioned caused him to look over his shoulder at me.

"Don't let one assh*le scare you off Avery." He walked over and knelt down in front of me, taking my hands in his.

"But he's not an assh*le Caleb, he's my baby brother." I couldn't get any of their faces away from my mind as I saw the hurt and the worry I caused them for years.

"Well he could have handled that a lot better than how he did. He's an assh*le in my books," he said.

"Maybe I should, I don't want to hurt them anymore and maybe me being here is causing them more pain." I hated feeling helpless, I wanted to make them all forget.

"Avery, you'll hurt them if you leave again and you know it. Your brother is just being a big prick but he'll get over it eventually," he reassured me. I looked up and peered into his beautiful eyes. I probably looked like a lost pup at the moment.

"Will he? Can you guarantee that?" I asked him.

He shook his head.

"No I can't, but are you willing to leave the rest of your family and hurt them again because of one person holding a grudge? That won't help you heal from this and it sure won't patch anything up with them so forget about James and focus on more important things."

"And what are those?" I asked, smiling lightly.

Caleb grinned evilly.

"Like how I'm going to take you with the whole pack noticing," he whispered before leaning up and kissing me firmly.

"Take me?" I questioned against his lips. He nodded, gripping my hair tightly in his hands.

"I think it's time you were on the receiving end of all our mind blowing sex, Avery," he growled.

What was he talking about? Was he really thinking of making me bottom this time?

"Oh and you think you can give it to me?" I teased. For some reason, the idea didn't scare me I was kind of intrigued by it.

"Oh I can give it like you've never known before." His tongue was tracing my bottom lip and I opened up for him but he skipped past my offering mouth and licked down my neck.

"Caleb, I don't think now is a good time though," I moaned through clenched teeth.

"I think you're bullsh*tting and trying to back out." Slowly, his hands ran under my shirt and up my chest until they pushed against me and lay me down. My legs were dangling off the edge of the bed as he crawled over and straddled me, taking my shirt off.

"Do you want to know what I feel like Avery?" he whispered seductively in my ear and my toes suddenly curled. What has gotten into him? The feel of his warm tongue tracing along my ear had me bucking my hips against his.

"Mmm . . ."

"Caleb," I groaned. His laughter filled my ear and my body tightened with its breathy sound.

"You didn't answer my question lover boy. Do . . . you . . . want . . . me . . . inside . . . of you?" With each pause, his hands caressed down my body till he held my hard member in his hands. "From the feel of it, I think you do," he purred against my neck.

"They're making dinner Caleb, we need to be down there soon." Alright I admit it, I was stalling. I was nervous as hell. I wanted it but I've never done this before. Caleb was more experienced in this area than I was, and with that thought, a growl rumbled through my throat. I didn't like the thought of him with anyone else.

"I think they'll understand if we were a bit late," he said, scooting off me to stand between my legs. Quickly, he reached down to the waistband of my pants and yanked them down along with my boxers until I lay there naked like a virgin sacrifice.

My breath was coming in gasps as I watched him lower his head towards my member and took me in that hot haven of his. I threw my head back as he took me deep.

"Oh God," I moaned, arching my back. He laughed again and the vibrations were delightful against my sensitive skin.

Pleasure was shooting through my fingertips as his tongue flattened under me and caressed my erection in smooth circles.

"F*ck!" I groaned as I reached down and ran my fingers through his long hair and grab it with my fist. He moaned at my actions and moved faster as I guided him to the pace I wanted.

This went on for who knows how long. I was bucking against his mouth, teetering on the edge of ecstasy but he stopped me and gripped the base of my member before slowly lifting his head to gulp down some air.

"Not yet," he panted, shaking his head at me. I groaned, dropping my head back on the bed as he kissed his way back up. His lips were warm and wet as they skimmed my stomach and chest. Surprising me, he took one of my nipples in his mouth and sucked hard.

A moan tore from my mouth as he moved to the other.

"You are the most beautiful man I have ever seen Avery and I'm beyond glad you're all mine," he said as he kissed his way up my neck. I looked at him through half-lidded eyes, seeing the lusty haze cloud his gaze. His tongue flicked the mark he gave me and desire crashed into me all over again.

I couldn't take it anymore so I began tearing at his clothes. His shirt and pants flew in different directions while his boxers slid from his body by my teeth. He bit down on his lip as he watched me. Ever so slowly, I kissed up his legs and thighs, purposely passing his hard-on. He was generously endowed in this particular region and my nerves shot up once again.

How was that going to fit in me?

"Are you nervous?" he asked, sitting up. I did the same but kept my face clear of any worry or nerves I was feeling. He smiled lightly and cupped my face.

"I promise you I will take it slow and do my best at pleasuring you to no end." I watched him lay me back down on the bed as he got up to rummage through his bag. Not soon after, he brought out a little bottle and climbed back on the bed next to me, rubbing the oil to where it was needed.

When he tried to roll me over on my stomach, my wolf decided to voice his displeasure about that. He was willing to let Caleb do this but he would not be put into such a submissive position. I let Caleb know this and he nodded.

Once he was positioned over me, I stared into his eyes taking deep breaths.

"I'll go slowly," he whispered in my ear and moved to kiss my lips as he cupped the back of my knees and bent them up so he could have access. He never broke the kiss, so when he pressed against my entrance I gasped in his mouth and he invaded in with his seeking tongue.

"Relax."

He pushed further and I wrapped my arms around his neck pulling him down and deepening our kiss, distracting myself from the oncoming pain.

I groaned as inch by inch he filled me till he was all the way seated inside.

"Ahh!" I cried in his mouth.

This was one of the most vulnerable moments I've ever been in but if it was for Caleb then I would gladly do anything for him, even if it meant stomping down on my wolf's domineering ways.

Caleb held still for a long moment till I finally relaxed under him. Feeling this, he began to move at a steady pace and right away I was lost in a sea of lust and passion. He had touched something deep inside and my world came undone at the feel of it.

I dug my nails into his back and moaned a bit too loudly. My curses and moans filled the room and I had to bite down on my lip to keep it down.

Caleb dragged his nose up across my neck up to my ear, moving faster in me as he consistently hit that same spot.

"This is what it feels like Avery." He was panting as he spoke. He licked the underside of my ear and I bucked into him, bringing him deeper.

"Oh God," I moaned.

"This is what it feels to have you inside of me and I want to share that gift with you," he whispered lovingly. Again he thrusted deeper and it was killing me. I didn't think I could survive something of this magnitude. But when I felt my climax peaking, I knew that I would surely die on the spot.

Caleb was moaning close to my ear and the sound of his pleasure upped mine about tenfold, his pleasure was my own. I felt him nuzzle my shoulder for a second before he licked his mark. He was close to release and wanted us to share it together. I accepted this and tilted my head, giving him more access while I panted and grunted under him, ready for his bite.

His canines sank into my flesh and I lost the grip I barely had on my control. The room became sharper right before it blurred with the blinding pleasure of my release. My claws grew, raking across his back as it brought a gasping cry of pleasure that escaped his lips as he joined me in ecstasy. His release was warm as it shot into me and I let out a deep breath before I collapsed back onto the bed. All the strength I had now ebbed from my shaking body.

I was vibrating with what just happened, my body sang with delight and even my wolf lay satisfied, too tired to continue.

Caleb rested on top of me, breathing heavily, and slicked with our sweat. I ran one of my hands lightly up and down his back, while the other combed through his soft brown hair.

"You think they know?" he asked softly, looking up at me with warm eyes. The front of his hair was sticking to his sweaty forehead and I couldn't help but lean up and kiss him softly.

"I think the whole pack knows." I smiled. He chuckled and laid his head back down on my shoulder.

"Good, now they know you're mine and I'll scratch any person's eyes out who thinks otherwise," he said.

I shook my head and closed my eyes, breathing deeply.

A timid knock at the door made us jump a bit as we both turned to look at the door.

"Um . . . honey . . . Dinner is ready." My mom's hesitant voice came from the other side.

"Okay!" I said loudly.

"I-I'll just wait downstairs." We heard light footsteps fade and Caleb let out a snort, finally making a move to pull out of me and sit on the edge of the bed.

"Well that wasn't awkward," he said then turned towards me. "Are you okay?" I nodded.

"I'm just letting my body heal up a bit," I told him. Slowly, he got up and stretched before making his way over to the other side of the bed and bent over me.

"By the way you were amazing," he said and kissed me firmly, running his fingers through my short hair.

"Glad to hear it." I smiled. He bit down on my lip lightly and his eyes sparked with lust again.

"I'm going to get ready, you can join me if you want." And with that he walked into the bathroom but not before looking over his shoulder for a second where he winked at me before cracking the door open. I let out a soft laugh.

'Man, this boy was insatiable.' I thought as I gladly followed him.

CHAPTER 29

CALEB

Sitting with your mate's family and eating dinner while knowing full well that they know what Avery and I just did was a bit embarrassing, but it was also exhilarating. Now the whole house knew that it was expected to leave him alone. That he was mine and no one else's. With a smile at that thought, I lifted my spoonful of soup up to my mouth, unable to stop thinking about earlier.

"Keep smiling like that and you'll end up looking like the Joker's son," Jim whispered in my ear. I rolled my eyes and pushed him away from me. He snickered and went back to his food.

Shaking my head, I looked up around the table. Avery's mom, Ivy was staring down at her bowl intently with a large splash of red on her cheeks. Lucian who sat at the end of the table was conversing with his Beta, his back straight and chin lifted high like the ever dominant Alpha, nothing affected him and if it did, he didn't show it.

Delilah was clueless; since she was only fourteen so she hadn't hit puberty yet, but I could tell she knew something was up. She was looking around the table but mainly her mom whose face would just redden even more when she looked at Avery and me. Let's not forget James who was all frowns and grumbles, his parents forced him to be here and he apparently wasn't very happy about it, like I give a crap.

"So, where did you two meet?" Alpha Chandler asked Avery.

"Blue Moon pack, sir," Avery answered. Lucian nodded.

"Isn't the Blue Moon pack under the new reign of the former Alpha's son?" Adam, the Alpha's Beta asked.

He was a big guy and was slightly younger than Lucian. He had dark brown hair and startling electric blue eyes that seemed to stare right into your soul. He had a large jagged scar down the side of his face which ran an inch from the corner of his left eye down to the middle of his cheek. He was a scary looking man until you got to know him. He was rough but pretty cool and had two sons named Brian and Asher with his mate Jessie.

Brian was around Avery's age and Asher was one year older than Connor, the latter had inherited his father's striking blue eyes but unlike his father's whose gaze resembled sharp blades, his were softer and more innocent looking. Jessie was a beautiful woman with black hair and light brown eyes whom Brian had gotten his looks from. They were a good looking family.

"Yes, Liam Moore, he was made Alpha just this year," Avery answered.

"And what of his mate, has he found her yet?" This time it was Alpha Chandler.

"Him sir, and yes Aiden Carlisle is a wonderful human mate to the Alpha."

"Oh, I see." Lucian nodded his head approvingly. I have to give this guy credit, he didn't let anything surprise him. Well, except when Avery and I came this morning, but besides that he took everything in stride. He gets points in my book.

"How is it that two males can mate? I don't understand this concept. Isn't the whole point of a mate to procreate?" Brian added his voice into the conversation. Avery shook his head.

"I don't understand it either but I'm not going to question what the Spirits do. They do these things for a reason and I'm grateful for it any way it plays out." He reached down to grab my hand. I smiled looking up at him.

"Well I'm surely grateful that they found someone for you, Avery," Lucian said. Adam nodded along with everyone else. Well, besides James who was still sulking and glaring down at his meal.

"I guess when you put it that way, but how are they going to continue the Moore blood line?" Brian continued.

"The human way I guess is through adoption or finding a willing surrogate woman," Avery said.

"How awkward for poor Aiden," Ivy said suddenly.

"When they decided to do this I think Aiden would be okay with it," Jessie reassured Ivy.

"How did you come to be in Portland, Oregan, Avery?" Lucian asked bringing a bite of steak into his mouth. "It's a pretty long way from England."

"I didn't get there till last year actually. I had a sudden yearning to go in that direction, I was currently in California at the time."

"So what was there?" Delilah asked.

"Aiden."

I shouldn't be jealous of this. It's not like he said Aiden's name in a longing or loving way but it kind of hurt to have him drawn to another man other than me. The things I had to go through to get him to just look at me was difficult, but it wasn't his fault. He was mateless and like all the others of his kind, they searched for a purpose, a reason for his existence. So in a way, I had to be grateful that he found Aiden because if he hadn't then I would never have found him. He wouldn't be here right now either and if he hadn't found Aiden, then he most likely wouldn't be on the earth with me.

My hand tightened in his, which brought his attention to me. He frowned in concern and I shook my head, smiling up at him.

"So it wasn't Caleb who you were drawn to?" Delilah frowned. Avery shook his head.

"No, but Caleb had his own problems at the time didn't you?" he asked to me. I blushed.

"Let's not bring that up," I muttered

"So who is this Aiden character to you?" Adam asked.

"Aiden is the person my wolf has been searching for. I had completed the Sayan's ritual with him and a few weeks later Caleb showed up and everything went crazy from there."

"You actually tied your soul to this boy but are mated with Caleb? How is that possible?" Ivy asked.

"That's a little complicated to explain at the moment, there are safety issues we have to consider," Jim answered this. Everyone looked at him with frowns.

He sighed. "Long story short since Avery is an Alpha, he has the right to a second mate, it's an old, long forgotten tradition but without knowing this Avery marked Caleb as his mate," he explained briefly.

"What about Caleb's mate?" Ivy asked with genuine concern.

"Like I've said before, this is a unique situation and safety is an important factor where these two are concerned." Jim smiled kindly but everyone knew when to drop it when they saw the hardened expression in his green eyes and the almost invisible edge to his voice. So just like that, it was dropped.

"Speaking of Alpha, did you come to regain your title?" Brian asked, peering at Avery from across the table. Avery opened his mouth to answer but he was cut off by the sound of a chair scraping against the floor before it pushed back and crashed onto the surface.

"He has no right!" James growled, slamming his hands down on the table as he stood. He was glaring at Brian before he moved his angry blue eyes towards Avery.

"James!" Alpha Chandler scolded but it did nothing to stop him.

"No, Avery has no right to even think he can just come back after years of abandonment on his own pack and take his place as Alpha!"

"James enough!" Ivy snapped, staring hard at her son but of course he ignored her.

"Were you not listening to the conversation James? It wasn't his fault, he had to leave!" Delilah exclaimed.

"What, are you thinking of taking up the position yourself, James?" Brian mocked with a smirk on his face.

"No, you all know I didn't inherit the Alpha gene, but Avery doesn't deserve it for what he's done." He continued, ignoring what his sister had said.

"Exactly, Avery is the only one who has the Alpha gene which automatically makes him next in line for the Alpha position, James. Anyway, you should know that he has a right to take up rule here." Alpha Chandler's voice was firm and final. James was huffing with fury as he glared at Avery, never taking his eyes away from him.

"This is bullsh*t!" he cursed then stormed out. I rolled my eyes, this guy was like a big whiny baby.

The room was silent for a moment before Lucian turned towards Avery.

"I'm serious Avery, you are heir to the position and it has always been here waiting for you"

That's when it hit me. What if he did take it? Would we be living here? Would we have to be part of the Sky Raven pack? I glanced over at Avery.

"I didn't come here to be the Alpha, I came here to make amends with you all." He sighed. "James is right though, I don't deserve to take up the position especially after what I have done to this pack. A leader is supposed to be faithful to its pack and stick by them at all costs and I ruined that trust when I left."

"And a good leader knows when they have done wrong and come to make peace," Lucian said, his eyes bright as he stared at his son. "And I couldn't be prouder of you." I knew that really hit Avery hard as he gripped my hand painfully.

"He's right honey, we need you back. I don't want you to go, I don't think I could bear it again," Ivy whimpered, behind her hand. Her eyes were brimming with tears.

Avery didn't speak, he didn't move but I felt the gather of emotions building inside of him, ready to explode.

"I think Avery needs a little bit of time to think about all this. It's a pretty big thing to accept after all," I said for him. Lucian peered over at me before he smiled softly and nodded.

"I understand, as long as the two of you stay for a while. Avery and I have some bonding to catch up on." He smiled. We both nodded at him.

"Great, that way you can meet our son!" I said excitedly and watched everyone snap towards my direction with widened eyes and open mouths.

CHAPTER 30

LEVI

"Levi." I heard a soft voice call from the doorway. I didn't move and just continued to lie on my side and stared out the window as rain pelted against the glass. Light footsteps approached me and my bed dipped slightly as they sat in front of me.

This is what my life has come to. I lie in bed day after day and stare out the window hoping, praying, and even begging for him to come back but he never does and never will. All I ever feel is the wrenching pain of his abandonment, the throbbing fire in my heart when it burns for his love, and the desire to at least get a glimpse of what it's like. I've become this pathetic excuse of a being who became nothing more than a shell of my former self and I wish I could quit him, forget all about him, and move on.

What have I done to deserve this? Why did the Spirits pick him for me? He could have had a great life with some beautiful girl, have kids, and love his life but he's forever connected to me and would never be able to love someone right.

I didn't know how much longer I could survive this way. Should I just end it now and be done with it? This is what he wanted after all. He didn't want me, so if I just end it for him, would he be pleased? Would he be able to breathe again if I didn't?

"Levi." A small warm hand brushed my hair back and I finally looked up to see Alpha Aiden gazing down at me with the most heartbreaking blue eyes I have ever seen.

"I know we're not close or anything, but Liam and everyone else were wondering if you wanted to play some board games with us. It's a pretty boring day and it will get your mind off things for a while," he said, his eyes begging for me to come but I was numb to the world and all its compassions at this point in time. I shook my head and shifted my gaze back to the window.

"Levi, will you please tell me what's wrong? I know you only really talked with Caleb, but from what I've seen, you're a very hyper and happy person so what's bugging you?"

"I just want to be alone." My voice was raspy from its lack of use.

He sighed and stood.

"If you change your mind, we'll be in the sitting room alright?" I didn't answer so he left.

Once he was gone I laid there for what seemed like hours till I pushed back the sheets and slowly got to my feet. I staggered, reaching out to hold myself up on the bed post. Taking a deep breath, I let go and shakily walked to the bathroom. My hand stretched out, fingers running along the wall as I stumbled to the sink and grasped the edge for balance. I was beyond weak from refusing to eat, well besides the times my dad would force-feed me. Slowly, I reached out and opened the cupboard, pulling out what I was looking for.

This is what he wanted, he didn't want me.

He didn't want me.

He didn't need me.

He hated me.

I loved him too much too but I'm in so much pain. Just looking at me disgusted him, what kind of mate would I be if I made him sick with just the sight of me? I flipped out the blade from my father's old fashion straight razor and stared at the glistening edge.

He didn't love me.

He never would.

I was just in the way.

Maybe if I wasn't here, he would come back to his home and finally be happy. I wish I could have seen him smile just once. The blade was kept sharp and I just stared at it.

This is for the best, to make Kyle happy.

A weak smile finally touched my lips after weeks of crying and cursing the world. I was finally going to make my mate pleased with me for the first time. I ran the tap with warm water and stuck my wrist under the flow before I lifted the blade and pressed it against my wrist. Taking another deep breath, I watched as the blade sliced clean through my skin, I did the same to the other before the blade clattered to the floor.

Dark red liquid started flowing from the cuts I've made. I should be scared at what I just did but I wasn't. My wolf pulled back from me, wanting this just as much. There was no Levi without Kyle and he knew that. Since I hadn't had a decent meal, exercised, or did anything a regular healthy wolf needs on a day-to-day basis, I knew I wouldn't be able to heal like one.

Slowly, the world began to tilt and I found myself staggering back and sliding down the wall next to the tub. The room was blurring before my eyes as warm tears slid down my cheeks.

"Please be happy now Kyle," I whispered roughly, hoping he could hear me from wherever he was.

Black edges started to form all around me, slowly enclosing me in as I dropped my head forward. The ground was a mess of red where some parts looked as if a bucket of blood red paint had tipped over, while other parts resembled the strokes of a paint brush. The canvas of my life was here on the floor bleeding out from me.

With that, I closed my eyes and felt my energy ebb out of me bit my bit till my body was just as numb as I have felt through all these long weeks. I didn't hurt anymore, my chest was no longer a burning ache that tortured me constantly, and it was slowly going away along with my fading heart.

"Kyle."

And with that I let go . . .

"Levi, Levi!"

*   *   *

MR. BLACKMAN

He wasn't here. I knew he wouldn't have left the room after all this time. The bed wasn't made and the sheets were pulled back. Slowly, I turned to see the bathroom door cracked open but not before I smelled blood. Frowning, I walked over to the door and knocked lightly.

"Levi?" I called out but got no answer. My frown deepened and I knocked a little harder, causing the door to swing open just a little bit only to see a mass of some type of deep red substance covering the floor. I froze for just a moment but in that moment, my heart stopped beating and my stomach dropped down to my feet.

Everything faded in and out and my whole being hummed in terror as I pushed the door wide open and saw my son, my beautiful dear sweet boy lying against the wall, practically transparent.

I felt like I was moving in slow motion as I took in the sight of the blood flowing from his wrist and onto the white tile floor.

"Levi." My voice cracked in a hushed tone, I was unable to believe what I was seeing in front of me, I didn't want to.

Then everything in me shattered, reality came crashing down on me and a deafening ring in my ears brought me back to this world and I realized it was me screaming my son's name.

"LEVI!" I ran to him as I fell on my knees, not caring that my pants were deep in a puddle of his blood.

"No, no, no, no Levi," I cried at him, taking his cold face in my hands. "Please Spirits, no," I begged, my voice raspy as I took his limp form in my arms where I held him and rocked. He was only eighteen, he was too young.

"Levi." I shook him desperately, tears streaming down my face. I pulled him close to me, his face was buried into my neck and I could feel his shallow breaths against my skin. Quickly, I staggered to my feet, slipping twice against the red liquid on the ground before I gently placed him on my bed, holding him close to me. I lifted his wrist to my mouth frantically and licked his wounds closed.

"Help!" I screamed, distraught at losing him. I didn't want to lose any more of my loved ones. My mate was gone and I'll be damned if I let the Spirits take my son away from me like this. I can't lose him too.

"Levi, you have to wake up!" I begged, tears clogging my throat. Brushing back, his long hair from his clammy cold skin, I noticed my hand was shaking terribly.

"Help me damn it!" I was in hysterics now. I was vibrating with fear, barely able to move with the sheer terror of losing him.

The door bust open and Wyatt, the former Beta and Robert, the former Alpha rushed in with Dom behind them.

"What happened?" Robert demanded and I shook my head, unable to get anything out. I still held Levi close to me.

"Marten, breathe," Wyatt told me softly. I was shaking and struggling for breath as I replayed the scene of finding my reason for still living on the floor with slashed wrists and it hit me hard. A sob climbed up my throat before a spine-chilling and agonizing scream ripped its way from my soul before I buried my face into Levi's chest begging, demanding that he live on.

"Dom, go get the doctor now!" Robert ordered and he was gone in seconds.

"Marten, tell us what happened," he said it like he was coaxing to a wild animal to show that he wasn't a danger.

"Robert . . ." Wyatt's worried voice sounded from the bathroom entrance. They both saw the mess and had a pretty good idea of what happened.

"I found him like this." I didn't even recognize my own voice.

"We're going to get him help and he'll be fine okay?" Robert said reassuringly. I just nodded against my son's barely moving chest.

"Please hurry." I cried softly.

It was all a blur as I watched them take Levi from me and into the pack's infirmary. They hooked him up to an IV and pumped him with blood. There wasn't much the doctor could do, so all we had to do was wait for him to wake up.

I sat at his side, holding his hand.

"You're so much stronger than this, Levi," I whispered to his pale sleeping form. "I wouldn't be able to handle you leaving me, I can't lose you too, Levi. I've only held on this long because of you, we can get through this together."

I felt new tears build in my eyes.

"We have to."

CHAPTER 31

CALEB

It's been a week and I haven't seen much of Avery lately but I didn't mind. I was forced to be with Jim everyday though and let me tell you, it was beyond annoying to say the least. We argued, we teased, and we got on each other's nerves but through it all, we made a special bond that couldn't be torn. He was starting to become like a brother, a big irritating brother, mind you and dare I say it, I'm sort of starting to like him.

Ugh! I need to wash my brain of such disturbing thoughts.

"Caleb." I turned from fixing the bed to face Jim, his expression was somber and I knew something was wrong.

"What's wrong?" I asked, suddenly serious as I walked over to him.

Jim shook his head.

"They're sending Connor over tonight." He was trying to smile but it wouldn't reach his eyes.

"Don't bullsh*t me Jim, what is it?" I demanded searching his face as I waited.

"Mr. Blackman and his son are going to be accompanying him." My mood brightened up at the mention of Levi.

"Seriously? That's awesome!" I exclaimed, grinning widely but it slowly faded as Jim's eyes drifted to the floor.

"They need you Caleb."

I frowned at him.

"What do you mean?" His green eyes found mine and I knew something was definitely wrong.

"Levi has passed his limits. He can't take this rejection from his mate any longer." I then understood what he was talking about.

"What happened Jim? Tell me!" I pleaded, gripping his arm.

"He uh, tried to . . . kill himself."

I froze.

He did what?

"His father found him in the bathroom. He took a razor to his wrist." Every word that came out of his mouth was being drowned out by the deep and loud pounding in my chest where every second it was ringing louder and louder in my ears.

"No." I gasped.

He couldn't have. Levi would never do something so destructive. He would never try to kill himself. He was the type to forgive and forget. Why would he do this?

Was this my fault for leaving him without helping like I said I would?

I did this.

I didn't realize I was swaying until Jim caught me before I collapsed on the floor.

"Caleb?" he asked, worried.

He gently set me on the bed.

"This is my fault," I whispered to him.

Jim frowned.

"No, Caleb it's not." He knelt down on one knee in front of me.

"Yes it is, I could have helped him before things got so bad." My voice caught as I felt the burn of tears make its way up to my throat and eyes.

"Caleb, stop. You had no idea he would do something like this."

I frowned at him, helplessly.

"Doesn't everyone though? We all know it's just a matter of time before a rejected or grieving wolf lose themselves and can't take it anymore. It's either they lose their minds and turn rogue or kill themselves. This was my first real action as an Elder and I failed. I failed you, and I failed Levi."

"You didn't fail anyone. He's alive and you have a chance now, look at it from a positive angle. He's still able to receive help."

"There is no positive angle, Jim, I let him down and now he's suffered for my carelessness I should never have left without seeing him first."

"Caleb, you can't save everyone and it's perfectly natural for a wolf to want to help his mate above all else." I didn't answer and just simply stared at the brown rug covering the floor.

"Okay, I'm going to get Avery and tell him you need him right now," Jim said before he stood up and placed a warm hand on top of my head.

"They'll be arriving tomorrow so don't worry anymore." And with that he left.

I stayed where I was, letting my thoughts race through my mind. How did it feel to be at such a low desperate point in your life that you'd attempt suicide then have your own father witness something like that? I knew Marten was only hanging on because of Levi. I knew this and I should have helped them both before I decided to even think about going on a plane and flying halfway across the world from them.

The sound of heavy urgent footsteps barely registered in my mind before I was swept up from the bed in a pair of strong arms along with the familiar scent of pine and sandalwood. The dam broke and a rush of tears came pouring from my eyes.

I wasn't one for crying. In fact, I hated it but I couldn't stop the sorrow and regret building inside. Avery tightened his hold on me as I lay in his arms, useless.

"Oh, Caleb," he whispered in my ear and I buried my face in his neck, my entire body shaking as sobs wracked my body.

"I should have helped him," I whimpered pathetically. Avery said nothing, there was really nothing he or Jim could say for that matter that could change my mind, so he held me and continued to do so throughout the night as I grieved over the terrible things my best friend has suffered because of my selfish neglect until I drifted off.

When night rolled around, I awoke with a headache. Avery's heavy arm was still around me as he lay behind me, so I turned to face him and snuggled deeper into his chest before I went back to sleep.

* * *

The day was going by slowly. I was pacing in front of the door, waiting for any signs of Levi, Marten, and Connor.

"Caleb, they're going to come so you don't have to post yourself by the door all day," Avery said from his seat on the staircase. I shook my head.

"Yes I do, I have to be the first one he sees and I have to apologize a thousand times." He should have never gone through this. As I thought about it more through my tossing and turning last night, I realized that it wasn't just my fault that Levi was like this, it was also Kyle's.

If Kyle hadn't left, Levi wouldn't be like this. If Kyle had accepted him like he should have, then Levi would be happy and content instead of attempting suicide. If I could, I would drag Kyle's worthless butt from his pathetic hiding place and force him to acknowledge his mate.

"Caleb you have to slow down and eat something. You haven't eaten anything since the day before yesterday." Avery's concern was present in his voice.

"I'm not hungry." And I wasn't. There was just something about hearing your friend almost dying that kills one's appetite. I heard him sigh but didn't stress the situation.

"Marten just called and said they should be close," Jim said as he walked down the stairs and towards me. I looked up at him.

"Really?" He nodded.

"Cool."

I walked to the large window that were on each side of the equally large door. I moved the heavy curtains to peek out.

An hour later I spotted a cloud of dirt form as a black car drove up to the front of the house, my heart started pounding at the sight.

"They're here," I whispered. I suddenly didn't know what to do.

"Then go out there," Avery told me gently.

"I can't move," I said, pulling the curtains back in place as I looked at him with fear.

He smiled reassuringly and walked up to me, cupping my face in his big tender hands as he bent to capture my lips with his. The kiss was warm and sweet and I forgot my worries for a moment.

"I'm right here," he whispered against my lips, repeating the same words I said to him before. I opened my eyes and stared at his warm brown ones.

"Okay." I took a deep breath and turned to grab the doorknob when Jim placed his hand over mine.

"Remember, you don't just go and bite him, Caleb. He has to accept help, and it has to be from his freewill for it to work." I nodded and opened the door to see Connor come flying out of the back seat and rushed towards me, before colliding into me like a battering ram.

"Oof!" I grunted as he slammed into me. His wild wavy hair was like a mop as he buried his face into my chest.

"I missed you so much!" he cried, tightening his arms around me. I smiled down at him and smoothed down some of his beautiful blonde locks with my hand.

"And I missed you." I knelt down to his level, staring straight into his wide crystal green eyes before I pulled him into a hug. "Yep, definitely missed you." I pulled back after giving him one more good squeeze.

"Go say hi to Avery." He nodded excitedly and rushed to Avery who laughed and threw him up into the air before he caught him in a bear hug. I heard Blondie's gleeful giggles as he wrapped his skinny arms around Avery's neck. I turned to see Marten and Levi make their way up the steps.

Time seemed to stop as I looked at Levi. The dark bags under his eyes were frightening, like he hadn't slept in years. His skin was white as a sheet which looked almost transparent and he looked so fragile and skinny that I thought he might fall over if a sudden gust of wind came through. He was like a walking skeleton. I moved towards him and engulfed him in a warm and gently loving hug. He just stood there, his arms still to his sides but his face was buried into my neck. I closed my eyes and held him tighter.

"I'm so sorry Levi," I whispered to him. He answered in a wolf-like whimper as he dropped his luggage to the floor before throwing his thin arms around me.

"Take it away, please," he pleaded in a heart-wrenching whisper. I felt the wetness of tears roll down my cheeks and nodded.

"Okay." He tilted his head to the side, giving me access to his neck. I didn't know how he knew I could do this but perhaps Jim told him. Nevertheless, I didn't wait a minute longer to figure that out, I wouldn't allow it.

Right there on the porch, I let my canines lengthen and moved his long hair out of the way before I bit down, causing us both to gasp.

In an instant, I could feel a wave of emotions burst inside me and my knees were close to giving way underneath the weight of it all.

Pain, sorrow, love, desperation, despair, worry, loss, and an overall sense of giving up attacked my very being. It rocked me to the core as it seeped further and further into my body and soul, and my head ached with a pounding so painful that I thought it might split.

I felt like I was literally being torn to pieces with every one of his emotions. I was ripped apart in separate directions as I continued. Levi's last few weeks flashed before my eyes along with all the suffering and pain he went through till he finally wanted to end it all. Yet through it all, he still wanted Kyle to be happy and to be pleased that he would not be there to anger him further.

I pulled away with an agonizing cry and staggered back from a swaying Levi.

Then everything went dark.

CHAPTER 32

AVERY

I moved quickly and caught Caleb before he could hit the floor. His face was completely white and his brows were scrunched together with pain. Sweat was building on his forehead so I pulled him up in my arms, holding him close as I looked over at Mr. Simons desperately. He didn't look surprised in the slightest, like he knew something like this would happen. For the first time in my existence, I growled at an Elder, not caring how disrespectful it was.

"Why didn't you warn us before making him do something like this?" My vision sharpened as I glared at him. His face was void of all expression as he looked at me.

"He had to experience this on his own without a heads-up, Avery," he explained bluntly.

"You put my mate in danger and expect me to accept that bulls*it excuse?!" My canines lengthened as I snapped them at Mr. Simons in warning. I watched him step back cautiously.

"He'll pull through Avery, it's just that every gift comes with a consequence."

"And you neglected to tell him this?" I snarled.

"What's going on?" I heard my father's deep voice come from behind me as he walked up, taking in Levi and Mr. Blackman who was holding his son against him as Levi tried to regain his balance. He then looked at Caleb who was cradled in my arms, then back at me before he blinked in shock.

"What happened?" he asked. I growled, turning my head towards Mr. Simons.

"Ask him," I hissed before turning around to march back into the house and up the stairs towards our room.

"Avery, is he going to be ok?" Connor asked from the doorway. He was wringing his hands as I glimpsed at him for a second.

"I-yes Connor, go downstairs and find my father," I said, brushing Caleb's hair away from his sweating face.

"But I want to stay with you." I closed my eyes and turned fully to him.

"I don't think right now is a good time." I walked over to him and placed a gentle hand on his back to guide him down the hall. "Ask Alpha Chandler if you can hang out with Delilah. They've all been dying to meet you." He hesitated, looking back at the door we were walking away from before he looked up at me with wide and tearful green eyes.

"Please make sure he's alright," he whispered before he rushed down the stairs.

I watched him for a second before going back to Caleb. He was withering and groaning on the bed. What was wrong with him? I touched his forehead and pulled back quickly, he was burning up. My worry instantly spiked up to new heights. Werewolves had strong immunities against illnesses, you rarely heard of our species falling ill so something had to have gone seriously wrong. If this is what happens every time he helps someone then I forbid it.

"You don't have to worry so much" Mr. Simons voice sounded behind me. Growling, I spun around and bared my teeth at him.

"What the hell do you mean I don't have to worry? He has a f*cking fever!" I snarled. Mr. Simons showed no signs of fear like any normal wolf would have and instead he just walked forward, ignoring the crouch I was slipping into. He was disregarding my warning of his presence near my mate.

"His body is expelling all the negative spirits that haunted Levi for so long. He had more than he could handle at the moment but it won't always be this way Avery, so calm down. I told you these powers come with consequences," he explained as I straightened my stance but kept a wary eye on him.

"So the cost of him taking these feelings from people is getting sick. Don't you think something like that would take a toll on his body at some point in the future?" I couldn't stop the rumbling in my chest as I talked to him. He put my mate in danger, something that Caleb wasn't even aware of. It was Mr. Simon's job to keep him safe or that's what he's been saying all this time.

"No, the cost is knowing the pain these wolves have gone through. He's going to have to share a little sliver of their pain in everyone he helps," he said.

I glared at him.

"And each little piece is just going to grow with every person till it consumes him and he turns like them, right?" I wouldn't allow something like that, not ever.

"Caleb wields a powerful gift and yes, the pieces do take a toll but not to his body or soul or anything like you would believe. He will be connected with those he helps Avery. He knows what they have suffered and he lives it with them in that split moment, then takes the majority of their pain away. It's hard to explain it correctly when you don't know from experience what these healing wolves do, but all I know is that he will be okay and that his soul will learn how to guard itself from the same event from recurring again, like all the others of his kind have. So don't fret over him Avery, he'll be fine once his spirit has gotten rid of Levi's grievances."

I didn't understand this all the way and I surely didn't understand how he could just stand there and tell me not to worry, because there's not a chance in hell I would ever not worry about Caleb especially when he's in this kind of state.

I sighed, turning away from Mr. Simons and back towards my mate who didn't look any better. A deep frown was forming between his brows and I used my thumb to caress it away.

"Please be okay," I whispered softly as I rested my forehead against him.

*   *   *

"How is he?" Levi asked, he was scared for Caleb and so was I. I had been looking after him for two days now but there were no signs of changes in his condition. I dropped down on the couch in the living room, finally leaving his side since the day he collapsed, and rubbed my face in exhaustion and frustration.

How long was this thing supposed to last? I've been watching him wither and groan every day, and wiped the sweat off his clammy skin. He was so pale that he was starting to blend into the sheets.

"No change," I grumbled into my hands.

"I'm sorry," Levi whispered quietly. "I didn't know this would happen to him." His confession only made me angrier with Mr. Simons.

"No one but Mr. Simons did," I growled.

The Elder had been hovering over Caleb and I, watching us from a distance since I wouldn't let him get too close to us. Mr. Simons probably thought he was doing the right thing, but to me he put my mate in danger without telling us crucial information. Maybe Caleb wouldn't have cared, but I did and I didn't appreciate his secrecy of something like this. He took the decision out of our hands.

"Alpha Liam told us what Caleb could do under Mr. Simons's permission, I'm sorry Avery, I wasn't thinking about what would happen to him, I just wanted it to go away." He dropped his head, ashamed.

I sighed, reaching over to place a hand on his shoulder.

"And has it?" I asked, both concerned and curious. He looked up at me as if he was trying to concentrate deep down.

"I . . ." He sighed and cocked his head. "I feel like a weight has been lifted, like I can finally breathe again but I can still feel the pain. It's just not as overwhelming as before. I think I can move on now." I was barely noticing the subtle changes from when he first came here until now. His skin had a much healthier glow, he finally bathed, and he was filling out his frame.

"I'm glad it worked for you, no one should have to go through something like you have." He nodded. Then I thought of something.

"What about his bite?" Levi frowned before his face cleared and he reached over and pulled his shirt to the side, his shoulder was clear of any marks.

"It healed like a regular wound would," he told me and I mentally sighed. I wasn't particularly fond of the idea that everyone Caleb helped would carry his mark. I selfishly wanted to be the only one that would bear his mark and no one else.

"That's good then."

"Avery?" I looked away from Levi to see my dad standing in the doorway. "Come here for a minute," he told me as he smiled at Levi.

I gave Levi one last glance before following him down the hall and into his office. He closed the door quietly then turned to me.

"Are you going to explain to me what the hell is going on in my pack house, Avery?" His voice was calm but assertive.

"I really can—" He lifted his hand. His dark eyes hard and catching fire.

"If you say that you can't tell me, I think I might lose it and you'll not like that side of me Avery, so I suggest you let me know what the hell is going on around here." There was no arguing with a tone like that. I didn't know what to do, I couldn't lie to my father but what I was protecting was my mate and even though I was furious with Mr. Simons, he was right in keeping Caleb's identity a secret. Elders were in more danger than regular wolves because they were powerful beings so taking them out made it easier for the hunters to off the rest of us.

"It's complicated dad and like Mr. Simons said, it's dangerous to explain."

"Avery if you think I would do anything to jeopardize your lives then I'm disappointed in you," he said tightly and it made me cringe. No one wants to hear their parents say those words but was it alright to tell him just because I want to make him proud? That's a bit selfish of me.

"It's not that, dad. If this information got out to the wrong people . . ." I trailed off, knowing he understood how important this all was.

"I'm the Alpha of this pack Avery and you will be too, if you ever answer me about that. No one here would ever do something to put you in harm's way, not you or your mate," he told me, his brown eyes serious but gentle as he gazed at me.

I sighed. *Should I? Was it the right thing?* I bit my lip remembering how Caleb was still in bed unconscious. Telling my dad wasn't going to change that.

"Avery." There was a trace of demand in his voice. I closed my eyes for a second.

"Caleb is an Elder," I whispered it but I knew he heard me. I looked up to see his face in complete shock.

"He is?" I nodded.

"This is why Mr. Simons and I haven't told you what's going on" Dad blinked a few times before nodding.

"I get it now but it would have been nice if you had trusted me and told me from the beginning so we could protect him the right way. Still, I understand your guy's reluctance."

He walked around his desk and plopped down onto it.

"And the reason these people are here is because of him right?"

I nodded.

"Levi is Caleb's best friend and he's been having a hard time with the rejection of his mate, so he came here for Caleb's help," I said.

Dad frowned.

"What do you mean?" he asked, folding his hands over the desk before he leaned forward.

"It's Caleb's ability. He can take the pain away from grieving wolves who have lost or have been rejected by their mates," I explained.

Dad's eyes widened.

"Is that even possible?"

"Well, he's healed Levi."

"How does he do something like that? So wait, you just forget about your mate and the pain goes away?" my dad asked, curiously.

"Well, no. You still know who they are to you and it doesn't take all of the pain away. Levi told me he still feels the pain, but it's not as heavy and overwhelming as it was before the bite."

"Bite?" he questioned.

"Yes, all Caleb has to do is bite the wolf where his or her mate would mark them. I don't completely understand all of this myself but once the bite is inflicted, the feelings are transferred to Caleb and he is able to work through them I guess and the wolf can get better." I was focusing on what Mr. Simons had told me as I explained it to the best of my knowledge while my father nodded. I guess he understood it as well.

"Caleb isn't damaged by this?" he asked in concern. I asked the same thing to Mr. Simons and a small smile lifted at the corners of my mouth.

I was about to answer when the door was suddenly opened.

"He will learn to block it out so nothing like this happens again." Mr. Simon's tight voice echoed from the doorway. He stepped in and closed the door behind him, his face was stern and cross as his eyes found mine.

"You've put your own mate at risk Avery, these walls aren't soundproof you know," he growled, as he glared at me then faced my father.

"Why didn't you tell me this earlier Jim? I've protected your secret all this time," he spoke. Jim met him with a serious expression.

"I know that Lucian but I'm able to protect myself if something went wrong. Caleb, however, may not." I never heard Mr. Simons sound so angry. Maybe he did care as much as he said he did.

"Well, don't blame Avery, I pulled the Alpha card on him." Dad shrugged. Mr. Simons shook his head and sighed tiredly.

"Whatever, what's done is done. Let's just keep this between us and no more speaking of it from this day forward," he demanded and we both nodded to him.

"By the way Caleb's up now."

CHAPTER 33

CALEB

I couldn't shake this weird feeling. It was like I missed something. I don't remember why I was lying in bed but Jim told me that I had passed out.

Passed out from what?

I looked around me and noticed I was in Avery's room. Where was he? I needed him. There was this weird feeling that was making me needy to touch him, to make sure that he was with me.

Slowly, I pushed the covers from me and sat at the edge of the bed trying to get my balance back. How long have I been asleep? It seems like forever since I last moved.

"Caleb?" The voice I heard was deep and smooth and I instantly relaxed, basking in its harmonious and deep rich tone. Avery turned the corner in my room and I felt complete. I lifted my arms for him, and he didn't even hesitate. I was then pulled up off my feet into his warm strong arms. I wrapped my arms around his neck and buried my face against it, taking in the earthy pine smell. Since he's been back home his scent has gotten a lot stronger and it was driving me crazy.

"Mmm," I moaned, inhaling more of him.

"Caleb, are you feeling alright?" Avery asked in concern.

I nodded.

"I just feel a bit woozy but it's going away now," I said as I ran my nose up the length of his neck and into his silky hair. He shivered and tighten his hold on me.

"What are you doing?" His voice was husky and strained.

"Inhaling you," I breathed, nibbling his ear.

"Ahh Caleb," he groaned.

"I want to go out," I told him, pulling back a moment to look up at him. He watched me with heavy lidded eyes.

"Like on a date?"

I shrugged. "That could be cool too but I meant running, you, me and our wolves." This caused him to smirk sexily.

"As you wish." He chuckled and leaned down to press a gentle kiss on my lips.

And just like that, the weird feeling of missing something instantly went away. I had everything I needed right here.

* * *

I was shedding my clothes an hour later after telling everyone that I was alright. It warmed my heart to know that they were all worried about me, even people from the pack I didn't know had asked if I was feeling better.

Jim and Avery told me what really happened the other day but when I saw Levi today looking as fresh as a freaking daisy, it didn't matter. If I could bring him happiness to his life again or anyone else's, it was worth it.

"Caleb?" I turned with a smile, recognizing Connor's sweet quiet voice. He may be fourteen but he acted a whole lot younger than that. I blamed it on that b*tch Lynn and her jackass father. They took his childhood away with the things they did to him. Just thinking about it now had my blood boiling.

I turned to him with a warm smile.

"Well if it isn't my son." I winked at him. His cheeks flushed a deep red as he dropped his gaze to the floor.

"Do you mean it?" he whispered but I heard him.

"What?"

"About me b-being your son."

This caused me to pause for a moment.

"Well yeah, if that's okay with you?" I didn't think about it before but what if that made him feel uncomfortable? I wasn't his real father but my wolf and I saw him as ours and always will.

"I'm very protective of you, Connor. From the very beginning you somehow wormed your way into my heart and my wolf sees you as his pup. I know that Avery agrees with that also, you don't have to call us dad or anything like that but—"

"Yes" He cut off my awkward rant. I cocked my head at him in question.

"Yes?"

He nodded.

"I want to call you dad, both you and Avery." His green eyes were sparkling and my heart melted all over again.

"Seriously?" My voice was shaking with a well of emotions, I couldn't hold back. He smiled and rushed towards me to give me a tight hug. I closed my eyes and held him close as I inhaled his scent, hugging him closer.

"I know I could never compare to your real parents but I promise, me and Avery will do our best to make you happy and safe."

"You already do." His muffled voice hummed against my bare chest and I smiled again. I heard the crunch of leaves and looked up at Avery who was in his large wolf form. He trotted up to us and rubbed up against Connor's leg and side, giving an uncharacteristic whine. I laughed.

"See? He feels the same way."

Connor giggled and ducked down to throw his skinny arms around Avery's neck.

"I love you guys," Connor said to us and my chest constricted with those damn emotions again. Avery purred and licked the side of Connor's face. Laughing, Connor shot up and wiped his face with his sleeve. Avery smiled wolfishly and moved to my side, nudging it with his large head. I glared down at him then looked back at Connor.

"We're going to go for a run alright?" I said and he nodded reluctantly. I sighed sadly.

"I wish you can come too." He shook his head, trying to put on a strong façade.

"Don't worry about it, I have a whole year before I can change so go have fun. I'm just going to go and bug Uncle Jim." He smirked.

I grinned, patting him on the shoulder.

"I knew you were special." Avery pawed at my jeans, this time almost making them fall off.

"Hey!" I warned as I spun around to glare at him again.

"I'm going now." Connor snickered before he turned to leave.

"We'll be back later tonight okay?" I called out after his retreating form, as I watched him disappear behind the trees leading up to the house. Once he was gone, I looked down at Avery and unbuttoned the rest of my jeans, pushing them down along with my boxers.

"Alright, let's go," I told him as I folded my clothes and placed them neatly by a tree. Avery walked up to me and licked my chest, sending tingles throughout my body. I stifled a moan and watched him trot off.

Tease!

Growling, I let the wolf take over as I shifted, letting the natural heat of the change submerge my body. A few seconds later I was on four legs and lifted my snout in the air, catching Avery's intoxicating scent. It surrounded everywhere I turned. This was the right time for our wolves to spend some quality time with each other so I let him go; and just like that, my wolf was running at full speed throughout the thick green trees, effectively tracking Avery through his delicious and distinct scent that sent us both in a frenzy.

I spotted his dirty blonde coat a few paces ahead of us and we growled in delight, which in turn only made Avery look back rather wolfishly before he took off once again. His fluffy tail was high, protruding dominance even when he's being chased. The dirt flew underneath my feet as the power my paws pounded closer to get to our mate.

I hadn't had the chance to run since we got here but I realized it was amazingly beautiful. The sun was out and high today, seeping through the top of the shade of the trees like rays of light. The soil was cool under my paws and there was a slight breeze along with the gust of air rushing against our fur as the chase continued. A yelp escaped my mouth from the excitement of the moment. I could hear Avery's laughter in my head as he hauled right ahead of us.

Damn he was fast.

I pushed harder till I felt like I was practically running on air. Everything around me was just a green blur up until we burst from the woods and ran along the beautiful green hills. I had no idea this was in the backyard. There were no trees here, just a large swaying grassy field that swished with our every movement.

Avery was closer to me and I finally caught up to him, taking the opportunity to jump with all I had as it was my only chance at catching him. We then sailed through the air eventually landing on his back. He yelped in surprise and we toppled down the side of the hill together.

If I could laugh I would so with glee as we rolled. I was so glad it was a slight hill too so once we stopped at the bottom, we had no injuries. Quickly, I shifted back on top of him.

"Caught you!" I laughed with a huge grin. He shifted under me and I was rewarded with the feel of his warm smooth skin.

"You did, so what are you going to do about it?" He panted staring up at me with royal blue eyes. My eyes widened at the beauty of them, I would never get used to his brown eyes changing to such a stunning mesmerizing color. My wolf whined in desperation to get at our mate and I felt the same way. I had that overwhelming sensation of wanting and needing his touch again. Avery groaned, reaching up and running his fingers up and down my back.

"I can smell your arousal, Caleb," he growled, his eyes glowing brighter now. I couldn't stop my canines from extending at this, not to mention his pine and earthy smell was wavering off of him, practically sending my body into a feverish state. I was hot and needy.

"Does it smell good?" I teased, leaning my head down to his neck as I took in his own scent.

"Yes," he groaned, sexily.

A strong breeze rushed through the grass, sending it swaying all around us as it hid us with its green earthy arms. I was on my hands and knees over him, staring into his handsome face before I laid myself down on him.

Slowly, I slid down his body, feeling his burning skin while never moving away my gaze from his. I was kneeling between his legs now and I let my lips trace a fiery trail on his delicious hard muscular stomach. I snuck a quick lick at his abs and his stomach tightened beneath me as he let out a loud moan. The sound vibrated through my entire being and soon, I was gone. My wolf was scraping at me for control now but I couldn't relinquish it. I couldn't let him have all the fun.

My hands ran up the side of his toned thighs all the way up to his sides. His body was flinching delectably with every scrap of my claws, my canines doing the same along his stomach. I dipped my tongue into the 'V' indention at his groin, nipping the side of his hip.

"Mmm," he moaned softly, lifting his hips towards me for more attention. I smiled at his desperation and I purred from it all.

I moved my lips passed his impatient member and left wet kisses down his thighs. He was such a beautiful specimen of a male. Nothing but hard and toned muscles, not to the point of revulsion, but instead perfectly lean and fit just like a werewolf of his caliber should be.

I kissed his inner thigh and slowly pushed them apart for my attention. He shivered again.

"You like that don't you?" I asked, huskily. He said nothing and just laid there, letting me do whatever I pleased.

I moved over to the other thigh and purposely licked there, dragging my canines across the skin. I felt his hand brush the top of my hair lovingly. I peered up at him to see him lean up on his elbows and watched me with dark lustful blue glowing eyes. The passion between us skyrocketed with that one glance. Smiling seductively, I moved right between him and took his stiff member into the warm haven of my mouth.

His head was thrown back and the sexiest groan I have ever heard fell from his gasping lips. His reaction only fueled my wanting to please him more and I took him deeper. His hand was gripping my hair painfully tight but I loved it. I loved how he lost himself in the pleasure and guided my head at how he wanted it. I loved how he bucked and withered till he couldn't take it anymore.

I lifted my head, not wanting him to reach a climax just yet. I moved up to his now heaving and sweaty body until I reached those plump lips of his.

"Mmm," I moaned in his mouth as his tongue invaded between my lips. I grabbed his hair in both hands and climbed on him, sitting myself on his lap. I felt him pushed up against me.

"I missed you," he whispered, parting from our kiss for just a moment.

"Three days is a long time," I panted. He kissed all along my jaw and bit down on my ear. I sank my teeth into my bottom lip, forgetting that my canines were extended as I punctured it. The blood dripped from the two holes on my lip and Avery's head snapped back, his nostrils flaring before his eyes now focused on the two ruby droplets. Growling, he raised his head up and ran his tongue across my bottom lip, licking at the wounds and healing it in seconds.

I groaned.

"You taste amazing." He hummed in delight.

Smiling, I kissed him and lifted my hips off him, ready to take him. My wolf was struggling against me, practically begging to take his mate. Avery caught the movement between our hot and passionate kiss, understanding what I wanted.

The moment he was seated inside, I started seeing stars. It had been so long since I felt him like this and I missed every moment of this. His touch was radiating though my skin with those amazing shocks and tingles that happened every time we touched. His large hands gripped my hips and his eyes flashed dangerously before he lifted me up along his length and brought me back down. With that, I was lost in a world of pleasure as I screamed wantonly. He made me make sounds that I didn't even know I could make. The friction between us was magnetic. It grabbed us down further into the heat till things between us became rough and frantic as we raced to fall off that cliff together.

He pushed me on my back and I wrapped my legs around his waist, riding out every thrust as I arched into his chest while my claws scraped down his back. His dirty blonde hair was sticking to his sweaty forehead, while his eyes were glowing like bright blue beacons.

"I-I'm close," I cried in his ear and he growled, feeling it roll in his chest.

"Let go with me then," he moaned, pushing deeper in that right spot and I lost it.

Avery collapsed on top of me, panting warm breaths onto my neck. Our chests were heaving and our bodies were slicked with sweat. The sun had gone down a while ago and the cool night air felt good against our hot skin.

"Is it just me or does this keeps getting better and better?" I laughed exhaustedly. Avery nuzzled against my neck taking in a deep breath.

"It's not just you." After a few minutes, he pulled out and I whimpered at the gesture.

He smiled, brushing back my wet hair.

"I know, I don't want to go either, but didn't you promise Connor that you'd be back tonight?" he asked.

I sighed.

"I did," I said sitting up.

"Right." He leaned over and gave me a gentle kiss.

"Have I ever told you that your accent is coming out the more we stay here?"

Avery laughed. "No, but that's interesting to know. How do you like it?"

I climbed on his lap again.

"Oh, I love it," I purred, running my nose along his jaw line.

"Good." He sighed, running his hand up and down my sides, causing shivers to wrack down my spine.

"Caleb." His tone was questionable and I looked down at him with a frown.

"What is it?" I asked, peering into his anxious brown eyes.

"D-do you like it here?" He was hesitant and I looked around me, taking the gorgeous hills, the tall grass, and the crisp air.

"I think it's beautiful here, I want to go sightseeing. We've been in England for almost a month and haven't gone anywhere," I confessed with a pout. Avery reached out with one hand and caressed a finger over my pouting lips.

"We will I promise, but I have to ask you a serious question."

I nodded.

"Would you like to live here?"

I froze.

Live . . .

In England . . . ?

"What about Portland?" I frowned at him. His hands made a slow trail down my thighs and he started rubbing the outer sides soothingly. I tried to focus on him and not his hot hands that were sending shivers everywhere.

"I-I realized since being here that it kind of gives me another chance to make things right. I am supposed to be Alpha. My father and a lot of the members of the pack want me to be. And since I've been here, my wolf has been persistent in taking the position. He wants you to be by his side . . . we both do."

I looked at him speechless.

Do I want to make a home here? I won't lie, the thought of leaving my sister all the way on the other side of the world was scary since we've never been this far apart before. But on the other hand, I was jumping at the opportunity. If Avery wanted to stay, I was all for it and my wolf agreed wholeheartedly.

But there was one thing I couldn't overlook.

"Avery, what about Aiden?" This caused him to look at me sorrowfully.

"I can't anymore, Caleb," he whispered and I frowned. He lowered his head in a shameful manner and I lifted his chin up with my finger, peering deep into his eyes.

"What does that mean" I asked softly. This was a sore subject, I could tell. He sighed.

"It's hurting you." I was about to deny it but he shook his head and continued. "Yes, it does and I can see it in your eyes every time his name is even mentioned and I can't do that to you. I have claimed you as my mate, my true mate and as such I will be damned if I purposely keep hurting you. So I've come to the decision to close myself off from him and my wolf agrees." He was assertive with his words. I shook my head.

"You can't live without Aiden, that's what we've all heard. Wanderers die without their purpose, isn't that the reason you are connected with him? What would happen if you cut off that connection?" I was worried. If that happened and I lose him, then what was the point of all this?

"No, Caleb you are my purpose, you're my reason now, not Aiden. Yes I care for him but I care for you much more. You can give me something he never can, a true connection with a mate, the beauty of living for another person wholeheartedly, and never letting go. True love."

I blinked back the burning tears in my eyes.

Damn him, he was going to make me cry, I hate crying.

"You're serious about this?" I asked shakily.

He smiled, cupping my face.

"Absolutely, I would give you anything Caleb, and that means all of me, not just pieces, just as I would ask of you and like you already have."

I sobbed, unable to hold it in and threw my arms around his neck.

"I love you," I whispered in his ear. "And yes I want to stay if you do." He chuckled and held me closer to him.

"Thank you."

Our mouth met passionately once more before we stood up.

"Can we visit Scotland? I've always wanted to go there!" I asked randomly, facing his tall frame. He looked down at me and smiled.

"That will be next on our list right after our tour of England," he told me and I nodded in delight.

So I guess this was our new home and you know what? I loved it.

"So have you ever tried haggis?" he asked, chuckling.

CHAPTER 34

CALEB

Avery was true to his word and took me, Levi, Mr. Blackman, Jim, and Connor all out sightseeing. The more I saw the spots he took us to, the more I fell in love with the place. We saw all the old buildings, the weird trolley bus things, and that huge clock tower named Big Ben or something like that. Avery told me the name like a hundred times but I keep forgetting through all the excitement. Whatever, sue me. Oh and let's not forget that I love the accents around here, whenever I see Avery talk to some random person, I always made him use it.

This was fun.

Connor was having the time of his life. His bright green eyes practically took up half his face as he looked at everything around him. I told him that we might be staying here for good, but if he wanted, he could go back with Levi and Marten. He of course, said no and demanded that he stay with Avery and I and who could ignore such a request? Upon hearing it, I pulled him into a huge hug and thanked him for being so cool with the idea.

"Hey, can we go in a pub?" I asked, turning towards the twentieth bar I've seen today. "I've never been in a pub before and I want to get that authentic feel." I smiled up at Avery.

He shook his head in amusement.

'I don't mind," he told me.

"Is Connor even allowed in one?" Levi asked. I shrugged.

"Oh come on, it's not like I'm going to buy him a beer or anything. Let's just go, they have to have water or orange juice or something." I noticed Connor stick his tongue out in disgust.

"Orange juice is nasty," he whined. I laughed, throwing an arm over his shoulder to pull him close.

"Then a beer it is," I joked and we all laughed.

We walked in and the place was buzzing with laughter, along with the clinking of drinks and blaring music. It was very homey in here with dark wood on pretty much everything. It was late in the day so the pub was starting to get a little crowded.

Avery and Jim asked us what we wanted, but I didn't know anything about alcohol so I let Avery decide while he told us to get a booth. Connor slid in first while Levi and his dad took the seat right in front of us. Levi had a smile on his face as he looked around, nodding his head to the fast pace song that was playing. I looked over at Mr. Blackman and he had the same tired and empty expression on his face that he always had.

I wanted to help him too. If it would make him feel better I would gladly help him just as I did his son. I opened my mouth to ask if he wanted that but Avery and Jim came back. Avery placed a tall glass of an orange-amber colored concoction right in front of me and a smaller glass of something bubbly towards Connor's smiling form. I frowned at him and he smiled before he sat beside me.

"Relax its apple cider," he told me and I sighed before I looked at my daunting glass.

"What is this?" I asked, moving the glass around in a circle skeptically as I glared at the slice of orange on the side. He laughed.

"Just try it," he said, pushing the glass towards me.

"I don't know . . ." I hesitated.

"You wanted to come in so drink the damn thing." Levi snickered at me as he sipped his beer. Glaring at him, I picked the cold glass and pressed it to my lips, giving Avery one more glance before I took a small sip. The taste hit my tongue and I cringed a bit before I relaxed. It wasn't all that bad, there was a distinct taste of orange and it was slightly sweeter than any beer I had before. I took another much larger sip and gave Avery an approving look.

"Oh, I guess we have a winner," Jim teased. I set the glass down licking my lips.

"What is it?"

"A blue moon," Avery answered. "I thought you would know that, what with the joke you made with my mom." He laughed while I blushed.

"Well, I've never tasted one before, I just knew there was a beer out there called blue moon." I ducked my head a bit and picked the beer back up to my embarrassment. Avery brushed my hair back behind my ear, chuckling.

"You're adorable."

"Stop," I whined, swatting his hand away. The table laughed and I turned my head away from them only to look over at Connor.

"How's your cider?" I asked, ignoring the *'awws'* they were cooing to tease me.

"It's good, do you want some?" He offered as I smiled and shook my head.

"No, I'm good."

"So you plan on staying, I see." I suddenly heard Jim say and I turned my attention back to the others.

"Yes, they want me here. They all expect me to be their Alpha," Avery answered. Jim nodded but his expression was serious.

"But do you want to be?" The table became quiet as we waited for his answer. When Avery inclined his head, I sighed in relief.

"Yes, it's always been my duty to take over the Sky Raven Pack. I can't deny the Alpha blood running through my veins. My wolf was meant to reign here and I can't stop the pull this place has on me. This is home, Mr. Simons."

Jim smiled, nodding his head in approval.

"Now the only person you need to prove this to is a certain brother of yours isn't it?" He chuckled, lifting his glass to his mouth.

Avery groaned. "Ugh, don't even remind me." He sighed in distress.

We stayed in the pub for a few more hours, talking about anything and everything we could. One of the nice workers even had Connor behind the bar as he poured drinks for people from the taps while teaching him how to mix drinks. He was having fun and a few of the customers were teasing and encouraging him. We were all enjoying ourselves including Mr. Blackman who let loose a bit. Levi and I were even dancing to the folk music that played through the pub, making fools of ourselves as we jumped around together. We even got some random girls to come and dance with us. During which, I'd occasionally glance over to Avery's direction, who would shake his head but never drop his smile. I've never seen him smile so much in all the time I knew him. I think coming here was a good thing for him.

After who knows how many blue moons and other different kinds of drinks, I was ready to go back to the pack house. It was around ten and I had to be the responsible parent so I took Connor from his job behind the bar.

"We have to go home now," I told him. Connor whined, a little reluctant to leave.

"Next time Connor," the bartender/co-manager said to him with a kind smile. "The kid is a natural," he told me. I smiled and rubbed the top of Connor's hair.

"Who would have thought?" I joked.

"Bye!" a few of the people at the bar said to Connor as we left. He waved back at them and the rest of us shook our heads.

We got a cab all the way out of London and back towards the pack house. We were halfway there when we told the cab driver that he could stop here and gave him his fare. We didn't want him seeing anything we couldn't explain. I was holding Avery's hand and watched Connor skip and run talking excitedly about Darren the bartender/manager guy and how cool he was to let him handle the taps.

The night air was still tonight and the stars were out and bright above us. I tightened my hand in Avery's hold and he smiled down at me. Jim was talking with Levi and Mr. Blackman in low tones. Connor was still jumping around, hyper from all the cider Darren let him have. Sighing, I let go of Avery's hand and went after my new off-the-wall son. I wonder if I can get adoptive papers for him, I should ask Jim about that later.

"Connor," I said sternly but he wasn't listening and I was practically chasing him around. I had to calm him down soon so he could go to sleep tonight. He was still sneaking in mine and Avery's room and I didn't want him all crazy when I'm trying to sleep. Trust me, I'm a grouch when I'm tired. Growling, I finally caught him by the shoulders.

"You are way too hyper." I laughed. He was looking up at me with wide innocent eyes.

"I love it here," he said to me and I smiled.

"I know, me too." I looked up to the rest of the group who were finally catching up to us when I heard a weird sound. It made a swooshing sound like a whistle and I snapped my head to the side as my eyes widened in horror. I quickly pushed Connor roughly to the ground, all while moving my body to cover him at the same time. I felt the sting hit my shoulder, and I let out a scream as the burn started.

I looked down at Connor's surprised face as he stared up at me as he lay sprawled out on the ground.

"Caleb!" Avery screamed, running up to me with Jim beside him as I dropped to my knees. The pain in my shoulder was like hot coals seeping through my veins and it was throbbing with white-hot aches. Again the sound came and I turned in fear, waiting for the pain to come back but it never came. Jim stood in front of my cowering figure, stopping the thing in midair before it dropped harmlessly to the ground. I didn't get a chance to look at it when he cursed harshly.

"Shi*t!" He turned his head sharply towards us.

"Hunters!" That one word was like a splash of ice-cold water in my blood.

I ignored the pain in my shoulder and stood up with Avery's help.

"Caleb, are you okay?" he asked, worry etched deep in his voice. I didn't answer and instead looked over at Levi and Marten.

"Get Connor and go!" I demanded. Levi frowned but took one look at the serious expression on my face.

"What about you?" Levi asked.

"Doesn't matter just get him out!" I growled and reached behind my back to tear the object away from my shoulder.

"Caleb . . ." Avery warned. I whimpered as the weapon tore my skin and blood began to seep down my back. I held the thing up and realized it was a silver arrow. The head was silver with spikes sticking out around it. Shakily, I dropped the offensive thing to the ground.

I peered up and saw Levi was still standing there while Connor was still on the floor. I growled, pulling Connor up roughly by his arm, making him yelp and pushed him in Levi's chest.

"What the hell are you still doing here? Go!" I snarled, putting as much authority in my tone as possible.

"Go warn Alpha Chandler."

Levi hesitated for a moment but when we heard the gun fire start, it caused him to jump and shift almost instantaneously, effectively scooping Connor on to his back with a flick of his large wolf head. His father soon followed after him and they ran as fast as possible.

"Go with them!" Avery growled at me as we hit the floor, ducking ourselves to prevent from being shot at.

"He's right," Jim agreed, keeping his eyes on the trees as he put up some kind of force field around us to protect us from being hit again.

"No, I'm not leaving you!" I snarled to Avery then looked at Jim.

The blaring of guns were getting closer and the ringing continued deafeningly in our ears.

"I can't hold them off forever!" Jim growled through clenched teeth. I looked all around us and slowly came to the conclusion that we were being surrounded. Men in black camouflage outfits were pouring out of the trees at an alarming rate, pointing several large guns and handguns straight at us. They all were dressed up in military gear with bulletproof jackets, cargo pants, and several handheld weapons strapped to each leg with an army knife in the slots, along with a belt full of bullet clips, night vision goggles and army boots.

"Well, what do we have here boys?" a man called out in a rather amused tone. I looked over to a rather large man. "Three little wolves that never made it to grandma's house," he chuckled, causing a chorus of snickers and malicious laughter to erupt.

Avery let out a petrifying chilling growl that had the hairs on my neck stand up on end. I felt my wolf cower from it.

"Guessin' we have a lively one here, don't we?" the man said again and I quickly noticed that it had an American southern accent. The huge guy took a step closer and Avery roared ferociously, stepping right in front of me. I was shaking now as the man didn't even flinch and just cocked his gun, pointing it straight at Avery's head that was a foot away from him. The man's lips were set in an angry sneer.

"You think I'm scared of you mutt?" he spat. I could see Avery's body was shaking dangerously close to shifting.

"You should be," he growled deeply.

"Avery," Jim warned, but he wasn't listening.

"Well, well, well, we got ourselves an Alpha, men. What are the chances?" He chuckled again, holding his gun steady and firm, completely fearless. I could tell these guys were legit and had done the complete training and everything.

"Look at those eyes would ya?" he teased.

"Freaky if you ask me," one man said.

"I haven't killed many Alphas in my day. You guys are pretty well protected by all those mangy slaves of yours." The guy continued.

"They're not slaves!" Avery snarled.

The man started laughing.

"I think someone's mad," he taunted. "That's the problem with you *wolves*, you have no restraint and kill whenever you want." His voice dripping in disgust.

"What are you talking about? We haven't killed anyone!" I exclaimed, jumping to my feet but staggered a bit from the loss of blood that was still pouring from my wound.

"Oh is that so?" He smiled, shaking his head. "Your kind is nothing but blood thirsty animals." The edge of his lip twitched slightly at this.

"You're wrong!" I yelled.

"Caleb, stop!" Avery boomed with an assertive tone in his voice and I shut my mouth quickly and shrank back.

"Looks like he's got his dogs on a tight leash!" someone shouted. Avery growled and jerked towards the owner of the voice but the man in front of us yelled.

"Hey! You stay your furry ass right where you are, you got me?!" he barked, jerking his gun threateningly. I whimpered, rushing to Avery's side as he wrapped a protective arm around my shoulder.

"Now unless you want to die, I suggest you get cooperative real fast. Bradley, Finn, tie them up," he ordered and two men came out of the circle.

Avery crouched, pushing me behind him as he and Jim now stood back-to-back.

"You're not taking us anywhere," he growled.

The man laughed.

"Oh but we are, there's no way you think you're getting out of this, son."

The men were walking slowly towards us like we were feral animals ready to attack and at this moment, they were right to act this way. My wolf was at the surface, ready to rip anyone who thought they could touch us and our mate. I glared at the man who was focused on me and I bared my elongated canines at him, daring him to come closer.

"Come here pup, let's play," said the guy who was staring at me through his goggles.

And just like that. All hell broke loose.

I couldn't hold my wolf back at the disrespectful taunting and instantly shifted midair, my claws going straight for his throat. We fell to the ground and wrestled. He was holding up pretty well considering I was a huge hundred and eighty pound wolf. Throughout the struggle, I could hear the others snarl and growl around me, along with the snapping of teeth and the grunts of men. I knew the others around us weren't shooting because their comrades could get hit in the cross fire. The man wrapped an arm around my neck tightly and I began twisting and rolling, putting up a hard fight. I snapped my teeth in his face and he jerked his head back quickly, laughing at how close I was at getting him.

Two arms came around my lower half and I looked down at another guy and quickly kicked him hard causing him to fly into a tree.

"Sh*t!" the guy holding my neck cursed. I raked my claw against his chest but got nowhere with the vest he was wearing. Turning my head, I noticed his other arm was open and I immediately clamped my teeth down on it where I was instantly rewarded with his loud screams of pain. His hold loosened and I ducked out quick, going straight for the kill when I felt the sting of something sharp at my side and I yelped. I spun around fast towards the bastard behind me, charging at him in fury when I suddenly staggered dizzily.

"Yeah, b*tch you didn't like that, did you?" the guy growled triumphantly, taking a hand gun from his boot as he pointed it at me and fired.

"*Caleb!*" a voice not my own screamed inside my head before I felt the pain hit me and I collapsed in darkness.

CHAPTER 35

AVERY

I watched Caleb hit the ground hard like deadweight. His body shifted back to his bare human form and my whole body caught fire. A red tint filled my sharp vision and my wolf howled vengeance through the night air. I wasn't even aware of my actions. My only thought was to get to my mate.

Men were flying towards me as I knocked them away with a swipe of my paw or butted them with my head. I caught someone's arm between my teeth and immediately rewarded then with a snap of my powerful jaw, causing them to scream and howl in agonizing pain.

"Put him down goddammit!" The man with the familiar southern accent yelled.

They didn't know who the hell they were messing with. They really thought that they could just come here and take us or kill us without a damn fight? Well they thought wrong. They messed up the moment they attacked my mate.

I was going to kill them all.

I felt the weight of a body jump on my back and I growled, thrashing everything in my way until he was finally thrown off.

"Caleb!" I called in my mind but all I got was silence. This caused me to move faster. I needed to be with him. There was a

pinch on my side but I ignored it as I dodged all the hands that were trying to grab me.

"Jim!" I yelled.

"Kind of busy here, Avery!" he answered back, sounding overwhelmed and exhausted. I couldn't chance it by looking at him as I watched two guys start to drag Caleb towards the woods. I roared furiously, knocking my large body into them. I tackled one of them down to the ground, putting all my weight on to his chest, crushing it. He gasped and screamed as I spun around, baring my teeth at the other man who now dropped Caleb roughly to the ground.

I stalked closer to him as he fumbled for something in his back pocket. I didn't give him time to take whatever it was he was looking for and I swiped heavily at his head, knocking him out as he flew into a tree. I ran to Caleb, nudging him with my nose. I couldn't help the whine pouring out of me in fear for my motionless and silent mate.

"Caleb?"

No response.

"Well it looks like someone has a soft spot for the mutt," the same familiar voice taunted and I snapped my head up, glaring at the man who seemed to be the one in charge here. He had his gun pointed to me and I stood over Caleb's body, crouching protectively as I growled lowly at the bastard. I shifted my eyes towards Jim who was putting up one hell of a fight and I watched the men in black go flying through the air as he charged to get to us.

"Go!" I ordered him. *"Go get help!"*

He growled.

"I'm not leaving you to these animals!" he snapped. He was getting closer, but out of nowhere, an arrow hit him knocking him over. He yelped and I watched his sides heave as he panted hard.

"Jim!" I screamed.

"See? You're no match for us, so quit being difficult and let's get this over with shall we?" the man said. I quickly glared back at him and he fired the gun.

Pain shot through me and the last thing I thought of before everything went blank was if this is how it ends, then at least I'll be with Caleb.

* * *

Groaning, I rolled on my side and could sense that it was dark and damp. A painful chill lingered in my bones from the hard cement ground I laid on. I grunted as I struggled in a sitting position.

My eyes were slowly adjusting to a dingy cellar room with just one door which appeared to be made of silver. There was no bed and no sink either, just four dirty grey brick walls. I didn't know how I got here but I had a major headache. I glanced down and noticed that my clothes had been changed to scratchy white scrubs while my shoes were gone.

The only thing I could smell was the musty and moldy air and nothing else. My wolf was starting to pace and whine anxiously.

Then the memories of everything that happened came flooding back.

The hunters . . . the guns . . .

Caleb!

I shot to my feet but staggered as the room began to spin, making me lean against the wall to steady my balance.

"F*ck," I moaned, holding my head and staggering forward.

"Mate!" I heard my wolf's cry ring in my head. I was breathing hard as I remembered watching Caleb crumple to the ground, so still and lifeless.

No! No he couldn't be dead! I raced towards the door then started to bang on it, ignoring the burns it caused on my skin.

He had to be alive, I wouldn't accept anything otherwise. I couldn't even think straight, every thought was on Caleb, and whether or not if he was dead or alive. A cry left my lips as I slid down the door to my knees.

"He can't," I whispered weakly.

Right there on that filthy floor, I broke. I was unable to stop the unforgiving familiar emptiness and loneliness from seeping into my cold body. Caleb brought me back, he helped me live for the first time in my life, and just like that he was yanked right out of it. No warning, he was just gone.

I lost my mate yet again and was left to live with the loss of both the people who could have made something out of me. No, Caleb did make something out of me. He made me see I could love and gave me a second chance.

With that thought I lost control.

"Ahh!" I roared, my body began to shake as my blood boiled with rage. My senses heightened to its peak.

They took my life when they took my mate from me. They stole everything from me and I swear they will pay. They'll all pay with their pathetic murderous lives.

I got to my feet, seeing nothing but red and kicked the door with my bare feet. The sound reverberated off the stone walls of my prison. I kicked again, nothing on this earth would stop my vengeance from tearing this place apart.

I growled. The sound was more animal than man as I raised my foot again, gratified with the dent that gradually grew with every forceful kick. I knew that if I did make it out of this door that I would do whatever it takes to make them pay. I might not survive but what else did I have to live for?

The silver door was now bent inward and the hinges were breaking off.

"Hey!" I heard someone yell on the other side as they came running towards my door. "What the hell?!" they exclaimed and the raging fire in me grew to new heights with just the sound of their disgusting voices.

I roared again, kicking harder than I had before and watched as the door caved in and flew out before it collided straight into the guard from the other side, slamming him into the wall right before it fell with the unconscious man under it. I was heaving and panting with anger and adrenaline as I walked out.

I looked down the hall. It was poorly lit with flickering fluorescent lighting on the ceiling. There was only one way out, so I marched down the hall towards the door, where not even two steps away, the door came flying open and two hunters yelled as they ran towards me.

I glared, taking the closest man around the neck and snapped it with ease. I dropped him and ducked as the other charged at me, swinging a metal bar. My shoulder slammed into the guy's stomach and he huffed out a gust of air.

I straightened my form, my hand gripping his throat tightly.

"Where is my pack?" I growled in his face, my canines on full display. I wouldn't leave my mate in the hands of these monsters alive or . . . dead, and neither would I leave Jim here. I glared at the guard and could see the fear in his eyes. He couldn't have been more than Caleb's age maybe even younger.

"I don't know—"

I snarled loudly, squeezing my hand tighter as he choked and gasped for air.

"Don't feed me that 'I don't know' bullsh*t! Either you give me what I want or I snap your weak little worthless neck." His eyes widened and he began to struggle, kicking his legs in desperation.

"Please, please don't. I'll tell you what you want just please." I sighed and stepped back, letting him fall to the floor. He gripped his neck, his body shaking as he gave loud wracking coughs. I growled impatiently and stepped towards him and he flinched.

"No, I'll tell you!" the boy cried before he huddled into the wall. "They brought two other bodies in last night and put them in the lab."

"Lab?!" I snapped.

"It's where they place the wolves with the freaky powers in. We were informed that the two they brought in were Elder wolves."

Jim.

"What do they do to them?" The boy didn't answer and instead refused to look at me as he kept his gaze to the floor. I growled furiously and balled the front of his shirt in my fist and yanked him off his feet.

"Ahh!" he screamed, pathetically slapping at my hand.

"Tell me!"

"They experiment on them!"

I frowned and glared at him in disgust.

"Like some sort of lab rat," I stated with a snarl. He looked ashamed but nodded reluctantly.

I know I shouldn't but I had to ask.

"Were they both alive when they were brought in?"

He peered up at me with terrified and confused brown eyes.

"Yes, they would be of no use to us if they were dead."

And with that realization, my focus changed from getting revenge to getting Caleb out of this hellhole alive. My rage was restored anew and I shook the boy hard.

"Where are they being kept? Give me the directions," I demanded.

"D-downstairs in t-the b-basement," he stuttered. With that I punched him hard in the face, knocking him out cold and threw him to the floor before I raced out the door. My Caleb was alive and was depending on me to get him out and I will, no matter what it takes.

I was running down long hallways, turning countless corner after corner when I realized that I was in an abandoned psychiatric hospital with many newly installed silver doors. I was afraid to look in any of them, worried that there were more captives like me behind each door so I focused on just getting Jim and Caleb out for now. That was my top priority.

I turned another corner and ran into the fifth hunter who turned towards me in surprise. I rushed towards him immediately before he could call anyone for help. Lengthening my claws, I quickly slashed him across the throat and moved on, not sparing a second glance.

I tiptoed to the next corner this time, peeking around to see two men standing guard right in front of a door where I instantly knew something important was behind it. Taking a deep breath, I charged at them, they were much more experienced than the others I have already killed.

One drew his gun and pointed it at me but was too slow and I was on him in a flash. I knocked his wrist up, kneeing him in the stomach where he grunted and bent over, giving me full view of the other hunter who was also pointing his gun at me.

I spun quickly into the groaning guard just in time as the other fired, the bullet hitting his comrade who I was using for a shield. The hunter's scream echoed down the hall along with the boom of the gun. I elbowed the guard away from me, causing him to collapse to the ground but not before I snatched his gun away from his hand and swiftly aimed it at the one still standing, shooting him straight between the eyes without hesitation.

It was then that I silently thanked the Spirits for all the different types of training I had to put myself through over the years on my travels.

I didn't waste time as I yanked the door open but came up short as I entered into the room.

"Oh Avery, we've been expecting you."

I was so stunned that I didn't notice a man was standing at the door behind me, but once it closed, he rushed out and slammed his fist hard into the side of my face. The gun flew from my hand and I dropped to the ground with a groan. I then felt a swift kick hit my side, and I was sure I gained a few broken ribs.

"Stop!" a voice I so longed to hear screamed and the continuous assault to my side ceased. I was rolled over to my back and as I lay there, and stared up at the one person who I least expected to be here, but then again, it made perfect sense.

With a painful whisper I forced out her name.

"Lynn."

"Avery," she answered smugly. "Well don't you look like sh*t?"

CHAPTER 36

CALEB

I woke up to a blinding light glaring down at me. With a groan, I tried to roll away from it but I was stuck or should I say strapped to a cold metal table. My vision was adjusting to my new environment and I looked down at my arms to see them strapped down to the table along with my legs.

A whimper left my lips at the terror of not knowing where the hell I was or what was happening hit me. Snapping my head from side to side, I managed to make out the numerous eerie needles and various disturbing tools on the table beside me. There were cabinets filled with vials and bottles full of drugs that I wasn't familiar with. I felt like I was in some kind of slasher movie.

How did I get here? The memory of a gun pointing in my face brought it all back along with the hunters, the fight, and then darkness.

The hysterics were hitting me hard at this moment. I was being held by hunters! And with that scary thought, I started to fight against the bindings, hoping that in some way I was strong enough to break them but the more I struggled, the worse the pain in my shoulder got, and my wrists were starting to burn.

"Tsk, tsk, tsk, I wouldn't do that." A stranger came through the silver door. The voice belonged to a man in a white lab coat and latex gloves who quickly came into view. Just the sight of him made me petrified.

"So, you're an Elder huh? You don't look like much," he muttered.

How did he know that?

I watched him walk to the table with all the instruments.

"No!" I cried, jerking against the restraints again. The man laughed.

"The more you struggle the more it'll hurt," he said as he walked towards me with a large intimidating looking needle.

"The straps have silver dust on it, so the more you yank on them, the quicker the silver seeps into your bloodstream. I hear silver is quite deadly to a werewolf." He snickered, holding the needle at eye level. Liquid sprayed from the tip, my heart was beating so fast that it was practically threatening to jump from my chest.

"Please," I begged. He stood over me unfazed.

"Sorry pup but orders are orders. I'm going to have to put you down but just not yet." And with that, he immediately stabbed me with the needle, causing a painful burning sensation to spread all throughout my entire body as I quickly passed out.

* * *

"Caleb?" My hearing was going in and out, but I heard the muffled whisper of my name.

"Caleb?" This time it was frantic. "Come on son, answer me!"

Groaning, I opened my eyes but everything was still dark. I was about to freak out but then I felt a piece of cloth tied over my eyes. I reached up to take it off but it shocked and burned me, making me instantly withdraw with a yelp.

"Caleb, are you alright?!" I recognized Jim's voice.

"Jim?" I asked, still disorientated.

"Yes it's me. How are you doing? How do you feel?" he asked.

I tried to sit up but the pain in my body was still burning.

"I'm burning all over and I'm tired," I told him, my voice was weak.

"It's the injections, it's laced with silver. It makes the shifting process too painful to endure."

"Where are you?" I cried, needing reassurance.

"Right beside you, here take my hand." I reached out blindly and swiped through the air.

"I can't find you!" I cried hysterically.

"Caleb just try and calm down. Move to the very end of the bars on your right." I took deep breaths and slowly touched every inch I could to the metal floor until I reached the bars. I then pushed my hands through them and soon felt his warm hand through the bars. I grasped it tightly, afraid to let go.

"There, we'll be okay," he told me but I could hear the doubt in his voice.

"Don't lie to me right now Jim. You know damn well that we're not going to make it out of here!"

"I'm trying to be positive here, Caleb." He sighed.

"There is nothing to be positive about!" I snapped. He said nothing else but I was happy he never let my hand go.

What was going to happen to us? Were we going to die in here?

Then I thought of Avery.

Oh no.

"Avery!" I exclaimed shooting to my feet but all I got was a bump on the head.

"What the hell?!" I exclaimed, holding my head with a hiss.

"We're being caged like animals," Jim growled. I could hear the anger in his tone.

"Yes you are, now come." A new voice made me jump in fright. How did I not hear him come in? The sound of a squeaky door opening caused me to turn towards its direction where two large hands grabbed me, roughly pulling me out of the cage and I yelped in surprise.

"No, leave him alone!" Jim exclaimed, banging against the bars.

"Oh shut up!" the voice snapped as he dragged my thrashing and squirming body across the floor.

"Jim!" I screamed, panic setting in but the guy just became more aggressive.

"Let him go damn it!" Jim yelled with a deep authoritative voice, one that could rival any Alpha as the cages around him raddled loudly.

"Hey Laura, shut him up!" the guy who was manhandling me said.

"Yes sir." Came a woman's voice.

"Get off me!" I yelled at my captor but all he did was grab me by the waist and threw me over his shoulder aggressively, knocking the air out of me. The door closed behind us and he walked down a hallway, the sounds of his shoes were loud and reverberating off the walls.

"We haven't done anything to you people, why are you doing this to us?" I felt the burning sensation in my throat slowly build up, a sign that I was about to cry.

"You're nothing but vermin who need to be exterminated. That is what we hunters do, we take out that which is plaguing our world with its unnatural repulsion. Your kind disgusts me. You're all just a bunch of mindless animals who take what you want and kill when the mood strikes."

I growled and paused in my struggle.

"I don't know who gave you this notion but it's not true. Wolves and humans are not that much different from each other. Both of our species have good and bad people. Yeah, we're able to change into something that you can't but we don't kill just for the hell of it. You are the ones who kill like mindless animals and hunt my kind down!"

"I've seen you wolves in action, too many of my friends have been killed because of you. I hate you all and I'll be glad to destroy every single one of you and put a stop to you from breeding those disgusting abominations." His voice was hard, sending shivers to climb up my spine.

The man came to a stop and opened a door. Once he finished, he unceremoniously threw me down to the floor and I grunted from the force of the landing.

"Here he is, boss," the man said.

"Excellent." My body froze. I knew that southern accent. "You can go," he told the guy.

Minutes ticked by before I was yanked to my feet and the blindfold was ripped off, causing me to hiss as it scraped my skin.

"You have a couple of guests here to see you," he told me as I blinked to clear my vision.

"What the hell are you talking about?!" I growled through clenched teeth as I finally saw his face without the night vision goggles.

He had cold black eyes and a short brown beard. His hair was cut and shaved at the sides and he looked to be in his forties.

"You apparently took something of theirs," he said with an amused smile and turned me around to face the two people I thought and hoped to never see again.

"If it isn't my sweet, sweet mate," Lynn purred as she walked up to me. I backed away with a horrified expression but was only pushed forward by the hunter.

"You did all this?" I asked, dumbfounded.

"No one says no to me Caleb, and you surely don't take what's mine. So daddy and I called these nice hunters to capture you." I couldn't believe it. She had put everyone and myself in danger with hunters because I rejected her?

"I'm sorry that you're a slut. Is that really my fault though?"

She laughed lightly as she came to stand in front of me.

"If I recall correctly, you were in bed with that guy . . . oh what's his name . . . ah, Avery every night doing God knows what."

I glared at her.

"You both are disgusting," she hissed in my face.

"I made it pretty clear that I didn't want you and you got butthurt over it?" I retorted. Her eyes flashed dangerously and she smacked me, scraping her claws across my cheek as she did so. My head snapped to the side and I hissed, cupping my burning cheek.

"You're a weak pathetic little mutt and I wouldn't want you for my mate, anyway," she growled.

I laughed.

"Then why go through all this trouble?" I taunted. She glared again and turned her head to look at something.

"Dad doesn't take kindly to threats and having his things taken from him." I shifted my gaze to the corner of the room by the door to see Alpha Collin standing tall and frightening. His eyes were a blazing grey as he watched me. I gulped before snapping my head back to Lynn.

"Connor is NOT a possession. He is not a thing. He is a living breathing being who deserves so much better than a couple of relatives who beat and humiliate him," I growled in her face. Her eyes widened slightly as she backed away a step, but composed herself quickly before she forced a smile.

"Oh does someone have a soft spot for my little cousin?" she said in a mocking baby voice. I jerked towards her, snapping my teeth in her face and she fell back on her ass in surprise.

"Enough!" the Alpha boomed and Lynn scrambled up to her feet, her cheeks flaming with embarrassment.

"So what are you going to do? Kill me now?" They both turned to me.

"I thought that was pretty clear with the hunters." Lynn rolled her eyes in annoyance.

"Well then what the hell are you waiting for?" I spat.

Just then a commotion came from the other side of the door and we all jerked our attention towards the grunts and shouts before a loud bang of a gun echoed, causing us all to flinch. Another barrel of sounds ensued, just as the door swung open, revealing my avenging angel with fiery blue eyes who stood there proud and tall.

My beautiful mate.

My Avery.

His eyes swept over us all as he stopped short in his tracks.

"Oh Avery, we've been expecting you," Lynn purred.

I didn't even get to call him before the door slammed shut behind as Alpha Collin was immediately on him.

I watched in horror as my mate fell to the ground and grunted with every kick the man sent to his side. Avery was curling into himself, trying to stop the assault, but the Alpha wouldn't back off and I shrieked for him to stop. The hunter held me to him tightly so I couldn't move at all.

"Stop!" I wailed at the top of my lungs.

Alpha Collin did stop but not before rolling him over roughly with his foot. Lynn walked over to stand over him. I watched Avery stare up at her in shock.

"Lynn," he whispered in a raspy strained voice.

"Avery, well don't you look like sh*t?" She cackled. I glared at her with such hatred that it could have easily sent her six feet under.

"It was you who called the hunters." Avery's voice rang with realization.

The man holding me sighed.

"Yes, yes, we've been over this boy, now how the hell did you escape my cellar?" he demanded. Avery struggled to his feet where Alpha Collin had him pushed up against the door in seconds, trapping him by the neck with his forearm.

"It wasn't so hard, I just kicked the door in." He snickered, blood dripping from his mouth and I cried in fear.

"Avery," I whimpered, desperately wanting to hold him against me. His glowing gaze met mine and softened.

"Caleb, are you alright?" The concern etched deep in his tone made my mouth form into a small smile.

"Yes."

He nodded.

"Aww well isn't that cute? The two homos are worried about one another," Collin taunted nastily. Avery glared up at him with so much animosity that I flinched.

"I'm going to tear your throat out," he spoke a matter-of-factly through clenched teeth. His eyes glowing an angry royal blue. His teeth bared and were sharp and dangerous. Collin laughed, pushing his arm harder against his neck.

"I'd like to see you try." He chuckled. "But if you don't mind I'm going to take my nephew back now. Right after I finish the two of you off." And with that he brought back his arm in a fast motion and jammed his now extended claws into Avery's stomach. I watched in wide-eyed terror at the scene.

"No!" I exclaimed, thrashing crazily against the hunter behind me. Avery was bent over as he coughed up a puddle of blood on to the floor and on the white scrubs he was in. Alpha Collin gripped the back of his neck and threw him across the room, causing Avery's body to slam into the wall which was hard enough to make the surface dent in and cause plaster to sprinkle in the air around him.

Unable to take it anymore, I grabbed the hunter's arm and thrusted it towards my face and bit down hard. A rush of blood filled my mouth as he screamed and let go. I then charged towards Collin with my whole body causing us to both collide into the wall and chair on the opposite side of the room.

The chair splintered with our combined weight as we crashed into the wall. I hissed as my head slammed into it, but I composed myself quickly, grabbing Collin by the shirt as I climbed onto him, sending punch after punch to his ugly face.

"Get off him!" Lynn's annoying voice yelled behind me but I didn't stop. He hurt my mate and I would kill anyone who put him in danger, even if I may be no match. The stupid shot they gave me was burning the hell out of my insides and I couldn't change even if I wanted to, so ripping his throat out with my teeth was out of the question. Suddenly, I was sailing through the air and I landed hard on the floor, the wind knocked out of me as I heard a terrifying growl emit from my punching bag.

"You little f*ck!" Collin growled, wiping the trail of blood from his mouth. I'm not going to lie, I felt a rush of satisfaction that I could bruise him up and make him bleed. He stomped over to me, snarling, and snapping his sharp canines at me. I scrambled back at his fast approaching form but hit something behind me. Quickly, I looked up and froze, it was the hunter with his bleeding arm. His face was drawn in a dirty scowl and he was pissed. He reached down and yanked me up to my feet roughly by the back of my hair and I yelped.

"How dare you bite me? You disgusting rat!" he hissed through his teeth. In a flash, he had his gun drawn and pointed it at the furious Alpha who was a mere foot away from me.

"Come any closer and I'll shoot a hole through your flea-ridden face!" Collin came to a dead stop, his eyes trained on the gun in surprise.

"What the hell are you doing?" he demanded.

The hunter laughed.

"We had a deal, Justin," Collins growled. The hunter 'Justin' laughed louder as he jerked and tightened his grip on my hair while I whimpered in pain.

"So? You really thought I'd make a deal with a couple of vile wolves and let you go? If you haven't noticed Collin, I'm a hunter and my purpose is to kill every single one of your kind." He chuckled and shifted his gun towards Lynn and fired right between the eyes. I watched her dropped to the floor in disbelief. Alpha Collin spun around just in time to see her lifeless body fall to the floor. I didn't see his face but the roar that erupted from him caused me to cringe back in fright.

"Lynn!" he wailed, dropping to his knees and holding her close in his lap but all she did was stare vacantly at the ceiling. When he looked back up to Justin, his eyes were a blazing crazed grey as his wolf surfaced.

"You son of a b*tch! I'm going to tear you to f*cking pieces! Why?!" he howled.

I didn't give a damn about Lynn or Collin though I could feel the anger and grief roll off him in waves. It was so strong that it reminded me of Levi. I looked over to Avery who I noticed was starting to stir and my heart lifted.

I needed to get to him but Justin's grip in my hair was painfully tight. The two men were arguing so I tuned them out while I tried to come up with a plan to escape this guy. My gaze travelled all around the office up until I noticed a window by the wall where Avery was at. He could have gone though it if Collins had thrown him a bit more to the left. Thank the Spirits we were on ground level so I didn't have to worry about jumping at some high distance.

Now how was I going to get Avery out of that window and not get us both killed by these maniacs?

"Hey, quit moving!" The hunter yanked on my hair and I yelped again, grabbing his wrist.

"Let go." I cried as tears filled my eyes.

"Oh shut up runt!" he snarled and pushed me to the floor, focusing his attention to a seething Collins. Without wasting time, I crawled to Avery, rolling him to his back and he groaned. His stomach was drenched in deep red liquid and was pooling around him.

"Avery." I cried in fear, placing my hands over his wound to try and stop the bleeding. His face scrunched into a grimace of pain. He moaned but nothing else.

My attention snapped at the yell and roar behind me where I immediately saw Alpha Collin and the hunter going at it. The Alpha kicked the gun from Justin and it slid towards the door where I quickly noticed another gun. There were two guns all the way on the other side of the room. Can I get them without being seen?

I hadn't moved my hands from Avery's stomach, afraid that if I did I'd lose him. I looked back at him with a deep frown.

"Avery, Avery baby can you hear me?" I whispered on the verge of tears.

I felt helpless, I couldn't change to protect him, and in this state I was as useless as a child. I didn't have fighting experience and I wasn't even a match against the two fighting behind me.

"Avery." I tried again and almost jumped for joy as his brown eyes began to open for me.

"Caleb." I could barely hear his shaky voice but I nodded.

"Yes." His face paled as he move to sit up and hissed in pain. "No, don't move!" I ordered.

"Where is Collin?" he asked, ignoring my warning.

"Fighting the hunter," I told him and looked behind me again. They were pretty evenly matched where the hunter had a knife and Alpha Collin had his claws drawn as they slashed at each other.

"Avery, there are two guns across the room, I think I can get them without being seen," I whispered to him and he snapped his eyes open completely.

"No," he growled at me and I rolled my eyes.

"It's our only chance, I can't shift right now." Avery snatched my wrist, holding it tightly as I tried to move.

"I said no Caleb, let me take care of this." And he struggled to stand on unsteady legs as he held his stomach.

I shot to my feet to help steady him.

"Damn it Avery! You're not in any condition to fight, just let me save you for once."

He shook his head.

"I swore to myself that I would get you out of here no matter the cost and that's what I'm going to do. A little scratch isn't going to stop me from protecting what's mine," he growled and I couldn't suppress the look of awe that came across my face. My heart fluttered and butterflies filled my stomach at those words.

"Fine," I said and turned towards the window. I unlatched it on both sides and tried to push it up but it wouldn't budge. I tried again, pushing with all I had until it finally moved up at about an inch.

"UGH!" I huffed, sliding down to my knees to take a breather.

"What are you doing?" Avery demanded in frustration. I stood and gestured towards the window.

"Making an escape," I said and went back to try and get the rusty thing to open. Avery sighed, glancing at the two fighters before he stood beside me and helped. The window was finally moving but it made the worst noise ever. The scuffle between the two never stopped so we continued. The window was about halfway open when I was suddenly grabbed away from it and pushed into a pair of steel-like arms.

Avery spun, growling at whoever it was that took me and he crouched defensively. I glanced around the best that I could as I struggled pointlessly in the guy's arms. With a heavy heart of dread, I watched the room fill with hunters. There were too many of them.

We weren't going to make it.

"Didn't go how you planned?" Justin's voice was grating on my last nerve. He dropped Alpha Collin, who had a deep slit in his gushing throat at his feet and stepped over him like he was nothing. "There's no escaping us boys so might as well face your fate." He smirked and I just wanted to rip it off his face.

The guy who had me was grunting as I thrashed around like a crazy person. I think I clocked him in the mouth at one point with the back of my head. He growled and crushed me to his chest with crazy strength, making it hard for me to breathe.

"Stop it!" he snarled in my ear and I froze.

It couldn't be.

"I don't know how you escaped my prison but I'll make sure there's not a next time!" Justin snapped as he glared at Avery.

All the hunters in the room were glaring at my mate and I felt my blood boil.

"I'll take good care of those Elders of yours," he chuckled and raised an extra gun at Avery's growling form. Immediately, I jerked forward but I was held back.

"No!" I yelled right when the gun went off.

"Avery!" I screamed, staring at him, expecting him to cry out and crumple to the ground but he was still standing there with his eyes closed like he was waiting for the same. Upon closer look, I noticed that the bullet had suspended in midair before it dropped harmlessly to the floor.

"What the—"

"Now!" The guy holding me yelled suddenly and jammed his elbow into one of the men's face beside him, causing the hunter to exclaim in pain and fall unconscious. I watched in astonishment as three other people from the group of hunters in the room turned on their comrades.

Avery didn't wait and went straight for Justin, grabbing him by the neck as he stood in momentary shock. His eyes met Avery's furious royal blue ones and with a flick of the latter's strong hand, Justin's head snapped to the side at an abnormal angle as he collapsed motionless. Avery didn't waste time and made a beeline straight to me, taking out everyone in his path.

The moment I saw a hunter fly past me and crashed into the window was the second I knew that we had a chance at getting out of here.

"Go, go, go!" the one who had started the fight behind me commanded and pushed me and Avery towards the door. Rapid fire was ringing in my ears as we rushed from the room but not one bullet hit us.

Out of nowhere, a hunter came at me as he turned around the corner into the room. I saw the glint of a knife in his hands and stopped in fear. No one had the time to stop him because he was too close, but as he raised his knife, his head was suddenly snapped with an audible crack and he fell at my feet.

"Go!" A familiar voice urged me on and I jerked my head to the side as I saw Jim run ahead of me.

"Jim!" I cried in relief.

He was okay. I thought as I ran behind him out of the room with Avery at my heels.

"Laura come on!" the guy from earlier said again.

Laura? I snapped my head back curiously as we ran out into the hall. That was the name I heard when that hunter dragged me away from Jim.

"Don't stop!" the leader of this group growled at me. I stumbled, trying to look straight again. Unexpectedly, I was scooped up into a pair of strong arms and was carried through the maze of hallways. I wanted to protest and say that I could run but I knew Avery would never do it, he'd just ignore me.

"This way!" the leader instructed and we rushed towards two double doors that flew open as we dashed out into the fresh dawn air.

The sense of freedom slammed into me and I wanted to cry.

The ground was littered with dead bodies and I closed my eyes, not wanting to see anymore deaths. I just wanted it all to be over so I buried my face in Avery's neck. His arms tightened around me in understanding as he and our four other saviors kept running as we finally got out of that creepy place and out of danger.

CHAPTER 37

CALEB

My suspicions were confirmed when we made it to the pack house and that the leader of our rescue mission was in fact, James. Alpha Chandler ran out of the house the second we arrived, fear evident on his face as he stopped in front of Avery, who was on his knees and bent over from his stomach wound.

"Avery!" he exclaimed, crouching to his level. Being the stubborn man that he is, he just waved him off.

"I'm fine, it will heal." I, on the other hand was holding him close to me and had my face buried in his neck.

"Go see the doctor, Avery," I kept telling him but he shook his head.

Finally, I looked up at Alpha Chandler and nodded. Lucian scooped his son from the ground, earning a groan from Avery and was hurried back inside with Ivy at his heels. I wanted to follow but couldn't seem to get any of my burning limbs to work so I sat in the grass looking longingly at their retreating forms.

"Caleb?" a woman's voice sounded behind me so I glanced around to see the woman Laura, who was holding a syringe in her hand as the whole terrifying ordeal came rushing back tenfold. Screaming, I crawled away from her as fast as I could, unable to get to my feet.

"Caleb, calm down!" James said, grabbing me and holding me tight. I struggled harder, beating at his chest, screeching for him to let go but he didn't.

"Shh," he whispered calmly in my ear.

"No, please," I begged. There was no way I could protect myself from him at the weak state I was in. I was too exhausted and I still couldn't shift. My body was still on fire. James pulled me in his lap and rocked me gently from side to side.

"There is no need to freak out Caleb. She's not going to hurt you. She wants to help," he reassured me but nothing he said was going through. All I could see was the man in the white coat taunting me, saying he was going to put me down as he stuck me with a needle where the pain and the burning sensation followed.

"I'm not the bad guy, Caleb," Laura said in a low, cautious voice. "James and I help the ones that were captured by the hunters. This syringe is an antidote I made to counteract the effects of the one that was given to you earlier." She stepped closer and knelt down. I watched her closely, never missing the slight twitch she made. "It will make you feel so much better."

My body slowly relaxed into James's once I looked into her eyes.

They were sincere and full of truth, but the one thing that made me stop my struggle were her eyes. They were the same deep brown as Avery's. I looked passed her then at Jim who just stood with a worried expression as he observed a few feet away. When he nodded, I peered back at her and gave her a slight nod of my head. She smiled when I gave in and leaned forward with the needle. I whimpered and cowered further into James, hiding my face into his shoulder.

"It's okay, she knows what she's doing," he spoke softly and rubbed my back soothingly as she took my arm and injected me. I flinched at the sting but a second later it was gone. I heard her quick retreat as the stuff she administered me with began to work. James took off his coat but didn't leave as my stomach began to turn and cramp up.

"Just let it out," he whispered, rubbing my back and that's just what I did. I threw up the entire contents of my stomach right there in the grass. Once I was too tired to move, I was picked up and brought back in the house.

"Take me to Avery," I whispered hoarsely to James receiving a nod in return.

"I will."

Avery was asleep on a hospital bed in the infirmary when I was brought in. He had bandages wrapped around his shirtless stomach that were beginning to stain red. James placed me on a bed next to his brother before walking towards the doctor.

"How is he?" he asked a tall lanky man.

"He's suffering from internal injuries and silver poisoning on his hands and feet but with time he will heal nicely since he's of Alpha blood. I put him under some strong anesthesia to help him with the pain and healing process. I say a day or two at the most, and he'll be back up and running again." James nodded, looking back at Avery. I could see the deep concern and affection on his face that I hadn't seen since knowing him.

"Thank you," he said and walked over to me.

"You doing alright?"

I nodded.

"I'm just tired," I replied, my eyes drooping down a bit. He smiled, patting my head.

"I'll tell the doc to let you stay here and get some rest alright?"

"Okay." I breathed out and glanced at Avery's handsome face as he slept, doing just the same.

* * *

AVERY

Two days later

I sat in the living room with my brother as he sat across from me with Laura next to him. Caleb was beside me, waiting for one of us to finally speak.

I sighed.

"Thank you for saving us," I said. James blinked before nodding.

"You're welcome." He shifted his body before continuing. "It's not like I could leave you there, I may be angry with you but I would never want you in the hands of hunters."

I wanted to smile.

"Well, I appreciate that." I cleared my throat. "So, how did you manage to impersonate a hunter and save us in the first place?" I had to ask. I know it couldn't have been an easy job.

"It's what I do. I help the wolves that those monsters capture. We have close tabs on them," he answered. Caleb sat forward, intrigued.

"So what, you're vigilantes?" he asked. James peered at him and nodded.

"You can say that. I work for the Elders." He reached over and took Laura's hand in his as they shared a loving gaze. "We work for them," he corrected himself.

"I'm the undercover agent, I've been under the hunter's noses for a few years now and was secretly gathering information that I can take back to the Elder council," Laura said.

"Why would the Elders trust you? You're just a human right?" Jim asked while he was standing in the back of the room.

She looked over at him.

"I used to be one of them. My father was a hunter and wanted to pass down the tradition of being a slayer. I didn't have the heart so I made it my duty to save these poor people who were being slaughtered. Soon after I was accepted in the hunter's society, I met James on one of our missions. I couldn't bear to see them hurt him so I covered for him. James was already part of the rescue team the Elders had put together and was on his own mission.

"Since then, we met up and exchanged info. Well after once we started to trust one another. Not long after he was completely sure I was on his side, he brought me to the Elder council. We told them that we were mates and we wanted to help, and what better way to infiltrate a hunter's lair than a hunter on the inside no one would expect? I had the information they needed and the smarts to counteract any poison they came up with." We all sat there in awe.

"Wow," Caleb whispered. I nodded in agreement.

"Why did you take up this task?" I asked James, completely worried for my brother's life. He constantly put his life in danger and I feared for him. His face dropped and was soon consumed with sadness.

"They've taken so many of us, Avery. I was tired of seeing my brethren killed, kidnapped, and tortured. I had to do something." His voice was full of desperation.

I nodded. He was already twenty so who was I to say what he can and can't do? In a way I was proud of him for his noble deed.

"I understand and I'm proud of you for what you do," I told him softly. His head shot up as his eyes stared at me wide-eyed like he'd never expect something like that to come out of my mouth. He ducked his head, causing his hair to drop in his face so we couldn't see it anymore. Laura had a sad expression on her face as she rubbed his back soothingly.

I knew this had to come sooner or later so I stood and asked everyone to leave us. Caleb frowned at me with concern before standing on his tiptoes to give me a chaste kiss and I watched him walk out with deep longing. I couldn't tell you how badly my wolf wanted to know how Caleb was completely unharmed and okay in a much more *intimate* way. The thought of it had my wolf nipping and scratching at the surface, desperate for me to let him out so he could check on his mate for himself.

I combed an anxious hand through my hair, messing it up more than it already was and finally turned to James who was now up from his seat. His back was turned to me as he stood in front of the large fireplace.

"I came to your room that night to give you a late birthday present. I was sad that I didn't get to give you one so I asked mom to take me to the mall the day after your birthday. I must have stayed there all day and complained about everything until I found this awesome t-shirt that I knew you would love. I was going to wrap it up and show you in the morning but I couldn't wait so I went into your room to surprise you and . . . you weren't there." He paused and I didn't say anything, I couldn't.

"I tried to find you and thought that maybe you went to sleep with Dee or mum and dad. The next morning I checked your room and down the stairs to see if you were there but you weren't. I asked mum and dad if you slept with them, but they just frowned and shook their heads and Dee did the same."

He then turn to stare at me with his bright blue eyes.

"You left. We searched for you for months and came up with nothing. Our best trackers didn't even know where to start. We didn't know if you were alive or dead and that was the worst part. Mum cried for who knows how long and poor father did his best to comfort her even though he felt the same. Dee didn't understand so she just kept begging us to go get you and bring you back like it was so easy. This pack couldn't function with its Alpha completely heartbroken over his son's disappearance. We all felt the ramifications and the sorrow we shared with mum and dad." I swallowed a large lump in my throat, forcing it back.

"I wanted to hate you," he whispered. His fists were balled in anger. "For what you did to us." I noticed the tears he was trying to hold back.

"I had my reasons," I finally spoke up. He scoffed and turned his head away from me. "I did James, if I had stayed I would have been a nuisance to you all." He stepped forward rather abruptly.

"How would you have known that? You didn't stay did you?!" I closed the great distance between us and captured his gaze.

"I was a wanderer, James. What was there for me to do for all of you? I couldn't take the Alpha position, I had no mate, and I couldn't stand the thought of mom, dad, and the pack watching me in pity. I was an empty shell of what I used to be before my maturity. I had to find a purpose in life since being the next ruler of the Sky Raven Pack was not an option anymore." He shook his head.

"You could have told us instead of running out at night like a bloody coward, Avery!"

"I was fifteen. It was all on impulse and hardly thought out. I'm sorry James," I said, grabbing his shoulder. He tried to jerk away from me, his tears falling freely.

"Let go, don't touch me Avery!" he screamed, struggling but I just slammed him into my chest and circled my arms around him tight, refusing to let go.

"I'm sorry, I am so deeply and profoundly sorry for what I have done to my family and mostly you," I whispered desperately in his ear. His struggles slowly died, and his face was now buried in my shoulder. His arms finally came around me and his hands gripped tightly at the back of my shirt. His body was shaky as he cried into my shoulder. I just closed my eyes and held him close.

"I'm always going to be your big brother and I love you for life," I told him softly which only made him cry harder.

"Don't leave again, I won't be able to take it," his hoarse voice begged and I smiled.

"I wasn't planning on it, actually what do you say about reconsidering your opinion of me to become the next Alpha Chandler?" James pulled back and gazed at me with a serious expression. I knew he wasn't too fond of the idea before, but I really wanted his blessing.

"I think it's where you belong."

EPILOGUE

CALEB

"No, don't leave!" I exclaimed, holding on to Levi's legs as I lay on the floor. He was practically dragging me along the surface as he walked towards the door.

"Ugh, my God Caleb. Get off me!" he whined.

"No, I don't want you to leave"

Levi had stayed a week after the hunter incident to make sure that I was alright. I was thankful for him and Mr. Blackman for taking care of Connor when we were captured.

The moment I woke up after Laura helped me with that shot, I immediately went to find Levi and my son. Man, that sounds weird to say but I loved it. I was relieved to know they made it and that I didn't have to go back to the hunter's lair to get them back, because I would have.

Levi set his suitcase on the side of the front door before reaching down and lifted me up to my feet. Man, was this guy strong.

"Dude, I have to go. This isn't my pack and I don't want to overstay my welcome," he explained but I just threw my arms around his neck, causing him to bend over and hug me back.

"I'm going to miss you like crazy," I whispered, saddened that it would feel like forever before seeing him again. He was going to be thousands of miles away from me. Who was I going to talk sh*t with? Who was I going to have my heart-to-hearts with when I wanted to complain about mates? Well, considering that would be a touchy subject for him, I don't think it would have been a good idea.

Wait, what if he does see Kyle back home? Will it all happen again? I frowned, I didn't want that to happen to him again. From what I felt before, it was literally killing him so . . .

"Why don't you ask Alpha Chandler to join this pack?" The look that crossed his face made me feel like I was crazy.

"Why the hell would I do that Caleb? Stop being a scaredy-cat and have your happily ever after with Avery. He's soon to be Alpha now and that means you stay here and I go back home. I'll visit you though so don't worry," Levi said as he pulled away from our hug and picked his suitcase back up.

I bit down on my lip as I walked behind him. His dad was waiting by the car with a smile on his face which only caused me to smile back.

I finally got around to asking him if he wanted me to help him with the loss of his mate. Levi was a big help with this because Mr. Blackman is a very stubborn man.

Three days ago

Avery was out with his dad, making the rounds around the territories. I was walking around with Levi, exploring more of the houses when we ended up in the library. I'm not a big book reader but Levi is, and we noticed Mr. Blackman was there sitting in a large green leather chair in the corner of the room. His head was in his hands and his shoulders were shaking. Levi and I frowned at one another before we rushed towards him.

"Dad!" Levi called, crouching at his feet before he took his dad's arm, trying to pull his hand away from his face.

"Dad, what's wrong?"

Marten lifted his head and I saw the tears stream down his face.

"Nothing, don't worry about me." He waved his son off. I felt the sorrow come off him in waves and I couldn't help but kneel beside him. It was like I was drawn to his pain.

"I can take it away if you want," I told him, completely serious. I knew this was hurting him and had been for too long and I didn't like it one bit. His tired eyes met mine and I saw the hope and resolve.

"I couldn't do that to you Caleb, not after what happened last time," he said in a raspy voice.

I shook my head.

"Don't worry about that. This is what I do Mr. Blackman and I need to help you, if you'd let me that is." Levi looked from me to his father and I saw the understanding.

"You would do that for him?" he asked with such awe that I blushed.

"Of course."

Levi turned to his dad and nodded.

"Please dad, let him help you" Marten stared at his son for the longest time before sighing.

"I'm only doing this for you, Levi," he whispered before he peered at me and gave me a nod.

"Go ahead."

* * *

I only ever want to see them happy and that's what I did. The bite that time wasn't like the first. I was still knocked off my feet, and I blacked out from the power of his sorrow and grief but that only lasted for about a minute. Avery found out and let's just say that he wasn't a happy camper for the past few days. I knew he was still pissed off about it so I planned to see him later today.

"You ready Levi?" Mr. Blackman asked, holding the door open.

"Yeah." Levi turned to me with a gentle and Levi-like smile.

"Thank you for everything Caleb," he said softly and leaned in, kissing me on the cheek.

"I'm glad you're alright., both of you," I said to him and his father. Levi placed his bag in the trunk of the car and walked to the back seat.

"See you around sometime, Caleb," he told me, his voice was strained and I could see the shine in his eyes. My throat was closing up and it was getting hard to breathe.

"Yeah."

"Caleb, thank you again," Mr. Blackman said for the hundredth time and I shrugged.

"Anytime," I answered.

And then they were gone as the car quickly made its way down the dusty road.

Sighing, I turned back and headed inside. The house was quiet as I trudged up the stairs and walked towards my shared room with Avery. Closing the door behind me, I kicked off my shoes and began to strip my clothes off as I made my way towards the bathroom, unable to stop my concerned thoughts for Levi. Maybe a nice warm shower would help me out.

Setting the temperature just right, I stepped in and sighed in relief. Yeah, this is just what I needed. I tilted my head back under the hot water, letting it soak into my entire body. Blindly, I reached down for the shampoo and squeezed a good dollop into my hands and started to scrub thoroughly through my hair then my face.

Suddenly, a pair of arms wrapped around me and I jerked in surprise.

"Ahh!" I screeched. Their body was shaking as their sexy laughter sounded in my ears.

"Sorry, I couldn't help myself," he told me, still laughing. His hands were rubbing my sides and chest as the water washed away all the soap in my face so I could finally see.

"What are you doing in here?" I asked though I already had an idea on why.

"I just wanted to see if you needed any help," he whispered in my ear and my body caught fire.

"Does this mean you forgive me?" I asked, turning my head to the side to look at him. His brown eyes softened as he gazed at me.

"I forgave you the second you did it. I just didn't want what happened last time to happen again."

I nodded in understanding.

"I'm sorry but I had to Avery." He didn't say anything and just buried his face in the back of my neck.

"Let me wash you," he whispered.

"Well if you insist," I teased nervously.

"I do." His words came out in a purr.

He spun me around to face him and I saw the deep lust etched in his handsome face. His eyes raked down my entire body as he continued to touch my back and sides. He grabbed a washcloth off the handle and soaped it up before he rubbed it across my chest and down to my stomach in slow circles. I stood motionless in front of him then closed my eyes, sighing in delight at the massage he started to give me.

When I was all clean, Avery's fingers still hadn't stopped touching me and were playing a dangerous game the lower they went. Avery ducked his head and pressed a kiss my neck, causing me to gasp and moan at the same time and dug my nails in his shoulder. Suddenly, I was no longer on my feet but was pushed up against the wall with Avery between my thighs as I wrapped my legs around his waist.

I was shaky as he trailed hot wet kisses down on one side of my neck and shoulder before he moved to the other. His tongue snaked out to lap at my jawline in a leisurely caress. My head fell back against the wall, giving him all the access he wanted.

"Avery," I whimpered. He pulled back and sported a pair of bright passionate blue eyes. I dipped my head to capture his lips to mine and that heated everything up tenfold. Nothing was slow or gentle as we both gave in to our primal instincts where we growled and bit each other hard enough to draw blood, adding further fuel to our lustful appetite. I reached down between us and took him in my hands, showing him where I wanted him as he growled sexily.

"Quit teasing me," I snarled at him and he smirked evilly.

"If you say so." And he slammed home. I threw my body up against the wall as he entered, the pain and pleasure causing me to see stars. I looked down at him with watery eyes and grinned as he moved. His grip was tight and hard around my waist and I knew I'd have bruises after this but I honestly couldn't care less at the moment.

I held on to him, wrapping my arms around his neck as he moved me against him rough and fast. My hands grabbed his hair and held it tight.

The water was starting to cool down but our bodies weren't as the passion between us hit new heights.

"Yeah, please don't stop!" I cried as I dug my teeth in his shoulder, unable to get over how amazing he made me feel. My hips began to join in the rhythm he had set which only made him go harder. I could hear him pant and growl in my ear as he continued to lose more control of himself.

He went deep this time and I felt the tingles and tightness in my stomach spread out as he kept his assault on that one spot that would bring me to that cliff of pleasure. The pleasurable heat was building up so fast that I didn't even have the time to breathe before I was forced over the edge and was slumped against the wall as Avery followed right behind me.

We were both out of breath as we stood there, trying to get our wits back. Slowly, Avery pulled out and set me back on shaky feet as he turned the now freezing water off. I couldn't move nor did I want to. I watched as Avery brushed my wet hair away from my face with his fingers and leaned down to kiss me softly.

"Come, let's go to bed," he said lifting me out and I laughed.

"I could have gotten out myself mister macho man," I whined while he wrapped a towel around me.

"Yeah well sue me for wanting to help my mate," he argued playfully. I rolled my eyes as I raised the towel to my hair to rub it dry before I collapsed on the edge of the bed. I felt Avery move the covers out of the way on his side and slid in. Curiously, I looked up at him and he was staring at me with a rather serious and thoughtful expression which made me frown.

"What?" I asked, crawling the rest of the way to bed so I could lay next him.

"What, what?" he asked. I shook my head.

"So have you asked Jim about the adoption papers for Connor?" Avery sighed, rubbing his eyes as he rested his head against the pillow.

"Well since his parents are already deceased and his relatives are now dead, he has no one to go to. I don't think we can get papers legally without bringing social services into this and that can go very badly, Caleb. The court will be involved and since we're so young, they won't let him stay with us, plus we aren't related in any way." My heart was sinking with every word he said and I quickly sat up.

"So you're saying that if they ever find him then they'll take him away from us?" I exclaimed. Avery nodded reluctantly.

"Yes."

"Can't we go to the Elder council? I'll be going there to study and stuff so I bet they'll help us, they have to!" Avery grabbed me and brought me down to his chest.

"We'll figure this out. I'm not letting anyone take him from us Caleb so don't worry about it now okay? He's ours," he reassured me.

How could I not worry? If Connor's old pack was looking for him and if they called the authorities then I could lose him. I've been through too much already and I didn't want him taken away from me. The minute I get the opportunity, I'm definitely crashing the Elder council tomorrow to get this settled. Avery began laughing and I lifted my head from his chest to frown at him.

"You're going to raise hell aren't you?" he asked which only made me smirk.

"You know it." He shook his head and pulled me up close, covering us with the blankets as I snuggled closer into his warm side. We stayed like that for almost twenty minutes before I interrupted our comfortable silence.

"So when is your dad letting you take over?" I asked curiously, making swirly patterns on his hard stomach. He moved his head over mine and spoke.

"I wanted to wait so I thought another year or so before I do that. Plus, I need to catch up on my studying on how to be a proper leader," he said into my damp hair and I scoffed.

"You don't need a damn book to tell you how to run your pack Avery, you'll be the best Alpha this world has ever seen," I said confidently and I knew I got a smile out of him as he kissed my hair.

"Thank you," he breathed.

"Anytime stud."

He chuckled.

The night was starting to take its toll and I slowly closed my eyes, resting comfortably with my wonderful mate on the verge of sleep when I heard it.

"I love you," he whispered.

My eyes snapped open and my heart stopped before it melted right there in my chest. How long have I been dying to hear those words come out of his mouth and there they were, just as sweet and amazing as I imagined. I moved my head up towards his and stared into his deep brown eyes. I could see the love and affection deep within them as I tried to hold my tears in.

Leaning up close to him, I pressed a gentle kiss to his lips.

"It's about time," I teased softly and he smiled that rare handsome smile of his that always made my heart race.

"I love you too," I whispered.

We fell asleep in each other's arms ready for our new life and family to start. We knew it would be tough but with him beside me, I could take on the world, though he might have to come and jam me out of certain situations from time to time, but I didn't care about that. I was happy. He was the one I marked, the one I wanted as mine . . .

And the one I get to love for the rest of my life.

all
it took
was one
look
T. LANAY

CHAPTER 1

AIDEN

Senior year, the last year of high school, but to me, it's almost the end of my four-year long prison stay. No, it was not because I didn't like school work. Actually, I was a straight-A student. It's just a constant reminder of my problem.

I knew the school like the back of my hand. That meant I knew the people. The thought of being picked on and thrown in dumpsters every day terrified me.

Why, you may ask, was I scared of my fellow classmates?

Well . . . I wasn't scared of them. I was wary of what they might do to me when they would fnd out that I'm the big G A Y.

Yeah, now you knew my problem. You could say I was ashamed of my sexuality. My parents always told me I should be proud. Yeah. Could you believe that? I was shocked, too.

Okay, okay. I was not totally ashamed. Maybe I shouldn't use that word. Here's a better one: scared. I was scared of it.

So here I was, incognito, playing the straight guy in my anatomy class and writing notes, being the awesome student that I was. The teacher was ranting on and on about medical studies and whatnot. This class was my favorite. I planned on going into the medical field. Jeanine, who I called J and my all-time best friend, was tapping her pen against the desk next to me which made me want to snatch it and throw it across the room. I gave her a narrow-eyed glare while she frowned at me.

I eyed the pen suggestively, hoping she would get the hint. I even raised my eyebrows at it. Apparently not, since she mouthed 'what' to me.

Rolling my eyes, I picked my pencil up and waved it at her.

"Oh," she mouthed and set her pen down.

"Finally," I said, heaving a heavy sigh.

"Mr. Walker, is there something you would like to share with the class?" Mr. Simons asked, giving me a stern look.

I shook my head and said a sheepish no. Jeanine giggled at me along with the rest of the class.

Glaring at her, I turned back to my notes grumpily. Why is it that I was always the one who gets in trouble when Jeanine and I talk in class? Slowly, I laid my head on my desk and ignored the rest of what Mr. Simons said because basically, I knew it already.

I suddenly found myself dozing off, and Mr. Simon's voice was starting to become a low mumble when a huge banging sound erupted. I looked up to see what was happening. Two well-built men burst through the door, practically breaking it down and tumbling to the floor. There was a collective gasp from the class along with a few screams from the girls.

Everyone quickly stood from their desks to see what was happening.

And of course, I would be caught up in the fight since I was the one right next to the door. They rolled too close to my desk, making it tip over with me on it.

I hit the floor with a hard thump and the pain came screaming in my wrist and head as the fight progressed next to me.

"Mr. Parker! Mr. Moore, stop this now!" Mr. Simons yelled at them while I was still struggling to untangle my legs from the desk.

"Aiden!" I heard Jeanine exclaim. I never had the chance to look at her before something hard hit my stomach, knocking the wind out of me and causing my head to hit the floor again.

I really needed to get up now! I screamed in my head.

Again, the person was slammed back into me, ruining my motivation to even move. I was waiting for it to happen again, but it didn't. Everything was quiet now, or maybe it was because I was trying to sort out my head. All I know was that I was having trouble seeing straight.

* * *

The nurse's office smelled funny when I woke up. I tried sitting up, but my head was swimming and pounding so badly. I decided that staying still was my best option.

I looked around.

'Why am I here again? And seriously, why does it smell so weird in here?'

"Aiden? Are you up?" Jeanine's voice sounded from behind the curtain.

"Yeah."

She pulled it back with a small smile on her face. "Hey, how are you feeling?" she asked taking a seat on the bed.

"Like hell. What happened?" I asked and watched as her face changed drastically to some sort of dark expression.

Uh-oh, I thought.

"You don't remember?"

I shook my head. "No."

"Well, those stupid jerks came barging in the room in a huge fight, making you fall from your desk. You hit your head pretty hard. Are you sure you're not feeling woozy or anything?"

Ignoring her concern, I asked who was fighting.

"It was Kyle and Liam."

I stared at her wide eyed. "You're saying that our school's star football players were fighting in our class, and I got dragged into it?"

She nodded.

"I'm lucky to even be alive right now!" I exclaimed.

"Yeah, Mr. Simons had to break them up because he feared for your poor pathetic little life," she said with an evil smirk.

"Haha, very funny. It makes me feel so good inside that you care." I rolled my eyes.

"I know, you should feel honored. No, but seriously, I'm going to get the nurse to make sure you don't need some serious medical attention." With that, I watched her disappear behind the curtain.

It didn't take long for the nurse to examine me and see if I was okay. When she released me, she told me she called someone so I didn't have to walk home. She gave me instructions on how to take care of my wrist and head since I had a sprain and might also have a mild concussion.

Jeanine walked me out and down the hallway. School let out ten minutes ago, and I was glad because I couldn't survive class with this major headache. As we made our way outside, J told me everything that went down in class since I missed most of it.

When we were passing the principal's office, I suddenly heard raised voices. I had this odd sensation that was begging me to look through the room's window, so I gave in and saw the principal, of course, giving a very expressive lecture to none other than the hooligans that squished me.

Maybe it was just because he had this look-at-me type of persona going on, but my eyes specifically trained themselves on Liam—well, his back. And might I say what a nice broad back it was? His hair looked ruffled and crazy from his earlier fight, but I had to say it was pretty sexy from the back. I was sure it was more so in the front. I had never really seen Liam up close, and the only reason I knew him was because he's the famous star quarterback. But from what I heard, he's a total heartthrob or whatever girls said about him. Personally, I never looked because I didn't want anyone to see me checking out dudes.

The abrupt tugging on my arm caught my attention.

"Aiden, what's up? What's wrong?" Jeanine asked, watching me with concern.

I shook my head. When did I stop walking? I was drawn to look into the window again and noticed Liam staring at me. He had a confused, shocked, and an almost angry expression. With a yelp, I moved for the front doors at hyper speed.

He saw me staring at him!

Oh god! Now he would think I was a freak or worse, he discovered I was gay! He's going to tell, and I was going to be best friends with the dumpster for the rest of my senior year. I was such an idiot!

Jeanine was staring at me weirdly. Her dark brown eyebrow was raised at me.

"What?" I asked innocently. "You know, that top really compliments your skin tone," I said, distracting her with the best extreme gay fashion designer impression I had seen on TV which always made her smile. But really, she was wearing a yellow blouse that went well with her light brown skin. It really did look good on her even though I know nothing about fashion. I might be gay, but fashion went over my head. If I could, I would still let my mom picked my clothes in the morning.

"Uh-huh, whatever. Your dad's here by the way," she said, pointing to the Mercedes waiting in the front.

"Crap. Thanks." I gave her a quick hug. "I'll call you later?" I said, slowly walking backwards towards the car.

She shook her head. "I have dance practice, so I'm going to be dead tired later."

"Oh, alright. I guess I'll see you tomorrow then." I opened the car door, ready to slide in.

"Yep, feel better," she said.

"I will." It was the last thing I told her before closing the door. Buckling up, I rested my head against the head rest.

"What is this fight I heard about?" my dad said as he started to drive. "Are you hurt badly? I know because the nurse called me and said you were knocked out. No need to go to the hospital?" he said, giving me a concerned sideways glance.

"No, Dad. I'm fine. I just have a headache, and I sprained my wrist." He nodded.

"Okay. We'll go to the store and get you a wrist brace and aspirin, alright?"

"Okay."

*　　*　　*

At dinner, I got a whole bunch of questions about what happened to me and answered them to the best of my abilities. My mom, like always, thought that a gay basher was constantly terrorizing me. Dad stayed quiet and just agreed with everything she said. It was really annoying. My fourteen-year-old sister, Connie, was sneaking text messages under the table since phones weren't allowed at dinner. My parents thought our generation was ruled by technology.

I know. Crazy, right?

My brother, Nash, was out with his girlfriend as usual. Since he went to the community college, he was still living with us. He hadn't heard what happened to me yet, and I was hoping it stayed that way. Ever since I came out to my family, my brother had been the most protective one.

Like this one time, the family and I were over at my great grandparent's house for a family reunion. Connie, Nash, and I were hanging out with our cousins. And you could imagine how everyone had a douchebag cousin, right? That one guy who always put you down whenever you're feeling vulnerable or a straight-up bully. Well, mine happened to be Brent. So anywho, Connie accidentally slip out that I was gay at dinner. She was only eleven and probably didn't even know what that meant yet or thought it wasn't a big deal.

So, like the douchebag Brent was, he made a huge scene, saying it was disgusting and wrong. He then did something I least expected. He called me a fag. No one had ever called me that before, and to be truthful, it was kind of traumatizing. I mean, if my own family didn't like who I was, how would everyone else take it? Bad, that's how. Nash's face had gone bright red as we all sat at the table, shocked. My brother had shot to his feet so fast no one had time to stop him as he socked Brent square in the face. Brent went crashing to the floor with his chair.

"Never say that to my brother again, you piece of shit!" Nash exclaimed, snatching Brent from the floor, and that was when a full-scale war broke out. My dad and his brother, Brent's dad, were struggling to separate them.

I remembered how afterwards everyone was arguing and pointing accusing fingers at me like I was the bad guy.

It took so much in me to keep myself from crying.

They told my parents to never come back with me. So my dad told them if I couldn't be a part of the family, then none of us would ever come back. He took my arm and walked out of the house with his dignity intact while mine crumbled and got blown away by the particularly strong wind that day.

The second we arrived home, my father instructed everyone to go inside while he kept me out with him. I could still remember how hard it was to look him in the eyes at that moment.

"Look at me, Aiden."

I shook my head, too ashamed at what I was. There's no way he didn't feel the same. I was a disgrace. No matter how much he tried to put on this facade to make me feel better, I knew I was a screwup.

"You don't have to pretend," I whispered. "You don't have to pretend that you love me." The sob tore through my throat as I said those words. Before I knew it, I was suddenly drawn into a bone crushing hug. Too shocked to say anything, I just let the tears come, sobbing in his chest as his arms tightened.

"I will never stop loving you! You are my son, Aiden. Nothing is going to stop this family from loving you unconditionally!" He pulled me at arm's length, and for the first time ever, I saw tears in my father's eyes. And just like the stubborn man that he was, he refused to let them fall. "They were in the wrong, not you. And I swear that I will never let them hurt you again. Do you hear me?"

I stared at him, unable to move nor speak.

"Aiden, I need you to understand. Tell me you do."

I then nodded, wrapping my arms around him tightly.

"I love you, Aiden. More than you'll ever know," he said, kissing my hair.

"I love you too, Dad."

That was the last time I had seen my dad's side of the family. My mom's side was more accepting, so now we had been going there for reunions.

* * *

I put my dish in the sink and headed upstairs to my room. I didn't realize how tired I was till my head hit the pillow. I was out.

BOOK YOU MIGHT ENJOY

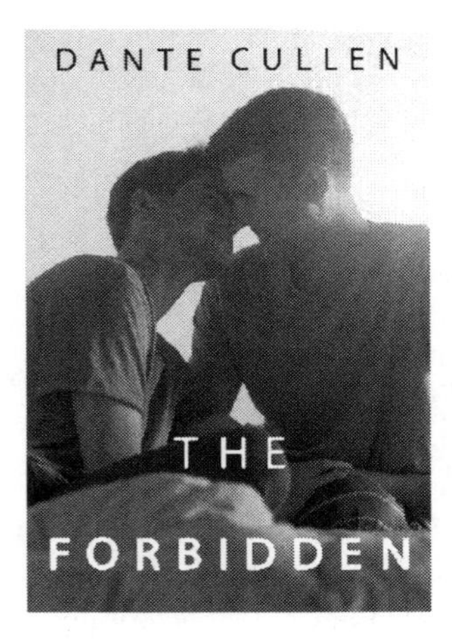

THE FORBIDDEN
Dante Cullen

Only fools rush in...

...especially if it's forbidden.

Zac Nielsen is your typical nice guy. The type who looks frailer than a porcelain chinaware.

On the other hand, Evan, also known by his stage name Cody Wilde, is the wild child that he is. The type who, out of spite, breaks the cupboard and its contents.

When these two opposites meet in Sapphire Town, things take an interesting turn, because despite their obvious differences, they actually find fun and comfort in each other's company. It doesn't take long for them to realize that something else has developed between them.

However, because of neglect, Evan has always forbidden other people to climb his walls, while Zac, because of disloyalty, is still hesitant to jump into a new relationship.

Will they let go of their fears and hold each other for the possible future? Or will they keep forbidding themselves of the very same thing they crave?

In Dante Cullen's The Forbidden, Zac and Evan learn to find themselves, to love and let go despite of the pain of the past and the opposition of society's norms. Their story is proof that at the end of the day, what truly matters is not the quantity but the quality of relationships we have, and that love—true love—will always be worth breaking our walls down.

BOOK YOU MIGHT ENJOY

LIFE SUCKS IF YOU'RE MARRIED TO A BILLIONAIRE

Krystel Grace

Kei Forest, a stubborn young man, is living an ordinary college life until he receives a letter that will change his life forever.

Recently turned twenty-one, he is now faced with a decision that will shake the very foundation of his life.

His parents had left him an unimaginable wealth but under one condition: He must marry the arrogant business magnate, Jace Langlois.

Will Kei put up with this ordeal? Or will he leave his husband after he gets his inheritance?

This is an LGBT book you shouldn't miss. Grab a copy now!

AUTHOR'S NOTE

Thank you so much for reading *A First Chance At Love*! I can't express how grateful I am for reading something that was once just a thought inside my head.

Please feel free to send me an email. Just know that my publisher filters these emails. Good news is always welcome.
t_lanay@awesomeauthors.org

One last thing: I'd love to hear your thoughts on the book. Please leave a review on Amazon or Goodreads because I just love reading your comments and getting to know you!

Can't wait to hear from you!

T. Lanay

ABOUT THE AUTHOR

T. Lanay aka Robokitt is the author of "The Blue Moon Series" on Wattpad. Born and raised in U.S. California, she loves reading and writing romance, LGBT, and supernatural romance books.